Praise for
Beastmaster: Myth

"*Beastmaster: Myth* opened my eyes to the immense world of fantasy! Richard Knaak and Sylvio Tabet took me to a world I had never dreamed of before and thrilled me with every twist and turn!"
— Patrick Wachsberger, Co-Chairman and President of Summit Entertainment, producers of the *Twilight Saga* films

"An action-packed fantasy adventure . . . Leaves the audience wishing [it] would never end! A phenomenal continuation of the Beastmaster story!"
— Mario Kassar, executive producer of the *Terminator* movies and TV series, the original *Rambo* trilogy, and *Basic Instinct*

"A fresh, dramatic, and thrilling tale of high fantasy adventure . . . that will intrigue and enlighten all the legions of this epic hero's fans, and will undoubtedly bring many new fans into the fold."
— Bestselling author Doug Niles

"Well-written, adventure-filled, action-packed!"
— *New York Times* bestselling author Margaret Weis

"*Beastmaster: Myth* is an elemental epic told with color, verve, and sparkle. I thoroughly enjoyed it. Then went back to the first page and enjoyed it all over again."
— Ed Greenwood, author of the *Forgotten Realms*®

BEASTMASTER
MYTH

RICHARD A. KNAAK
and SYLVIO TABET

POCKET BOOKS

New York   London   Toronto   Sydney

Pocket Books
A Division of Simon & Schuster, Inc.
1230 Avenue of the Americas
New York, NY 10020

First Pocket Books trade paperback edition December 2009

POCKET and colophon are registered trademarks of Simon & Schuster, Inc.

For information about special discounts for bulk purchases, please contact Simon & Schuster Special Sales at 1-800-456-6798 or business@simonandschuster.com.

The Simon & Schuster Speakers Bureau can bring authors to your live event. For more information or to book an event contact the Simon & Schuster Speakers Bureau at 866-248-3049 or visit our website at www.simonspeakers.com.

Designed by Akasha Archer
Illustration from Shutterstock.com

Cover art by Boris Vallejo and Julie Bell

Manufactured in the United States of America

1   3   5   7   9   10   8   6   4   2

Library of Congress Cataloging-in-Publication Data is available.

ISBN 978-1-4391-4417-6
ISBN 978-1-4391-5768-8 (ebook)

To my children, Maya, Sylvio Sharif, and Kim,
and to all the Beastmaster fans

ACKNOWLEDGMENTS

I would like to express my thanks to all who, over the years, believed in the Beastmaster and supported me in my project.

For many years I traveled to India to meet my yogi. I would like to thank him and the yogis I met and did not meet. They inspired me to live the magic and the reality that is part of the Beastmaster and our lives.

I would like to thank Don Maass, my literary agent, and, especially, Richard Knaak, with whom I had a great collaboration and who shared my vision in this incredible adventure. I look forward to working together with him on more Beastmaster stories. Thanks to Jaime for editing our "beast."

—Sylvio Tabet

This novel could not have existed without the dedication of Beastmaster fans everywhere. I hope you enjoy this new tale!

Particular thanks must also go to Sylvio Tabet, my co-author and a man with a dream. I am pleased to have been a part of the fruition of that dream and hope that we can do this again. This novel became more than just a story for both of us.

My gratitude also to Don Maass—there to bring in timely suggestions and support—and our patient editors on this project, Jaime and Marco.

—Richard A. Knaak

INTRODUCTION

Around 1982, two young filmmakers approached me with an original script about a man—a king—born through magic from an animal and who can communicate with other creatures. His only family consisted of Ruh, the tiger, who became his strength; Sharak, the eagle, who was his eyes; and Kodo and Podo, the ferrets—the thieves—whose tricks turned out to be very helpful when needed. With them, his mission was to defend whoever needed his help against the evils of his world.

The Beastmaster was created, and the film that I produced became one of the most replayed movies on television. More movies followed, then a pilot, and at last a series of some sixty-six episodes—all of which are still playing around the world. *The Beastmaster* became a cult hit with countless followers.

And then I decided it was time to share with the public the true meaning of the Beastmaster, this hero who has captured the fascination of so many, in a new, original novel.

Beastmaster is also a story of persistence. It took many years to finance the second movie, the third, and then the series. Twenty-five years have passed and now the novel has come to fruition. It proves that certain heroes don't die—they truly become myth. Their stories are told and repeated forever. Thanks to Richard Knaak, that persistence has finally been rewarded in this, the tale you hold.

I was immediately drawn to Dar's character and the link between the animal and human aspects. Animals do not know greed, anger, or jealousy. We humans are more complex, and unfortunately, our dark side creates all the turmoil that the world experiences. Dar is a mixture of both, and thus, he is our best representative to bring peace and order to our world. Still, as a human by birth he has his doubts and ever searches for his true nature, just as the rest of us must do.

At its roots, Dar's world is truly magic and sorcery. There is no past, present, nor future—there is only the *now*. Set in a "time where time does not exist," this novel explores through Dar the essence of good and evil and the true meaning of life and spirituality . . . and, of course, also provides an exciting epic adventure with characters old and new.

We hope that the myth will transport you to a world that will become part of your daily dreams and escape, and that the Beastmaster will be back for more adventures . . . and dreams.

—Sylvio Tabet

1

ONCE UPON A TIME . . .
   It was a way storytellers from the very first began their tales, whether true or of their own imagining. It was always some version of those words.

Once upon a time . . .

Yet, to a sage such as Baraji, time did not happen once, but *always*. There were as many moments of the same bit of time as there were sands in a desert. More even, for, in truth, time was endless in all directions.

But that did not mean that a single moment might not affect all the rest and that such moments might indeed determine not only the fates of men, but *worlds* and more.

The bald, skeletal figure muttered under his breath, breath that came out in thick clouds, for the icy cave in which Baraji meditated was situated high upon a snowcapped peak of dank Harrath, north of even chill Andereas. Baraji himself did not, of course, notice such a mundane thing as the cold, for he had long ago progressed past such human frailty. His mind, his soul, was focused instead on the many realities beyond perceived reality, and the nature of all that, which was imminent to the future.

The tiny fire before him was surrounded by perfectly circular black stones that themselves formed a perfect circle. The power of the mandala shone in the pattern of the stones and even the flames within. Baraji leaned forward to examine the center of the fire not with his weaker mortal eyes, but with the invisible third one that could see beyond this one plane of existence.

It was as he had thought. Nodding satisfaction, he gathered snow from the icy cave floor and tossed it onto the flames.

The fire erupted with a squeal. A shape suddenly burst from the center—tendrils, like grass, blossomed into red, inquisitive orbs lacking pupils, fearsome orbs that stared in all directions for the space of a breath . . . and then turned into a crimson-tinged mist that swiftly dissipated.

"It is the moment," rasped Baraji. "But is it?"

In truth, that was not for him to decide; that was for another. And so, Baraji reached into the snow again and removed a single brown and black feather buried within it. Released with a flick from his cadaverous hand, the feather bobbed on the heaving halo of fire before being swept into the flames. A plume of thick, acrid smoke burst forth from the now bloodred blaze.

Baraji inhaled deeply, inviting the mystic powers of the smoke to flow into him. As he did, a faint, familiar voice emerged from within the fire, a voice that cried the same question over and over.

Who am I? it asked. *Who am I?* repeated the voice, and though it was strong of timbre, it was rife with uncertainty.

And from the smoke arose a ghostly visage that continued to mouth the question. The face took on the semblance of a lithe man in his prime—square jaw, angular features, and bright, guileless blue eyes set under a brooding brow. For a moment, the ghostly vision confronted Baraji . . . then flung forward, enveloping the sage's own face.

In that instant, Baraji's countenance became that of the man in the smoke. His bald pate was suddenly crowned by thick, brown locks that framed the sturdy, clean-shaven face. Yet, where once there had been a haunted, questioning look, now was an expression of self-knowledge.

"I *am*," Baraji mustered through the magical mask. "I *am* . . ."

But no sooner did he answer than the other face sloughed off, plunging into the fire. The voice dissolved into ash as it implored once more the same earnest question.

With a toothless smile that held no humor, the sage drew a small mandala in the frozen ground between him and the fire— circles within circles surrounding triangles and, in their very midst, a rounded mouth. Baraji muttered under his breath once more and, in the center of the mandala, saw simultaneously many things, many places, and many times.

Lastly he saw a great glacier . . . and on it, a tiny figure. The young man from the smoke.

Baraji let himself become the vision. The harsh, swirling land-scape surrounded him. The winds roared with abandon, whip-ping across the barren glacier and over the naked figure seated cross-legged in meditation. Snow and ice draped the man as if he had been there for a great period . . . which was truer than even the figure knew himself. His body was lean and well-muscled and so very pale that most would have thought—rightly so under the circumstances—that he had long ago lost his battle against the fero-cious elements.

But Baraji peered close and saw the faint, telltale puff of breath every few minutes. The man was deep in a trance, journeying through the worlds within him as the sage had taught him.

His teacher was much pleased by the dedication, much pleased by the effort. Back in the cave, the physical Baraji nodded at his student. He opened his mouth—and unleashed a deafening roar like that of a great jungle cat.

DAR'S BODY FLINCHED ever so slightly. Deep within, he stirred from the contemplations that had consumed him during his trance. His subconscious felt the echo of an animal call . . . and yet not. He tried to return to the relative serenity of his meditation and the search for answers to his constant question . . . *Who am I? What am I? Am I a man? An animal? Both? Neither? What is my purpose in this world?*

Those who had met him in the real world called him not by his name, but most often by how legend had marked him. They called him the *Beastmaster,* for Dar had the ability to become one with any animal, the ability to speak with them and see through their eyes. The creatures of the jungle would even stand with him in battle against sorcerers and other evils he encountered during his endless journeys throughout Ancor. In the space of his twenty-plus summers, Dar had become a mythic figure, his epithet woven into countless fantastic stories, both real and embellished by those who recited them.

Dar had not asked for such abilities; they had been thrust upon him before he had even been born. Dark sorcery had ripped him from his mother's womb—brutally slaying her in the process—and had implanted his fetus into the womb of a cow. After his birth into the arms of his wicked captors, Dar was marked for murder—a ritual of fire that would keep him from fulfilling his epic prophecy. But the fates intervened, and instead Dar was rescued and raised by a simple villager, a farmer with no knowledge of the infant's royal blood or of his natal link to animal kind.

Dar's incredible abilities manifested themselves while he was but a child . . . a fortunate turn of events that enabled him at the time to rescue his adoptive father from the clutches of a hungry bear by facing the ursine giant and silently commanding it to leave. As the boy came of age, there were more and more incidents—most of them minor in event, yet still astounding for simply being what they were.

And so began the legend of the Beastmaster . . .

It had taken many summers for Dar to discover the truth of his origins—summers in which he became known far and wide for his abilities and deeds, and one particular summer in which he not only lost his adoptive father but most of his village to a bloodthirsty barbarian horde. He helped the survivors to resettle, but, haunted by his failure to save his father and his village, he left shortly thereafter out of personal shame.

What had been intended as only a short journey became an endless one with only intermittent visits to what remained of his home. Some of the people he met during his distant wanderings accepted his existence with gratitude, others with fear. Many of the former even offered him friendship or a place to stay, but ever the Beastmaster moved on from village to village, realm to realm. Like the many creatures he encountered, Dar could never tame the restlessness within himself, a restlessness that he finally understood had come not just from the loss of the only human family he had ever had, but—in some ways yet more significant—not knowing where he belonged among the men and animals of his world.

Thus, in search of answers, the Beastmaster—a "legend" that believed little in his own tale—had journeyed up to the mountains of Harrath, northernmost of all realms, to see the sage of whom many wise men had spoken. Baraji would be the one to help him, they had said. Baraji *is* enlightenment, they had insisted. From him, Dar would find the answers. And he had begun to . . .

But his meditations now struck a desperate and frightening impasse. Vivid dreams assailed his mind. Like an enemy army waiting, ready to spring, eager to catch its target unaware—in one fell swoop the visions overpowered Dar. He struggled to regain the peace and composure for which he had so long earnestly fought, but the dreams—nay, *nightmares*—would not let him. Dar was bombarded by horrific vision after horrific vision, most of them filled with things that seemed impossible for his imagination to create.

He saw his beloved world, his Ancor, shrouded in black, monstrous smoke billowing from vast, jagged wounds in the earth. The gust of thick plumes covered more than a mile and filled the heavens with a dread eagerness. It was a wonder there was light at all, for the sun could surely not shine through. The only source of light in his nightmares radiated from the holes themselves, where red and gold flames and flashes of what appeared to be blue lightning illuminated the permanent night.

And in the wicked glow Dar saw fiends and demons of myriad shapes and evils. Giant metal golems—each a three-legged cyclops whose lone eye was a blazing, azure orb that spit lightning—strode over burnt trees, seeking movement. Helmeted and armored demons short of stature but broad of build scurried along the ground, bursting fire from weapons held within their clawed hands. In the manic strobes of illumination, their bulbous-eyed helmets with protruding elephantine hoses gave the impression of some grotesque giant insect.

Shadows moved that might have been spiders—had they not been tenfold the size of a man. More fearsome creatures followed in the wake of the helmeted warriors, which Dar's distressed subconscious could not identify as akin to anything that had ever walked Ancor.

Then, through the thick smoke enshrouding the heavens, fell a fiery rain of huge rocks.

Meteorites.

They struck the lands in Dar's nightmares with relentless precision, wiping out towns, villages, kingdoms. High stone walls shattered like eggshells and mighty palaces were crushed into dust. A blistering inferno gorged all in its path and belched only ash, as the gargantuan missiles buried themselves deep in Ancor's ravaged soil.

And from those enormous pits erupted more wicked black plumes, transforming the sky into a horrific shadow. Dar fought to see what lay in the bottom of the nearest crater, for he could not fathom that these massive plumes were simply the result of impact. There was something darker, more evil, at work within. He pressed forward, nearing the edge.

He squinted hard into the choking, black smoke—but just as the stinging haze enveloped him, the Beastmaster awoke with a scream that echoed beyond the stark, lifeless glacier, beyond even the nearby peaks.

Dar's body, which Baraji had suggested he strip naked in order to better relive the experience of birth and beginning, was encrusted in glittering layers of ice and snow—the accumulation of many a storm. Even the bright sun could not diminish the biting cold, and Dar, shaking off the icy white shroud, quickly scrambled for his garments and the thick brown fur that his teacher had given him for this journey. Even then, the lean fighter was clad in little more than shin-high leather boots, a dark-tanned kilt fitted with metal tabs, and matching wrist guards. Like his animal brethren, Dar lived simply, taking from the world only what was required for survival.

As full reason returned, Dar suddenly realized that he was alone. He quickly surveyed the chill area, but found no sign of his trusted comrades. Concentrating, he tried to touch their minds, but failed.

Baraji, Dar immediately thought. *Ruh and the others must be with Baraji!*

From a powdery mound to his left, Dar dug out a pouch and a long, wooden staff. His sword he had left in the care of Baraji, who had suggested that Dar's only conflict atop the glacier would be that within himself.

But Dar was puzzled by what had manifested in his nightmares.

He stared down at his feet, where, still clearly etched in the hard snow despite the weather, a mandala—a circular pattern Dar had drawn according to Baraji's earlier tutoring—yet beckoned. The mandala, with its inner circles in which lay pyramids and crisscrossing lines, had been the Beastmaster's focus for his meditation. Mandalas were key to the self-awareness that Dar sought, if only because they opened up what Baraji called the *chakras* within him. Releasing each of the chakras—nexuses to one's inner energy and being— were the first steps toward that understanding.

Yet as the stiffness in Dar's limbs softened after what seemed like days of meditation, he felt no closer to the truth. He wondered if he had been wrong to see hope in the sage's lessons. As far as he could tell, all he had garnered was a frozen body and dread dreams that, thankfully, could have nothing to do with the true world. Nothing at—

His bright eyes widened in shock as Dar glanced toward the south—and saw a sky as black as pitch. The Beastmaster uttered no sound. The monstrous horrors from his nightmares ran through his mind.

He began to run. Like a nimble mountain goat, Dar raced along the glacier to the distant slope he had initially ascended. The shrieks of the dying resounded in his ears, and he could not help but think that each fading voice had been true, after all. Baraji would know; Baraji would tell Dar if his sinister dreams were actually based in reality.

Baraji, the Beastmaster prayed, would surely tell him that he was only imagining.

Consumed with ever-swelling anxiety for both his dear friends and his beloved Ancor, Dar ran recklessly, frantically. His foot cracked through a thin layer of frozen snow and wedged into a narrow gap. He stumbled, and the slick ice beneath thrust him forward. Dar lost his footing, lost control . . .

He plummeted to the glacier's edge, sliding toward a drop of well over a thousand feet. Dar jammed his staff into the snow, trying to halt or even slow his fall, but the wooden stick abruptly cracked in two. The Beastmaster clutched at the ground, seeking a handhold, but his grasping fingers only came away with icy powder.

The wind howled harder in his ears, a sign that the edge was near. With his mind, Dar called out to those who were his cherished family, his comrades in arms—but they were oddly absent. The mental link with each had been severed as if they were dead.

He struggled for traction again, but encountered only empty air. Dar flew off the edge—

And awoke *again*.

Now he sat cross-legged in a familiar place, his sword over his lap. The ice-covered stalactites and stalagmites gave the sage's cave the semblance of a giant mouth with savage teeth—a mouth about to swallow him whole.

Baraji paid him no mind, the hairless elder gazing into the tiny fire he always kept. Dar sat opposite his teacher, a position he recalled from numerous occasions, before Baraji had sent him to the glacier.

Or had Dar ever actually left?

"It is . . . but is it?" muttered the wizened figure as he reached down beside him and took up a tiny bit of snow. Baraji tossed the hardened flakes into the fire. An eruption of multicolored flames illuminated a sudden apparition—a round-eyed, demonic face that appeared ever so briefly above the fire.

Baraji nodded as if the already-vanishing sight explained all things perfectly. "It is . . . it must be . . ." He suddenly looked up, meeting Dar's startled gaze. "It must be . . ."

"What—what must be?" Dar was startled by his own voice, which sounded as if it better belonged to one of the great frogs of the Myrnean Swamp. Swallowing, the Beastmaster tried again. "What must . . . be?" His nerves grew taut as he recovered from his astonishment at finding himself in the cave rather than plummeting off the glacier, and recalled the vivid dreams of slaughter and devastation. "Ancor! Does it have to do with Ancor?" He leaped to his feet. "I dreamed—"

"Dreamed you did, but lived you did," sang the sage darkly. "Awaiting the moment, if the moment is here. Several summers, two hands worth and some, your waiting, for—"

"So many?" Dar blurted, staggering back. He shook his head, refusing to believe that he had heard correctly. "Master Baraji . . . you must tell me . . . you speak as if . . . as if it has been so many seasons since I last walked the jungles . . . that the trance . . ."

The elderly figure nodded. "Ten summers and some, the Beastmaster has dwelled in his timeless quest while Ancor has seen light turn to darkness."

So very long. Dar turned from his teacher, trying to come to grips with what Baraji claimed. It could not be true! This must have been some new lesson that the master sought to teach him . . .

As if hearing him, Baraji said, "All is as it had to be, my student; all was necessary."

Dar spun back to face him. "Why? This was not what I asked for! Why?" He thought of the changes, the losses, that could happen in one season, let alone as many as Baraji hinted at. Who was alive? Who was dead? Who—

The nightmares came back to him. "They are real, aren't they? Everything I saw!"

Baraji stared into the fire, saying nothing. It was answer enough for Dar. He all but lunged toward the emaciated man.

"Master Baraji! Why? What is happening to Ancor? And why let me be ignorant of all of it?"

The sage tossed another pinch of snow into the fire. There was a rush of air and above the flames momentarily appeared a blackened jungle and the ravaged remnants of huts. Although the image lasted but a breath, it remained burned in the Beastmaster's head.

"Destiny is happening," Baraji murmured. "And that is why it had to be so long, Beastmaster . . ."

Dar had heard enough. He had accepted the sage's vague remarks during his studies, seeing in them guides to his own personal search. Now, though, all Dar wanted was explicit answers. Ancor was and had been under assault by demons or some other terrible magical power, and yet Baraji had left him in his trance not just days, weeks, or even months, but—impossible as it was to believe—years. All those who Dar had cared for, all those he had sought to protect, might already be dead.

The Beastmaster shivered. Even the ones he most needed now . . .

"And where are the others?" he demanded, aware that animals did not in general live as long as men. Dar fought to restrain himself from shouting but was sickened at the thought of losing those he considered his family without even knowing of their passing. "Where do they lay now, Baraji? And for how long? When did Sharak fall from the sky, or Ruh, Podo, and Kodo crawl off into the wilderness? Do any of them still live?"

At last the naked figure peered up again. "The Beastmaster without his beasts?" Baraji shook his head. "Destiny demands you all, my pupil, and your friends, of course, would demand to wait for your return . . ."

He gestured deeper into the cave . . . where, for the first time, Dar beheld four tranquil white mounds.

Ice coated what had once been soft snow, turning the latter into a crystalline mantle that glittered in the flickering illumination of the tiny fire. Dar could not stifle a gasp. One hand went out to the mounds, then quickly withdrew.

"I feel nothing," he stated baldly. If they were alive, as Baraji had indicated, there should have been *something*.

Attention again on the flames, the sage commented, "They are merely deep asleep and must be called . . ."

Brow furrowed, Dar stared at the rounded shapes that were supposed to be his dearest friends. *Merely asleep?* He doubted that very much, yet clung to the remote hope.

Ruh . . . the Beastmaster called with his mind, for it was not words with which he generally spoke with the animals, but rather emotions and thought. *Ruh . . . Kodo . . . Podo . . . Sharak . . .*

Nothing happened. Dar nearly gave in, but could not accept that they were truly lost to him, not with so much else in turmoil.

Ruh . . . Dar imagined the powerful, majestic tiger racing through the forest. *Kodo . . . Podo . . .* The wily ferrets had always traveled with him in his pouch, ever ready to lend their skills at thievery for good causes. *Sharak . . .* The sentinel in the sky, the magnificent brown eagle, who had always given Dar warning of threat.

Ruh . . . Sharak . . . Podo . . . Kodo . . .

Dar felt Baraji's eyes trained on him. Stepping closer, he tried to connect with the four animals as he had always done.

One of the two tiny mounds trembled. Dar held his breath as the mound stilled again . . . then renewed its shaking. Cracks appeared in the icy snow. From within came scratching, faint at first, then much louder, more active.

An inquisitive black nose broke through to the surface. It twitched several times and focused on where Dar stood.

Kodo smashed his way out of the rest of his chill cocoon, then scurried over to Dar. He leaped into the Beastmaster's waiting arms, nuzzling Dar on the face.

Dar hugged the black and golden brown ferret, then sensed Kodo's desire to be put on the ground again. He understood why.

Kodo ran back to the other small mound, which had also begun to shake. The ferret used his sharp teeth and claws to penetrate the solid glaze. Seconds later, a second ferret—a female—emerged and the two animals licked one another happily before racing for Dar.

"Kodo . . . Podo . . ." he murmured, his eyes moist. Grateful for their return, he set aside his sword and clutched both ferrets as though they were his children.

As he did, the smaller of the remaining two mounds cracked open at the top. As if emerging from an egg, Sharak thrust his head out and squawked a greeting to the Beastmaster. Then, with a flapping of his wings, the eagle dispersed the rest of the snow and fluttered into the air. Dar let the ferrets climb into the sack that was their home, then held out an arm for the powerful bird.

Sharak landed on the leather guard. Folding his wings, he gave Dar another squawk, and the Beastmaster stroked the bird on the head.

A muffled yet still powerful roar suddenly escaped the depths of the cave. The final mound shook with such vigor that icicles above it broke free, splintering on the ground. A massive, striped tiger surfaced. With a great roar and shudder, Ruh flung the moisture from his sleek fur, baring incisors as long as Dar's hand.

The great cat sniffed the air—his rich, amber orbs quickly fixing on the Beastmaster. Unlike the others, Ruh strode toward Dar in a most casual manner, as if seeing the human was not so special a matter to so tremendous a cat. Still, the moment he reached Dar, the tiger pressed his face against the Beastmaster's leg and purred like a happy cub.

For a moment, Dar forgot his troubles as he reveled in the animals' return. There were those he loved among humans, but no more than he did these four. But the moment of relief passed quickly.

Dar thought of the thick, black cover over the southern sky, and Ruh and the others quickly registered his concern. The tiger let out a growl of fury and puzzlement, emotions mirrored by the ferrets and Sharak.

His concern only for Ancor now, Dar retrieved his blade and turned to leave. Despite such an incredible length of time without sustenance, miraculously he felt no hunger. With luck, he and the animals could reach better climes before they needed to eat.

As Dar stepped past the fire, Baraji extended his bony hands toward him. In them was a small, oblong stone almost bronze in color with small gold striations in the middle. An iron chain was attached to each end of the stone.

"There is magic in this, my pupil," the skeletal sage murmured. For the first time, Baraji showed a true human concern. "Carry it with you as you seek the truth and your destiny."

Dar had faced magic many times in the past and sensed that Baraji did not exaggerate when it came to the stone. The Beastmaster respectfully accepted the gift. If what he had dreamed was the terrifying truth—and at this point he had no reason to doubt it—then he would need anything that his mentor could provide.

The stone felt pleasantly warm in his palms, almost as if he held a small, living creature rather than a simple piece of mineral the size of a thick plum. Dar brought the chain over his neck and let the stone settle on his chest. The warmth above his heart gave him some slight hope.

"What does it do?" he asked.

Baraji shook his head. "It is not what *it* does, it is what *you* do—what you *are*, Beastmaster."

Grunting at Baraji's typically ambiguous statement, Dar nodded to the sage, then turned. He needed to descend to the lowlands, to see the extent that his nightmares mirrored reality. He needed to see if there was yet something he could do for those below.

With the ferrets at rest in his pouch, Sharak on his arm, and Ruh at his side, the Beastmaster headed for the mouth of the cave. Outside, the wind howled mournfully, as if presaging what Dar would find.

Just before he stepped out into the flying snow, Dar glanced back over his shoulder.

The cadaverous figure was no longer there.

Standing in his place was a handsome young man with hawklike features and hair the color of a raven's feather. The bearded stranger was clad in robes that shimmered with the colors of the rainbow. His face, dark of complexion, was filled with honesty, intelligence, and, most of all, wisdom.

Dar recognized that this was indeed still Baraji.

"Through all else, continue to seek the answers to your own inner quest," the sage calmly remarked, "for it is intertwined with your fate to help all others." Baraji smiled like a father before his son. "And it may be the best hope for all Ancor . . ."

"What—?" was all Dar managed to utter before the wind outside suddenly rushed into the cave, buffeting the Beastmaster and his companions before reaching Baraji. With a gentleness it had not shown for Dar, the wind encircled the robed figure. Baraji smiled wide as he transformed into flakes of snow that were plucked up by the wind and carried out of the cave. At the same time, the gust extinguished the fire.

Stepping outside, the Beastmaster watched as the snowflakes dispersed among the mountains. Dar touched the stone hanging over his chest and felt in it a hint of his mentor's presence.

Dar hefted his sword and let Sharak take to the sky. The eagle circled once, then, with a mighty cry, headed in the direction of the trail descending the side of the peak.

Taking a deep breath, the Beastmaster charged through the cold and snow, already wondering how he—a lone warrior with questionable magical abilities—might be able to combat the titanic fury engulfing what seemed all of Ancor.

Assuming that it was not already far, far too late to do anything at all.

2

JALAN RAN. HE DARTED THROUGH THE DARKENED JUNGLE AS fast as his young legs could still manage, but always felt as if the demons and monsters were at his heels, ready to devour him or strike him down with the terrifying blue lightning bolts they fired from their hands.

A fleeting *whoosh* was Jalan's only warning before the trees beside him erupted into an inferno that lit up the the entire vicinity. He stumbled to a halt and crouched behind a thick tree, gaping at the carnage.

The horrific explosion that had shaken his village again flashed through his mind—and with it came images of his family's thatched hut ablaze and his mother, her cloth dress on fire, screaming his name.

The boy shivered as the sweat of heat and fear trickled down from his black hair, stinging his eyes.

His heart jumped as he recalled the jolt he had felt when his father, Garas, had suddenly hoisted him up and carried the child of ten summers out of the village. The barrel-chested farmer had blindly navigated through the thick smoke to safety in the nearby forest. As the pair had begun to fight their way through the jagged undergrowth, the screaming from the village ceased and all became eerily silent save for the deafening roar of the inferno.

That was when the first of the demons had materialized.

FITTED WITH SLEEK, metallic armor and an oversized helmet, the toadlike creature had been shorter than Jalan's father by at least a foot but as broad at the shoulder as Olydius the blacksmith. They had watched in horror as the demon swiftly raised a gauntleted hand toward the pair. From it, a tube perhaps as long as the boy's forearm sprang forward.

With a cry, Garas—who had oft regaled his son with tales of serving as a soldier for the then–child king of Aruk, Tal—threw the youth to the side and kicked out at the demon. As the monstrous warrior staggered back, from the tube erupted an earsplitting lightning bolt that would forever be a part of Jalan's nightmares. The treetops burst into flames, and his father seized Jalan, shouting, "Run, boy! Run to Iloth!" referring to a village to the north. "And if you get lost, keep running!"

Jalan wanted to stay, but he had always obeyed his father and knew that Garas would be disappointed with him if he did not go. The boy ran, fast as he could, knowing his father would soon be close behind.

But then . . . he heard a dreadful cry. A sickening blue light illuminated his path, and Jalan halted, looking back over his shoulder—

Just in time to see a second terrifying blue flash engulf his beloved father.

Jalan screamed, too, but kept running. As he thrashed through the woods, his father's horrific death repeated itself over and over in his mind, never once lessening in dreadful intensity.

Suddenly, a grinding sound filled the jungle, tearing the boy from his nightmares. He knew that sound. With a fearful glance over his shoulder, Jalan caught sight of a giant metal-clad golem.

It moved on three jointed legs so long that they stretched high over what trees remained. Armless, with a round, squat body and short head, the giant's face consisted of one huge, blue orb that swept constantly over the vicinity as the titan's head turned around in one unsettling circle after another.

Jalan ducked behind a tree, praying that the giant would not see him. The monstrous creature had one menacing eye that flashed the same deadly blue lightning whenever it blinked. Its very glance could send death as far as Jalan could run in a hundred breaths.

The terrible glow of the giant's eye shifted past him . . . then froze. The frantic boy held his breath.

With a grace its shape belied, the metallic titan's legs turned in the direction of the gaze. The demon started to hum almost merrily.

Jalan cringed.

The orb blinked.

Blue lightning shot forth, striking the area at which the behemoth stared. Along its path, the streaming bolt set ablaze more treetops.

And as it struck its distant target, a human shriek arose that drained the blood from Jalan's face. It sounded like his father . . . too much like his father. But that could not be. Garas was dead. The demon had slain another. Apparently someone else had survived Karith . . . at least for a few frightening hours.

Heart racing, Jalan stumbled back from the tree.

The evil orb veered in his direction.

Jalan threw himself to the side just before the light washed over where he had been standing. Pressing himself against the ruined trunk of another tree, the boy bit his lip and waited.

There was a pause . . . and then the giant moved on in search of other prey.

Trembling, the boy finally turned away and resumed his flight. Garas had given him a command; Jalan always obeyed his father.

Even if his father was dead.

But several ominous shapes abruptly filled the burning jungle around him. Jalan recognized the outlines of demon warriors identical to the one his father had fought against. There was also something else among them, something flitting about almost like a malevolent ghost. It was clad in black and gray shrouded robes, its face—if the ghost had one, Jalan thought with a shiver—utterly obscured.

And then the shadowy figure spoke. In low, sibilant tones that reminded Jalan too much of a snake, the hooded form commanded, "Send the Oculon further northeast! Now!" To one of the helmed figures, the ghost gestured with a cadaverous hand, "I want all you Pygmesians to scorch the area clean, then set up the landing markers! Hurry, lest you incur *his* wrath as well as mine!"

The demon to whom the figure spoke made an odd clacking sound like that of the large horned beetles that lived in the trees near Jalan's lost home. Then the—*Pygmesians,* the ghost had called them—fanned out even further.

Two of them rushed toward his location.

He had no choice but to run, although it immediately put him in plain sight of the monsters.

But just as he leaped out, from the treetops came a merry squawk and a flurry of feathers illuminated by the nearby fires— bright red and blue. The parrot dove down between the two Pygmesians, utterly distracting them from Jalan's presence. The demons clacked angrily as they tried to aim their tubes at the bird.

The boy did not waste the miracle. He ran as hard as he could. Behind him, Jalan heard the *fwoosh*ing sound of the demons' lightning sticks and the parrot's continued cheerful call. The bird laughed in a most human manner, a sound punctuated by more lightning.

And then the ghastly sounds receded as Jalan shoved on. He was now far off the trail to Iloth, but that did not matter. Jalan did not expect to find the other village any more intact than his own. He had to keep running. His father had oft spoken not only of Aruk, but an even mightier kingdom: Edurac. In Jalan's young mind, surely one of those lay ahead. In it, he could find sanctuary. In it, he could find safety.

Something swooped just over his head. Jalan nearly shrieked in terror but then recognized the squawk of the parrot. The bird alighted on a low branch, then eyed the wheezing human. In desperate need for some contact, Jalan stretched out a tentative hand toward the friendly parrot. He wished the colorful avian would come to him, if even for a moment.

The parrot fluttered off the branch, then landed on his outstretched arm.

Momentarily distracted from the death and devastation around him, Jalan used his other hand to gently stroke the parrot's back. He had always had an affinity for animals, often knowing what ailed them even when his father did not. The parrot rubbed his head into the boy's hand.

"Seto . . ." Jalan blurted. For some reason, he wanted to call the avian by the name, which meant "happiness."

"Seto!" squawked the parrot quietly but merrily, as if tasting with pleasure his new title. The round eyes blinked. "Seto!"

Then, to Jalan's dismay, the bird leaped from his arm and flew off ahead. The boy stifled a gasp of fear; he did not want to be left alone again.

But Seto only flew back to the branch upon which he had previously perched. He settled there, then looked back at Jalan.

"Seto!" the bird called in a quieter but still cheerful voice.

At that moment, Jalan heard the sickening roar of the demons' relentless hunt. He started to run again, instinctively racing to where the parrot perched.

Seto fluttered off the branch, landing on another a short distance farther. Jalan followed, finding the path an easier one than the one he had used thus far.

"Jalan!" squawked Seto as he took to the air, once more alighting on a branch a little beyond the boy.

Hearing the bird call to him, Jalan took heart. He picked up his pace, Seto already his lifeline, his hope.

And not once did the boy even question how the parrot had learned to speak a name it had never heard uttered.

DAR MOVED WITH the swiftness of an antelope as he first left Hagras, then crossed the nearly as inhospitable wind-tossed plains of lower Andereas. In Andereas, though, there was at least some plant life and game, sparse though the pickings were. Sharak and Ruh stalked and caught a pair of white-furred hares, and they and the rest fed on this meager fare.

The Beastmaster paused to give thanks to the spirits of the hares, aware of their essential role in the chain of life. Hunting to survive was no sin, but it was also proper to respect that which kept you alive and healthy.

Dar respectfully placed the polished skulls facing west, the direction of the new day and a symbol of life and birth. Murmuring a prayer of gratitude over each skull, Dar set them in the middle of a mandala he had drawn in the earth. The last was his own addition to the ritual, for surely the teachings of Baraji applied to the life and death of even these small but significant creatures. Dar's mandala bore symbols of various animals, each surrounded by a circle representing the sun.

Sitting back, the Beastmaster raised his hands, palms up in the direction of the hidden sun, asking in silent gesture that it take the spirits to their next lives—

The skulls quivered.

Dar pulled back. Kodo and Podo, who had been by his side, scurried behind him. Ruh let out a low growl, which was echoed by Sharak's squawk.

The skulls slowly began to turn in a circle, animation that Dar had never witnessed before. His ritual was not one of magic, merely reverence.

But now the bones of the rodents moved as if seeking something. The skulls suddenly pointed south . . . no . . . southwest. Dar gingerly touched one, and although the weight of his finger alone should have been able to turn it, the skull remained resolutely fixed on that particular direction, quivering all the time.

It came as no surprise to find that the black shroud was darkest over that part of Ancor.

Dar hesitated, conflicted. His original intention had been to head west, straight to where the survivors of his village had settled, but this startling new sign beckoned to him. He stepped from the mandala and the bones . . . and the moment he did, the skulls stilled.

Dar knew he could not abandon those who had known him most of his life. Although his adopted father was long dead, there were others in the village who had been special to him. There were even some friends among the Touargang tribe, the seminomadic hunters who had become the villagers' neighbors and trading partners. The chieftain's young daughter—Tara was her name—had been especially fascinated with his ties to all animals. Of all of the Touargangs, the wide-eyed princess had seemed to understand Dar the most.

He shook his head, clearing away the memories in order to consider what land lay south of him.

Edurac. One of the mightiest of kingdoms, ruled by King Leardius. Dar had never been to Edurac, but he knew its lofty reputation. It was strong and surely could defend itself long enough for the Beastmaster to pass through his own village first.

Determined to help his people, Dar led Ruh and the others on toward the looming jungles to the west. Ahead, the thick, churning cloud cover stretched closer and closer toward him, as if eager to swallow the Beastmaster up, as it had all else.

As it seemed poised to do with the rest of Ancor . . .

What sounded like thunder continually rumbled from the dark lands ahead, but Dar knew well that what he heard was nothing so harmless as that. There was too much regularity to the horrific sounds, and from dread experience the Beastmaster understood them to be explosions or crashes. The nightmarish images of fiery missiles plummeting from the heavens returned to him, and the human immediately picked up his already swift pace. When at last he reached the lowlands and the first hints of the jungle, Dar breathed easier . . . but only briefly. As he entered the vast, growing darkness, he sensed for the first time something so unnatural that it made him shiver.

Yet still the Beastmaster pressed on, the ferrets in his pouch, Ruh and Sharak spreading out ahead to scout. They were essential to Dar's efforts; while the eagle could see far ahead, it was up to Ruh to determine just what might lurk hidden in the undergrowth of the jungle.

But after the first few hours, Dar wondered if *anything* lurked in the benighted land. Ruh sensed no other animals and only the occasional insect. The skies were equally devoid of winged folk, including Sharak's kind. It was as if anything intelligent that could have fled already had . . . or, worse, perhaps been taken.

Fearful of the last, Dar bent low to the soft soil, searching for tracks. He found them quickly and in great numbers. There *had* been a mass exodus of the jungle's denizens toward the west, toward the lands beyond fabled Edurac. The footprints of grazers mixed freely with those of the beasts that hunted them, a sign of just how desperate the creatures had been.

It was yet another sign that the Beastmaster should also journey in that direction—and Edurac, of course—but his heart overpowered his instinct. First the village, then the great kingdom.

Dar continued on the trail. He was still days from the village, precious days. Even at a pace that no other human could have maintained, it would be five or more before he reached his goal . . . assuming there was anything left to reach.

It was only minutes later that Sharak demanded his attention. Dar's mind instantly became one with that of the eagle, his view suddenly shifting to a perspective far above the ground. The avian's eyes not only took in far more of the landscape than Dar's could have, but magnified it as well.

And what it took in was a gargantuan shape far in the distance, a thing that Dar thought made of metal. The Beastmaster's hands tightened; he had seen sorcerers conjure to life metal constructs of different shapes. Golems, they called them.

But never had he seen a golem so huge or so complex. Even from Sharak's distant viewpoint, Dar saw the ease with which it moved. The legs swiveled like those of a man and the massive arms smashed away any impediment in its path. The hands ended in metal talons that ripped through solid wood with great ease. It had a head that seemed to blend right into its torso. Of a face, there consisted but two massive, blank orbs. The rest was an insidious mass of metal and softer materials that seemed reminisicent of some great beast's trunk sealed to the chest.

What looked like metal horns but moved like the ears of an animal jutted from the top. Other, solid horns, thrust in a row from the top down the back of the head. Dar kept especially still as the animated horns turned. He was certain that the golem was listening for intruders.

The creature's armor was covered in intricate metalwork that the Beastmaster recognized also had some function. Those coursing over the chest gave the golem the added appearance of something skeletal despite its great girth.

The horns/ears stilled.

The golem suddenly turned its inhuman gaze to the sky.

Dar instinctively warned Sharak, but the great raptor was already banking.

Lightning—*blue* lightning—shot forth from a tube on the golem's arm. Dar stood astounded, never having seen lightning that flew up, never mind with such evil precision. The wicked streak shot so closely past Sharak that through the eagle Dar was able to feel the incredible heat.

He summoned Sharak back, ignoring the bird's desire to stay aloft. Sharak was no coward; he did not like to run and hide from any foe. However, Dar knew that the eagle had been fortunate—the next time the golem focused on him, there was no promise that Sharak would survive.

Even as the raptor descended to him, Dar touched Ruh's mind. Now the landscape transformed into a variety of shapes that each emitted a hint of heat. That heat, along with the astounding smells that the tiger picked up, identified everything for nearly a mile around.

Ruh prowled the jungle at a dizzying speed, twisting around torched trees and maneuvering through gaps that should not have admitted an animal of his tremendous size and girth. In the jungle, Ruh was monarch. No lion, no hyena, could match him. The only threats to him in the past had come in the form of men—hunters, soldiers, and spellcasters.

And with Dar at his side, none of those had prevailed.

Yet, although he moved with the utmost confidence, the white, orange, and ebony cat was never careless. Each slight movement received an imperceptible but penetrating glance, each sound a purposeful flick of the ears, each scent an analyzing inhalation from the nostrils. With senses more acute than even those of Sharak or the ferrets—and certainly any human—Ruh gave Dar the ability to survey the world as few other creatures could.

At the moment, those senses were touching upon things so unnatural and unknown to both man and tiger that Ruh actually hesitated in midstep. Dar, too, paused. The scents that assailed Ruh made the cat arch his back in distaste. There was a notion of foulness, of something that should not be. Ruh bared his fangs and the Beastmaster, mind still locked with the cat's, unconsciously imitated the reaction.

Then Kodo thrust his head out of the pouch, his nose sniffing at something in the vicinity of Dar and the rest. Podo popped out a moment later, imitating the male's reaction. With reluctance, Dar broke the link with Ruh and studied the darkness ahead.

"What is it?" he asked, reaching back to rub the ferrets' heads.

The small animals seemed agitated. There was something in their midst—an eerie presence. The Beastmaster's nerves taut, he sent Sharak to the trees, readied his sword, and carefully stepped forward.

A monstrous howl filled Dar's ears, and something that reminded him of a gigantic flying squirrel or bat sought to envelop his head. A flurry of leathery wings covered the Beastmaster's face, and Dar found his mouth and nose blocked.

He seized the creature by the back, only to pull back his hand in sharp pain. Small, curved quills dotted the thing's spine, quills as deadly as spear points.

Clutching the hilt of his sword with both hands, Dar slashed at the creature's side. All the while he sought to reach its mind in order to find out what it was and why it sought to hurt him. Yet all the Beastmaster sensed was the foul aura that he and his companions had noticed earlier. It was as if the creature was not what it appeared—that it was less animal and more like some crafted abomination. Dar was immediately reminded of the distant golem.

Vicious talons tore at his shoulders while a circular mouth full of hooked teeth attempted to rip out his throat. So close, the Beastmaster beheld a savage face that was indeed some monstrous parody of one of the wolf-headed bats with which he was more familiar. The grotesque eyes were as wide as saucers and the ears long and pointed like the tips of spears. The snout was long and wrinkled. The round mouth continued to snap madly at his flesh, a long, serpentine tongue flickering in and out between attacks. So insistent were the attacks that Dar had no choice but to cut deep into the beast's thick, coarsely furred torso despite his desire never to cause any animal harm.

But what gushed out of the winged terror and over Dar was not blood as the Beastmaster knew it. It had a stench like sulfur and, indeed, was of a yellowish tint recognizable even in the shadowy light.

The fluid stung his skin, and Dar quickly hurled the writhing body from him, scrambling to wipe away the sticky liquid. Hooked claws left bloody lines in Dar's shoulders as the dying creature hit the ground with a thud.

Far ahead, he sensed warning from Ruh. With a hurried glance through the tiger's eyes, the Beastmaster saw Ruh leap up in a vain attempt to snag a fleeting form with his claws. The cat's frustration washed over Dar.

Sharak let out a shriek. As Dar glanced up, three more flying shapes came darting toward him—the creatures that Ruh had sought to catch. As they closed in on the human, the eagle seized one in his talons and an aerial combat ensued.

Swinging hard, Dar forced the remaining two fiends to veer

away from him. For the first time he saw their huge, round eyes, like those of nocturnal beasts—yet these creatures did not blink. Glancing at their vast obsidian pupils, Dar found nothing with which to communicate. If these abominations had been born of nature, they were far past that now.

Sharak and the third flyer continued to spin among the trees, colliding with branches as they sought to rip one another apart with beak and maw. It was only the swiftness of the eagle's wings that kept them from being snared by the claws of the creature. Sharak had a fierce hold on his adversary, but each time the bird attempted to bite at the thick area that passed for the other creature's throat, the toothy maw was there to meet it.

Dar's blade cut through the air, barely missing the head of one of the flyers. The two fiends continued to dart around the Beastmaster in opposite directions in what he knew was purposeful distraction. At any moment, one would use the confusion to strike.

The first of the abominations flew past him again. Dar corrected his stance to fend it off . . . then realized that the second had disappeared.

A spine-chilling flutter of leathery wings brushed the back of his neck—and as he jerked his head, two squealing creatures landed atop the flyer, sending it hurtling to the ground next to Dar. Podo and Kodo attacked with a ferocity their little forms belied, ripping into the tough hide while somehow avoiding the quills that had given the Beastmaster trouble.

Now able to focus on just the one, Dar managed a slash that cut deep into the left wing. Spitting viciously, the flyer veered about and darted back into the jungle, a splatter of its burning life fluids sprinkling Dar in the process.

As the Beastmaster turned, he saw Sharak finally score a mortal strike at his foe's underside. Ignoring the gush of burning blood, the eagle tore with abandon into the flyer. Both the eagle and the dying creature descended to the jungle floor, where Sharak finished the grisly task, then screeched in triumph.

As for the ferrets, their adversary was long dead, but both continued to worry the corpse, just in case. Dar finally ordered them back so that he could inspect the carcass. Kodo and Podo had done their work well, leaving less than even Sharak or Dar had with their own foes. The ferrets constantly spit and rubbed their faces in the soft earth as they attempted to remove all traces of the distasteful fluids from them.

The second flyer was identical to the one that Dar had initially slain. Even in death, it radiated a wrongness that made the hair on the nape of his neck stand. Once this had been an ordinary animal, of that the Beastmaster felt certain, but where it had originated, he could not say.

But what mattered was its purpose here—and that of its companions. It had not been fleeing the evil sweeping across Ancor; it had been part of it. A small but deadly part of it.

Dar cleaned his blade and abandoned the corpses. The dark jungle beckoned . . . and he had no choice but to continue on.

Continue on and pray for all those those who lived in it.

THE SOLE SURVIVING flyer darted through the jungle with desperate speed, its wound more deadly than the human could have imagined. Weaving uncertainly, the round-orbed creature probed ahead for what it sought . . . and as its strength flagged, the flyer finally found it.

Breath coming in pants, the abomination awkwardly landed on a branch. Its yellow life fluids continued to drip from the wound; the Beastmaster had severed a vital artery, but the purpose for which the flyer had been crafted did not permit the fiend to do anything but seek to fulfill its duty. Once that was accomplished, the flyer could die.

Eyes widening to twice their initial size, the creature let out a low, continuous hum.

MILES AWAY AND near the area where Sharak had noticed the distant golem, a second flyer perched in a tree suddenly opened wide its own orbs. It repeated the hum for a moment, then abandoned the tree. It flew through the jungle, soaring above ranks of helmed Pygmesians systematically scorching the earth, under the legs of the metallic giants scanning the distance for prey, and past others of its kind in the process of gathering information . . . the most essential purpose of all flyers.

Then, sensing the one it sought, the winged abomination descended. As it did, an ethereal arm wrapped in a dark, flowing sleeve reached out to give it perch. The ghostly figure, face obscured by his voluminous hood, leaned close so that the eyes of the flyer filled his view.

"Show me . . ." he hissed. "Show me what is of so much interest . . ."

And the eyes of the flyer transformed, in them images—murky at first, then much more defined—flashing by. The first were simple ones, mainly jungle, but then came the first that caught the hooded one's interest.

Images of a great cat, a raptor, some smaller animals . . . and a human with a sword—Dar and his companions, viewed through the eyes of the invaders' sentinels and spies.

Images that caused an intake of breath from the ghostly form.

"So!" he rasped. "It must be he! Surely . . . it must be . . ."

3

DAR DID NOT HAVE A PLAN, SHOULD HE MANAGE TO EVEN reach the place where the survivors of his village—of lost Emur—had long ago settled. More and more, the Beastmaster suspected that he was too late for them, that what lay ahead would be well beyond anything with which he had ever come to grips. By rights, rather than continue west, Dar should have turned south—now northwest from his current location—and moved on to Edurac. Edurac was the logical, perhaps the *only* choice left to him.

And yet, his innate desire to hope . . . to help . . . kept him moving even as he wondered if there was anyone or anything at all left. Even though it had been so very long since Dar had been there, just knowing that part of his past still existed had always been comforting. The thought of Emur falling a second time, the last of its people slaughtered, was too much for him.

Ruh ran well ahead despite the Beastmaster's admonishment

that the tiger not stray far. Dar could barely sense the great cat, so much further had Ruh already gone. High above, Sharak helped the human keep abreast of the distant golem—and other shapes of mysterious and dread form—further to the south.

Dar felt a cold, moist nose on his neck. Podo licked his skin, the ferret inquisitive.

"No, you two stay with me," the Beastmaster murmured. "I've enough to worry about with Ruh and Sharak."

His concern shifted back to Ruh. The sense of foreboding had grown so great that Dar distrusted even the shadows surrounding every tree. Yet Ruh refused to return to the others.

Sharak squawked a warning.

As Dar linked to the eagle, the jungle shook with horrific vigor. Trees toppled over with monstrous ease. The Beastmaster barely escaped being crushed. The sack slipped from his back, but he snagged it before it could roll away with Kodo and Podo inside.

A searing hiss filled the air, momentarily forcing Dar to cover his ears until he could become accustomed to it. He felt the ferrets' distress at the high-pitched sound but could do nothing for them. Indeed, Dar knew he had to push even closer to the source.

A fiery glow filled the sky ahead of him and created even more macabre shadows in the jungle. A stench arose . . . no . . . a number of unsettling scents mingling together to create one so foul that the Beastmaster had to cover his nose and mouth for fear that he would lose what little food his stomach held. Dar recognized some of those scents and his heart and gut twisted, for they included burnt and rotting flesh.

He cautiously slipped among the trees to garner a closer view, trusting to Sharak's gaze at the same time. The eagle sighted something huge ahead, but flying low as the Beastmaster had ordered, Sharak could not identify it.

Dar stepped on a thick branch that cracked under the weight

of his muscular form. Frustrated by the noise it caused, he glanced down.

With utter repulsion, the Beastmaster stumbled back. What he had taken for a branch was a human bone.

Whether it had been man or woman, Dar could not attest, so thoroughly had the victim been burnt. The bones were black and like fragile kindling. Dar realized that he had stepped on other pieces without even noticing. The smaller bones had simply crumbled to ash.

Whatever had so thoroughly scorched this poor soul had also wreaked havoc on the nearest trees and even the ground in which the remains lay. Dar's blood began to boil and he swore under his breath at such an awful deed.

Something moved in the firelit region ahead. Dar crouched, awaiting whatever demonic foe might be approaching.

A winged form fluttered onto one of the nearest branches and merrily chirped, "Seto!"

A parrot. The bird's sudden appearance completely startled Dar. With all other creatures gone or slain, how could it be that this single avian flew about the jungle as if nothing was amiss?

He started to reach out to the parrot . . . only to have a figure about half his height come charging toward him from the south with reckless abandon. Dar raised his weapon, then saw that it was only a young boy.

The boy collided with him. Dar used his free hand to still the lad. Sharak screeched.

"The demons come!" the boy cried. "The Pygmesians . . ."

"Pygmesians?" Dar repeated. "What—"

He got no further, for at that moment the jungle to the south filled with the shadows of a score of macabre, armored figures.

"Jalan!" the parrot cried, then fluttered to a branch behind Dar. The boy tore from the Beastmaster's grip, running after the bird.

Dar let him pass, knowing that the youth was safer behind him and more concerned now with what swarmed toward them. He was enraged, knowing these were some of the villains responsible for the terrible death and destruction around him. Podo and Kodo popped their heads out of the sack, ready to aid him as he charged the shadowy forms.

A macabre figure suddenly thrust up in front of him. The Beastmaster glimpsed an oversized helmet with bulbous eyeholes. An armored hand jabbed toward him, a sinister tube jutting out from the palm.

Dar leaped aside, at the same time praying that the boy was far out of sight. He could not worry about the boy and fight at the same time.

A blue streak of lightning burst from the tube, shooting past where the human's chest would have been. The streak set ablaze two trees just beyond Dar.

The Beastmaster's blade whirled about. With an expert eye, he aimed for what he thought the weakest link in the demon's odd, sleek, green-and-black armor.

The elephantine hose—stretching down to the chest from where Dar assumed the nose and mouth were—severed with ease. A sulfuric odor briefly wafted under Dar's nose, stinging it and causing him to cough.

A horrific clacking sound escaped the demon as it grasped futilely at the severed hose, then collapsed. Even as it tumbled, Dar instinctively spun to his right, striking with the pommel of his sword.

The iron pommel crashed through the eye of another attacker's helmet. Dar caught a better glimpse of this creature, a fearsome warrior who, albeit shorter than him, had the muscular build of an ape. One hand clutched the Beastmaster's sword arm, squeezing with merciless strength.

Kicking out, Dar sent the armored figure crashing into the brush. Another Pygmesian grasped Dar's sword arm, while a second raised splayed fingers at the human's throat.

Again proving that his own strength well-matched his foes', Dar swung the two Pygmesians together.

From the splayed fingers shot forth four thick but swift darts. They plunged into the neck of the second of Dar's struggling adversaries . . . and exploded, ripping apart the hapless Pygmesian.

Fragments of armor and bits of stench-ridden flesh rained upon everyone. Without hesitation, Dar threw himself forward, tackling the creature who had fired. They collided with three others and all fell to the ground in a tangle.

Out of the corner of his eye, the Beastmaster saw another Pygmesian—hand clutching a lightning tube—looming over him. However, Sharak dove into the face of the new attacker, ripping with his talons and sharp beak at the hose. The Pygmesian clacked furiously and grasped for the eagle, but Sharak managed to grab the hose and rip it from the armored hide.

A streak of blue lightning darted past the Beastmaster from yet another direction, Sharak its intended target. The avian veered away just in time, the wicked bolt instead turning the Pygmesian with whom the eagle had been struggling into an inferno.

The warrior who had just missed Sharak now turned the tube toward Dar—and was in turn assailed by two sleek, scurrying forms. Kodo and Podo scampered over the assassin in opposing directions, frustrating the Pygmesian's attempts to seize one or the other. As they moved, the ferrets also chewed or tore at anything that would give to their teeth and claws.

The desperate Pygmesian tried to fire over its shoulder at Podo, but instead scorched the midsection of a great tree. The trunk collapsed, falling into the fray.

Warned by Sharak, Dar struggled free of the collapsing tree's path. A Pygmesian holding tight to his leg was not so fortunate. The trunk crushed its back with an audible crack.

Sharak again dove in among the demons, distracting several of them. The Pygmesian upon which the ferrets clung began to spin in what was almost a comic series of circles before Kodo bit into a line stretching from the creature's back to the arm that wielded the tube. A harsh flash of light accompanied the bite as the wire flew free, sending the male ferret dropping to the ground with a squeal. Podo leaped down to join him just as the damaged wire touched another connection on the Pygmesian's armored back.

The connection exploded, ripping apart the upper half of the Pygmesian with such quickness that it left the bottom half still standing.

But there were still more of the grotesque figures surrounding Dar. The Beastmaster's eyes teared from the smoke rising from the flames. Through his watery orbs, his adversaries grew more grotesque, their too-large helmets bespeaking of equally repulsive heads and the bend of their bodies making Dar think not of apes anymore, but of giant frogs learning to walk like men. The tubes reminded him of snouts and he could only hazard to guess what abhorrent method of breathing the demons used.

Yet, for demons—if that was what they truly were—they had proven quite mortal. They had flesh that cut and something that passed for blood. They could be slain just as any man could.

But there were still far too many of them for him to defeat.

Though all too aware of that, the Beastmaster fought with all his might. With a great roar, he brought his blade up and across another tubed throat. Kodo and Podo scurried beneath his legs, then intertwined themselves between those of the next nearest adversary. As the warrior stumbled, Dar ended the villain's life.

But matters turned for the worst from there. Sharak sought to also come to the further aid of his human brother, but two of the

Pygmesians now focused specifically on the eagle, nearly burning Sharak more than once. Others encircled the ferrets, cutting them off from Dar. The Beastmaster faced the rest alone and although he charged bravely into them—severing the head of another adversary in the process—he realized that he was doomed.

One hand caught tight his sword arm. As Dar struggled to free himself, he was grabbed from behind by two other foes. Sinister helmets clustered around his face and the fiendish clattering that sounded like speech threatened to deafen him. In the glass eyes of the helmets, the Beastmaster saw his own strained face multiplied many times over.

One of his captors pressed a tube against Dar's chest.

A roar resounded in the jungle. Several of the armored demons turned in the direction of the sound—

A huge, feline paw with curved claws as long as Dar's fingers easily slashed through the creatures' odd armor. Two Pygmesians crumpled, their backs ripped open and a foul, blue liquid spill out. The one wielding the tube turned just in time to have its hose—and its throat—ripped out by great fangs.

Ruh, his jaws and body already stained with the blue liquid that likely passed for the villains' blood, tore into the invaders like a mad storm. Helmed bodies were thrown in all directions. The Pygmesians lost all order. The tiger moved like a huge scythe, reaping the enemy like wheat for the harvest.

The Beastmaster flung aside his remaining captor, then skewered another. The invaders finally broke, scattering back in the direction from which they had come. The survivors numbered few and, with a final, powerful swipe, Ruh made certain that they counted two less. Dar would still have followed the Pygmesians if not for the boy.

The Beastmaster called Ruh back with him, but the tiger proved most unwilling to abandon his prey. Now linked to Ruh, Dar finally understood the reason for the huge cat's disturbing absence. The tiger had come across other Pygmesians during his distant scouting and had been forced to fight his way through them before he could come to his human friend's aid.

"We must go!" Dar again urged the reluctant cat. "Ruh, there will be other battles! It's best we go . . . there is an innocent . . . a young boy . . . to consider, too. We must find him!"

Heeding the human's words, the tiger made one slap at a limp body, then, along with Kodo and Podo, followed the Beastmaster.

Dar feared that it would take another hunt to find the boy, but Sharak, flying ahead, linked to him. Through the eagle's eyes, Dar beheld the brightly plumed parrot perched in a treetop as if waiting for the others to catch up.

With Sharak to guide him, the Beastmaster rushed through the jungle. He soon came upon the boy, who stood pressed against a tree, his breathing rapid and his face twisted in fear. His black hair and light skin did not particularly mark him to Dar, who had seen such in a hundred different places. Like Dar, he was clad in a loincloth and sandals. The boy was healthy, but very weary. He had likely been fleeing for days.

The young eyes watched him warily. Dar knew how he must look to the lad. Blood from a half dozen shallow wounds mixed with sweat, dirt, and the foul blue substance that ran through the veins of the Pygmesians surely made the Beastmaster appear as devilish as his foes. Despite that, Dar dared extend his empty hand, saying, "Have no fear. My name is Dar. I am a friend. Come with me. We need to leave before those creatures return."

But the boy continued to stare. Dar saw death in his eyes and knew that the child had witnessed things no child should.

The pouch squirmed. The ferrets popped out, Kodo peering over Dar's left shoulder and Podo over his right. The boy's gaze immediately went to the two furry heads and his expression softened.

Dar seized on the ferrets' initiative. "These are my friends."

He patted the female on the head. "This is Podo. She likes to be scratched behind the ears." The Beastmaster shifted so as to pet the male. "And this is Kodo. He likes to eat . . . and eat."

Podo climbed out. With astounding dexterity, she made her way along Dar's arm so that the boy could see her better.

From a nearby tree, Sharak screeched. The boy glanced at the eagle.

"That is Sharak. A brave hunter in the sky." Thinking of the parrot, he added, "You like birds, don't you? Sharak is my friend as the red one is yours . . ."

The young eyes seemed to grow less wary. Both Kodo and Podo caught his attention again.

At that moment, Ruh made his regal presence known. Of all Dar's companions, he was the most impressive, the most fearsome. The boy immediately pressed against the tree again. He looked to the Beastmaster for help.

Ruh padded up to Dar, then at Dar's silent urging, rolled on his back like a huge kitten waiting to be scratched on his belly.

"See?" The Beastmaster grinned. "Nothing to fear from Ruh! He's just a big, playful baby who protects his friends! Here! Want to scratch him?"

Fascinated despite his fear, the boy stepped closer. Following Dar's example, he carefully rubbed the tiger. An innocent grin spread across his tired face.

"What's your name?" Dar asked.

The boy finally found his voice. "J-Jalan . . ."

The Beastmaster's brow furrowed. The parrot had called out that name. Things made more sense to him. Indicating the colorful avian, Dar asked, "And that's your bird?"

Jalan shook his head. Dar frowned but let the matter pass.

Not to be left out of any scratching, the ferrets scurried down the Beastmaster's arms to where Jalan crouched. Without hesitation, the boy rubbed both behind the ears. His grin grew wider. The ferrets accepted their rightful share of scratching, then raced off to investigate the area for anything of interest.

"Are you alone?" the Beastmaster had to ask. He knew the answer but wanted to be absolutely certain.

"Just Seto," Jalan murmured, glancing back at the parrot. Seto spread his wings, then cheerfully bobbed his head several times.

Frowning, Dar sought to make contact with the bird. The Beastmaster's mind suddenly filled with bright and quickly shifting images. Dar fought to steady himself as visions of a hundred Setos in various avian antics washed over him. Seto flying. Seto clinging to a branch . . . sometimes upside down. Seto trying to crack open a tasty nut, often unsuccessfully.

And more and more . . .

With some relief, Dar broke the link. Accustomed to the orderly thoughts of Sharak, the parrot's simple and, in many cases, *comical* mind made the Beastmaster feel as if he had nearly gone mad. Seto appeared to be a creature of the moment more than any other animal with whom Dar had communed. His thoughts were more those of an infant than an adult.

As if to verify this further, the parrot chose that moment to let himself swing to the underside of the branch. Jalan, who had followed Dar's gaze, laughed at the bird's actions. The parrot imitated the boy's laugh, which amused Jalan even more.

Sensing that the boy was more at ease, and confident that the animals were on the lookout, Dar took the chance to question his new companion further. There was so much he had wanted to discover—he thought perhaps Jalan knew something of import.

To his surprise, the boy knew more than just "something." Jalan, it seemed, had an astounding memory and had witnessed much during his own flight . . . each event as tragic as it was incredible.

The boy recounted the horribly graphic tale of his parents'

demise, from his mother's fiery death to his father's heroic yet doomed struggle against the Pygmesians, which had at least enabled Jalan to flee. He went on to speak of what he had witnessed of his village's utter destruction, then his desperate escape . . . and all in such precise, emotionally charged detail that Dar was completely astounded.

The Beastmaster learned also how his new companion had discovered what their attackers were called. Jalan shivered as he described hearing the hissing voice of the ghost through not only his ears . . . but his thoughts, too.

"Do you recall exactly what he said?" asked Dar, well aware from past experience that even the slightest word might be of the greatest importance. Words were power, whether magical or not.

Jalan shivered, as much from memory as from the night mist that had begun to settle over the jungle. After a moment's hesitation, the dark-haired boy nodded. "He said . . . he said . . . 'Send the Oculin . . . Oculon . . . further northeast! Now!'" Jalan gestured, evidently repeating a movement of the sinister speaker. " 'I want all you Pygmesians to scorch . . . to scorch the area clean, then set up the . . . the landing markers! Hurry, lest . . . lest you in-incur *his* wrath as well as mine!'"

It was clear that Jalan did not understand many of the words that he spoke, but he spoke them well, nevertheless. Yet the boy's remarkable memory made Dar in some ways pity him, for clearly Jalan would not soon forget what had happened to his family or his village . . . just as the Beastmaster still could not forget the fate of his even after so many years.

To Dar's far right, Podo sniffed the air, the ferret's sense of smell sharper than that of many creatures. Kodo joined her, tasting with his tongue a mist-enshrouded breeze that had just risen up. With an inquisitive squeak, Podo scampered into the underbrush while the male waited. Each of the Beastmaster's companions was part of a very thorough, well-coordinated sentry arrangement. They would alert him should any danger threaten the two humans.

Secure in that knowledge, the Beastmaster went back to mulling Jalan's tragic story. The sorcerer—Dar had no other word for the ghostly, robed figure commanding the Pygmesians—was a particular point of interest. Not the master, according to Jalan's words, but a servant of high status. The sorcerer had also spouted a disturbing name—the Oculon—that the Beastmaster suspected likely referred to the enormous golem he had seen in the distance.

Evidently disturbed by the cold mist, Seto fluttered down to Jalan's shoulder for better warmth. The boy, one hand scratching the bird's head, stared at Seto's bright plumage and muttered, "It was . . . it was so *red* . . ."

"Your village?" Dar responded, assuming that his companion spoke of the fire that had razed his community.

"The hole . . . the *hole* was so red . . ."

The Beastmaster stirred. "Hole?"

Still gazing at Seto, Jalan, seemingly mesmerized by memory, went on, "It was . . . it was so deep, too. I couldn't see the bottom . . . I could only see the big gray bug! It kept shrieking as it dug deeper and deeper into the ground like it wanted to go all the way through to the other side . . ."

Tensing, Dar leaned forward. Jalan's description reminded him of only one thing. The worst of his initial nightmares . . .

The boy had seen into one of the monstrous pits.

"Tell me more," Dar urged, hoping he was not pushing Jalan toward anything that might upset him too much.

But Seto seemed a calming influence on Jalan. Still scratching the avian's head, the youth said, "I was running. Running. I found . . . I think it . . . it was the village Father told me to run to. Iloth. But it . . . but it was all gone! And there was . . . a red glow rising up from ahead . . . like Seto's feathers—"

"Seto!" squawked the parrot, always pleased to hear his name.

Undistracted by the interruption, Jalan continued, "—and gold like the sun and . . . and lightning—" He faltered. "Blue lightning . . . like when Father—"

The parrot nuzzled the boy's head. Dar put a comforting hand on Jalan's arm, murmuring, "It's all right. Can you tell me more about what you saw in the hole? What about the gray bug you saw digging in it? How large was it? What did it look like?"

The child's eyes widened again. "As huge as a mountain and made . . . of metal! It was round . . . round like a ball . . ."

Once more, a thing of metal, not flesh of any sort. Another golem, perhaps, but one far greater in dimensions than the Oculon. Dar refrained from shaking his head in both amazement and concern. What power their unseen master wielded! Who was he? Where did he come from?

Kodo emitted a squeak of curiosity, which the Beastmaster took as a reflection of his own questioning mind. The animals understood humans better than the latter realized, Dar's animals most of all, thanks to their innate link with him.

Taking a deep breath, Jalan continued. He had never meant to stumble to the very edge of the hole, but sinister shadows nearby had made him fear that Pygmesians or other even worse fiends approached. He had stumbled to the ground at the very edge of the pit, praying that he would neither be seen nor fall into the vast gap.

And although Jalan had not wanted to, his gaze had been irresistibly drawn to what lay deep within.

That was when he had seen the gargantuan "bug" at work—its long, cylindrical mouth spitting the foul blue lightning that both the Oculon and Pygmesians had wielded. Propped in place by a dozen segmented limbs clutching the sides of the huge pit, the behemoth burned away rock and stone as it slowly but relentlessly descended deeper and deeper into Ancor's interior. Its lightning had set everything around it ablaze, sending up bursts of red and gold flame, and the monstrous plumes of smoke that eventually filled the sky.

For Jalan, the glimpse had been a short one, for immediately after he had heard a sound to his left. There he had seen the helmed figures of Pygmesians outlined in the fiery illumination—Pygmesians heading in his direction. He had had no choice but to push himself to his feet and run again. Run with all the strength he had—strength fueled by fear . . .

And Jalan had not stopped running until he had collided with the Beastmaster.

Dar said nothing as the boy finished. For what purpose had the invaders harnessed such might? What reason did they have for desiring to dig not just in one part of Ancor, but seemingly many?

Sharak let out a low warning screech.

Dar leaped to his feet. The Beastmaster lunged toward Jalan, snatching up the startled boy. Seto fluttered up into the air, then surged ahead with Sharak while Ruh protected the rear.

"Kodo! Podo! To me!" Dar shouted.

He felt Kodo's answering thoughts . . . but not Podo's. Indeed, the male ferret radiated some concern for the female.

A sickening blue light from above washed over everything and a moment later, a metallic squeak filled Dar's ears.

Even without looking back, he knew that one of the gargantuan golems was on their heels.

Glancing around, the Beastmaster saw Kodo still hesitating. "Kodo! Come! Podo will be right behind us!"

A mere heartbeat later, an explosion rattled the area. Flames leaped high into the air. Jalan smothered a cry as he and Dar were thrown forward. Kodo finally abandoned his vigil to return to his human friend.

The dread light again swept over their vicinity, creating sinister shadows in the thickening mist. The Beastmaster pulled Jalan away just as light reached them.

From the jungle came the ominous clacking that was the Pygmesians' speech.

Ruh let out a roar, pacing rapidly and ready to pounce, but Dar summoned him away. "No, Ruh!" the Beastmaster shouted. "I need you here! Hurry!"

The tiger raced to him. Dar threw Jalan atop the great cat, commanding the boy, "Hold tight!"

As Ruh raced off with his startled passenger, the Beastmaster, ignoring the threat of the golem and the warriors, desperately sought Podo. But the only sign of the female's presence was a small patch of disturbed soil and a few prints leading into the thick vegetation.

Then his search was cut short, for with an earsplitting crash, one massive leg of the golem came down nearby. The light began to sweep toward Kodo and him. Pressing the ferret against his chest, Dar ran furiously after Ruh. The light just missed his heel as he entered the thick underbrush.

Kodo squeaked his concern as the Beastmaster hurried on. Gritting his teeth, Dar growled, "She's probably tracking us at this moment! She'll meet with us later!"

That was what he hoped, at least. As much as Dar desired to turn back and search for Podo one last time, he could do nothing but run. Run all the way to Edurac. There, with what Jalan knew, perhaps he could find some answers to what was happening.

And long before then, Podo would surely rejoin the party . . .

THE PYGMESIANS SWARMED over the area where Dar and the rest had been, seeking clues, seeking enemies. However, the humans and the animals had made good their escape . . . for now.

A leathery-winged shape flew among them, a toothy flyer such as the one Dar had earlier fought. It soared over the heads of the hunters, seemingly unconcerned when some of the Pygmesians and the hooded sorcerer glanced up.

"Come to me, my *horath* . . ." the figure hissed in a voice Jalan would have known well. "Come to me . . ."

The flyer dropped toward the ghostly form. As it came closer, it released from its claws its burden.

Long, skeletal fingers grasped the furred form eagerly. The sorcerer chuckled darkly as he inspected the female ferret. Podo's chest rose and fell, then rose and fell again.

"Excellent . . ." murmured the sibilant voice. "Perfectly executed . . ."

4

FOUR DAYS THEY HAD TRAVELED SINCE ESCAPING THE OCULON, and Dar remained troubled that Podo had not yet caught up. Kodo constantly hung his head out of the pouch, always looking back, and the Beastmaster could sense the male's worry. Even Jalan radiated concern for the animal he had known for so little time, the boy very empathic when it came to all creatures.

More and more he reminded Dar of his young self. Jalan's gift was not exactly the same, but near enough that Dar began to keenly sympathize with the boy's struggle. Not merely the tragic deaths of Jalan's parents and fellow villagers—a striking similarity to the Beastmaster's own past—but the obvious signs that animals, not people, had been the child's closest friends.

Indeed, as much as Dar was frustrated by the comical mind of Seto, the parrot seemed to fill a void for Jalan. Dar was glad for that, especially considering how arduous the trek had become.

The lands they roamed now appeared free of the invaders—invaders whom Dar now guessed were not actually demons despite their monstrous nature—but there was still very little game. Thus far, the predators in the party had been forced to make do with a few small reptiles caught along the way. Dar had located fruit and nuts on which he, Jalan, and the ferret could sup, but Sharak and Ruh needed more meat and before long, so would the rest of the party.

Putting that concern aside for the time being, Dar finally called a halt to the day's journey. Once settled down, he continued his questioning of Jalan. Each time the two talked, the boy remembered more details. Dar was curious to know just what else the boy might still have to reveal.

However, before he could even broach the subject, Ruh, who had gone out to hunt, suddenly alerted him to an unexpected find not far from their location.

The Beastmaster rubbed Kodo's head. The ferret looked up, his continued dismay readily apparent to his human brother. Kodo and Podo had been two parts of one creature; the male was at a loss without her.

"She will be with us again, Kodo," Dar murmured. "Now I want you to be a brave warrior and keep Jalan company while I go see what Ruh's found."

Kodo rubbed his nose into Dar's hand, then scampered over to Jalan. The boy gently scratched the ferret's neck.

"Seto!" squawked the parrot, the only one to keep a cheerful disposition amidst so much horror. Dar supposed the bird was indicating his intention to also watch over Jalan, but the Beastmaster did not link with Seto to find out. One glimpse into the parrot's chaotic mind had been enough.

"As you like," he absently answered the avian. To Jalan, he asked, "Will you trust me if I promise that you'll be fine while I am gone?"

Jalan nodded. Indicating the parrot and Kodo, he added, *"They're with me. . . ."*

Dar nodded, then left, determined to be back as soon as possible, food or not. In his brief contact with the Beastmaster, Ruh had hinted at a possible source of sustenance, but the cat had not revealed just what it was . . . other than that it lay by a river.

The river naturally made Dar think that it had to be fish, but if so, why would the tiger not indicate that? As he neared, he sighted Ruh at the banks, avidly gnawing at something. Just beyond the cat, the river roared along, its waters so wild and its width so great that Dar gave thanks he and the others did not have to cross it.

Ruh looked up as he approached, the tiger eagerly licking his lips. Despite the lack of much illumination, Dar saw something around the cat's mouth that glinted as if struck by the absent sunlight. Something *silver*.

"What is it you've found, old friend?" Dar glanced at the spot near the resting animal's forepaws, but saw nothing but flattened grass. Whatever the tiger had been supping on, he had utterly consumed it . . . bones and all, assuming that it *was* fish.

Letting out a low rumble, Ruh indicated the river with his head. Dar stepped to the edge of the bank and peered into the racing waters.

Something that gleamed of silver leaped out of the river at him.

Having left his sword sheathed, Dar managed to catch whatever it was with both hands. A fat, silver fish as long as one of the ferrets briefly wriggled in his clutches, then grew oddly placid despite its obvious doom. Dar eyed the mirrorlike scales that seemed to glow with a light of their own, astounded to see his face repeated in the fish's hide a thousand times and more.

Only belatedly did he notice small markings near the tail. The Beastmaster frowned. It was very likely the trick of the odd gleam of the scales, but the markings almost looked as if they formed a crude mandala. Dar chuckled, wondering if he should thank Baraji for this sudden, almost mystical bounty.

A second fish leaped from the river.

Only Dar's swift reflexes enabled him to switch the first to one hand, then catch the second with the other. The new fish was identical to the first. *Absolutely* identical. Dar had caught enough fish in his life to know that such could hardly be possible. To one with his expert eye, there were always minute variations. Yet, down to the last scale, this pair looked to be twins.

A wondrous light abruptly shone from deep within the rushing water. Setting aside his catch, the Beastmaster stared in awe as the entire section of the river nearest him turned a bright silver. Under the surface, he saw scores and scores of glittering fish just like the ones that had leaped to his hands. They swam against the current, maintaining positions right before the stunned human.

The river's roar grew louder . . . and Dar suddenly heard *words* in the rush of water. The odd, bubbling voice ebbed and flowed with the current, but after a moment, Dar realized that the words were aimed at him.

Beastmaster . . . Beastmaster . . . the river called. *Protector and friend . . . protector and friend . . . we give that you might live . . . we give that you might fight . . . so that you might help turn the dark back into light . . .*

Dar peered at the fish below, then along the rest of the river. Rivers themselves did not speak, but there were beings—spirits or elementals—who could do so for them. He had met some of their like in times past but had not expected to find one here.

The fish continued to maintain their positions, as if waiting for some signal. Above them, the surface foamed.

A face appeared in the foam . . . or at least gaps that seemed like eyes and a mouth, the latter wide enough to swallow either Ruh or Dar.

Beastmaster . . . protector and friend . . . the face mouthed. *We give . . .*

Two more fish leaped out of the river, landing at Dar's feet. Another pair immediately followed, then two more.

In seconds, there was enough to feed everyone, including the voracious Ruh.

The face began to recede into the river, but Dar reached out, calling, "Wait! Don't leave!"

The face hesitated.

"Thank you," the Beastmaster first said. "I thank the guardian of this river—"

We thank the Beastmaster for protecting the land . . . we thank the Beastmaster for his devotion to Ancor . . . and we beseech him to do anything he can to thrust back the evil descending upon Ancor . . .

"I will do what I can. That is all I can promise."

That must be enough . . . the face solemnly replied. *We will hope . . .*

"Is there—is there anything you can tell me?" Dar asked. "Anything about those who come with the darkness? Are they demons? What do they want? What can we do? I must know!"

We but flow where the water goes . . . but demons they are not, we know that much . . . the face distorted as if angered. *But demons could be no smaller evil . . . and the stars feel guilt that they bring the burden of Ancor's ill sister to her . . .*

Dar did not understand most of what the guardian said, but he did register that as he had suspected, the invaders were not demons despite their look and powers. They were mortal . . . and yet, more evil still for that reason.

"What do they want? Do you know any way to stop them?" The last question was a desperate one, but Dar saw no reason not to ask. If the river spirit had any notions, the Beastmaster was more than happy to hear them.

But the face only veered to the side, saying, *Edurac . . . that way lies Edurac . . . and the prophet . . .*

Two of the gleaming fish leaped up in the direction of the distant kingdom, then disappeared in the water again.

With their return to the water, the face vanished.

"Wait!" But it immediately became obvious that the guardian was gone. As Dar watched, the silver fish also disappeared, the school finally letting the current take them down river.

Dar stood there for a moment, then glanced at Ruh. The tiger, already finishing off another morsel, grumbled, then looked eagerly at Dar's catch.

"Yes, there is still more for you, my good glutton." Dar scooped up as much fish as he could carry, leaving what remained for the eager cat to devour. It took some doing to return to Jalan without dropping any of his burden, but Dar was not about to lose one bit of the precious food. There was no telling when next such a miracle might happen. At the very least, everyone would eat well this one evening.

Tomorrow was another question.

BUT IN THAT regard, the fish proved to be far more miraculous than even Dar expected. The river guardian had been very generous and, even taking Ruh into account, a fair amount had remained after the evening meal. Dar had expected to leave the rest to whatever scavengers might remain in the area, but, upon waking, had discovered the fish as fresh as if they had just been caught. That had given the party a stronger start for the day's journey. More important, as the hours passed, no one, not even the tiger, felt the least bit hungry. Indeed, even by the end of the day, none in the weary party had any desire for more food, just sleep.

They rested around the fire Dar had built, Sharak and Ruh keeping watch in the jungle. Seto had settled on a branch near Jalan and a still-distraught Kodo nuzzled Dar for comfort.

"Was there really a face in the water?" Jalan asked, not for the first time. His eyes were more animated than the Beastmaster had ever seen them. "Was it really a spirit?"

"Or an elemental or something else," Dar returned. "There are many unusual creatures and fantastic beings in Ancor."

"I wish I could've seen it!"

Jalan continued to press the Beastmaster for details concerning the events at the river, even though Dar could tell him no more than he already had. Still, the boy's eager curiosity infected Dar as well, lightening the warrior's mood for the first time since Podo's disappearance.

Then a slight movement—perhaps the shifting of a branch at the wrong moment—set Dar's nerves taut.

He surreptitiously reached for his sword.

Jalan caught his action. "What—?"

Silencing the boy with a look, the Beastmaster cautiously started to rise.

Armored riders, wearing crested helmets and breastplates emblazoned with the image of a hawk, burst into the campsite from all directions. From the jungle, Ruh released a challenging roar, but the Beastmaster could not do anything for the tiger. Instead, he grabbed Jalan by the arm and ran for safety.

But wherever Dar turned, the riders were there. Many had spears, which they used to prod the two humans back.

Dar swung Jalan behind him, then attacked. His powerful slash enabled the sharp blade to sever the heads of three of the spears, briefly giving him and the boy an opening.

"Come!" Snagging Jalan's hand, Dar plunged forward. One of the riders sought to grab him, but he sorely underestimated the Beastmaster's swiftness and agility.

Kodo, who had clung to Dar's chest, now scurried atop his shoulder, snapping at any other hand that tried to reach his human brother. Seto flew behind Jalan, bobbing in the faces of one rider after another and all the while laughing merrily.

Sharak dove in from the treetops, his wings blinding a rider who had just veered around to pursue Dar. Dar gave thanks to his animal friends as he headed for the thick, black jungle. Safety was not far—

A net fell upon the Beastmaster and his companion.

Stifling a curse, Dar tried to cut his way free. Sharak landed atop him, seeking in vain to pull the net up. Kodo chewed hard on the ropes that made up the net, but the ferret could not make a gap large enough for his friends to slip through.

Go! Dar commanded Kodo and the eagle. He did not want them captured with him. Sharak obediently seized Kodo, then rose into the air.

Despite having sent the others away, Dar did not by any means give up hope. He managed to cut through one section, then a second. The hole was nearly large enough to enable him to slip out and take Jalan with him.

But a second net fell upon the first. Dar's sword became entangled. Two riders seized the ends of the net and quickly rode in a circle around the captives, further snaring them.

Jalan slipped. The Beastmaster tried to help him but fell instead.

The nets tightened, preventing the pair from moving. One of the riders leaped down and quickly bound the ends together, leaving Dar and Jalan looking like game caught in a hunt.

From the jungle came a muffled roar from Ruh . . . then, a dread silence.

Dar cursed his carelessness. Caught up in Jalan's tragedy and his own nightmares, he had not paid enough attention to their surroundings. He had thought that they were far enough away from the invaders . . . and thus had made a fatal blunder.

"Bind the net well," growled a hirsute figure atop a dark brown charger. Like the rest, his helmet obscured much of his countenance. In the flickering light of the campfire, only the snarling mouth was visible. "They escape and it'll be your hides!"

But unless something unexpected were to happen, Dar saw no hope of escape. Another rider joined the one binding the nets and between them they raised that end up. Dar expected them to drag the pair behind their horses and feared what bodily harm that might cause, especially to Jalan—but then the familiar rattling of a horse-drawn wagon gave him some slight hope.

"Load 'em in with the other catch," commanded the leader. "Hurry!"

"Is that a good idea?" asked one of those securing the nets. "That thing might tear these two to shreds!"

"If you damned fools secured it good enough, there'll be no harm!" He leaned over to leer at Dar and Jalan. "Besides, he only wants these spies of Xorot's to live long enough for Orestian to find out whatever they know . . ."

Spies? Their captors thought they were spies? Dar realized that these warriors were not the foes that he had thought them to be. "Wait! We're not spies! We are friends! Listen!"

But the lead rider only growled at his declarations. "As were the vermin before you, eh? They said they weren't spies . . . and then twenty good men were torn to bloody gobbets by some sorcerer's device they carried before we cut them down!" To one of those working on the nets, the leader roared, "Fessac, you fool! Get 'em into the wagon and hurry! Spy or not, the king or Orestian will make the decision, right, lads?"

There were several mocking "ayes." Dar and the boy were un-ceremoniously dumped into the wagon . . . where the Beastmaster discovered that the fearsome creature the riders had captured was none other than Ruh. The tiger was also in a net, bound even more tightly than the humans. Ruh radiated his frustration and dismay with a roar that shook the vicinity.

"By the gods!" cried one man. "That can be no animal, but rather a demon!"

"'Twould explain why it roams in a place where even the smallest scavengers can no longer be found," returned the captain. "Never mind that now! They're Orestian's problem!" He waved the party on. "One thing there's no doubt of: King Leardius'll be pleased with this catch!"

Leardius! Dar again sought to speak to the riders, but the wagon jerked and he and Jalan collided with Ruh. The rattle of the moving wagon was so loud that the Beastmaster knew it would be futile to try anything more.

Dar grunted in pain as another bump battered him against the side of the wagon. He wondered at the tricks of fate and if the gods were now laughing at him.

The Beastmaster had wanted so desperately to reach legendary Edurac to speak with its king, noble Leardius. And now . . . he would have his chance, and would likely die in the process.

THE FLYER SURVEYED the scene of Dar's defeat, drinking in every action, every word. When the riders took off with their captives, it carefully followed for a pace, avoiding the sharp-beaked hunter and its furry companion soaring high in the dark sky. It had been warned about the one human's bestial comrades and how dangerous their bites were. Yet, even with such risk, a horach obeyed its prime purpose. Slaughter those that were only worth slaughtering; watch and learn about those that were more dangerous.

And, especially, keep watch on the one that so interested its master.

When it had seen enough, the horach turned from the riders and their catch, heading south with incredible speed. It had orders to bring what it knew back to the sorcerer, back to *Kyrik* . . .

Knowing where the sorcerer was—as all the horach did, for they were bound to Kyrik from their birth—the monstrous flyer soared without pause night and day, eventually coming upon the infernal place Jalan had so graphically described to Dar. Once it had been a village called Cartuus, but now it was a series of numbers and letters as dictated by the sorcerer's own master. It was one foul site among many, all chosen for one reason, one purpose.

The horach sensed Kyrik near. It descended into the hellish realm, soaring over the heads of Pygmesians marking the perimeter of the region with small, pyramid-shaped crystals that glowed a deep emerald, then under the legs of an Oculon surveying what remained of the nearby jungle for any unfamiliar movement. It flew past others of its kind, who immediately turned expectant eyes to it. However, there was no need to pass on the knowledge to them at this point, not with Kyrik almost within—

A short, black lance thrust up just as the horach passed from the sight of its fellows. The lance expertly caught the flyer in a nerve that not only weakened the wings, but prevented the creature from calling out to either its own kind or to the sorcerer.

Wings flapping feebly, the horach struggled to escape the lance. A slim, feminine hand grasped it by the back of the neck and with great force made the horach stare ahead.

"What makes you fly so urgently to Kyrik, little spy?" a throaty, seductive voice asked the wounded captive. "I'd like to see first what compels you so, hmmm?"

She turned the orbs to her own slanted, golden ones. The eyes were but one part of a striking, if severe, countenance both beautiful and deadly. Full, crimson lips pursed in amusement, their blood-red color a sharp contrast to her ivory, unblemished skin. Her nose was short and narrow, yet it was clear that no scent escaped her. Nor did any sound, for she had been bred from birth to be the master's chief hunter, letting no one stand in her path.

A lush head of scarlet tresses framed her face, her forehead topped by a strong widow's peak. She wore the thin armor that the Pygmesians did, although hers was cut tighter and pleasing in those places the master most preferred. Her slightest movement was like that of a feline preparing to pounce on prey.

"Show me . . ." she cooed to the horach, who, even though a beast created more by science than nature, knew well enough not to disobey. It revealed through its saucerlike orbs all that it had seen regarding Dar . . . especially his capture.

Her brow arched as she absorbed all that the flyer had seen. When the horach finally finished, she chuckled, then murmured, "Well! How amusing . . . I don't think I'll send you on to Kyrik after all . . ."

With a single twist, the huntress snapped the flyer's neck, then carelessly tossed the remains into the vast, burning hole. She touched a small metal clasp at her throat and stared up into the smoke-filled heavens to what she knew waited above.

"I must see our great lord," she said to the air. There was a sight clacking sound at her left ear, as if some minute Pygmesian had taken up residence there.

The huntress's body suddenly glowed gold . . . and in the next breath, she vanished.

5

To the people, Ancor was not merely their world, but *the* world. What else was there, after all? Ancor was their existence, their life, and had been the life of each of the generations preceding them. It fed them, it clothed them, and—being balanced in all things—even took them unto death when their chosen time came. Since time immemorial, there had been only Ancor . . .

But a few . . . merely a few . . . had looked in their minds, in their imagining, beyond Ancor, beyond the skies to where the stars blazed. They did not see the stars as gods, the homes of gods, torches set upon the ceiling of Ancor, or a thousand other suggestions birthed by storytellers or priests. They pondered those stars and wondered if, as the sun shone upon their world, did these likewise do so upon other Ancors?

They would have been right . . . and wrong. For while there

were other worlds that might have once looked like Ancor, her very sister—her very birth twin—had long ago become something that no man or creature of Dar's world would have recognized as kin.

The black smoke had spread over much of Ancor, but in those places where the night sky could still be glimpsed, astrologers would have noted another light in the sky. Had their scrying lenses been stronger, they would have noticed fainter ones around it.

And, had they been able to peer even closer, they would have seen that all of those lights, those apparent stars . . . slowly moved, with apparent purpose, like ships.

Which was what they were, though like none ever seen upon the face of Ancor.

Akin in shape to the mantas that swam Ancor's seas but individually far larger than a great king's vast palace, the black metal vessels constantly hovered around another vessel that dwarfed them as the elephant did the ant. In contrast to the sinister swarm that served it, the sleek, crimson and black leviathan was far longer than it was wide, though even in its breadth it measured a hundred times more than the next largest ship in the swarm.

All the star vessels bristled with menacing appendages, some of them akin to larger versions of the lightning tubes wielded by the Pygmesians. Others resembled the mechanical arms of golems or the cutlasses wielded by pirates, though their uses were far more fantastic. However, the flagship—for, like in any navy of Ancor, it surely had to be called that—carried upon both its front half and the high tower at its center ominous gigantic shields inverted toward anything that approached it and on its side were wide, arched openings from which constantly radiated a fiery force that barely seemed contained.

In the silence of the dark void beyond Ancor, only that ever-stirring force and the multitude of tiny lights on each vessel gave hint that life existed out there. Within each star ship, the ranks of invaders awaited word to descend to the once-pristine realm below, word that could be given by only one among them.

A FLASH OF gold presaged the startling materialization of the flame-tressed huntress. She formed like a ghost before two Pygmesians and a third, even more bizarre creature—a gaunt, multilimbed thing whose half-dozen, almost serpentine appendages constantly moved from one part of a metallic display of lights to another. From the top of its armored head, two red globe eyes solemnly stared at her.

The huntress strode past them without a word, the stark, iron wall before her melting along her outline as she walked through it as if it were air.

She entered an equally dark corridor devoid of any decor, any touch of humanity, and lit by a low, red aura that filtered out from the very walls themselves. The wide, arched corridor was filled with Pygmesians marching to their training sessions; small, metallic creatures with spindly legs racing along the walls like hyperactive spiders; and hulking, reptilian figures with faces only vestigially human who bowed their crested heads to her in respect to her position. Though hunters like her—with weaponry both hooked over their shoulders and hooked *into* their bodies—they knew she was their superior in both rank and skill. Few among their ungodly corps would challenge her, and none could have done so successfully.

But if there were two who might have, they were those given the honor of guarding the entrance to the chamber she approached. The doorway stood almost like a shrine, its outline a blending of bloodred and midnight black with dark gold bordering both. A savage black slash cut across the center of the doorway, the symbol of both the invaders' world and the one with whom that world was synonymous.

The utterly yellow eyes of the broader of the two reptilian forms acknowledged her from under a thick brow ridge that rose to the high, bony crest beginning atop his skull and running down to the middle of his back. The mutated hunter had no nose, merely two diagonal slits that flapped open and closed as he took in her unique scent. The lipless mouth widened into a death's-head grin, revealing tightly clamped teeth as sharp as daggers.

"Zzzzorrrennna . . ." he greeted her. A six-fingered fist slapped against the unclothed chest, where he had willingly seared the mark of the master into his scaled flesh.

"Drayz . . ." she greeted back, two predators acknowledging each other's deadliness.

The other guardian imitated Drayz's gesture, then rasped, "Huntress, you wish an audience with the lord?"

"I wouldn't be standing here staring at your ugly faces if I didn't, Kuln."

Though not as broad as Drayz, Kuln matched him in height. In contrast to his comrade, he also wore more than the black leather loincloth and sandals that Drayz preferred. Kuln was clad in the thin but resilient armor of the Pygmesians. Like them, he also had a wide array of tubes and wires running along his chest and back—but in his case each was set to a hidden weapon available at his command with but a thought. He had no crest, but otherwise his features were enough like Drayz's to make them seem brothers . . . which they were in a sense, having been awakened at the same time in the vast artificial hatcheries of their home.

"Weaponsss down . . ." commanded Drayz, who, save his clawed hands, looked unarmed himself . . . but certainly was.

"I would do no less," Zorena retorted with a shake of her long hair. "For am I not first servant in his eyes?"

They bowed to her words, though not without a little envy. Only she stood higher than them among the master's warriors.

The huntress blinked. Around her there momentarily flared a slight, red aura.

Drayz nodded. "Enter hisss prrresssence . . ."

Without any more acknowledgment of the pair, Zorena walked through the door, which melted around her outline as the previous had. But the huntress also felt a slight tingle as subtle energies bathed her body, seeking any weapon, any tool, that she or any other entering this sanctum might have tried to hide. But those energies failed to find any fault with Zorena, for, after all, she was her lord's favorite . . . and no fool.

Darkness greeted her at first, but then the same low, crimson light she had witnessed in the corridors emanated from the surrounding steel walls. It brightened as she approached what to any ignorant stranger might have appeared to be nothing less than the interior of a tomb.

On one side, three tall, vaguely humanoid statues stood in a row, the trio looking like guards protecting the dead. Their odd appearance made it seem as if some artisan had started one, quit work upon it after barely carving the basics, then begun the second, only to quit again at the same point, and try, equally without success, a third time. Zorena frowned at the statues, then dismissed them from her thoughts.

In all the flagship, this was the only chamber adorned with what might have been called personal effects, though they were hardly that. On each side of her and illuminating as she passed them, images hovering an inch or two before the walls moved about with a three-dimensional fluidity. Zorena glanced at one—the vision of a fiery mountain overlooking an endless track of featureless, square, metallic buildings and other equally stark structures from whose long, slim stacks poured dark plumes akin to those now enshrouding most of Ancor. Those plumes mixed with a greater cloud arising from the volcanic peak in the background.

Zorena recognized that particular vision well, though it was similar in appearance to a thousand others of her world. *Voranamar,* greatest of cities in all the world of *Ishram* . . . and the place of her own birthing.

The drastic contrast between Voranamar—all Ishram—and Ancor reminded her of her duty. Zorena strode toward the center of the chamber, where the crimson glow was abruptly supplanted by a stronger silver light that bathed the focal point of the room.

And there, set upon a pedestal of the blackest onyx, lay the coffin-shaped container. It was tilted at an angle so that the head of the occupant rose toward any who entered. Within, the body of a muscular man a foot taller than the two mutates guarding him lay in repose—the sharp, angular features both handsome and impos-ing tilted slightly to the side. His black hair was shorn almost to the skull. The lower half of his body was clad much like his warriors in that he wore the sleek, flexible armor—though in his case gray-black—and boots, but his upper half was naked save for a leather weapon band running from the left part of the waist to the right shoulder.

The light above suddenly changed to a deep azure that washed over the still body. At the same time, scores of intricate mechani-cal arms with varied ends came into play. Some precisely cut small incisions in the torso, where others thrust in and performed unseen services. These were followed by yet more that sutured the cuts so perfectly that it was as if the incisions had never existed.

The closer Zorena drew, the better she could see other things. Minute, almost transparent tubes stood attached to the throat, the chest, and the skull, each feeding a different color liquid into the body. Other small arms performed injections, either adding or with-drawing substances.

The energies bathing the body altered every few breaths. Zorena hesitated, observing the face.

The eyes opened.

Though she had lived her entire life gazing at them, the huntress still let out a gasp. Their silver, mirrorlike finish was the result of the greatest sciences Ishram could offer and they allowed her lord to see well beyond what other men did. He could even see the energies at play throughout reality.

But although the eyes stared directly at her, they did not yet see Zorena. Instead, another small arm from the mechanism that treated him stretched before the eyes, shining a red beam into one, then the other.

She knelt at the foot of the coffin, her arms bent behind her, her head gazing at the floor.

"*Vorannos . . .*" Zorena intoned. "Vorannos . . ."

As she spoke, the many mechanisms at work on the giant suddenly finished their tasks, then withdrew into hidden slots in the coffin.

"Vorannos . . ." the huntress solemnly called a third time.

Though she did not look up, Zorena sensed the mirror eyes flicker shut, then open again. She heard the slight intake of breath, as her lord returned to waking.

"Is that my Zorena I hear?" came a deep, deep voice augmented by devices beyond even her ken.

There was a hum that was also her signal to rise. The huntress watched in respect as the back of the coffin rose up and toward her while the bottom descended to the floor.

Vorannos, lord of Ishram, lord of *all* things in the universe, stepped from the coffin as if from the softest and plushest of beds.

"My Zorena," he rumbled, her awestruck face reflected in his eyes. "My huntress supreme . . . you have something to report to me?" His eyes literally glowed with anticipation. He cupped her chin in his hand. "Perhaps . . . have you found the way?"

"I am near to success . . . I feel it," she replied.

The grip tightened painfully. Vorannos's mouth twisted into a savage, mirthless smile. " 'Near to success' is as far away from it as failure, my Zorena . . . I grow weary and frustrated with so little to show for the destruction of this pathetic world and so many, like yourself, searching and searching . . . in *vain*, it always seems . . ."

"It is . . ." She struggled to speak, for his fingers had now gone from her chin to her throat. "It is the primitive . . . the one who seeks for us within his own ranks . . . he demands more for his bargain . . . more and more . . ."

The mirror eyes flashed again. "Offer him what he desires, then, my Zorena . . . offer him all he wants . . . so long as he fulfills his part."

"Yes . . . my lord . . ."

Vorannos released her. As the huntress inhaled, the lord of Ishram, his expression now utterly calm, quietly added, "You will not fail . . . you know what failure means . . . you all know . . ."

"Yes, my lord . . ." Zorena knew very well what it meant. Death was the least of Vorannos's punishments, and even that never came with mercy. An eternity of unrelenting pain was often the reward for those who did not live up to the expected devotion of their glorious lord.

"You have other news of importance," he said, his tone indicating that anything less would be to her regret. "Tell me."

She took a deep breath. "It is the *one*. He is marked."

"Ah?" the eyes brightened, but this time in anticipation. The shadow of a smile graced Vorannos's handsome but cold features. "How marked?"

"He speaks with the animals of this world and they with him. They fight at his side and call him brother."

"And a name?"

Her confidence buoyed by his obvious interest, Zorena answered, "A name, I did not hear. But there is a legend that speaks of a title . . . a champion of Ancor called . . . called the *Beastmaster*."

Vorannos tasted the word. "Beastmaster . . . yes . . . he must be the one . . ."

"He is on his way to Edurac even as we speak . . . but as a prisoner . . ."

The lord of Ishram roared with amusement. "*This* is the one who must champion this mud hole? He does not promise much hope for a fine duel if he falls so easily to rabble!"

Zorena echoed his laughter, ceasing when Vorannos did. He looked to her, expression turning cunning. "Edurac, you say . . ."

She anticipated his thoughts. Falling on one knee, the huntress declared, "I will see to it, my lord."

"Yes . . . let this . . . Beastmaster . . . be tested. Let it be shown if he is worthy of me . . . and worthy of being slain by me . . ."

Vorannos had slain hundreds, even thousands, by his own hand, and among those had been the heroes of countless previous worlds. The lord of Ishram had met all of them with a great eagerness, as if they were the only things that could fill his life until his true prize was found.

Yet once each was slain—even if Vorannos had taken special care to make their deaths so entertaining and pleasing—it ever became clear that he was not satisfied. The battles never gave what he wanted of them.

But the champion of Ancor . . . perhaps he could indeed satisfy her master.

Rising again, Zorena stepped back. The huntress sensed movement behind her and knew that Kuln and Drayz had entered. Vorannos had silently summoned them for some purpose known only to him.

The lord of Ishram gazed imperiously at his loyal trio. "Zorena's task is clear, but I have one for you now, my good mutates."

Drayz let out a hiss of anticipation. Kuln murmured, "At last . . ."

The pair had seen little of Ancor since the invaders' arrival. They and Zorena were not to be wasted on razing jungles and slaughtering primitives. The Pygmesians and other lesser mutates were more than sufficient to clear the path for the burrowers and eliminate most resistance.

Vorannos indicated the huntress. "You will work with her on this."

No one gave any sign of disgruntlement, though Zorena cared as little for the pair as they did her. Indeed, Vorannos liked to make use of their competitive nature, as he did the rivalries among most of his followers. It kept them eager, kept them hungry.

"The *prophet* is the next step," the lord of Ishram simply said. "Find him or her. The prophet, the text, or the Beastmaster . . . one of them must be the ultimate key to the Fountain."

He turned away without warning, dismissing the trio from his interest so simply. Zorena and the others bowed their heads low as they backed out of the chamber. The red-tressed woman caught a last glimpse of her master as he turned toward the three statues.

She bared her teeth, not at Vorannos, but rather the figures. In a whisper too low for any other to hear, the huntress hissed, "Kyrik . . ."

THE LORD OF Ishram, of *all* things, paused before the statues, then glanced at the panoramas next to them. They marked to him the great victories he had wrought in forging Ishram into the glory it was now. With pleasure, he surveyed the moving images of great war machines grinding along the churned soil, of the endless and gloriously identical metal cities that now covered most of its surface. Gone was the disorderly growth of nature and in its place arose the absolute symmetry of the technology that Vorannos saw as the true ultimate use of the universe's energies and resources.

Indeed, Ishram had once been exactly like Ancor, its twin and its sister in all things. But now the blue skies were gone, covered by the thick black clouds of endless construction on the machines Vorannos demanded for expansion of his domain. The seas were great sewage reservoirs for the by-products, all water needed for survival refined through more machines. Food was no longer grown on insufficient farms or in forests and jungles . . . in fact, neither farms, forests, nor jungles even existed anymore. Instead, as with all things, sustenance was the miracle of chemical processes, of the ingenious creation of injections and pastes, supplemented by engineered solids mocking the extinct fauna and flora of not just Ishram but all the worlds to come under Vorannos's sway.

Even the air itself was a thing refiltered and refined, as were those who breathed it. The Pygmesians were the ultimate example of the last, they had transformed to partake—without breathing devices—of the sulfur-rich air of Ishram and a thousand other remade worlds.

The same air that would eventually encompass what remained of Ancor once Vorannos's quest for the Fountain came to fruition.

"The Fountain . . ." he murmured, returning to the three statues. "Eternity . . ."

The mirror eyes fixed upon the center of the trio. Vorannos grinned darkly.

"Kyrik! Kyrik, you dog! Attend your master!"

There was a moment of stillness . . . and then the center statue took on a hazy appearance, as if becoming only mist. Its outline altered, growing taller, gaunt. A long, flowing cloak and hood formed over the statue.

The blunt, unfinished hands stretched long, the fingers tapering. Under the hood, a cadaverous, birdlike countenance shaped itself. Slitted, ebony eyes—both the pupils *and* what surrounded them—flickered into unholy life.

"Lord of Ishram . . ." the sorcerer, Kyrik, hissed. He bent his head very low, the utterly subservient hound of the huntmaster. Kyrik, perhaps most of all, embodied those that served closest to Vorannos, those that feared the cruelly handsome, ageless—thanks to the machines within and without that constantly kept time, disease, and other failings at bay—lord of Ishram, but believed it better to follow the charismatic, powerful conqueror than stand in his path. Besides, the rewards for doing so could be quite enticing . . .

"I have not heard from you, sorcerer. Why is that?"

The absolute master of technology, Vorannos did not see any contradiction in referring to Kyrik as a master of arcane energies. Magic was to the lord of Ishram another element of his sciences; Kyrik was merely adept at manipulating the natural energies of the universe with his will, his unique mind. Vorannos could do the same with the mechanisms running through his entire refurbished body. He found Kyrik, however, very proficient at certain tasks and, in places such as Ancor, the sorcerer's skills blended well with what the locals wielded.

"I have . . . been tasting the energies of this world, this, the primal world, my lord." Looking much like a vulture who has just discovered a particularly appealing piece of carrion, the ghoulish figure added, "It's a rich, full world, my lord. Very delicious . . ."

"You have been indulging yourself, you mean. You have been playing, when you were supposed to be seeking, dog . . ." Vorannos bared his teeth.

"I never meant any disrespect . . ." replied the other, bowing lower yet.

The lord of Ishram raised a hand and Kyrik cringed, though he only existed in mental form here—the statue but a host for his consciousness to possess. Even from so far away, his master could strike him dead with a glance.

But instead of striking the sorcerer, the lord of Ishram gestured at the far wall, which stood blank compared to the rest.

The wall vanished as if torn away . . . and the stars and ships greeted their liege.

The stars, the ships, and, below, Ancor.

"I have conquered world upon world upon world in order to satiate that thirst, Kyrik! Not a realm exists between Ishram and her sister, Ancor, that has not been remade in my glorious image . . ."

"Such gifts you have brought to so many undeserving . . ."

Vorannos stepped up to the edge. So vivid was the image of glittering stars and savage warships that it seemed as if one could step out and touch them. Yet the wall still remained. The view was the result of more of the technology that was Vorannos's "magic."

But the countless stars and the fleet that moved by his whim were of no interest to Ishram's master. Rather, Vorannos only had eyes for the green and blue planet.

"It's there, dog. After so long, I know it's there. The Fountain of Eternity or Life, some call it, the Fountain beside which all else pales. Immortality, endless knowledge, endless power, the restoration of perfect health . . ." His fingers touched his chest where one of the latest sutures had been sealed. "Perfect health . . ." He angrily pulled the fingers back. "It gives all that and so much more to the one who commands it. It is the key to the universe, and those who drink from its waters are said to have *Creation* at their fingertips . . . as you, who have been longest with me on this hunt and whose life I hold so easily in my hand"—Vorannos shut his hand tight as for emphasis—"most understand . . ."

Keeping his shoulders humbly hunched, Kyrik inched just to the side and a step back from his lord. "And truly you are the only one worthy of partaking of it. Only you, Lord Vorannos, only you . . . despite even what the fragments that were uncovered on our grand and beloved home world of Ishram said about it . . ."

Twin Ancors were reflected in the warlord's gaze. Yet he no longer saw the world below, but rather the ancient script, far older than even him, that said, "Only the pure, only the redeemable, only the good, may taste of the waters and be touched by them. Those that would seek for their gain, for evil, for conquest . . . the Fountain is forbidden them always . . ." Vorannos's lip curled in renewed vehemence. "*Nothing* is forbidden to me. I will raze Ancor to the ground, bombard it from the sky until nothing remains, burrow through its soil . . . until the Fountain is mine. It is *here.* I will have it if there must be ten-thousand holes before one penetrates to where it is hidden."

"It could be yours already," soothed Kyrik in his ear. "What causes Zorena to fail and fail so? Did she not properly seduce the primitive who claimed to have clues to its whereabouts? Did she not offer everything available to her to find out? Better we had crushed this Edurac first, ripped its secrets from it—"

Vorannos glared over his shoulder, silencing the sorcerer. "And thereby likely destroyed them, is that what you want, dog? To destroy perhaps the key to the path?"

"Nay, my lord, nay!"

"Edurac will be reduced, as all things here will be," the lord of Ishram growled as he turned upon Kyrik. "And you who speaks of Zorena's faults, what do you give me but empty hands, you cringing vermin? What? At least from her, I know that He Who Must Be Faced, he who the fragments dictate somehow as being of Ancor as I am of Ishram, is near this accursed kingdom also, and that he is a prisoner of the very folk who should be pleading for his aid! He is as the texts described, a master of animals, a child of nature, a warrior raised by the primal world to stand against all evils!" He chuckled. "To stand against me. Zorena's served me well with such knowledge—"

"Knowledge she stole from me!" Kyrik spat. "Ripped from the eyes of one of the horach!"

"And you would have done no less in hoping to please me . . ."

The sorcerer acknowledged this truth. "I knew of the one, my lord, before she did! I knew even that his title was Beastmaster and that his birth name is *Dar of Emur*! I held back this knowledge until

I had prepared a trap for him, so that I could either present the primitive for your pleasure . . . or at least give you his rotting carcass, should that be the case!"

Vorannos whirled. His right hand pointed toward one of the remaining statues.

Smoke arose from the statue and a hideous hissing sound filled the chamber.

The statue curled within itself, what vague human features it had twisting into something ungodly. It curled into a fetal position, almost like a living thing writhing in agony.

Kyrik was blinded by a flash of light . . . and when the sorcerer looked upon the statue, there was little left but quickly dissipating vapors.

"There are but three hosts remaining to house your spirit, my bodiless Kyrik. It is your own foolishness for choosing your sorcery over your original mortal form. They give you protection from ordinary weapons, but not my wrath. Spare me words and show me why they should not be reduced to two in number."

The sorcerer was quick to respond. He revealed no regret at the loss of a valuable host even though the cost to forge another artificial body was high. Instead, with renewed guile in his voice, Kyrik bowed low, then withdrew his hands into his voluminous cloak. Though he in truth stood upon Ancor, what he brought forth next so caught Vorannos's interest that the lord of all nearly reached out to touch it despite it being merely an image of the true thing.

It was a beast. A small, furred vermin the likes of which had once existed on Ishram . . . until it and all else had been better engineered to serve the glory of Vorannos.

"This Beastmaster, this Dar of Emur, there is the great possibility that, despite being presently a prisoner of ignorant Edurac, he will still stand against your wishes, my lord!" Kyrik's own dark eyes danced with anticipation. He held the animal up. It was brown of fur and long of body. Barely noticeable was the rising and falling of the chest. "And when he does . . . it will be this . . . this that shall bring him to your feet without you so much as needing to raise a finger . . ."

The mirror eyes surveyed the image of the creature, all details memorized in a breath. Vorannos rarely marveled at anything, but he did find himself curious about this tiny creature and how it could wield the power to bring down the only possible impediment to his search for the Fountain.

"What is it, dog? What is it called that so promises victory?"

Kyrik smiled like a jackal. "It is called a Podo . . ."

6

BOUND AS HE WAS, DAR SAW LITTLE OF THE JUNGLES AND other landscape leading to Edurac, but one significant change from the ruined regions through which he had most recently journeyed quickly became obvious. The creatures of Ancor had not yet completely abandoned those areas through which the party now passed. Life still had a strong hold on this land.

First to make themselves noticed were the higher insects . . . the bees, the butterflies, and such. They fluttered around Dar, drawn to his true nature but unable to do much for his situation. Dar was not even certain that they understood what was happening.

Then the voices of the birds could be heard, some songs calling to the Beastmaster. *What can we do? What can we do? What can we do?* they asked, so very willing to assist in his freedom. Yet Dar warned them away, for they could not aid him as he desired.

But, shortly after, he finally sensed the larger animals and they him. Like the birds, they offered—through distant and not so distant roars—their strength and skills to the Beastmaster, but Dar asked that they keep hidden, for he could not think of any way by which they could presently help.

What was still most important for him was to speak to either the king or this Orestian—whose position was still unclear, although it seemed to be a combination of royal advisor and court mage. Then surely all matters concerning the mistaken capture would be cleared up and the deadly threat already encompassing most of Ancor could then be focused upon.

The soldiers did not speak to Dar, Jalan, or even much to one another, and it was only when the jungle suddenly gave way to some of the only clear sky remaining that the Beastmaster knew that Edurac lay just ahead. New sounds, the sounds of civilization—especially voices—grew from a faint whisper to a veritable roar as the wagon neared its destination. Through cautious maneuvering, Dar managed to enable both himself and Jalan to see over the edge of the wagon wall.

And just as he did . . . above the two captives appeared the imposing stone walls of the kingdom.

The thick, towering walls radiated an air of security that comforted even Dar. Surely more than a yard in depth, the high walls—built of stone and clay—rose at least four stories, possibly five. The Beastmaster caught glimpses of helmed and breastplated guards upon the battlements even as the latter peered down to see what catch the hunters had brought.

The standard of King Leardius fluttered above, upon it the same fearsome hawk that the Beastmaster's captors had worn. Dar had heard much about Edurac even though he had never been to it in the past; nearly every land knew of its glory and might.

Swarms of travelers on foot, horse, or wagon were steered aside as the hunters demanded preference for entering. Many of those on foot were ragged and dirty and had clearly journeyed a long distance. Their hollow eyes bespoke of horrors and suffering beyond what he once could have imagined . . . until his encounters in the jungle.

The wagon passed between the two wide, iron doors that comprised the front gate. Tall buildings with wide archways then surrounded the wagon, the huge, round windows of the upper levels like eyes inspecting with suspicion anything entering the kingdom.

The wagon jostled, momentarily throwing the two humans and the tiger together. Ruh uttered a growl of frustration, but the Beastmaster quieted him again. He did not want to stir up their captors' wariness even more.

A horn sounded. Regaining his view, Dar glanced toward the source of the sound.

"What is it?" Jalan murmured, the boy speaking for the first time in hours. He had been unusually calm and seemed to follow Dar's lead in all things. The Beastmaster hoped that Jalan would not live to regret that decision.

"The palace of the king . . ." he finally answered to his companion's question. "It can only be that."

It was the largest and most imposing of these structures Dar's limited vision was able to make out. Four towers marked the palace's sharp corners and at the center a massive dome spread across for as far as he could see. At the top of the dome, two stone hawks peered down over the populace.

Fluted columns flanked the high, sculpted entrance, where marble warriors in friezes high above engaged in battle with falling foes. To reach the huge bronze doors, a fit soldier would have to march up a monumental flight of marble steps at least half the length of the vast dome. Dar wondered if the hunters would drag him and the others up the steps or at least unbind them first.

But as they passed through the massive, iron-bar fence protecting the perimeter of the palace, the wagon veered sharply to the left. Guards on duty all along the way kept wary attention on the prisoners as the wagon headed toward a lower, less intricate bronze door located in a wall that was part stone, part earth, revealing that the palace not only soared well above Edurac but extended well below, too.

Dar began to suspect that it would not be Leardius to whom they would be presented.

At the door, a dozen guards with black helms and breastplates marked with an owl stepped forth. Their leader wore a faceless helmet from which came a disturbing, almost monotone voice.

"What do you bring?" he asked of the party's captain.

"Spies, demons, intruders, odd strangers . . . take your pick, Zyun, but just take 'em to your master as you're damned supposed to and see if they know anything."

From the two narrow eye slits—the only markings on the face plate—a pair of dark black eyes studied the trio. "They'll be surprised by what they know."

It was time to speak. "Listen to me," Dar interjected, raising his head. "I am no enemy. We escaped from the darkness to the south. I must speak with the king or, if need be, the one called Orestian."

"It is Orestian to whom you'll be speaking . . . and speaking much, outlander." Zyun looked over Jalan and Ruh. "Demons, not likely. Spies for Xorot, more than possible."

"I know of no Xorot—"

Zyun signaled the other faceless guards forward. "Silence him, then drag this sorry catch in to the master."

Ruh stirred, stretching the net holding him to its limit. Dar touched the tiger's mind, warning Ruh against coming to his defense.

The hilt of a dagger sent the Beastmaster into darkness.

· · ·

THERE WERE SOLDIERS skirting the jungle, soldiers in such numbers that they could only be going to war. Although the slim, raven-tressed woman recognized the kingdom of their origin, she did not step out to greet them. Even the familiar was suspect in this dire time. It could very well be that for reasons unknown to the watching figure, the young, square-jawed king astride the golden charger allied himself with the opportunistic despot, Xorot of the Claw. The flaxen-haired rider would not be the first of the "civilized" rulers to do so. There were those who believed it was better to serve the darkness than be consumed by it.

And, from what she had seen, the female warrior could not necessarily disagree with them, though she herself would still fight to her last drop of blood against the fiends emerging from the fiery pits.

The warrior, with her tanned skin and agile movements, slipped back into the deeper recesses of the jungle, her dark green top and short, matching skirt helping her blend into her surroundings. With sandals of thatchgrass enhancing her naturally silent movements, the watcher moved on, leaving no hint of her nearby presence.

Perhaps she had been wrong to avoid speaking with the armed riders, but, assuming they were not with Xorot, what she had seen thus far made her doubtful in their ability to do anything but briefly stall the fiends of the dark. Armed fighters could do only so much against the creatures that had dropped from the stars. In truth, she believed there was only one hope.

A hope that the female warrior also knew was long dead.

"Then it must fall to me," she murmured sternly. "It must fall to me."

It was a mantra that the young woman had repeated for days upon days, weeks upon weeks, as she had roamed the jungles in search of answers, of strength.

And it was a mantra in which, despite her tone of conviction, she did not have any faith.

"SO IT IS," declared a drawling voice that reminded Dar of a jackal's cry. "So it is, but what is it?"

As he stirred to waking, Dar instinctively reached for his head in order to stop the march of elephants through it. That is, the Beastmaster *tried* to reach, only to discover that his arms were bound by leather straps at the wrists and stretched far to each side . . . as were his legs.

His surroundings began to take shape. He was in a huge, stone chamber with no windows, which likely meant that it was well beneath the ground. He could tell from the many veinlike cracks in the walls that the place was ancient. Torches in niches illuminated the rounded chamber, revealing to his right a series of scorched and stained tables upon which were set vials, black boxes, and other arcane items that set Dar's nerves taut.

And to his left, he heard the voice again. "This fool is no more a spy for Xorot than the tiger is a demon, I think."

"As I thought, too, master." The second voice was all too recognizable as being that of Zyun.

Dar turned his head to the pair . . . but focused his eyes immediately beyond them as something else snared his attention. In a cage set against the wall behind his captors, Ruh and Jalan peered anxiously back. Although the pair were held together, Jalan had no need to fear the animal. Indeed, the guards standing near the door of the cage were more of a threat. Still, seeing his friends so made Dar struggle in vain against his bonds.

"A poor sense of focus, hmmm . . ." A stout figure in long, emerald robes trimmed with blue moved to cut off the Beastmaster's view. "Merely some primal barbarian of the jungle, perhaps."

"My name is Dar," the Beastmaster said with some defiance.

"And I am no enemy of Edurac. I come with warning about the creatures to the south. The ones who have destroyed entire lands—"

The faceless Zyun slapped him across the jaw. "You speak only to answer the master's questions!"

Ruh's growl erupted from behind the robed form. Dar bared his teeth at Zyun, then looked to the man next to the guard.

Orestian—for it surely could be none other than the king's spell-caster—was a round-faced, middle-aged man with a wisp of a gray beard on the tip of his chin and an equally thin crown of brown circling his otherwise bald pate. His mouth was pursed and his nose reminded Dar of those of the wild pigs that rummaged for jungle mushrooms. The Beastmaster might have marked Orestian as of little consequence had it not been for the man's eyes, which were very much like those of the patient and silent hunter of the forest, the great snake. Green with flecks of gold, those orbs observed everything about the bound Beastmaster that was worth observing. Dar, in turn, knew that of the two men, Zyun, for all his outward menace, was the least of the prisoner's concerns.

"Dar of the jungle, you have something of the smell of a magician," Orestian declared. He turned to gesture toward the cage. "A tiger may be tamed to obey a mere man, but a hungry tiger would make of a youth—if that is what he truly is—a quick meal. No, not all is what it seems here."

"They are my friends," the Beastmaster replied simply. "And thus, friends of each other. That is why Ruh will not touch him."

The spellcaster's brow furrowed in amusement. "And friends do not devour one another when the opportunity or need presents itself? The jungle is more straightforward than the city, then, to be sure."

Dar sought to bring the conversation back to his own need. "Master Orestian—for I think you are him—again, I come only to speak of the enemy to the south and offer my skills in fighting—"

Zyun bent his hand back to slap the prisoner again, but Orestian shook his head. The guard immediately dropped his hand to his side.

"My good King Leardius has legions of armored warriors on horseback, ten times as many spearmen to follow them, and archers in such numbers that you would not believe. What skills do you offer besides impudence and your uncanny cat?"

"Perhaps the boy is actually as you suggested earlier, master," Zyun snarled. "A sprite or elemental of the forest in service to this jungle magician. It may be that if he's no spy for Xorot, that he is one for Xorot's obscene lords, those who smother the sky—"

Once more struggling against his bonds, which were tethered to tall, wooden posts on each side of him, Dar growled back, "The boy is no sprite or elemental! He is a child, orphaned by the evil we should be fighting together! He—"

"Speaks with an avian who speaks as a man as no creature born of mortal Ancor could," Orestian broke in. He pointed upward.

Dar, following his gesture, beheld a small cage hung from the ceiling.

In it, Seto merrily flapped his wings at the Beastmaster.

The suggestion Orestian had made concerning Jalan and the parrot was so incredulous that Dar could not help laughing despite the severity of the overall situation.

"He shows his true colors in his madness!" Zyun snapped. "A magician or a magical being himself . . ."

It was the two men who had to be mad, for their accusations held no logic that the Beastmaster could see. Dar ceased laughing. "Let me speak with Leardius and all will—"

The spellcaster snapped his fingers. In addition to silencing his prisoner, the action brought four other guards to Dar.

"There is only one certainty with this one," the bald figure uttered. "The trial of the pit."

Zyun chuckled.

As one, the other guards began undoing Dar's bonds. Lest the Beastmaster think that he was being released, Zyun drew a sharp sword and set the point at the prisoner's throat. The other armored figures first released Dar's ankles—enabling him to stand—then his wrists.

Behind his concealing helmet, Zyun's eyes dared Dar to try to fight his way to freedom.

And so, the Beastmaster did just that.

None of the guards were ready for his audacity, not even Zyun. Perhaps they expected a halfhearted attempt, but not the swift, feline twist that sent one of his other captors into the sword point Zyun thrust forward just a moment too late.

The two armored men should have only collided, with the blade bouncing harmlessly off the breastplate of Zyun's underling, but the guard leader, determined to get his foe at all cost, twisted the point upward at the last moment. He impaled the second guard through the throat even as Dar threw two of the remaining men into one another.

Orestian calmly backed away as his former prisoner turned to him. Dar had no desire to hurt anyone, and even the one death— though not his doing—already weighed heavily on his conscience, but the spellcaster and his guards had given him no choice.

He spread his hands as he closed on Orestian, trying to show the man that he meant no harm. All Dar desired was to have the robed scholar lead him to Leardius.

Zyun threw himself at Dar. The Beastmaster stumbled back as the armored figure collided with him with the force of a charging bull.

His left foot encountered only air. Dar lost his balance and grabbed for anything to keep him from falling. One hand seized Zyun's forearm.

But the lead guard proved insufficient to counter Dar's imbalance and, in fact, fell with him.

The two men dropped into a wide hole.

Dar did his best to twist into a position that might save him from some harm once he hit bottom, but the collision that followed still sent shock waves through his bones and left him stunned. His shoulder pounded with agonizing pain and tears left him blind.

It was the scraping of metal against stone that cut through the haze and forced him to fight to focus. He heard a grunt, then sensed movement toward him.

Through blurry eyes, the Beastmaster watched Zyun coalesce. The guard's helmet was gone, revealing the man beneath to be as grotesque as anything Dar had ever seen. Much of Zyun's nose and one side of his mouth had been ripped away and healed over, with even some bone showing. He wore a permanent leer. His yellow hair framed his face as a lion's mane did the great beast's visage.

Dar expected Zyun to come at him, but though the Eduracian had regained his sword, he seemed not the least interested in the Beastmaster. Instead, he was frantically looking around, seeking escape.

From behind Zyun there came a low but powerful hiss.

Sword up, the fearful Eduracian turned . . . but too late.

A scaled paw with four sharp claws slashed at the guard's head . . . which then went flying past Dar's startled eyes.

Zyun's torso, blood from the open neck spilling over the black armor, stood quivering for a moment before crashing to the floor. In its collapse it revealed just what had removed one threat from Dar and now presented a far greater one to the injured warrior.

The reptile was as tall at the shoulder as the human, but at least six times as wide, with a body half-covered in a spiked shell that gave the creature some semblance to a turtle. But no turtle had such a long, almost crocodilian maw with overlapping teeth that measured as long as Dar's hand. The moss-green behemoth waddled as it moved toward the new prey, behind it dragging a long, thick tail with more of the sharp spikes running along to the very tip.

Although Dar had never seen its like before, he felt no fear, only wariness. The Beastmaster stretched a hand toward the giant, seeking to link with the reptile as he did with all animals.

But a voice above interrupted Dar before he could attempt anything. "I mark you now," Orestian said, pointing down at the prisoner. "You are an enemy of Edurac, at the very least, though whether spying for Xorot, demons, or some other force, you may confess now. It is the only way by which to save your life . . ."

"I am no spy, no enemy!"

The sorcerer steepled his fingers. With an almost pious look, he shook his head. "You condemn yourself . . ."

The slavering reptile charged Dar. The Beastmaster reached out to its mind . . . and found an intangible barrier that kept his own from linking to the creature's.

Only then did Dar realize that the reptile had paused when Orestian had spoken, then moved again once the spellcaster had decided he would trouble no more with the prisoner. Orestian utterly controlled his pet's simple mind, which meant that Dar was in far more peril than he had imagined.

The giant lunged for him, great maw snapping at the human's chest. Better prepared than the late Zyun, Dar nimbly dodged the bite. However, the pit was limited in width and length, and avoiding the reptile was only a temporary reprieve. Dar glanced at the walls, but they had been purposely rubbed smooth and were too high for even someone was agile as him to jump up and grab a handhold at the top.

With another hiss, the reptile suddenly lurched on its hind legs and swatted at Dar. The great claws came within inches of doing to the Beastmaster what they had done to the unlamented Zyun.

Dar sought the death of no animal or man, but like both he believed in his inherent right to defend himself. He backed up, then took a tremendous leap that startled the shelled behemoth, for the Beastmaster landed atop the creature's spiked crest.

The giant swerved as it tried to snap at the small annoyance on its back. The tail suddenly flashed backward, the spikes narrowly missing Dar.

He leaped again, this time landing to his massive foe's far left. Zyun's decapitated corpse lay barely a foot from him.

Seizing the guard's weapon, the Beastmaster turned just as the reptile maneuvered around to pursue him again. Dar met the animal's snapping maw with the sharp blade, rewarding the reptile's eagerness with a bloody gash under one nostril.

The great beast momentarily retreated, clearly not accustomed to prey that could fight back. Seeing the dripping wound, Dar regretted what he had done. If there could have been any method for him to avoid injuring, much less slaying, the reptile, he would have been happy to make use of it.

Once again, Dar sought to make contact with his adversary, and once again Orestian's spellwork prevented him. Dar glanced up, but there was no means by which he could disrupt the watching sorcerer's concentration.

The reptile lunged forward, this time using its front paws. Dar parried thrusts from both, then cut at one appendage. Unfortunately, his blade bounced off the armored hide.

There had to be more vulnerable spots than just the tip of the snout, but other than the yellow-red orbs, set so deep that they appeared little more than slits under the thick brow ridge, Dar could see nothing. He had no desire to go plunging his arm into the long, toothy mouth in the hopes of reaching something vital further toward the gullet.

Once more, the reptile lunged toward him. Dar retreated, only to feel hard rock against his back. The creature had him penned in. Dar had to make a choice about his avenues of attack and whether he was truly committed to killing an animal even if the other choice was his own life lost.

Then a brightly colored missile dropped between the two combatants. The reptile pulled back as a winged form, fluttering before its eyes, merrily called out, "Seto! Good Seto!"

"How did that avian escape?" Orestian demanded. One of the other guards produced a crossbow, but the sorcerer snapped, "No! You may injure the *karkuuran* . . ."

Seto continued to hover above the reptile—or karkuuran, as Orestian had identified it—distracting it from Dar's presence. The parrot laughed as the huge predator twisted its long head up to snap at the infuriating speck. Seto looked as though he thought he and the karkuuran were merely playing.

But the parrot's antics did more than just give Dar a reprieve. They revealed at last what Dar believed to be the reptile's most vulnerable spot. Just above the throat and at the base of the lower jaw was a soft, unarmored area normally hidden by the karkuuran's massive head. Now, though, with the reptile focused on something above, the soft tissue was open to attack.

Dar hefted the blade, but hesitated. He knew that each moment meant losing the one opportunity he had, but the Beastmaster could not bring himself to slay the karkuuran, who only followed instinct and Orestian's enforced commands.

Withdrawing the sword, Dar kicked at the unshielded location.

The karkuuran let out a bellow that mixed outrage and pain. It waddled back, its bellow transforming into a deep, hacking cough.

Although he had not done enough to permanently harm the reptile, guilt still swept over Dar. Still, he moved toward the beast and crouched, hoping for another chance.

Seto gave it to him again, the parrot once more diving down

before the predator's furious eyes. Despite its injury—or perhaps because of it—the karkuuran again tried to snap up the irritating morsel.

The moment the vulnerable area revealed itself, Dar kicked again.

Outraged and obviously in tremendous pain, the armored creature tried to crush Dar beneath one massive paw. The Beastmaster grunted as the claws just barely scraped his left leg. Even the minor strike was enough to jolt Dar, causing him to drop to one knee.

But the karkuuran did not fall upon him. Hacking, the reptile also slipped to its knees. As the Beastmaster pulled himself up, he saw that the angle in which the karkuuran lay left the injured area readily accessible. A simple sword thrust would end the battle here and now.

Dar threw the sword to the ground, more concerned with the karkuuran's life than his own. He tried yet again to reach into the armored creature's mind and almost thought that he finally felt something.

"What's happening?" Orestian called out. "What's happening?"

Dar saw that the struggle between him and the karkuuran had led them toward the overhang from which the creature had first emerged to slay Zyun. The Beastmaster quickly surveyed the karkuuran's home even as he debated what to do about the stricken giant. However, the overhang extended only so far, ending in a shadowy, rounded area that led nowhere.

The karkuuran continued to hack. The unprotected area had proven far more vulnerable to Dar than the human had thought.

Let me help you, he called with his thoughts to the immense reptile. *Let me help you . . .*

The karkuuran let out a mournful rumble, but whether in acknowledgment of Dar's kindness or some other reason, the human could not say. Regardless, Dar decided to risk the savage teeth and rending claws to see if he had done anything that might yet cause the reptile's regrettable doom.

Above, Orestian shouted something else—not only was it unintelligible, but at that moment the Beastmaster cared about nobody else save the one he had been forced to injure.

The creature's throat throbbed red, but as he ran his fingers across it, Dar did not sense any damage beyond the superficial. The karkuuran would recover with time. Still, listening to its labored breathing, Dar regretted even that much stress to the animal.

He suddenly felt eyes upon him, eyes from the direction of the reptile's makeshift burrow.

It was not a guard, as his first instincts insisted, but an extraordinary figure—an elderly, white-bearded man. The anemic figure wore a plain tunic that reached to his knees. His feet were bare and callused. He was bald of head, and his kindly features reminded Dar of the farmer who had raised him.

In the bright, ivory eyes that met the Beastmaster's gaze, the figure conveyed compassion and understanding. The bearded man nodded. Dar read approval in the elder's expression and understood somehow that the stranger was pleased with the warrior's decision not only to spare the life of the huge predator when offered the chance to slay it, but for Dar's also offering to aid the distressed animal. The Beastmaster had remained true to his beliefs in the sanctity of even the reptile's life. Only men truly gave him no choice but to fight to the death.

Dar opened his mouth to speak, but the elder raised one white hand toward him. Upon the open palm, the Beastmaster beheld something with which he had become familiar through his studies with Baraji.

A mandala. It was emerald of hue and consisted of several rounded edges encircling crescent moons and other patterns too tiny for Dar to make out from where he was. Yet the more the warrior stared at the pattern, the more he thought that the center moved of its own accord.

No . . . not merely the center. Now it looked as if the entire mandala turned from left to right. It also appeared to vibrate—

The pattern flew with astounding swiftness from the bearded elder's palm to Dar's chest. However, it did not strike Dar, but rather went *through* him.

Something stirred within the Beastmaster's heart, something he only then realized had been asleep all his life. He stood there in wonderment, feeling a sense of contentment rare to him.

Only after a moment did Dar notice that he was again alone in the pit. Of the pale elder, there was no sign whatsoever, although where the figure could have gone was impossible to say.

Behind the gasping karkuuran, Dar heard movement. Glancing over his shoulders, he saw four guards slip down by ropes into the pit. Two already had their weapons drawn.

Worse, above all of them, Orestian began to mutter words that Dar knew had more threat to them than double the number of foes encroaching on him. Against swords the Beastmaster could fight, but Orestian's sorcery was a threat for which he had no counter.

However, before either the guards or their master could strike, there suddenly arose a clamor from far beyond Orestian. Barely a breath later, a sturdy voice resounded throughout the underground chamber.

"Stop! Stop all this at once!"

At the same time, a winged form darted down past Orestian, heading straight to Dar. However, it was not Seto, as the Beastmaster first imagined.

Sharak alighted on his brother's arm.

7

ARMORED SOLDIERS RESEMBLING DAR'S ORIGINAL CAPTORS
quickly surrounded the perimeter of the pit's top. The
guards, poised to attack the Beastmaster, sheathed their
weapons and looked to Orestian.

As for the spellcaster, he took on an expression of devotion,
bowing to a figure yet unseen by Dar.

A silence followed, a silence broken by the jingle of armor as
someone strode with haste to the pit. A stern warrior with a trim
black beard just beginning to gray at the edges peered down at the
prisoner. His breastplate and silver-tipped kilt were both ebony, with
the hawk emblazoned in red on the former.

"By the oracle, give that man aid in climbing out before that
monster regains its senses or it'll be all your heads!"

Instantly, the new contingent began taking command of the
ropes used by Orestian's guards. Two ropes were immediately

dropped down to where Dar could make use of them. Sending Sharak up, Dar seized one and quickly climbed to the top.

Orestian, meanwhile, was seeking to explain things to the steely-eyed man who had put an end to the madness. "Your Majesty, this incident was unavoidable. His appearance, his companions, and his vague references were very reminiscent of the Tyrean trouble. You recall how many good men perished before we put an end to Xorot's infiltrators."

Dar eyed the newcomer, who surely had to be the legendary King Leardius. The Beastmaster gave the dark-maned monarch a solemn nod, but did not kneel as perhaps some there would have expected.

The corners of Leardius's mouth crept upward. He gave Dar an approving nod in return, then somewhat impatiently added, "You've been stalwart in protecting us from a second debacle like that, Orestian, and so I won't fault you even though I see two men dead and another almost devoured."

The round face grew more apologetic. "The guard was a tragic accident. Zyun . . . Zyun was . . . overimpetuous, and he paid for that." Orestian suddenly turned to Dar. "And to you, I beg forgiveness. If his majesty sees such reason to preserve you by coming himself to your rescue, I must conclude that you are a valued friend of Edurac."

Leardius chuckled, some of his impatience dissipating. "He's more than that, Orestian. He's a *myth* come back from the dead. You know of whom I speak."

The sorcerer pulled back with a gasp. "The animals . . . my lord . . . I—I should have recognized the clues myself! A myth come back from the dead, indeed . . ."

Dar winced at being called a myth. "Your majesty, I am merely a wanderer who's come—"

The armored figure let out a bellowing laugh. Even in the dim light of the chamber's torches, his armor, traced with gold and silver on the edges, glistened. A small but intricately cast circlet around his head acted as even further mark of his august position, each segment of it alternating between triangles of gold and small diamonds cut into shapes.

Sharak called out from above. The eagle returned to a grateful Dar's shoulder. Sharak, knowing that Dar had wanted to see the king, had located Leardius. But Dar wondered how the avian could possibly have gotten the lord of Edurac to come to Dar's rescue.

But movement elsewhere distracted Dar from asking. From beneath the purple cloak fastened to Leardius's armored shoulders and draping down his back, a familiar ferret emerged, one who quickly scurried down to the floor, then raced to rejoin the eagle and their human brother. Kodo nuzzled Dar's face, both so happy to see each other that they paid little mind to the watching Eduracians. Yet seeing the male ferret made the Beastmaster once again wonder about Podo and her fate. Unfortunately, Kodo knew nothing of his mate.

The unique reunion made Leardius even more relieved. He cleared his throat, calling himself to Dar's attention. "I was told the legends and know one teller in particular to speak them as truth, but still, they were always to my own self mere stories—myths!" The king shook his head. "Yet the oracle did warn me to watch for when a servant of the sky and a furred thief would appear in my royal chambers and mark their presence with actions more human than animal. Then I would know that *he* had come and that the myths were fact! You can be sure it took little prompting for me to believe when these two came just as predicted! Praise Ontas for his gift!"

"Brother Ontas!" Seto exuberantly called out from above as if seeking to join the conversation.

Orestian remained silent throughout, eyeing Dar from the side as if studying a fascinating insect. Dar wanted the king to stop speaking, but he could hardly think of any way to bring that about without causing a scandalous scene.

Leardius only made it worse, abruptly dropping to one knee. "I greet you, lord of the animals, protector of the jungles, of all life! I greet you and welcome you to my realm!" He slapped his fist against his breastplate. "Hail, *Beastmaster!*"

Several of the guards started at their ruler's use of the title, and all, including Orestian, fell to their knees in imitation of his action.

Dar was grateful that Edurac no longer saw him as an enemy, but he was equally distraught by this continued display of awe. He had no idea what Leardius meant when he spoke of an oracle's words, but he recognized that the king saw in him some sort of champion that would aid the realm against the tide of darkness descending upon it.

It was a role Dar felt was far greater than his meager shoulders could bear.

"Please, Your Majesty! Do not kneel to me! I am only a simple warrior who comes bearing warnings and seeking answers! My skills I offer to Edurac, yes, but—"

Leardius appeared to be only half listening. Gazing over his shoulder, the bearded monarch roared, "The boy and the tiger! By the gods! Release them now!"

A pair of soldiers rushed to obey. Orestian took a step back as Ruh and Jalan exited the cage, but the cat only growled displeasure at his former captor.

Jalan ran to Dar, hugging him tight. "I knew you'd save us!"

In Dar's opinion, he had done nothing. Worse, the boy's gratitude only served to heighten Leardius's opinion that he had found himself some legendary hero who would vanquish all evils.

"Let us leave this place for better surroundings," the king continued. "You look in need of sustenance, and I wish to speak with you concerning the dire events facing Edurac and Ancor. Orestian, we'll deal with this later . . ."

"Yes, Your Majesty," the bald man replied, bowing low.

Dar surrendered . . . at least for the moment. He let Leardius guide him from Orestian's sanctum, the king's guards, Jalan, and the animals close behind.

They exited through a bronze door whose broken fastenings spoke of Leardius's determination to reach his mythic champion before anything happened to him. From there, they ascended to a mysterious sliding panel that opened to reveal a glistening marble hallway with high fluted columns and a statuary depicting what the Beastmaster had to assume were the great kings of Edurac.

The panel slid shut behind the party and when Dar looked for it, he saw only solid wall.

"The chambers below were secret prisons used for torture," his august host conceded with regret. "For the private pleasures of ancestors long dead and just as long shunned."

Dar had met good fathers with sons willing to do great ill and good sons with abhorrent fathers. There were few bloodlines that could, had they the knowledge spreading back through generations, truthfully claim that no evil existed in them. The Beastmaster nodded, his understanding seeming a tremendous relief to Leardius. The king clearly wanted nothing to deter his chosen hero from aiding Edurac.

"But those chambers find much more just use these days, aiding us in protecting the good people of the realm from the demons and villains throughout." The bearded monarch bowed his head in disgust. "Although I must apologize again for the terrible mistake made against you and your friends."

"I regret that two men died for no good reason," Dar returned. Zyun had been fanatic in his duties, but the Beastmaster felt that surely the man had meant the best for his home. "I'll mourn them, but otherwise will speak no more of this."

"You benevolence is commendable," Leardius replied with a solemn smile. "Ah! Here we are!"

They entered a sumptuous chamber that Dar assumed was where Leardius entertained other royal guests. Several guards lined the walls and those who had followed the party there immediately resumed stations in areas that they had clearly vacated earlier. A vast wooden table filled with fruits, meats, and varied wines was the centerpiece of the chamber, more than two dozen chairs of the finest oak surrounding it.

From an arched entrance at the back of the room, four young, veiled women in gauzy blouses and flowing skirts silently rushed forth, each taking up a place near the largest and grandest of the chairs at the table's head.

"My wives," Leardius revealed proudly. "I was preparing to come here to sup just before your friends visited my personal chambers." He gestured at the dark-eyed women who, despite the thin veils, were obviously beautiful. "As they would have served me when I arrived, so shall they now serve the two of us—and the boy and the beasts, too, of course!"

Dar was never happy letting others serve him, but this was Leardius's realm, and again he did not wish to offend his host. The king's wives obviously were used to this role, a custom the Beastmaster knew of from other lands.

The women appeared anxious when Ruh sidled up to his side, but the king was unperturbed. Clapping once, he shouted, "Be at peace, my wives! This is a hero, a champion, and his faithful companions! The tiger is nothing to fear!" But in a lower tone strictly for Dar, Leardius asked, "He can be safely fed here without any trouble, yes?"

"Ruh will not harm anyone."

"Excellent!" The armored monarch clapped again. "Prepare the meal for eating, and see to it that enough is brought for all my guests!"

Two of his wives immediately left through the arched entrance—not simply to obey, but very likely because it gave them a
reprieve from the tiger's presence. The other pair immediately set
additional places.

One woman pulled back the chair in which Leardius was to sit.
The hawk emblem covered most of the richly carved back.

The king shook his head. "Not for me. Not for this day."

To Dar's increasing dismay, the man guided *him* to the chair.
"Your Majesty—"

"You will do me this honor, Beastmaster. It's a small thing compared with what Edurac must ask of you . . ."

Trying not to swallow hard, Dar acquiesced. As he sat, his host
turned to Jalan.

"And you, little one. You would prefer a seat next to your friend?"

"Yes, please!" the boy piped up.

"Yes, please!" echoed Seto from Jalan's shoulder, imitating the
human's voice perfectly. "Yes, please!"

The king chuckled. "Astounding! Small wonder some thought
the bird magical!"

"He is . . . full of surprises," the Beastmaster had to admit.

With Jalan on one side of Dar, Leardius finally seated himself
unceremoniously on the other. His two other wives returned with
more food and wine.

"I honor them in other ways," the king remarked, having apparently caught some slight reproving glance from his guest. "And
in these times, there're none I could trust to see that my meals are
safe than those I know best." Leardius took up a golden goblet that
one of his wives had filled with rich, red wine. "Now! First we sup,
then . . . then, with our stomachs full and our minds sharper, we
speak of the salvation of Edurac, eh?"

Dar would have preferred they leap straight to the second part,
but, despite Leardius's clear anxiety, the bearded fighter would not

hear of it. The king dove into his own food, refusing to speak at all until Dar surrendered and joined him. Jalan, eating as if he had never tasted food before, emptied his plate twice before Dar managed to even devour half his fare. The boy handed tidbits to the parrot, who would turn them over and over as if inspecting every detail before putting them in his beak. Sharak and Kodo, more direct, accepted Dar's offerings immediately.

From where he lay, Ruh rumbled inquisitively at Leardius.

The king chuckled. "Do you think I've forgotten you, my feline friend? I would dare not! Your—uh—feast simply took more time to prepare."

And, at that moment, Leardius's wives returned again, this time with a huge platter of fresh, raw meat. Dar could sense their uncertainty as they neared the tiger and when the king rose to help them, Dar did, also.

"Thank you, Majara . . . Callisti," Leardius murmured soothingly to the women. "That will be all. My thanks."

Dar also thanked the women, then placed the meat before Ruh. The tiger nuzzled his arm, then made a purring sound toward the women. One dared touch his fur near his hindquarters before both retreated from the chamber.

"You see?" jested Leardius to the cat as he and Dar seated themselves again. "A feast fit for a monarch among predators."

Ruh gave him an approving grumble, then tore into the fresh meat.

Leardius's expression suddenly altered. He notably shivered and his gaze turned vacant.

Rising in concern, the Beastmaster blurted, "Your Majesty! Are you ill?"

The bearded monarch blinked. Though his face remained pale, he was more himself again. "Forgive me . . . it came upon me unexpectedly. I was suddenly there again . . . at the last battle. When we sought to save Gaeloth, the kingdom of my cousin, Lored. You know the realm?"

Dar shook his head, which caused Leardius's sadness to deepen. "And none shall know it now, save in story . . . assuming any of us survive. My cousin's dead, having stood with his valiant warriors at the gates while others led many of his people on to Edurac." He looked much older to Dar now. "The sky was black, but we could see them so clearly, the demons . . . or whatever they were. Some moved like men, though they were not as we, others were like creatures out of my worst nightmares. And what spilled out of them when we did manage to slay them was not like our blood, but it spilled nevertheless. There were so many, though . . ."

"How did the rest of you survive?"

The king leaned forward. "That's just it. We only survived because they came to a *halt*. It was as if their master had wanted the land around Gaeloth and had no care at the time for anything else." He shrugged bitterly. "My scouts later reported that nothing remained of the entire kingdom but one of those damned fiery pits . . ."

A fate, they both knew, that possibly awaited Edurac as well. Yet Dar had to wonder why the invaders, having proven themselves so powerful, had not yet fallen upon the greatest of Ancor's remaining defenders.

Both men recognized that it was time to discuss the terrible events sweeping over their world. Leardius indicated Jalan. "He should leave . . ."

Jalan suddenly looked frightened. Before the boy could say anything, Dar interjected, "He has seen enough to earn his presence here, Your Majesty. And from him we may also learn something more."

Jalan relaxed. Dar had not included the fact that he knew the boy had come to see him as his guardian. Dar intended to correct that, but for now he did not have the heart to send Jalan off among people even more unfamiliar to him than the Beastmaster.

But soon . . .

"Very well." Leardius turned toward his guards. "Leave us. Wait outside the doors."

After the men had obediently marched out, the king, brow furrowed deep, hesitantly admitted, "I'd like to hear your story first, Beastmaster, before I tell you of Edurac's situation. Though I am pleased by your appearance, I am still not certain whether I speak to a man or a shadow or what. The prophecy said I should watch for you, but I expected one more my age than yours. You are myth . . . legend. How do you come to be here at this time, your semblance that of one much younger than you should be?"

"I have been here and not here, Your Majesty," Dar replied. "In truth, I have never left Ancor, but at times, I was not part of it." He petted Kodo on the head. "But that story is not what matters. I am here, King Leardius, because Ancor is in strife. Not only do my brothers and sisters of the jungle suffer, but so does our very world. I can be *nowhere* else but here. I *must* be here now . . ."

"So the prophecy said. 'He will come, the master of all beasts, when his time and ours collide. He will come to Edurac, his messengers in the guises of a great hunter, a small thief, and a winged king, the last two of whom will be the ones to mark his coming to you, lord of the realm . . .'" Leardius grunted. "That was the part most direct, a rare thing from Brother Ontas. When the eagle entered my chambers carrying with him the ferret, I knew that the first part of the oracle's words had come to pass. The rest of the prophecy becomes more muddled, though, speaking of the world turned inside out, of the search within oneself to find hope for Ancor, and of the water of life being also the key to death . . ." The king suddenly blinked. "A fool I am! You can hear all yourself!"

Rising, the bearded monarch called out. A nervous guard immediately burst through the doors.

"Bring the fire bird!" Leardius commanded. His visage darkening, he added, "And poor Feronin, afterward."

The guard was not long in returning. He and a comrade carried in their grip an ivory cage in which a splendid snow-white dove perched. As beautiful as it was, Dar did not know why the dove might be called a fire bird until he caught sight of the brilliant crimson plumage at the tip of the tail.

"So you know, we did not cage it. It caged *itself,*" his host explained. "And I realize now that it did so in order to wait for you."

Dar puzzled this last over. With the cage set on the huge table, the guards retreated out of the room. Leardius reached for the door of the cage, but suddenly the fire bird cooed. It gazed at Dar. Then, its prison shimmered . . . and the bars and door faded away like so much stardust.

The dove stretched its wings, then flew gracefully toward Dar. He tried to touch its thoughts, but they were hidden from him. The Beastmaster wondered how he was to learn more of the prophecy from this unique avian.

The bird veered just before it would have reached him. As it did, the crimson plumage seemed to catch on fire. Yet Dar suddenly saw that it was not fire, but rather a flash of light formed in the wake of the creature's flight.

They were images . . . visions. Each in itself was motionless, but so swiftly did the dove circle around that it seemed the array moved. Moreover, although there were no spoken words, Dar began to hear the prophecy in his head just as Leardius had told it to him.

Though the images were like those out of dreams, he instantly recognized himself by both stance and action. But there was also something in the prophecy about the Beastmaster that disturbed Dar, for that other self looked physically caught halfway between human and animal. His legs were those of a swift antelope, his arms those of a great ape. His eyes were akin to Ruh's.

Then the part of the prophecy he already knew vanished and his attention was caught by what followed.

And the twins, dark and light, the Beastmaster suddenly heard in his head, *will stand at their gates and open the way to the blending of the gray. There, the choice will be made . . .*

Dar saw two of himself, one a dark shadow with hints that metal covered all the flesh. He was reminded of the golems. The twins locked hands and lightning and thunder arose between them. They battled in the midst of a vast sea and Ancor itself floated on that sea, as if a tiny bit of flotsam.

And if the dark defeats the light, the world will turn in on itself, and cold metal will replace warm earth . . .

Ancor now filled the vision, but an Ancor covered in smoke and endless ranks of cold, metal structures. The people of Ancor moved about, but they were no longer human. Their bodies were bent and their faces were masked . . . masked in a way that brought to Dar's mind the Pygmesians.

His mouth opened in preparation for a gasp—and a mad cry burst from the hall beyond. The fire bird turned suddenly and flew without erring through a high window. Dar tried to summon it back, but the dove paid him no heed.

The visions vanished unfinished. King Leardius did not look angry at the costly interruption, but rather more sad.

"Poor Feronin . . ." To the guards without, he called, "Bring him in."

The four armored figures that obeyed dragged with them a man—or a shell of a man—whom Dar could see had once been a stalwart warrior. The shaggy-haired, skeletal figure now wore only a soiled old metal and cloth kilt. His feet were bare and highly cal-lused. Unsettling green circles marked his breast and also the back at the base of the spine. They looked as if some monstrous leech had adhered itself to the unfortunate, seeking his blood.

But what most struck Dar was the man's face. It was devoid of any humanity. The mouth hung gaping and the eyes stared without blinking. He could scarcely believe that any sound, even the cry, could have come from this empty shell.

The guards started to direct the cadaverous figure to the floor, but Leardius grew angry.

"Feronin was one of you once," he rumbled. "Give him a chair from my table."

The more he saw of Feronin, the more uneasy Dar became. Ruh, Kodo, and Sharak also sensed the wrongness in this disheveled man, the tiger even inching back.

"Who is he?" asked Dar.

"The only of my emissaries to return alive . . . or at least pretend to be. Know you, Beastmaster, that I did also seek some parley with the lord of the growing darkness, hoping to discover not only the truth of why he sought Ancor's devastation, but also what could be done to stop it. Feronin was the bravest of the brave and he volunteered after three other men and their escorts had vanished forever into the shadows. He brought a message of peace and understanding . . . and returned with a message of madness and evil."

Feronin let out another cry. Jalan ran to Dar's side. Even as they recovered from the madman's sudden outburst, Feronin suddenly spoke . . . but in a voice that could not have been his own.

"There is only one thing I wish of your pathetic world, king of Edurac. The Fountain. There is no value to Ancor save the Fountain. For the Fountain, your lives will be spared. For the Fountain, all Ancor will be granted the bliss of my rule and the joy of my power. For anything less, the agony will be endless . . ."

Dar shivered, but not just for the reason that Leardius might have thought. He shivered also because the voice had reminded him of his own, but without any humanity at all.

"Give me the Fountain and you will be forgiven," Feronin's mouth went on. It was now evident that the man himself did not even exist. "You will be made anew, made better . . . made to serve my glory. Such is the fate of all, if they are fortunate. Such is the fate they will plead for, if they are not."

The eyes abruptly turned to the two men. For the first time, Dar saw that some sort of mirror finish covered the actual orbs. They served to make what was left of the emissary even less human.

"Give me the Fountain . . ." the voice calmly demanded.

Feronin's mouth clamped shut. Once again, the dead eyes stared unseeing.

Only then did Dar realize that he was sweating. Jalan had grown pale and still, and King Leardius stared at the floor. Even the animals were silent.

All except Seto, that is. The chamber had only been quiet for a moment when the colorful parrot suddenly flapped his wings and cheerfully cried out his own name.

The king stirred. Wordlessly signaling the guards, he had them remove the broken emissary. Dar watched as the man was led out as if he were a puppet on strings.

"So Feronin speaks whenever in my presence," Leardius finally said when they were alone again, his fists so tight the knuckles were white. "So he'd speak again in a few minutes if we but wait. That's all his purpose seems to be. To tell us to give them this—this mysterious Fountain—and what'll happen whether we do or not."

"It ties in with the prophecy; that much is clear."

"Aye, Beastmaster, but that's all that's clear. Edurac is obviously tied to Ancor's fate. I'm grateful for every ally, for that reason . . . and filled with hate for those who would stand against her—fools and madmen like Xorot, they who would be the carrion crows feasting on the invaders' carnage!"

Dar had heard the name before. "Who is this Xorot?"

"Xorot of the Claw, that's the title by which he's best known, Beastmaster! King of the Vorundites, a half-savage people. Xorot once sought Edurac for his prize, but we beat him back hard, sent he and his warriors licking their wounds, I'll tell you that! But he's rebuilt his damned horde and added to it others like himself, petty kings and lords who think they saved their hides by joining with the darkness!" Leardius stretched forward and clasped Dar's forearm. "But now the Beastmaster is among us and woe betide Xorot's crows!"

"Your Majesty—"

"Each day the darkness draws closer!" Leardius suddenly implored. "You are in the prophecy! You've seen that! You are the hope of my people, of all Ancor! You can turn the animals against the invaders, lead an army in battle such as never has been known! I'll make you commander of the combined realms! Then—"

The Beastmaster slammed his fist on the table. "Your Majesty! I am *only* one man. Who is this oracle who demands so much of me? By what right does he throw all this on my shoulders?"

"He is a hermit by the name of Brother Ontas and though in the past his prophecies were more vague, on you he spoke with uncommon precision. He is also the one who first foretold that Edurac was the invaders' desire as well as its bane . . ."

"Brother Ontas!" chirped Seto.

As Jalan sought to shush the parrot, Dar asked. "Where is the Fountain? Do you know?"

"That question I've no good answer for," admitted the bearded monarch. He spread his hands in frustration. "Edurac has always been known for its worship of knowledge. We are the site of the Dunolian libraries, whose ancient writings speak of Ancor's earliest days, when magic was far more prevalent than man! From Brother"—Leardius glanced at Seto, who seemed to be eagerly awaiting his next word—"from the hermit, we're aware that these demons seek knowledge of the mystical Fountain that they believe is contained in the libraries . . . but the trail ends there, Beastmaster. Not even Orestian, who leads the hunt, can find anything more than hearsay! Even if we wished to give this Fountain over to the darkness's master, we couldn't!"

The king slumped back, thoughts obviously racing. As Dar contemplated his words, Leardius murmured to himself. The lord of Edurac was going over his explanation, trying, even now, to make more sense of it himself. The Beastmaster heard only a few of those words, but they struck him with interest nonethelesss

"Birth . . ." Leardius whispered. "Life . . . forever flowing . . . *eternity?*" The king shook his head in frustration.

So much destruction, Dar thought, *for something that might only exist in myth?* But then, he was supposed to only exist in myth, too.

Dar could only think of one thing to do. "This oracle . . . he must know more . . . I would speak with him. I would know exactly all he can tell about this dread time. Is it at all possible to summon him, Your Majesty?"

"Alas, he does not reside in Edurac or I'd have him here before you already! He is to be found—somewhere—in the jungle lands, but I cannot say where. Men I've sent in search of him have found nothing. He sends by bird missives bearing his prophecies; in fact, I'd not know him by face even if he were with us now."

"You've never actually met Brother Ontas?"

The parrot spread his wings. "Brother Ontas! Brother Ontas!"

"Shush, Seto!" Jalan pleaded.

But instead of obeying, the avian fluttered up above the party. Spreading his own wings, Sharak let out a shriek filled with reprimand but remained near Dar.

Seto headed up to the same open window the fire bird had used, all the while jubilantly calling out, "Brother Ontas! Brother Ontas!"

And only then did Dar recall that the first time the hermit's name had been mentioned, Leardius had not used the word "brother" . . . yet the parrot had called Ontas by that title even then.

Seto alighted on the base of the opening. The bird peered down at the humans and animals, the round eyes filled with a naïveté Dar no longer quite believed. The parrot began preening his feathers.

Dar's eyes narrowed. He focused on the parrot. But before he could try to link with Seto, the bird returned to Jalan. The boy gave the parrot a piece of bread, which Seto stuffed into his beak. Jalan murmured in the avian's ear.

Nodding grimly, Dar looked to his host. "It appears that the oracle has given us the means by which to find him . . ."

KING LEARDIUS WAS a cautious man, something that the many guards surrounding him and his guests epitomized. Other guards outside of the chamber guaranteed that no one other than he, Dar, Jalan, and the animals knew what they discussed. Even Leardius's wives had been sent away before one word had been spoken.

And yet . . . near to the king's seat, behind one of the very guards seeking to protect the ruler of Ancor, a tiny listener took in all that passed between the Beastmaster and his host. It had burrowed deep into the wall from outside, sent there to discover what would transpire.

With its multitude of tiny, hooked legs and its segmented body, it might have seemed akin to some of the scavengers of the jungle, but no denizen of Ancor carried atop it a head that was a thing of *metal*, not flesh. Eyeless, it bore instead a single, round indentation in the front designed to detect even the drop of a feather.

Ishram was this burrower's birthplace, a machine the womb from which it was born . . . and if any Ancorite had seen the listener and called it a demon, they would not have been that far from the truth. Only in the realm of Vorannos could such a creature have come into being.

Not only did it listen, but, much like the winged horach, it could relay those sounds, those words, to the one who had sent it . . . and who was not all that far away.

The burrower's master grinned both at what he now heard and the astounding magic by which he had been able to do so.

"She will be pleased . . ." Orestian murmured, steepling his hands. "*He* will be pleased . . ."

8

THE KING INSISTED THAT DAR AND HIS COMPANIONS MAKE the palace their home that night, even though the Beastmaster had never truly felt comfortable sleeping anywhere save the outdoors. Yet Dar could not in all good conscience refuse Leardius and so he chose to accept—and suffer—the bed the ruler of Edurac offered him. And as the animals and Jalan had no any intention of leaving the Beastmaster, all were to stay in the vast chambers that Edurac's monarch had saved for his most determined ally yet, but who would not arrive for some days.

But before rest could be his, the Beastmaster was confronted by yet another sudden and potentially troublesome event. Leardius and he had come to grim agreement on many matters, yet there were others who, Dar quickly discovered, were not at all pleased at the abrupt—and very secretive—appearance of a single warrior whose value the king appeared to place over their own.

They were Leardius's most powerful allies, five of the strongest of those kings who had pledged to stand with Edurac. On their own, each was influential, and together they presented a force that Leardius *had* to heed. That made it even more of an outrage when they had discovered that they had not been included in his sudden and mysterious dealings with this newcomer.

Scattering guards aside, they burst into the palace just as Leardius started to lead Dar and the others to their quarters. With a fearsome, bald man of elder years at their head, the five confronted Leardius and his guests in the main hall.

Their leader paused only to drink in the sight of the king, Dar, Jalan, and the animals, then bellowed, "Leardius! Leardius! Is this the way those who have sworn their blood to you are to be treated? News came to some of us that you meet in secret concerning the defense of all our peoples, a stranger said to be tied most directly to the oracle's damned prophecies! For such a gathering, your good allies should surely be included . . . or are we no longer key to Edurac's survival now that this rumored legend's come to you?"

"Heratos!" Dar's host angrily shouted in turn. "Still your tongue! Make no claim so base! All of you remain my good, stalwart comrades and partners in the defense of *all* Ancor . . ." Leardius indicated the Beastmaster. "His arrival was unexpected and I admit I was caught up in the astonishment of it, but you should all be well aware that anything I've discussed with him I'll certainly tell you now!"

"Aye . . . after the fact! After all discussions and any decisions have been made!" There was a rumble of agreement from the other four, all men of a similar cut as Leardius and Heratos, but with a slight bit less of their fire. Yet, with Heratos to lead them, Dar saw that they were clearly a potential threat to the cohesion of any force seeking to stand against the darkness.

Hands on his hips, the bald giant strode boldly to the Beastmaster, even ignoring Ruh's warning grumble.

The jingle of Heratos's mail armor accented his next words. "And so you are the lord of the animals spoken of by the oracle? The one who shall somehow save us all? Yes, the tales of your exploits are known to all of us—even those who've come from across the sea and beyond the mountains to the west—though I've always found them questionable, to say the least."

"Children's tales, I always said . . ." growled another king, his long, bound hair swinging as he spoke. "Children's tales heard too often some years back, as I recall, eh, Heratos?"

"To be sure, Akuran, to be sure! A man who talks to the animals!" Some of the others chuckled as Heratos added, "A circus performer could pretend to do the same, eh?"

"The tales are true," Leardius returned solemnly, his temper clearly barely held in check. "*Dar* is true."

"He had better be, if we're to place our lives in his hands, my friend. That's what bothers me so and the others, too. A strong enough lad from the looks of him, but if we'd been invited to your meeting, we'd have had a better chance to judge the truth. He could be anything, as far as we can see . . ."

"A madman, mayhaps, even," argued a stout, red-haired fighter whose iron breastplate bore the mark of a hungry, scarlet wolf. Of the group, only he also wore a helmet, open-faced and with a lupine skull adhered to the top.

"You shame me . . ." Dar's host declared, losing the calm he had briefly attained. "All so lacking in trust in my judgment of this man . . ."

Once more Dar stepped into the conversation, seeking to keep the alliance from falling apart because of his arrival. Feeling Heratos's great influence, he focused only on him. Perhaps the others would come around if Heratos did.

"My lord Heratos," the Beastmaster began. Baraji's teachings also came to the forefront, mollifying Dar's own frustration with the narrow-minded monarchs. "Your concerns are very reasonable. I would have such concerns myself were I in your place."

Leardius's eyes gave a hint of suspicion, but, to his credit, the king of Edurac kept still.

Heratos nodded. "You do well to speak to me with such respect, but words or tone alone will fail to sway us. We must have more proof."

"Words are not all I intend, my lord. Actions alone will serve to convince you and the rest. Let me show you."

With that, Dar linked to Sharak, who had patiently perched atop his shoulder. The eagle listened to his thoughts and his whispered words, then, at the Beastmaster's signal, fluttered through an open window.

Heratos did not appear to be impressed. But Dar had only just set the events into motion, and so he endured not only the visiting kings' disbelief, but also Leardius's growing concern.

Time seemed to stand still. Silence filled the chamber as everyone waited . . . for something . . .

And then the great doors swung open again, their low creaking causing Heratos and some of the other kings to start. A guard rushed into the chamber.

"My lord Leardius!" he declared, falling down on one knee. "There are . . . there are *creatures* outside the doors of the great hall!"

"Creatures! Of what sort?" The gathered monarchs stood poised, expecting, Dar realized, some threat from the south.

"Animals," he said quietly and calmly. "Animals, Your Majesties."

Heratos frowned. The other kings looked to him for guidance but all he could do was shrug as Dar indicated the men should turn to the doors.

"Animals . . ." Heratos finally managed, but before he could say anything more, odd footsteps echoed in the hall without.

A horse thrust its head through the doorway.

"Baliphon?" Heratos blurted. The horse, a brilliant white stallion, gave a snort and started forward.

Behind the steed came two greyhounds, a chestnut mare, a pair of hunting birds . . . and a dark brown wolf. Sharak, who had helped guide them here, returned to Dar's shoulder. Leardius could not smother a grin as the other monarchs muttered among themselves and watched uneasily as their favored animals entered. Baliphon nuzzled Heratos's hand, then, to his master's surprise, moved on to Dar. The other beasts did the same.

Dar nodded, grateful to the animals for having come so quickly at his summons.

But not all were willing to see his efforts for what they were. "Witchery!" proclaimed one king. "Drak!" he futilely called to one hound. "Come to me!"

"So you accept that he *can* summon the creatures of nature," Leardius responded slyly. "Whether by magic or some other ability, that surely makes him the Beastmaster."

"Not necessarily." Heratos eyed Baliphon and Dar. "Tell me something that only my steed and I would know. Tell me something that will convince me. I've heard of no witch or wizard who could gain such knowledge from any animal."

It was just what Dar had expected to be asked. He did not have to wait to answer, having asked the horse such a question even before the steed had reached the palace. "Baliphon recalls many things. He remembers the time the two of you fell while hunting a stag and how you had tears for him when you thought his leg might be broken and that you'd be forced to slay him. He remembers when you first chose him to be your mount, how you trained him like a father, using care rather than brutality when he could not at first learn the commands you wanted . . ." Heratos's softness when it came to his horse had surprised and pleased Dar. Up until then, he had feared the type of allies Leardius had drawn to him. "There is more detail . . ."

Heratos gaped. Dar used the man's hesitation to focus on the other kings, to whom one by one, he named events and emotions to which only the animals had been privy. Dar chose only good memories and, fortunately, the animals had plenty of those.

An awkward silence followed as each man drank in what he had been told. The powerful lords looked to one another for some guidance, but found nothing.

"It is . . . as you say," Heratos finally managed, visibly shaken. "If you are not called the Beastmaster, then who could be?" Leaning closer, he said more quietly, "We can only hope that they didn't tell you *too* much."

"Only what was necessary, my lord." That brought a relieved chuckle from the giant Heratos, a reaction immediately repeated by his anxious companions. "I have respected the privacy of all of you beyond that."

"And I find it impossible not to believe that, Beastmaster. What say the rest of you?"

With Heratos in his corner, Dar faced no objection from the other monarchs. They looked almost sheepish as they nodded agreement.

Heratos looked from Dar to Leardius. "He is as you say, but how can he aid us?" Returning his gaze to the Beastmaster, he respectfully asked, "What will you do?"

"The Beastmaster is part of the prophecy," Dar's host said. "The oracle declared that he would come to us. He's an integral part of our salvation, our redemption. Come morning, he will go in search of the oracle himself."

"I may be able to do something else," Dar added. "The animals will help, I believe. I will do what I can with them before and during my quest for answers from Brother Ontas—"

"Brother Ontas!" Heratos interrupted. "You'll have a devil of a time with him. Brother Ontas makes *nothing* clear." Dar shrugged, and in response, the foreign ruler lifted his hands in surrender. "So it must be . . . but I miss the days when wars were simple affairs. Never have I enjoyed the involvement of oracles and magic . . ."

"Who would?" offered Dar, and his question received nods of approval, which made him hopeful that they regarded him more as one of them than one of those unnatural things of which Heratos had just spoken.

Jalan suddenly yawned, not so surprising a thing considering how long and exhausting the day had been. His sleepy appearance further softened the other kings and made even Heratos laugh. "Aye, it's late, as this boy shows. Very well, Beastmaster. If it's to the oracle you must go, then we'll not let you tarry. The skies grow darker with every day."

"I will leave at dawn."

"May the gods guide you," retorted one of the other kings. "Time is running out, and more men die each day fighting a foe unknown to them with weapons of the like we've never seen before . . ."

"Oracles, witches, and sorcerers," grumbled Akuran, the most cynical of the lot. "From such as these must we look for solutions? What we truly need more are miracles—"

"And speaking of *Orestian*," Heratos interrupted, with a grunt of disdain. "How goes that sorry sorcerer with his endless digging through dusty tomes, Leardius? Has he found anything at all of value about this Fountain? Its location . . . that would surely help."

"Men, we must not let these thoughts destroy our faith. You must trust me that Orestian is looking. He promises—"

" 'Promises.' Always some 'promise.' Glad I am now to have this one"— Heratos gestured at Dar—"Beastmaster. You mentioned your animals helping. Our men are outnumbered and weary. The darkness is almost upon Edurac, meaning worse fighting than ever. *Your* 'friends' could be of help to us in battle . . ."

"They will fight . . . and more will come."

"I pray to the gods that you're right." Heratos took Baliphon's reins. "We'll leave you two, then, and I for one will feel better now. Fare you well, Beastmaster, and good hunting for the elusive Brother Ontas—"

"Brother Ontas!" squawked Seto, flapping his colorful wings. The parrot danced back and forth on Jalan's shoulder. The boy yawned again, then petted the bird's head.

Heratos chuckled at the sight. "Good to find something light in this time of darkness. Come, my friends . . ." He bowed respectfully to Leardius, as did his companions. The foreign monarchs were clearly apologetic over the way they had barged in and treated their host.

Heratos led the other kings out, the horses, hounds, wolf, and birds trailing alongside their individual masters. The Beastmaster had made certain that each animal knew the safety of these men was paramount. Already loyal, they would do their utmost to protect their humans. Dar noted subtle glances and movements that marked how differently each man now perceived his animal companion. The foreign monarchs, even Heratos, were forever changed.

If only all else could be so simple, Dar thought wearily. This band of animals was a start, but only a start. Dar would have to do much more . . . if he could.

Leardius slapped him on the back. "Come, Beastmaster! By that look, you are done in more than the boy. If you're to leave tomorrow at first light, you'd best get rest now."

"That would be good." Dar's burdens again weighed heavily on him, this new quest especially concerning him. He wished there were someone else who could be entrusted with the matter, but the only one that came to mind was the sorcerer, Orestian. As a man whose calling involved much study and research, the sorcerer would have been a reasonable choice to seek out the oracle and then puzzle out what would no doubt be murky answers.

But the Beastmaster could not bring himself to even suggest that to Leardius. Dar would hunt down the oracle with the parrot's aid and leave the search of Edurac's ancient library to one better suited. Perhaps . . . perhaps while Dar was away, Orestian would indeed find some other answer that would aid the defenders.

Dar wished the sorcerer the best of fortune. If something *should* go terribly awry with the Beastmaster's search for Brother Ontas, than there was at least still the sorcerer upon which to lay Ancor's hopes . . .

ORESTIAN PLACED THE recovered burrower in the small, metal container in which he had first received it from *her*. She had given him exact instructions on both the use and care of this astounding magical creature—and also a warning of what would happen if he failed to heed those instructions.

It was as much for her as for all that her master had offered him that Orestian had obeyed the instructions to the letter. Cursed with an uncomely appearance and manner, Orestian's encounters with females of any sort were reduced to those paid or forced to be in his company. Yet she, on the other hand, listened to his words with interest, leaned close when speaking, and did not show any repulsion when the two of them did touch. Her throaty voice sent his blood coursing, and although Orestian knew she used him, he was more than willing to be used . . . to a point. After all, there had been promises made, promises of power and prestige such as he could never otherwise obtain.

Leardius thought him satisfied to live below the ground and serve at the king's whim, but Orestian had never been pleased with doing so. He was far more clever than the lord of Edurac, and it had always chafed him that he had to bow and scrape to one who was superior to him only by birth, not ability.

But that would all soon change. What he had to report to her and her lord would elevate him in their eyes, prove that he was worthy of the rewards they had dangled before him.

None of his personal guards remained in the chamber. They were not partner to his great duplicity. When commanded to leave, the warriors had eagerly obeyed, each no doubt certain that the sorcerer had intended some particularly disturbing spell.

They would not have been entirely wrong. With the burrower replaced, Orestian turned to a locked cabinet on the far end of his sanctum. Removing the thick, iron key from a pocket, the spellcaster unlatched the heavy lock sealing the two gilded doors together.

And as Orestian swung those doors open, the monstrous, glassy eyes of a helmed Pygmesian head stared back at him from within.

Orestian had nothing but contempt for the Pygmesians, however fierce they were in battle. In his mind, they were like worker bees serving the ruler of the hive. They lived and died at the whim of their lord . . . and were even sacrificed when other uses were found for their corpses.

The helmeted head was perched on a small, brass pole, small bits of withered, now-green flesh still dangling from beneath the severed neck. She—his adored Zorena—had personally removed it from the unsuspecting creature while Orestian had watched in amazement.

"The minds of Pygmesians are especially susceptible to the currents of your world's natural magic," the fiery-haired goddess had explained . . . though the sorcerer had admittedly not understood all of it. "Through the head, your thoughts will be clear to the great one. No words of lie, no misguiding gestures, will avail you should you betray him during times of communication. He and I will know that all you speak is truth, sorcerer. Remember that well each time you peer into the glass lenses . . ."

Orestian leaned close. He had never actually seen the Pygmesian's true face, for that was unnecessary to contacting either Zorena or her unseen lord. He needed only to touch his fingertips to the metal plates on the sides—just where the ears would have been on a human—and begin the spell of his own crafting.

At first he saw within each lens his own distorted face, one in some ways as grotesque as he assumed that of the creature whose covered skull he now used. But as the words of power spilled from his tongue, another face began to overlap his own . . . a face far more fair than the stout sorcerer's.

"Well, my sweet little prey . . ." she purred, her beauteous image pressing closer in each lens. "I've awaited your call with longing . . ."

A hand fell upon Orestian's shoulder.

He turned to find the huntress standing tall behind him.

"You've called, and I've come, my sweet little prey . . ." Zorena stepped around the sorcerer's shoulder and eyed the macabre means by which he communicated with her. She ran one finger longingly around the edge of the Pygmesian's ravaged throat where the sword now sheathed on her back had keenly cut through armor and flesh. "You have something for me? Something that will please our lord? I promised him great things from you, said you were the seeker of knowledge that we needed. I spoke so highly of you, my sweet little prey . . ."

"And I've not failed you," Orestian breathed, intoxicated by her dangerous presence. He puffed up his chest, trying to sound commanding. "But the value of what I've gathered demands a greater reward and the right to stand before *him* when I tell it."

Zorena displayed no shift in temperament despite Orestian's sudden and outrageous demand. Through veiled eyes, she murmured, "It must be much, indeed . . ."

His hand slipped to her side, but although she pressed close in response, somehow the sorcerer yet failed to gain the kiss or touch he had desired. Zorena moved from his grip as easily as if she were air.

"Much . . ." he responded.

The huntress gave a slight nod . . . then her hand moved with astounding speed. The sword came out, and before Orestian could even gasp, the blade struck.

There was a sinister flash of black energy and the Pygmesian helmet and skull split in two. As the gruesome remains—still crackling—plummeted to the stone floor, they dissipated into black ash. A sudden gust of air swept them away with a force that Orestian noted could not have arisen by natural means so deep beneath the palace.

The long, thin blade flared black once more, this time at Orestian's throat. Then Zorena sheathed the deadly weapon and said with a smile, "If all you say is true, my sweet prey, then we are done with that bit of offal. It's time you did receive all that you've earned . . ."

As Orestian watched, Zorena murmured to the empty air. After nodding as if to some unheard voice, she smiled like a cat and reached out to the sorcerer.

"Come. Clasp my hand. Do not let go if you value your life."

A thrill ran through Orestian's spine as their hands touched. But all carnal desires vanished as an aura of gold almost but not quite as brilliant as her glittering eyes surrounded them both. Orestian had seen the aura envelop Zorena in the past, but as it swallowed him along with her, he was momentarily shaken. Yet he held fast, guided not only by his lust for the huntress, but his lust for what her master would grant him.

And in the next second, their surroundings transformed. Gone was his sanctum and the comfort of its familiar surroundings. Instead, he stood in a place of cold metal—

Orestian let out a gasp at the monstrous creature standing near them. Two crimson orbs bigger than his palm eyed him with dread indifference, as its horrifying number of serpentine limbs played with a metal altar covered in odd levers and buttons.

"Pay it no mind," remarked Zorena as if speaking casually of the rain. "Follow."

He did, but halted in shock again a mere breath later as she walked *through* the nearest wall.

"Such powerful sorcery . . ." Orestian gasped, then realized that the only one who could hear him was the ghoulish octupoid at the altar. Gritting his teeth, Orestian barged headfirst into the wall.

He could not contain the sigh of relief once he stepped through. Zorena awaited him, but, despite his desire for her, she was the least sight of interest. Behind her stretched a long corridor, also of metal, and filling it were demons and creatures of varying shapes. There were several reptilian men and these observed him most. Orestian tried to stand fast, but the vein in his neck pounded anew with anxiety.

"My brave, sweet prey," Zorena whispered in his ear. "Walk beside me. He knows of your coming."

That information made all else pale. Orestian pulled himself together, thinking of the exalted position he would gain for his part. There would be no one in all of Ancor as powerful as he, not even that fool, Xorot. Xorot was a useful pawn, but merely a pawn. Zorena had assured him of that fact, whereas the sorcerer—he was more in not only her eyes, but those of the master. He was their great source of knowledge concerning the fabled Fountain. He was the one who would give them Ancor, for which he would in turn rule in the master's name with the huntress as his queen.

Chest out, Orestian strode among the demons as their superior, not one who should fear them. Zorena was a lithe cat beside him, each movement calculated yet perfectly fluid.

There was no doubt in the sorcerer's mind when they reached the sanctum of Zorena's master. The entrance was obvious enough in its austere grandeur, but Orestian paid more attention to what he sensed. There was a vast array of stunning forces in play around the vicinity, forces such as the sorcerer had never experienced in all his years of study.

I await you . . . came a voice so commanding that the bald spell-caster nearly fell to his knees right there. Only Zorena's hand kept him on his feet as she brought him forward.

Exactly how he entered, Orestian could not say. Suddenly he stood in darkness, well aware that he and the huntress were not alone.

"You have brought me the Fountain?" the voice asked, this time filling his ears, not his thoughts. In the darkness, there formed the shape of a throne, but one unlike that upon which the simpleton Leardius sat. This was of metal with intriguing wires and patterns throughout its design.

Zorena knelt and Orestian, needing no hint, followed her example.

Upon the shadowed throne there formed the outline of a giant. Orestian sensed the energies from earlier gather in greater force, concentrated where the great figure sat, and as they did, Zorena's lord began to coalesce. The sorcerer openly gaped as the giant's features grew distinct and he, for the first time, gazed upon the one for whom he had sold Edurac and, very likely, all Ancor.

The face was so perfect that Orestian instantly envied the god-like figure. With such a face as that, a hundred Zorenas would have fallen at his feet without hesitation.

"My lord Vorannos," the huntress intoned reverently.

"My lord Vorannos," repeated the sorcerer.

"You have brought me the Fountain?" the giant asked with deathly calm. "I can see no other reason for you to stand before me, Orestian of Edurac, than that."

The sorcerer swallowed, then, deciding that he held the cards, dared to stand and face Vorannos directly. "I have the Fountain and more."

For the first time, there came a hint of eagerness on the stern, godlike face. "Tell me . . ."

"I've been promised great rewards, my lord Vorannos."

"And so you have been." Vorannos gestured. A light akin to that which had brought the sorcerer to this place arose to Orestian's side.

And in that light, a pile of gold coins nearly up to the Ancorian's knees now glittered. Orestian could not help but be drawn to them and as he stared close, he saw on many the faces of kings who had never walked his world, kings long crushed by the lord of Ishram.

That the hoard of gold was so huge did not overwhelm Orestian. There was a spell by which he could make the gold more manageable in size.

"And more," added Vorannos. Next to the pile of gold, a small, metal chest sealed by emerald bands materialized like a ghost. The sorcerer felt the emanations from it and knew the contents for what they had to be.

"The seeds of power," Zorena's master remarked offhandedly. "The ability of transmutation . . . the knowledge that a hundred generations of your craft have searched in vain for."

Orestian started to reach for the box, but a warning crossed Vorannos's expression. "You've promised me much, too."

Smoothing his robes, Orestian said, "The Fountain does indeed exist. The key was all the time in the Dunolian libraries within Edurac." Now it was Orestian's turn to amaze. He gestured and the air before him glowed a bright orange. Vorannos's brow rose, but otherwise the giant remained still and silent. "Behold . . ."

Letter by letter, ancient script burned to life between the sorcerer and the one with whom he had bargained. Word after word in the language of Creation spread before them. It had taken Orestian long nights to properly re-create them.

Orestian thought to translate all for Vorannos, but Vorannos began muttering in the old tongue as soon as the words appeared.

"Kylither zo idridia nuum . . . Zensu zo nuum gera . . ." Vorannos went on and on, speaking with a fluidity that astounded the sorcerer. A rapt expression spread across Vorannos's face, an almost childlike expression. Line after line, the invaders' lord read what Orestian revealed.

And when he was done, Vorannos let out a hard breath and smiled as if he had already sipped from the Fountain. Orestian had drawn enough hints from Zorena's past words to be certain that Vorannos was incredibly ancient. The lord of Ishram lived by means of his power and his mechanical sorcery, but those had their limits. This discovery surely gave him a breath of hope such as could not even be imagined.

"You see," Orestian finally said.

"As it was written on Ishram, so it is written on Ancor. Yes, I see, sorcerer. I see that you've granted me much I sought."

"The Fountain is beneath Edurac itself, but cannot be reached through any path near it. Indeed, the nearer to Edurac you strive to the Fountain, the farther you are from the goal—"

Vorannos leaped to his feet. He had been imposing before, but now he towered over Orestian. The sorcerer shut his mouth tight, letting Vorannos vent just as he had expected.

"Then what, spellcaster, is the use of all you bring me? Ancor is half-ravaged already! How do I gain admittance? You do nothing but taunt me!" His hand came up, enveloping Orestian's chin. The flesh burned where Vorannos's fingers touched. The lord of Ishram scattered the gold with a harsh kick. "For this I should reward you?"

"There is more!" Ancor's betrayer blurted. Vorannos's anger had far surpassed the sorcerer's calculations. He had to talk swiftly to regain control. Orestian recovered his aplomb as the fingers loosened. Vorannos was obsessed with the mythic Fountain. He would not treat the sorcerer so, not when Orestian held the answers for him. "My lord Vorannos, you must be just a little patient. I would not come to you if I did not have something worthy of your time . . . and worthy of perhaps even more than we agreed?"

"You desire a greater reward, sorcerer?" Vorannos's expression calmed again. "More than governing for me? More than the riches I offered through Zorena?" He chuckled, a sound as ominous as thunder. "More than . . . Zorena?"

Orestian smiled back, far more confident now. Yes, he could demand anything he wanted of this one, no matter how powerful Vorannos might be. All Orestian had to do was leave just a little out so that his benefactor would forever be beholden to him.

"I know the Fountain's promise. I would have that as well, my lord. I would share in its promise of eternal life and might."

Vorannos paused . . . then, "You shall never have to fear death again if the way to the Fountain you have uncovered for me. You shall never want for power, either."

Orestian nodded. With calculation, he began, "It concerns the one of whom you once warned me. The one we know now is called the Beastmaster, the one who is Leardius's chosen champion—"

Vorannos looked to Zorena. "You see, my dear huntress? The One Who Must Be Faced plays his part yet! Ha! All happens as it is written and I've predicted . . ."

Nodding to her master, Zorena murmured to Orestian, "He holds the key? Is that what you say?"

"Nay, but he will find it! There is an oracle, called by some Brother Ontas . . ." The sorcerer then went into the story of Dar and all that had happened as Orestian knew it from the burrower. Vorannos laughed at some parts, brooded over others, but when Orestian was finished, the calm once more governed the lord of the invaders.

"All comes to pass as it must come to pass," Vorannos declared again. He patted Orestian on the shoulder, a painful moment for the sorcerer. "Knowledge worthy of your reward."

Vorannos extended his hand to the scattered gold . . . and as if each piece had come to life. the pile re-formed itself. Indeed, it was even noticeably larger to Orestian than before. His heart pounded and a covetous sweat spread over his brow.

"There is more . . . but its later telling is my guarantee of the rewards . . ."

The giant's expression did not alter. "Indeed? It must be something of tremendous importance, then."

Orestian's confidence was at its peak. "Very, for even though you might find the Fountain, attaining it requires great effort . . . and such knowledge costs dearly."

"More than I've already promised?" The hand again touched Orestian's shoulder, but this time did not move away. It squeezed tight. "More than I would have ever granted a worm like you, anyway?"

A terrible heat coursed through the sorcerer. He screamed and tried—unsuccessfully—to pull away.

"Fool primitive." Vorannos's mirror eyes reflected Orestian's countenance. The lord of Ishram's voice was dead of emotion and his mouth was twisted into a grin worse than that of a death grimace. "Did you think I had not seen those words before? Or that I knew not the fact that the path is a myriad one? In truth, the only actual knowledge you give me—and its value is beyond compare, yes—is that He Who Must Be Faced, the Beastmaster—will be the one to provide me with the key to reaching the Fountain . . ."

The sorcerer tried to speak, but his body was no longer his to control and all that emerged was a choking sound.

"You have served well, Orestian of Edurac, and so I shall reward you as I always planned. I told you that you'd never fear death again and that you would never desire more power, either." Vorannos's eyes were terrible to behold, for in their mirror finish the sorcerer saw his own doomed face. "For, once executed, neither of those concerns will have any more merit, wouldn't you say?"

Somehow . . . somehow Orestian found the will to speak. "You promised to—to—"

"I promise now to grant you the greatest gift of all: a swift, merciful death that the rest of Ancor will envy . . ."

The hand moved as if it were the wind, the palm abruptly flattening against Orestian's forehead.

The bald spellcaster's blood boiled. His mouth stretched wide, wider than humanly possible. Orestian tried to counter with a spell of his own, but the only effect his efforts had against Vorannos was to make the giant briefly glow red. Some other force utterly shielded Vorannos from him.

Then all the sorcerer could do was howl wordlessly for his life, though his cry only served to make Vorannos smile wider.

Orestian's body sagged. His flesh dribbled on the floor, then melted. With the flesh went sinew and bone, all turned to liquid. A terrible stench arose, but neither Vorannos nor Zorena was in the least affected by it.

Even the sorcerer's garments melted, mixing with what had formerly been his body. The howl lasted far longer than should have been humanly possible, reducing to a whimper, then, finally, silence.

The dark pool that then lay at Vorannos's feet quickly shriveled in size as the mechanisms hidden in the walls and floors of his sanctum worked to automatically clear any and all refuse from the great one's vicinity. A slight but steady current of air even washed away the remaining stench.

Vorannos shrugged at the last bit of Orestian to vanish. "Do forgive me, sorcerer. I did say it was supposed to be quick and without pain. My error . . ."

The huntress rose, some slight concern in her tone. "My lord Vorannos . . . the knowledge he claimed at the end . . ."

The mirror eyes focused on her. "There is nothing I need know once the Fountain is before me. So close, I will make it mine no matter what."

"As you say."

"Besides, the primitive had grown much too greedy to be of any more use. There can be no room for such greed, such desire." His gaze trailed off. "There is only my desire . . . and it shall be fulfilled."

"It shall be . . ." Zorena repeated.

"You know what you must do." As she bowed in acknowledgment, Vorannos continued, "And Kyrik . . . he shall know what to do . . ."

"The hunt begins, my lord?"

Vorannos's mirror eyes crackled with dark energy. His grin was that of a hungry wolf. "Oh, yes . . . it begins . . . and with the champion's blood, I will anoint the Fountain . . . and make *all* mine . . ."

9

As if to mark the urgency of Dar's search for the mysterious Brother Ontas, the sky the next morning began its day nearly as dark as the not-so-distant blackness to the south. Dar could sense the moods of the people he passed shifting with the overcast, though Leardius kept a confident front.

Dar's farewell to the king was a short one, as both were well aware that time was of the essence for everyone.

"Heratos reminded me that you must beware in the jungle," Leardius said. "Even when the enemy is not upon us, his scouts—in many foul shapes and forms—haunt the region."

"I will keep a careful eye," Dar promised. "and I will make this journey to the oracle a swift one."

"And we will stand vigilant . . . and pray, too."

They clasped hands, and the Beastmaster led his party off into the jungle.

Dar and his companions followed Seto's flight path. The colorful parrot would fly several yards ahead, then alight onto a tree until the rest caught up. Now and then, he would alternate between calling out Brother Ontas's or Jalan's name.

Sharak flew high above, monitoring the lands ahead. The eagle circled continually, always adjusting his flight to where the parrot was leading the others. Ruh remained closer to Dar and Jalan, the tiger willing to run ahead to safeguard the jungle, but less able to co-ordinate his movements with Seto's abrupt shifts in direction. Kodo, still mourning Podo's absence, voiced his opinion of the trail with a series of squeaks as he rode in Dar's pouch.

They journeyed on foot along a path so narrow it precluded horses. Dar was concerned about Jalan keeping pace, but the boy scrambled through the rugged terrain with relative ease . . . even more so than the Beastmaster at times.

As they traveled, Dar concentrated on another promise to King Leardius. Edurac's defenders would be strengthened, though many would at first wonder at their startling new allies.

"I will speak with every animal I find," the Beastmaster had said to his host. "They will come to Edurac and they will fight as they are best able to fight. Let all your warriors, all your people, be aware of what the animals of the wild will give in support, for they will give everything they can . . ."

"There will be a declaration of alliance, I swear!" King Leardius had returned, eyes wide in awe at what Dar proposed. "And great the punishment for the fool who breaks it!"

"The same must be demanded of the other kings of our cause."

"Heratos and the others will agree. You've proven your reputa-tion to them. You have my word, Beastmaster."

There had been no doubt in Dar's mind as to the strength of Leardius's word, and so he was determined to live up to his own. The Beastmaster began reaching out to the denizens of the wild as soon as he and the others entered the jungle. One by one, animals, birds, and others responded to his unmistakable call. There was initial reluctance on their part, for men were more often the enemy than the friend, but they listened nonetheless. Listened . . . and then began the migration to Edurac.

Yet, as the day waned, Dar found himself highly unsatisfied with the pace of his effort. Thus far, he had been able to summon individual creatures, but Edurac needed much more than a handful, even if that now included some of the large cats and even a roaming bear.

And so, after night fell and the party had long called an end to its travels, Dar seated himself cross-legged at the edge of camp with his eyes shut and his breathing barely perceptible. Ruh and Sharak guarded him from nearby while Kodo kept watch from atop Dar's shoulder. Trees surrounded him as if also guardians. A sleepy Jalan kept Seto quiet with treats, the better for Dar's concentration.

Though his eyes were shut, Dar began drawing with his left index finger a perfectly formed mandala identical to the one he had received in the reptile's pit at Edurac. The image had come to him instinctively. The Beastmaster used it to help himself focus, then reached out with his thoughts to the creatures of the jungle, reached out to them in every direction. He sensed the many minds tense at his astounding intrusion, then calm when they realized, as those earlier had, just who and what he was. Once satisfied that he had his audience, Dar told them what was happening.

Whether or not they had any trust for humans, the birds and beasts were as bound to the fate of men as the latter were to theirs. And perhaps because they were animals and followed instinct more than desire, they understood what he meant and thus *did* readily agree when he asked them to go to Edurac. Dar sensed a much vaster migration begin. From far beyond the limits of his sight, creatures of all shapes and sizes began walking in step with those already on their way to the kingdom. As they moved, they also passed his desire on to those beyond his mind's reach, and they, in turn, summoned more. The numbers swelled as they could not have in a hundred days if he had continued to touch one mind at a time.

They would fight beside the humans, just as he asked. They would seek, with their sharper instincts and natural weapons, the weaknesses of the invaders and use those to their utmost advantage. They would also make use of the attacks by the humans of Edurac.

Throughout the night and even into the morning, Dar sent his plea to every animal who stirred or came within the reach of his outstretched thoughts. He sent out the call until he was absolutely certain that none could have missed it. Only then did he open his eyes and exhale, exhausted but relieved.

"It will build now," he whispered to himself. "It will build . . ."

Dar was grateful to the animals for agreeing to do as he asked, although a part of him was unsettled by what he sensed was part of their reason for doing so. They had initially agreed to listen only because they saw him as one of them, as an animal of the jungle. He was not *human,* not in their eyes. Even Ruh and the others did not truly see Dar as completely human. To them, he was something in between.

Neither completely human nor completely animal . . . Dar felt the old, agonizing questions arise anew. *What am I? Who am I?*

With visible effort, Dar shook off the uncertainties . . . at least for the time being. He reminded himself that he had kept his promise to the king; the animals were on their way.

But despite his success, the Beastmaster knew that those he had summoned would still not provide nearly enough support. Nor would those human allies yet to arrive prove any more sufficient. This quest *had* to succeed.

"Brother Ontas!" Seto squawked cheerfully to Dar from Jalan's shoulder.

Certain that the parrot was reading his thoughts somehow

despite no mental link between the two of them, Dar nodded. "Brother Ontas, definitely."

The bird let out a human chuckle, then began preening himself. Dar joined Jalan for food, then, despite not having slept, led the party on again.

But their path turned for the worse as the day progressed, the uneven, tangled landscape and a fearsome storm forcing them much farther south than Dar had intended. Now they journeyed at the very edge of the black shroud covering the sky.

"Stay close," he reminded Jalan, though surely the boy knew that well. There was no hint of danger, but Dar felt uneasy.

Now well beyond the limits of his earlier summons, Dar began reaching out anew to any animals in the area. Ruh and the others helped spread the word as they could, though it meant that they, too, often roamed beyond Dar's mental scope.

Although they followed Seto's chosen route, Dar was also able to sense within himself that they were indeed on the right path. He innately felt that this was somehow related to the mandala. He wondered if perhaps this Brother Ontas could shed some light on that.

A weary Jalan chose that moment to ask, "Do you think we're almost there?"

"Ask Seto."

The boy blinked. "I tried. I don't think he understands distance too well."

Sharak called out from above. Through him, Dar saw a pack of wild dogs scurrying through the underbrush. They were not native to this region and clearly had moved up from farther south.

The Beastmaster touched their minds cautiously. As he suspected, they were skittish and at first tried to reject his presence, but gradually realized that he was no threat. Dar sought out the dominant female and informed her of his desire.

She was hesitant, the pack having suffered more than once from hunters' weapons. However, with some effort, Dar convinced her of the necessity. The female finally led her pack on toward Edurac.

Dar took a deep breath. He was exhausted, but not because of the traveling. It took no effort to touch the minds of any animals, but convincing them—convincing *every* beast—had proven much more difficult. The link with the pack leader had set his head to pounding, not for the first time that day.

"I'm thirsty," Jalan piped up just as Dar ceased communication with the wild dogs.

The Beastmaster smiled weakly and handed him the water sack. The boy drank deeply. Dar knew that Jalan was exhausted, but the boy was well aware that they had to keep moving . . . not only to continue their quest, but also to avoid possible threat from the invaders. They had seen none thus far, but always there were hints in the air, scents that Dar could not recognize save that they were not natural. The dark shroud to the south also seemed to be moving a little closer each day.

Dar touched minds with Sharak once more, observing the likely trail ahead. They would have to go even farther south, close enough to the ruined lands and the invaders for his taste. Fortunately, from there the path turned a more northeasterly—and presumably safer—direction, finally taking them away from the tainted realms.

He reached out to Kodo and Ruh to inform them of the necessary change in direction. Ruh acknowledged his advice immediately, at the same time alerting Dar to the recent scent of a rhinoceros. With their plated bodies and stubborn attitudes, such horned giants were terrifying to behold in combat. Even a single one would be valuable to King Leardius.

Kodo had also volunteered to use his skills to scout around, in great part because he could not rest easy since Podo's disappearance. Dar had appreciated his decision at the time but now found the male more reckless than he had ever seen him. More than once Kodo had gone beyond the human's limits to contact him, for which Dar had admonished him.

Keeping his senses in part on a search for the new beast, Dar called to Kodo. The ferret did not respond. The Beastmaster frowned, then made another attempt . . . which fared no better.

Dar immediately reached out to Sharak. The eagle let out a shriek in reply, then veered around in the direction the ferret had last been seen.

Ruh also turned off his own path, the tiger as eager to find his small friend as Dar and Sharak were. The Beastmaster then recalled the wild dogs, the only other animals in the vicinity at the time. Ruh and Sharak would never harm Kodo, but perhaps . . .

However, a quick link with the dominant female proved sufficient to reveal that the dogs had been nowhere near Kodo's location. Dar broke the link.

"What is it?" Jalan asked. "Is it Kodo?"

That the boy could guess that much reminded Dar once again how sensitive Jalan was to the animals. "Call Seto to you."

Jalan did just that, accepting Dar's lack of any other answer as necessary to the moment. With Jalan right behind him, Dar turned off the path. He had to find Kodo. The Beastmaster still ached inside for not having rescued Podo.

Before he could tell the tiger and eagle what he planned, Sharak—keen eyes on Ruh—led Dar to where the tiger was already investigating the missing Kodo's trail. Ruh inhaled the ferret's scent, started off toward the east, then turned back again.

"What is it, striped brother?" Dar joined the huge cat, both sniffing the air as Ruh had done and studying what prints he could find.

Those prints told him that Kodo had turned southeast, yet, as with Ruh, the Beastmaster smelled the ferret's scent to the east, too.

Ruh growled, suggesting what Dar also wanted to propose but dreaded—that the tiger's human brother should remain on the parrot's trail while he followed Kodo's scent.

Caught between his concern for Kodo and for Ruh, the Beastmaster hesitated. Unfortunately, Dar knew that his priority was still to find Brother Ontas.

He took a moment to kneel down and hug the tiger tightly around the neck. As Ruh lovingly ran his rough tongue up his cheek, Dar whispered, "Be wary . . ."

The great feline gave him a snort. Ruh was a most skilled hunter. Ferrets could be distracted, not so him.

With Jalan at his heels, Dar wended his way along where Kodo's tracks headed. Yet, he only got a few yards before they completely stopped in mid-run.

Dar bent down, frantically searching. "No . . ."

Podo's earlier loss was still an all-too-strong memory. Indeed, all through the journey, Dar had still on occasion called out with his thoughts in the wild hope that the female would answer. Now the male's sudden disappearance sent renewed shivers down the Beastmaster's spine. He could not lose Kodo. Dar began tearing through the dark underbrush, seeking some hint as to where the ferret might have gone.

Picking up on his concern, Jalan also began combing the vicinity. Dar at first tried to keep an eye on the boy, but seeing that Jalan never seemed to go far, began to concentrate more and more on Kodo again.

Just as the trail seemed as cold as the glacier upon which he had meditated, Dar noticed a single paw print in the soft soil. Most hunters would have missed it in the darkness, but the Beastmaster's eyes were nearly as sharp as any animal's.

It was a ferret's paw print, and although part of it was not shaped Kodo's, there was no other member of the ferret species nearby. It had to be his missing friend. Hopes rising, Dar began to follow in the direction of the paw print.

Something moved among the plants ahead of him. A long, sleek form scurried out, eyes fixing on the human—

At that moment, another creature landed heavily on Dar's shoulder and in his ears Dar heard a familiar voice shout, "Brother Ontas!"

Dar instinctively turned to the parrot, irritated at the interruption. He just as swiftly shifted his gaze back to the other animal . . . only to find it gone.

Rushing to the spot, the Beastmaster searched the ground thoroughly . . . but found no tracks, no sign at all that what he had seen was real.

The ferret that he had glimpsed had looked not like Kodo . . . but rather the lighter-brown-furred *Podo*.

Seto had fluttered up into the air the moment that Dar had lunged forward. Now the parrot returned to the Beastmaster's shoulder, this time merrily squawking, "Jalan!"

Spinning around, Dar realized that Jalan was nowhere to be seen. He ran back to where he had last seen the boy, calling out as he did.

A dark figure popped up from the underbrush. "Dar?"

Greatly relieved, the Beastmaster gripped the boy on the shoulder and murmured, "I'm sorry . . ."

Jalan misunderstood him. "I'm sorry, too. I couldn't find Kodo, either!"

Dar shook his head, but did not explain. He had been ashamed that he had left the youth alone even for a few scant minutes. Whatever had caused the ferret to vanish could just as easily have taken Jalan as well.

"It's okay!" the boy added, clearly trying to sound encouraging. "Ruh will find him!"

The tiger was indeed their best hope at this point. A cry from the sky alerted Dar to Sharak's presence. The Beastmaster immediately bonded with the eagle, seeing through the avian eyes the area where Ruh hunted.

The great cat was not immediately visible, but Dar was not concerned just yet. For all his size, Ruh was skilled at blending into the jungle. It was part of what made him such a skilled predator.

Dar asked Sharak to descend to just above the treetops. As the eagle obeyed, through Sharak's eyes the Beastmaster caught sight of the great cat just as Ruh slipped among the trees, vanishing again.

Sharak shrieked. A hidden Ruh growled in reply.

"This way!" Dar commanded Jalan. He seized the boy by the hand in order to avoid the two becoming separated. Ruh had found something. There was not a moment to lose. It would take the pair off the trail to Ontas, but surely only for a few moments longer. The Beastmaster felt he had to risk that much for his friends. Only a few moments . . .

Sharak kept him abreast of the tiger's whereabouts as Dar and Jalan ran. Fortunately for the two humans, Ruh was being cautious in his tracking and so did not move at his full speed. The Beastmaster and his young companion quickly cut the distance.

The parrot flew ahead, landing, as he always did, on a branch several yards ahead and then waiting for the pair to catch up. Seto would call out Jalan's name, then preen his feathers before setting off for the next branch. The parrot seemed to understand that Dar intended this as only a very quick deviation from the quest.

Suddenly Sharak lost sight of Ruh. A call from the eagle was greeted by a muffled growl. The raptor dropped in among the trees and spotted the tiger's tail just vanishing in the underbrush—

"Jalan!" Seto called, the bird now swooping down to the Beastmaster's face. Dar raised his free arm to avoid a collision with the parrot.

A huge creature with more than half a dozen long, tapering legs rose up from Jalan's right.

Dar threw the boy forward, hoping that Jalan would be able to keep his balance and keep running. Dar drew his sword as the multilegged creature loomed over him. Though the bottom part of the torso reminded him of a spider or some other sort of arthropod, the upper part was more human—if a human could possess a torso twice as wide as his, two long arms ending each in a trio of talons, and a head that, in the dark, looked to be nearly flat on top.

Leardius had warned him of the monstrous scouts of the invaders. The Beastmaster could only assume this abomination one of them. In his concern for his missing friends and the need to reach the oracle, Dar had grown careless . . . now a possibly fatal flaw.

The combination of night and the fiend's own dark hide made it impossible for even Dar to note much detail in the face, but from wherever the mouth was, there emerged a throaty sound that sent shivers through the human. One needlelike leg darted at the warrior and only the Beastmaster's reflexes saved him from being impaled.

As he rolled back onto his feet, Dar slashed with the blade. The keen edge cut through the limb. A foul substance sprayed over Dar, but he stifled his disgust and charged forward.

However, as he neared the lower torso, another sharp limb skewered his shoulder. Dar cried out. The sword dropped.

The abomination bent down and seized him with its talons, the points digging painfully into the Beastmaster's shoulder and arm. Dar's monstrous adversary pulled him close.

Two round, multifaceted orbs stared at him. There was no nose, and more unsettling, when the mouth opened, it not only opened sideways, but revealed a sharp appendage whose purpose the human did not wish to discover.

The creature abruptly turned its gaze from him. Uttering an angry growl, it peered down past the Beastmaster.

Following its gaze, Dar discovered Jalan—the sword held as adeptly as possible in the youth's two small hands—clumsily attacking the underside. The boy brought the blade up again and again. Although the weapon was obviously much too large for Jalan, he had evidently wounded the creature at least once, for a thick, dark substance dripped from the tip of the blade.

"Jalan!" Dar managed to shout, despite his pain. "Run! Go!"

But the boy did not heed him, determined, it seemed, to stand by his friend. Seto tried to aid Jalan in his efforts by darting through the air in front of it and shouting his name.

Paying little heed to the bird's efforts to distract it, the grotesque arachnid—surely tied somehow to the invaders, for Dar had never seen or heard of its terrible like before—used one pointed leg to attack Jalan. However, Jalan was a shorter target. He ducked the leg, then dragged the sword to another part of the monster's underside.

Two more limbs bent to stop the boy. Although Jalan avoided them again, his fortunes were clearly turning for the worse. He had at least managed to buy Dar a momentary distraction and the Beastmaster now made use of it by reaching up and bringing the edges of both hands hard against the abomination's throat.

The arachnid let out a fearsome choking sound as it flung Dar to the ground. The Beastmaster collided hard with the earth, his breath shoved violently from his lungs.

Jalan tried to bring the sword up, but at last one of the macabre creature's limbs caught him a powerful blow across the chest. Losing his grip on the sword, the boy tumbled back.

The eight-legged nightmare ignored Jalan thereafter, Dar clearly of far more interest. It quickly loped over to where the Beastmaster lay, obviously intent on a swift finish to the struggle.

Dar sought in vain to rise as the creature leaned over him. It snared his shoulder again, renewing the agony. The savage mouth opened wide—

From the dark treetops above, a lithe shadow fell upon the arachnid's back. The beast snarled and dropped Dar as it sought to turn toward this unexpected adversary.

As Dar slowly regained his bearings, he saw the darkened figure cling tightly to the arachnid's torso. The monster spun about in a mad circle, claws seeking what always remained just out of reach. The newcomer held in one hand a long spear, with which it now sought to drive into the fiend's back.

But although the monster could not reach its foe, it did not simply wait to die. Suddenly, the behemoth fell on one side. The action nearly shook the warrior off its back and did succeed in causing the Beastmaster's would-be rescuer to drop the spear.

Gasping, his body wracked with pain, Dar struggled after the fallen weapon. The arachnid discovered him anew, its other attacker now of lesser importance to it. With a baleful call, it righted itself and lunged for the Beastmaster.

As it did, the figure on its back pulled free a dagger. The blade sank in where the human torso met that of the giant spider.

The arachnid shivered, then hissed. One set of claws nearly raked the shadowy form's chest.

Dar snagged the spear but had no good angle at which to aim it. He stood there, desperate to find a vital spot.

"To me!" the other shouted. "Hurry!"

The Beastmaster instinctively obeyed, throwing the spear with expert aim to his partner in peril.

The dark form caught the weapon with equal expertise. Skilled hands immediately turned the sharp point downward.

With a cry, the other warrior buried the entire spear head into the arachnid's human back.

The wiry legs instantly flailed. Dar sought to avoid them, but, caught between two, was struck hard on the side of the head. Once more, he fell to the ground, this time landing close to a still stunned Jalan.

"Seto!" cried out the parrot, fluttering down to the pair. Seto landed on Jalan's chest and the boy's eyes opened.

Another winged form appeared. The long-missing Sharak. The eagle let out an apologetic squawk to Dar, then dove in front of the arachnid who, despite its obvious death throes, was conscious enough to seek to take one or both of its adversaries with it. Dar, the most evident in view, might still have had to fear being torn apart by savage claws if not for the eagle's daring. The avian flew directly in the face of the dying monster, Sharak's talons clawing at the eyes.

At the same time, the shadowed warrior pulled free the dripping spearhead, then, for good measure, thrust it in again.

The abomination gasped . . . then all eight legs gave way. As the gigantic corpse fell over, the warrior nimbly leaped off, landing just a few feet from the Beastmaster.

However, almost immediately there was a gasp from the darkened form as it faced Dar. The spear that had just saved both of their lives abruptly spun about to aim at the Beastmaster's throat.

As he reflexively stepped back, Dar's head cleared enough to enable him to note what should have been obvious from the start: both the voice that had spoken earlier and the shape now standing over him made it clear that his rescuer was female.

And as the spearpoint hovered over him, the female warrior blurted a single, disbelieving word. *"Dar?"*

10

THE VAST HORDE MOVED RELENTLESSLY TOWARD EDURAC. With riders by the thousands and warriors on foot numbering several times that, Xorot of the Claw commanded a force with which to be reckoned. Behind him rode the kings of more than a dozen realms, some of whom had once looked down upon him as a barbarian and likely still did. Yet they had sworn oaths to him, of adding their might to his own already considerable force. After all, it was obvious to any but the most foolish that the lord of the invaders was sure to conquer all Ancor.

And very soon the last of those fools would be crushed by Xorot's warriors.

Xorot was a bear of a man, both in size and by the thick, black hair that covered much of his body. He wore a new breastplate with a vulture's claw etched as the centerpiece, the armor forged for his new role as grand leader. His helmet was made of scaled leather and shaped like that of the same bird, the sharp, crooked beak acting as part visor.

Clad otherwise in red kilt and sandals, Xorot was a sharp contrast to many of the more cultured monarchs now serving under him. Yet none visibly showed their disdain. Crowns or helmets atop their heads, the foreign kings were interested in but one thing: to take Edurac without destroying its famous Dunolian libraries. That was most key. Lord Vorannos wanted only the libraries. All else of Edurac could eventually be razed to the ground—and the riches within shared among Xorot and the other kings—but the libraries had to be preserved.

That meant care at first when attacking, but Xorot still expected enough blood and plundering to satisfy his thirst. He had waited a long time to repay Leardius for his past shame.

He might have waited forever, if not for the shadowy envoy sent by the invaders' lord. The ghostly Kyrik had been quite adept at displaying for the warlord the many reasons to join in the conquest of Ancor. Riches, of course, had appealed greatly to Xorot and the Vorundites, as, naturally, had revenge. Yet the power Kyrik's master offered was the most enticing reason. Xorot would be the ruler of an empire spreading across the world.

There was also the simple and, to Xorot, obvious fact that failure to join was to embrace horrible death. Kyrik, through his spells, revealed vivid images of those lands that had refused the generous offer. The barbarian had relished the variety of tortures the invaders had used on those who had defied them.

It had not then been difficult to rally other rulers around him, including even the more "civilized" ones. Men were men, and greed and fear were powerful bargaining tools. Aware that Xorot had the favor of the invaders—as shown by his realm remaining untouched while nearby ones lay scorched—the other monarchs had fallen into line quite readily.

The warlord unleashed a yellowed grin as he sighted a set of hills in the distance. The dark blanket covering the sky made it difficult to see very far, but he recognized the landmark.

"We near the Caldar Ridges," he roared to the others. "Edurac, it is not far beyond."

The others grunted satisfaction; they had been promised rewards once Edurac was taken. In addition to being granted shares of its legendary wealth, they had been told that each would gain territories greatly dwarfing what they currently ruled. From kings they would all become emperors. The sooner the Edurac fell, the better . . . so long as the libraries remained unharmed.

To the surprise of his companions, Xorot signaled to a guard. Raising a curled goat horn, the warrior blew hard.

"We stop?" growled one of the other kings. "Why?"

"Not long, it is," Xorot responded. He spoke in the Common tongue, though it ill suited him compared to the rasping language of his people. Still, it was required so that the fools with him understood. "We only wait for them."

"Them?" asked the same king, a cloaked, birdlike man with beady eyes. He glanced at the others and saw no comprehension from them, either.

Xorot's grin widened. He had kept this bit of news from his so-called allies. The horde was to gain additional reinforcements.

He smelled the air. Xorot had an excellent sense of smell, necessary, he thought, for a good warrior and hunter. He doubted the others could smell much other than the sweating bodies around them.

But he sensed the new additions coming . . . and a moment later, sighted movement.

Leaning back in the saddle, Xorot indicated the direction. His smile was that of a jackal. "Them," he repeated. "They come now . . ."

And slowly the other kings and warriors in the ranks saw it. Horses stirred uneasily, some forcing their riders to struggle for control. Hardened fighters, even those of his own people, gritted their teeth and looked as if they would prefer to be anywhere else.

The newcomers slowly but relentlessly converged on the horde. The front ranks coalesced into the broad-shouldered, toadlike figures with helmets that covered oversized heads. They appeared to have no weapons, but Xorot knew that they carried hidden ones.

Row after row of the creatures called Pygmesians marched toward the assembled throng, frightening to behold in their unnerving similarity to humans. Behind them came other *things,* some of them apparently flesh, others metal, and too many macabre combinations of both. They marched on two legs or more or rolled on metal wheels or even flew above the ground. Some were as tall as trees, others dwarfs.

Xorot nodded to the other rulers. "Now," he growled merrily. "Now we ride again . . . to Edurac . . ."

"YOU CAN'T BE!" the female warrior growled a breath later. "You wear his face, but just as I remember it, not as it should be now, older and more worn!"

The spear jutted closer.

"Leave him alone!" Jalan shouted. The boy threw himself at her, but the slim figure easily avoided the collision without pulling the spear away.

Sharak dropped down, flying in front of the woman. Yet the eagle was oddly careful not to cause her any harm. Instead, the bird landed before the spearpoint, as if ready to take it in place of his human brother.

The female warrior hesitated. The spearpoint shifted slightly to the left. Clearly startled, she blurted, "Is that—can that be—?"

Taking advantage of her evident confusion, Dar rolled to the side. Ending in a crouch, the Beastmaster prepared to attack. He knew that this was no enemy, and, in fact, there was more and more about her he thought familiar. Dar wanted to know more, but not, of course, at risk to himself or Jalan.

"I am indeed Dar!" he warily called to the figure. "If you are someone who knows me, tell me your name and I will try to place you!"

"Dar . . ." she murmured again. The spear did not lower, but it did pull back slightly. "We knew each other well, though I was a child then." The lithe female stepped closer, finally enabling the Beastmaster to use his exceptional night vision to see her clearly enough.

And there *was* something familiar. She had a tanned, oval face and deep dark eyes that could easily snare any male. A lush mane of black hair bound tightly behind her fell all the way to the small of her back. Her nose had an upturned look that reminded him of a people he had once known.

"You . . . you are Touargang."

Her severe expression lightened a bit. Full, round lips fought back a hopeful smile. "I'm Tara, Dar. Tara . . ."

"Tara . . ." Visions of the young princess coursed through his memory. Now Dar could see in the warrior the child, who was now a beautiful woman.

Sharak squawked. The eagle alighted onto the arm Tara suddenly stretched out. Lowering the spear, the Touargang stroked the eagle on the back of the head.

"Sharak always favored you," Dar commented as he straightened. "I remember when you wanted him to teach you to fly and were upset that you could not learn . . ."

"I was very young and foolish . . ." Tara trailed off, staring at the Beastmaster anew. "It really is you, Dar . . ."

She dropped the spear and let Sharak take flight. Before Dar realized what was happening, Tara was upon him, hugging him like that small child he recalled. He felt moisture on his chest and knew it was from tears.

But Dar quickly realized that her tears had to do with more than just him. "Tara . . . what is it?"

The raven-tressed woman looked up, her face moist. "We're all that's left, Dar! The Touargang, the survivors of Emur . . . they're all dead!"

He stiffened, the blackness he had felt so many years ago when his father had died now suddenly filling him anew. The survivors from his village had given life to his father's memory.

But now . . .

"How?"

"How else?" she snapped, though her bitterness was not focused on him. "By the same evil that makes the sky in the day nearly as dark as night! We had no warning! Suddenly the flames were everywhere! All—buildings and people—were burned to cinders in moments!" Tears streamed down her face as Tara considered her next words. "My parents, Dar—I didn't even see them die! I only heard the rush of wind and then all exploded into chaos!" Her face was twisted with grief. Dar's heart dropped. Her pain reminded him all too much of his own past.

Tara took a deep breath. Her shaky voice took on a sinister tone. "Then . . . then the monsters came, the things that look like demons but bleed like men. We fought them, those of us who didn't perish immediately, but they had weapons of magic and there were so many of them. We finally tried to flee, but they were everywhere!"

Dar could scarcely believe it. "And what of wise Juji'at? What of the old shaman and his magic?" he asked incredulously. "Was that not worth something?"

"It is the only reason I live. Juji'at, he came in his great bear cloak and cast a spell of thunder when the creatures hunted for those of us left. The entire area exploded. We hoped to escape during that, but there were more of the enemy than a thousand Touargang tribes could battle! I was struck . . . and when I awoke . . . all were burnt as the villagers were. I lay under Juji'at's cloak and can only think that the magic in it hid me from the monsters' eyes. Of he, I never found any trace, alive or dead . . ."

Dar thought again of the powerful shaman and hoped that he still lived. Ancor was not without its potent energies, but it would need all of them now. He gave thanks for the miracle that had saved Tara even as he mourned all those lost, including his good friend and her father, the chieftain, K'atos.

And I am supposed to save Ancor? Dar again thought bitterly. *As all I know die horribly?*

Pulling herself together, Tara added, "I swore by my father and mother that I'd see the invaders—those *monsters*—" she corrected with disgust,— "dead, though I don't know how that might be done. Many I've killed as I've moved along, but those numbers mean nothing to what their evil lord commands."

"So I know too well," returned Dar. He looked around for Seto. Regardless of events, Dar knew he needed to move on after the oracle. "Tara, I must—"

"Dar . . ." Tara moved back into his view, the Touargang noticing his sudden desire to leave. "Even though I swore to be Ancor's protector and avenger, I knew deep down that I'd not be enough!" She reached for his hand and clasped it tightly in hers. "I prayed that somehow there'd be another miracle, that you might still be alive, even though for many years now they said you weren't . . ." She suddenly embraced him again, this time in pleasure. "But you *are* alive and untouched by time! Ancor surely must've planned this!"

Dar shrugged, not wanting to take time to explain all of it. "I am here and I am me. The rest is of no importance. What matters is that I reach the oracle."

"The oracle?"

He sighed, seeing that it would be impossible to keep her in the dark. As they walked, Dar quickly explained as much as he could, condensing it and hoping that Tara would not ask questions. Fortunately, in this one aspect, she had changed from the inquisitive child that he had known. Now the female warrior simply took his word with everything, no matter how fantastic.

He finished with the beginning of his quest for Brother Ontas, then the vanishing of Kodo.

"First Podo, now Kodo?" blurted Tara at last, recalling the ferrets fondly. She immediately spun around. "There must be a trail to follow—"

"There is no more time. Jalan and I must reach this Brother Ontas. Ruh might still be following—Ruh!" In his astonishment to discover Tara, Dar had momentarily forgotten the tiger. He immediately linked with Sharak.

The eagle took to the air, heading to where Ruh had last been sighted. As Sharak raced on, he gave Dar glimpses of the darkened land far ahead. Yet nowhere was there a sign of Ruh. The hair on Dar's back rose and he almost veered off the path again. First the ferrets, now the tiger? It could not be possible! How could Dar have been so careless?

No! I will find you, Ruh! And you, Kodo, and even Podo, too! He suddenly grew fearful for Sharak and warned the eagle to take care.

And even while linked to the avian, Dar sought out Ruh with his mind. Once, he thought he sensed the great cat, but the moment passed so swiftly that he could not be certain that it had not been his imagination.

Despite his swelling fear for his animal friends, Dar also kept track of Seto and the path. True to the character of the girl he recalled, Tara, having made herself part of the group, watched over Jalan as if he were her charge. She had instinctively realized what Dar needed to do and that he could not entirely watch the youngest of their party sufficiently because of it.

They moved through the jungle to a more open area. Dar sensed that Ruh had also come this way—Kodo's supposed trail apparently having changed direction again—but the cat's scent was very faint. Indeed, much more faint than should have been possible, considering how recently the tiger would have passed.

Squatting close to the dirt, the Beastmaster ran his fingers over the upturned soil as he smelled the various odors of the vicinity. Again, there was the faint hint of Ruh. Sharak, however, could find no more visible sign, though the eagle circled the area slowly and carefully.

Dar gently touched the lowest branches of a nearby tree. Something had gone by recently, but not, he felt, his friend. This had no scent whatsoever and had left no trail on the ground. Only the breaking of one tiny branch gave hint.

Dar tried to imagine what could move so while possibly carrying the tiger with it.

Sharak suddenly alerted him to a new presence.

There were riders in the jungle, armored men in growing numbers.

Through the eagle's eyes he saw their shadowy forms. They appeared to be either searching or scouting. Dar might have avoided them, but so close to where both Kodo and Ruh had disappeared, he dared not do so. They might be the cause and, thus, his only hope of rescuing the animals.

To Tara and Jalan, the Beastmaster whispered, "Stay here! There are fighters in the jungle. They may know what happened to the others. I must find out."

"No!" gasped Jalan. "I want to help! They are my friends, too!"

"My friends, too!" Seto repeated in Jalan's voice.

"It might not be so wise to separate," Tara also suggested. "Look what happened to the ferret and the tiger."

Dar did not want to leave them, but neither did he want them in danger should the men ahead be responsible. From Leardius, Dar already knew that many kings had pledged their might to the master of the invaders, some for self-preservation, and many for greed. Dar knew firsthand what greed could do to a man, and he dreaded facing these traitors of humankind. He and his companions had traveled a far distance, and the risk of confronting some of those betrayers increased with every step.

"Stay far back, then," Dar finally conceded. "Tara . . . if there is any danger at all, you take the boy here—Jalan is his name—and race to Edurac. Understand?"

She gave him a reluctant nod. Not at all satisfied, the Beastmaster nevertheless started toward the nearest of the riders. Sharak monitored the oncoming warriors, marking for Dar their various locations.

Wending his way to one rider separated from the rest, Dar studied the black figure. He could make out no distinct markings, and though he suspected that this was an enemy, Dar did not want to take the chance of harming a possible innocent.

But the debate as to what to do was suddenly taken from him as the mounted warrior's steed suddenly snorted. Dar cursed, sensing that the wind had just shifted, sending his scent to the animal. He had no time to soothe the horse's concern, for the rider immediately urged the animal toward him.

With a roar, the armored figure pulled a broadsword free and slashed at the Beastmaster. Dar rolled under the swing, then came up behind the horse. The rider tugged hard on the reins, forcing the animal to a quick and likely painful turn.

But in doing so, the rider left himself open. Dar leaped up, tackling the warrior. Both men tumbled off, crashing hard on the ground nearby.

Despite Dar's hopes, the fall did not stun his adversary. The Beastmaster struggled against a strong opponent. Dar had several maneuvers that could put a quick end to the fight, but he still feared accidentally injuring someone who might not be a true threat.

Then the rider drew a dagger, and Dar had to forget any concern for the other's life. He barely caught his foe's wrist. The tip of the blade hovered inches from his nose.

Dar gave the wrist a sharp twist. The wrist did not break but came very close to doing so. Crying in pain, the armored figure lost his grip. The dagger fell next to Dar's ear.

Other voices shouted in the distance. Dar swore, well aware that his situation was growing precarious. He hoped that Tara had had the good sense to already take Jalan and run to safety.

A feathered form dropped on the rider's covered head. Sharak beat at the helmet, his wings getting in the man's face in the process. The rider struggled to fend off the eagle while still struggling with Dar.

The lower edge of the Beastmaster's palm slammed into his foe's chin. The armored figure rolled backward.

Dar punched him hard in the jaw before he could recover. The other warrior finally collapsed, unconscious.

But another rider appeared just as Dar extricated himself from the body. He, too, tried to run the Beastmaster down—

With a cry, Tara flew out of the shadows, her feet expertly striking the new foe directly in the chest. As he fell, the Touargang seized the saddle and spun back atop the animal, mounting it as if she were its rider. She then drew from her belt her own dagger, preparing to throw it at a third scout just approaching.

"No!" Dar called. Even now, he feared a terrible mistake, though he had no reason to think why.

Tara hesitated, then turned the dagger around. She threw it at the oncoming rider . . . and it struck him in the face pommel first. He dropped to the jungle floor near the others, injured but not dangerously so.

"Get out of here!" Dar shouted. To his horror, though, he now saw Jalan off to the side, the boy holding tight to a piece of wood as if it were a mace or war club.

Then Tara froze in the saddle. She suddenly called to Dar, "They're not enemies! Dar! We must make peace, and quickly!"

Hearing that, Dar gave thanks for his instinctive restraint. Still, though he was glad that Tara could at last identify the riders, Dar now had to find some manner by which to rectify the terrible misunderstanding.

A horn sounded. The jungle filled with yet more riders. Several carried torches, any hint of natural light a thing of the past now that night was fully on the jungle.

Before they could attack, Dar raised his hands palm outward with fingers splayed so that the riders could see that they were empty. "We mean no harm! This was all an accident!"

At first, the riders seemed disinclined to listen, but then one of those wielding a torch commanded, "Hold! Everyone stay back!" To Dar, he added, "Keep your hands visible, barbarian!"

The officer urged his mount toward them. As he passed Tara, he muttered, "A Touargang. One of you still lives, eh?"

"If one lives, all live," she responded.

The rider grunted his indifference to her opinion. He reached the Beastmaster and thrust the torch forward. Dar kept his instinct to bat the torch away in check and was grateful neither Sharak nor Jalan did anything foolish. The sooner he proved himself of no threat to these men, the sooner he could renew the hunt for Ruh and Kodo.

But no sooner had the torch illuminated his face than the officer swore. "King's blood! Samuon! Signal His Majesty!"

A horn blared. Within moments, a legion of new riders spread throughout the area, no doubt making certain that no threat hid nearby. However, far too many circled the Beastmaster. Dar, all but blinded by the torch, wondered what about him had so startled the first warrior. As with Leardius, did these men, too, know of the stories concerning him?

"Captain Arturius!" came a regal voice. "What is it? Spies of Xorot's? Fiends from the south?"

The captain sounded shaken. "Nay, Your Majesty . . . more like ghosts of the past . . ."

"Hmm?" The riders' king rode up beside the captain. Dar could not see the other's silhouetted visage, though he certainly heard the exclamation that followed . . . as did likely everyone else.

"By the witches of Maax!" the king rasped. He pulled back on the reins, further reducing himself to a half-seen shadow from Dar's point of view. "'Tis not possible!"

"It's possible," Tara interjected unexpectedly. "For in this time of darkness, surely Ancor herself is capable of miracles. You of all people should know that . . . King Tal."

"*Tal?*" Dar had thought it astounding enough to come across Tara . . . but here was one who made that reunion pale.

Tal. Ruler of Aruk.

Tal. His own brother.

To be accurate, Tal of Aruk was Dar's half brother, the younger son of their birth father through his second wife. Long ago, Dar had saved Tal as a youth and, years later, helped him retain his throne after treachery and sorcery had nearly stolen it away. Although they had met only those times, the brothers shared a close bond between them. Yet Dar had purposely stayed away, fearing that the troubles that seemed to follow him would cause Tal more harm.

"Pull that damn torch away, captain. Let my brother see me as I see him."

"But can it truly be him, sire? I recalled his face, but it's untouched, unaged!" The officer shook his head. "Nay! I was foolish to call you, Your Majesty! This must indeed be some fiend in his guise!"

Dar's mounting frustration vanished as Tal stubbornly replied, "I know my brother, Captain! Whether through magic or other means, he looks as he did years ago . . . but he's most definitely Dar!"

"As you say, sire," The officer withdrew next to the king, taking the torch with him.

And so, in the light of that torch, Dar at last beheld his younger brother . . . who now looked at least as old as him. A round helmet with a chin guard framed a face more lined, more experienced. Tal had the noble, handsome features of a hero out of a children's story, with a strong jaw, angular features, and brilliant blue eyes. A scar now lay beneath one eye.

Wisps of brown hair stuck out from under the helmet, which resembled that of the other riders save a circlet of gold and red gems that surrounded the short, curved visor. Tal wore a shining, silver breastplate with intricate scrollwork along the edges and with it a metal kilt and sandals. Attached at the shoulders was a crimson cloak. From his left side dangled a sheath containing a long, no doubt well-honed sword.

Tal continued in turn to stare at Dar, in all likelihood yet digesting the impossible vision before him. Then, without warning, the king leaped from his mount and rushed the Beastmaster.

"Dar!" Tal clung to him as tightly as Tara had. This second reunion, combined with the vanishing of Ruh and Kodo, proved almost too much for Dar. The Beastmaster quivered and nearly fell into Tal's arms.

"Ancor truly watches over us!" the king uttered. "There is hope! There must be! How odd such an encounter otherwise!" He rubbed his chin in sudden thought. "Or is it? It was Om's sudden suggestion that we veer this direction. Captain! Summon the general for me!"

"Yes, sire!"

"I left Om to keep order over the soldiers," Tal explained. "But this demands his presence. He seemed determined that we go this way and no other, despite the jungle slowing us some."

One of the other riders respectfully approached. "Sire, all is clear in the immediate vicinity. We're sending out scouts further into the jungle now—"

"Take care!" Dar interjected. "Tal, this area is not safe! Before we came upon your men, I was desperately searching for Ruh and Kodo, taken by the darkness!" He quickly spoke of the arachnid and the vanishing of the two, adding in at the same time the earlier disappearance of the female ferret.

Tal cursed. "I remember all three well and fondly . . . and what you say only makes me more determined to send out scouts and searchers . . ."

"No, Tal, this is not your concern—"

"My family, both human and animal, is always my concern." Turning from Dar, Tal ordered more of his men out into the jungle, telling them to especially watch for the tiger or ferrets. The searchers left in bands of five or more as a safety precaution that the Beastmaster did not think sufficient. Dar himself wanted to go along, but knew that Jalan and Tara would follow him if he did.

That brought up a further consideration concerning Tara. Leaning close to Tal, he murmured, "It is late and there is no choice for us but to stay the night, but come the morning I must go on immediately. I must not only hope to find Ruh and the others, but an oracle who may hold the secret to the survival of us all. When I leave, please keep Tara with you, or else she will follow me into danger. I have no choice about Jalan; his parrot is the key and only the boy can speak with him. But Tara, she must stay behind . . ."

"As must I? We are blood! Dar, you saved my life more than twice over! You tried to save our father, even after the priest of Ar, Maax, drove him mad!" The king vehemently shook his head. "Brother, the Touargang may stay behind—if that is even possible—but I am going with you!"

Dar could not permit Tal to do as he planned. "You are heading for Edurac, are you not?" He realized that Tal was the major ally that Leardius had been awaiting. "Edurac must be defended. If it falls, there is nothing left! You know you must go there, and not with me . . ."

Tal frowned in frustration, obviously disappointed with Dar's words. But he finally nodded. "You . . . you are right . . . but . . . but we've only just rediscovered each other! For you to leave already come the dawn—"

"If it is fated, we will meet again."

"I despise fate. It destroyed our family . . ." Tal looked grim. "I'll do what I can about the Touargang . . . and, yes . . . I'll continue on to Edurac." He cursed again. "Damn General Om and his directions! I'd almost wish this encounter had never happened . . ."

"Cursed I am by my king, I see," came a voice from nearby. "Is there no greater dismay for me?"

The voice was slightly high-pitched, but filled—despite the words—with a great calm that recalled to Dar his mentor, Baraji.

Tal turned in the saddle. "Ah, General Om, I've a question I hope you've got a very good answer for."

"Answer it, I shall do my best!" a rider approaching the pair replied. From his mount, the general, his uncovered head shaved close, bowed first to his liege, then to the Beastmaster. As if to make up for the lack of hair on his skull, Om wore a thick, lengthy mustache that hung down both sides of his mouth past his chin. "In all things, King Tal, I am your loyal servant . . ."

The general looked up at Dar. He *had* to look up to most men, even when saddled, for Om was short, very short.

Shorter even than Jalan.

"And your servant also," the dwarf said to the Beastmaster, fierce, oval eyes glittering in the torchlight. "*Brother* to my master . . ."

11

HOW DO YOU KNOW THAT I AM YOUR KING'S BROTHER?"
Dar demanded.

The dwarf was not disconcerted by the question. "My
ears are sharp. I but heard it mentioned as I neared . . . and King Tal
has often spoken of the Beastmaster."

"Om is right, Dar," admitted Tal. "That is no mystery . . . but
this detour you sent us upon, General—why here and why now?"

The dwarf grinned. Despite his build, Dar saw that he was obviously not one to be underestimated. His eyes held a deep cunning,
but not, in contrast to Orestian, a cunning that made the Beastmaster wary. They also had a calmness to them that Dar envied.

"The scouts reported sightings of Xorot's own watchers. He will
reach Edurac before us, but it would be best, yes, if he could do so
not knowing we are at his heels. This path took us out of sight of
those watchers."

"And coincidentally brought me to my brother."

"The circle that is all Ancor benefits from coincidence by making it happen," Om stated.

The cryptic remark reminded the Beastmaster of Baraji. He studied the dwarf anew. Om had a patience about him that made Dar certain the man had studied a similar path such as Dar had sought from the sage . . . Only, Om appeared more advanced in those studies.

"If Ancor makes it happen, how can it still be considered coincidence?" came Tara's voice. Like a panther, she strode silently up beside Dar. "Then it is not coincidence."

Om smiled wider. His eyes took in the Touargang, but not in any impolite manner. Instead, he seemed to be measuring something within her . . . measuring it and seeming pleased by what he found. "Is it not? Then one might as well say that destiny and coincidence are not brothers . . ."

"That makes no sense—!"

Tal interrupted, "Debating Om is an endless and futile thing and I've found that he is generally right." He grinned.

The dwarf accepted the compliment but added, "This young warrior is correct to question, sire, for truths change all the time, and we must be aware of that." His gaze returned to Tara. "And destinies we must question most of all, yes?"

Dar wanted to ask more questions himself, but Tal ordered that everyone come to the encampment while the searchers finished securing the area. Dar left reluctantly, Sharak echoing his dismay at not being able to pursue the disappearances of their friends. But clearly someone sought to keep Dar from the oracle, which meant that he had to double his efforts . . . and pray that he would yet be able to rescue Ruh and the others.

His hope there lay in the fact that no bodies had been found. The invaders were merciless; had the animals been slain outright, there would have been remains. Someone knew how important they were to Dar. They had to be captives, not corpses . . .

Once they were settled in by a fire, Tal did much of the talking, the Beastmaster's brother buoyed by Dar's appearance, whatever the cause of it. Dar continued to study Om, who appeared more interested in conversation with Tara. The two had become involved in a discussion of destinies and chance. Again, the general reminded him of Baraji, albeit not so advanced. Yet, as Baraji had chosen to teach Dar, Om seemed to be encouraging the Touargang.

"The focus inward best enables us to see better the world around us," the dwarf told her as they returned to the main column of soldiers. "So long as that focus is not upon our desires, but our needs."

Those words reflected well on Dar, too, and emphasized that seeking Brother Ontas was more important than even his friends. There would be no Ruh, Kodo, or Podo if there was no Ancor.

Yet, still he ached inside . . .

Dar also learned much news as he and the others ate the food offered by Tal. None of that news was good.

"Falizan has fallen," Tal informed him. "They were supposed to join our column, but the skies rained down upon them three nights before our meeting and the darkness enshrouded the region." He spat in the fire. "We come with less men than anticipated, but we come." His expression shifting to one more childlike, the king suddenly asked, "Will we be enough, Dar?"

"We must be . . ." was all the Beastmaster could say.

The conversations trailed off after the meal, and Tal reluctantly sent his guests off to sleep. But sleep was an uncomfortable thing, with nightmares assailing Dar. He saw his world in flames and his animal friends tortured. Twice he woke up with a cry, the second time to find Tara leaning over him. The flickering flames made her face appear more spirit than mortal. Her eyes glittered from the light, as if they contained stars.

"What is it?" she asked. "Tell me." The concern in her eyes touched Dar more than he could imagine. He remembered how much she had cared for the ferrets and Ruh.

Tara read his expression and understood. "We'll find them . . . and this oracle of yours, too."

Her soft touch on his chest soothed him and he fell back to sleep.

Well before night gave way to day, Dar awoke and set himself in a meditation position facing where the sun, though shrouded, would rise. He hoped to clear his mind for the coming day, but, come the morning, his efforts proved only partially successful. Still, considering the circumstances, Dar supposed he should be grateful for anything.

He and Tal said their farewells. Om and Tara spoke some distance away and Dar at first thought that the general was acting on orders from Tal to keep the Touargang with the column, but then Tara rejoined Dar. From the smile she gave him, it was obvious that though she had found much of interest in her conversation with Om, the woman warrior was not going to leave the Beastmaster.

Yet Tara could not help talking in admiration of the dwarf. "He knows so much," she murmured. "He talked almost as if he knew me all my life . . ."

"I trust no one more than Om," Tal returned. "No one, that is, save my brother."

The two men hugged. From Tal, Dar had gained new supplies. The Beastmaster slung these over his shoulder as he quietly smiled one last time at his sibling.

"We'll meet again," Tal insisted.

Dar only nodded.

The next morning, as the column moved on, the Beastmaster led his party deeper into the jungle. Even Seto's ever-cheerful calls and Tara's nearby presence did nothing to diminish Dar's depression. Tal's departure, while of necessity, added to the weight of his other losses. He prayed that this Brother Ontas would have the answers he needed.

The day passed in more darkness, the shrouded sky of the south mixing with storm clouds in the north. Despite a heavy rain that struck late, the black blanket above remained undiminished. That left Dar in a mood nearly as dark, and each time the parrot called out Brother Ontas's name, he grew more and more angry at the avian. The Beastmaster wondered if Seto had led them astray, that he really did not know where the oracle lived.

Tara brought this up also. "Can we trust this bird?"

"Seto's telling the truth!" defended Jalan. "He's just—he's just not very good with distances . . . or days."

"Hmmph." Tara wrinkled her nose at Dar and he smiled back.

That day ended as futile and wet as the previous one. Dar located an overhang that provided the trio and the birds with some protection. Huddled together, they fell asleep shivering from the constant moisture.

It was Dar who awoke first, the sensation that he was being watched verified by the parrot's colorful form perched atop his leg. Seto studied the Beastmaster meticulously, then mumbled, "Brother Ontas . . ."

Neither Tara nor Jalan stirred. Dar rose, sending the parrot to the nearest branch. Seto preened as the Beastmaster smelled the air for a possible source of water. He turned to the north and heard the faint sound of trickling.

Following the sound despite knowing that he should not leave the others, Dar descended into a thicker part of the jungle. Although he sensed no danger, he drew his sword, just in case. However, the area into which he stepped seemed to belie any notion of trouble. Bushes taller than him vied with the trees for their share of whatever light remained. Lush red berries dotted many of those bushes, bright yellow flowers the others. If not for the lack of any animal or insect sound, the Beastmaster would have found the area quite tranquil.

Then one of the bushes caught his attention. It was roughly his height and slightly wider. What interested Dar, though, was how the leaves in the crown had grown to almost give it a face. There were eyes, a nose, and even a smiling mouth.

But such fanciful displays of nature were not why he was there. Dar stepped back to study the area in full again—only to turn to the bush once more as something within him insisted that he look closer.

And as he did, the Beastmaster noted that the face fused by the leaves looked even more real, more human.

"I know you," Dar declared, though he could not say how. "I know you . . . oracle . . ."

The bush shook. Leaves fell away, yet others formed together, creating a figure in weathered, forest green robes.

An elder, cherubic man stood before the Beastmaster.

"Welcome, welcome!" he called in a jovial voice.

Seto suddenly alighted onto a branch overhanging the miraculous newcomer.

"Brother Ontas!" the parrot called from the tree. "Brother Ontas!"

"Seto . . ." The oracle held up his left hand and the parrot alighted on it. "You've been a very good boy, Seto . . ."

The avian let out a purring sound like a cat, then rolled his head into Brother Ontas's forearm.

"Then . . . you . . . are the oracle of King Leardius," Dar blurted.

"Yes, yes . . ." Without warning, the robed figure strode past him. "Come! We must see how the others are getting along!"

Brother Ontas returned to where Dar and the others had been sleeping. As they neared, the Beastmaster noticed something different with the landscape. To the east, the ground rose into a small, squat hill that he could not recall from the night before.

But that was not all. In the side of the hill there now stood the mouth of a cave, and, judging by the footprints leading into and out of it, one likely occupied by the oracle.

Ontas grinned at Dar. "Aah! Your friends are awakening!"

Sure enough, despite the conversation and Seto's cry, Tara and Jalan were only now just stirring. Sharak, too, only belatedly became aware that something was different. The eagle fluttered from his perch in the overhang to Dar's arm and squawked his frustration out at Seto . . . who utterly ignored him.

"Such language!" Ontas reprimanded Sharak, though with a twinkle in his eye.

Soothing the eagle, Dar waited while Tara and the boy joined him. Jalan's eyes were huge saucers staring at Brother Ontas as though the latter had done some wonderful magician's trick . . . which perhaps was not all that far from the truth.

"Please, will you break fast with me? Surely you must be hungry!" Ontas gestured toward the cave. A pot with some sort of porridge stood boiling over a tiny fire and next to it, set on a long, flat stone, was a fresh loaf of bread and a large jug.

None of it had been there a moment before, though Tara and Jalan did not know that.

The boy eagerly headed for the food, Tara following. Dar lingered, eyeing Brother Ontas.

"Ancor provides all," the hermit cheerfully commented before stepping to the pot and doling out the contents in clay bowls that had also miraculously appeared.

The food was surprisingly tasty for what appeared simple fare, and what Dar drank from the mug presented him by his host reminded the Beastmaster of a sweet wine he had tried in a western port town. He frowned slightly when Ontas offered another mug to Jalan, then saw that the boy's drink was of a different hue. Tara's, in addition, looked more like water.

All had come from the same jug.

Brother Ontas did not explain, but again there was a twinkle in his bright green eyes as he also drank.

"Did you sleep well?" he asked with genuine interest.

"We slept on your very doorstep, it seems," Dar responded. Although he had taken an instant liking to the oracle, one thing bothered the Beastmaster. "Brother Ontas, how can you be so calm and cheerful? How can you even sit there? You of all people know that Ancor is burning . . . people are dying . . ."

Brother Ontas immediately looked more solemn. "And few know the full torture of that better than I, Dar of Emur. I live each day the lives lost and the lives that will be lost. I dream each night of the encroaching darkness and the fiends from the stars who dwell within it. Over and over I view the horrors that have been, are happening, or might be. Should I dwell too deeply in them, madness will surely take me . . ."

"Did you say from the stars?" Jalan blurted, mouth filled with food.

"They're demons, after all," Tara growled.

"Demons? If by demons you mean men who have either sold their souls or were forced to in exchange for evil deeds, for relentless bloodshed, then . . . yes, they are demons. Yet if you mean as in summoned from some burning underworld . . . no . . . even those that look so monstrous are but men of a different face, mortal and able to kill and be killed. As you both know. Only their lord . . . only he would I truly call a demon in every sense of the word."

"Men . . . from the stars?" Dar tried hard to imagine that.

The hermit bowed his head. "I've seen a world and it is Ancor's twin sister. But the twin is twisted, made so by her dark lover. Ishram, she is called, once meaning 'the gate that stands tall.' But now she is the entrance to abomination and hell . . ."

"And these . . . these invaders . . . they all come from there?"

"Oh, no! Many are from other worlds along the path between the sisters—little sisters, perhaps—made over one by one in Ishram's terrible image." Ontas shook his head. "Forgive me. In *his* terrible image, for if evil can take form, it is that of the lord of Ishram."

Dar leaned close. In but the space of a moment, he had already learned much about those he faced. For the one whom Leardius had claimed to be very obscure with his knowledge, Brother Ontas had been very forthcoming thus far.

"Who is he? What is his name?"

Ontas chuckled. In some ways, his round face was reminiscent of Orestian's, but far less guarded, far less secretive. Also, Ontas had hair, if only a silver ring running from the sides and back of the head. Dar could not help liking the oracle, even if he did not yet entirely understand him.

"A name? A name? Would that my visions were always so precise! Ha! I gathered the name of Ishram from a hundred different dreams, piecing it together from common links!" He gently thrust a finger toward the Beastmaster. "As for what he might look like, he could be a giant or an ant, but he is bound to you as if he were yourself, though his heart is made of cold metal—statues there are that are more flesh than he. In him is only blackness, no hint of light whatsoever, just as the light is you and burns away any touch of evil that might seek to reside in your soul . . ."

Again, that hint that somehow he and the monstrous leader of the invaders were related, despite also being such opposites. Dar gritted his teeth, wanting no such tie, but aware himself, somehow, that it existed.

"Do you see Ancor ending like this sister of hers?" the Beastmaster asked, trying not to think of the sinister bond. "Is our quest to be futile or is there truly hope?"

"There are many visions that show Ancor more foul than Ishram, Dar of Emur, but these visions, they are of futures not yet written in stone. There's a chance, although it grows slimmer with each day. I wish I could say more, but what I see are only bits of what will or might come. I do my best to make sense of them for others . . ." He smiled. "But I can say that if you reach the Fountain first, you will have a great chance of restoring all that's been lost."

Dar thought of his missing friends and wondered if Ontas included them in that last statement. He also wanted to know more about the Fountain, which Ontas had finally mentioned.

"How did they reach us from the stars?" Jalan interrupted again before Dar could ask his own question. "Did they jump down from them?"

"Ha! Precious thought, lad! They traveled as any must travel, in ships that sail the winds of the sky!"

Tara snorted. "You're jesting with us now! You're as much story-teller as you are soothsayer!"

The hermit chuckled. "And you have a better explanation? Would you rather they had wings to fly . . . which some, I believe, do, by the way."

"We have no time for such talk," Dar interjected. "You know why I have come—"

"I know why *all* of you have come. Make no mistake, Dar of Emur; you are not alone in this quest. All those who are dear to you play their part. To be alone . . . that is to accept defeat willingly."

The Beastmaster ignored his words. "Just tell me about the Fountain. It does exist, doesn't it?"

"Does *Ancor* exist? Be at peace! Be at peace! Yes, the Fountain exists. Some call it the Fountain of Eternity, others the Fountain of Truth. There are a thousand names I could mention, but they all fall short of fact. Know only that the Fountain, as we need it to be, does exist in the depths of our world, set there at Creation to be safeguarded and to safeguard."

"And how do we reach it? Where is it?"

Brother Ontas steepled his hands. "To reach it is not merely a matter of distance, Dar of Emur. You must be *prepared* for it. You walk the path already, as Ancor needs. You have been taught . . . and you have prevailed. To truly reach the Fountain, there are seven distinct mandalas that must be earned and, most important of all, must be understood."

"Seven—"

"Ah, did I say seven?" The robed figure chuckled again. "Only six for you, Beastmaster, for one you've already received for your learning. Recall you the pit and the bespelled creature you fought . . . and that which came after?"

Tara and Jalan turned curious eyes to Dar. Even the boy, who had been in Orestian's sanctum, had not witnessed the Beastmaster's battle nor certainly his encounter with the elderly figure.

"The . . . the sage I saw . . . he showed me a pattern . . . a mandala, yes . . ." Only now did it make sense to Dar. "But you say I have already received that one? How?"

"Because, in understanding compassion, you did not slay the animal when it would have seemed better to do so." Ontas leaned back. "Because you *are.*"

"I am what?" The Beastmaster began to feel as if he were speaking to Baraji.

The oracle eyed him under his thick brow. "You've been on this path for so very long. Many lifetimes, in fact, Dar of Emur, for you and Ancor will always be intertwined."

"So, I have no choice in this matter?"

The hermit shook his head. "You've every choice . . . and that is why you were chosen. You *are.*"

Now Brother Ontas was sounding much like Leardius had described him. Dar surrendered to the inevitable. *I am,* he thought to himself. *Always, I am.* He looked again at Brother Ontas. "And there are six more I must find? How do I earn them? How?"

"You have the answers, not me. I can tell you only this. Find and earn. *Earn,* Dar of Emur. To simply take them, that will spell failure for you. They must also be the true ones, for there are as many patterns as there are grains of dirt. More, even."

It sounded so daunting. Ancor was under siege. "There must be some other way. Something quicker and simpler."

"If there was, then it would be simpler for he who covets the Fountain . . . and Ancor would already be lost. Thus it must be, for it can be no other way." The oracle sipped from his mug. "And it will be my place to travel along with you on the path for a time, hopefully to offer some little guidance."

For the first time, Dar heard something he thought truly promising. "You'll lead us to the mandalas?"

"I? Nay. It's you who must lead. You who must find the sages whose task it is to guard the mandalas, which are but mortal symbols of the chakras they truly represent." Brother Ontas's hand went to the base of Dar's spine. "The one you have is here. Compassion. The mandala is visible when it must be, but the chakra it has opened up within will always be a part of you, regardless, Dar of Emur . . . and that is our hope for success. Our hope for a future. It will help your animal instincts guide you to the next and the next and so on."

The Beastmaster grunted. Once again, the fate of all rested entirely in his inadequate hands. Setting down his empty bowl, he asked, "If that is the case, can we not just begin now?"

"Be not so eager, for this journey will cost you, too. Listen closely. You cannot earn the mandalas and thus open the chakras without sacrifice . . ."

Dar shuddered. Glancing at Jalan and Tara, he declared, "Then you two must go back, probably to my brother Tal. You will be safer there." He looked up at Sharak. "And you, too, old friend. Better you keep looking for Ruh, Kodo, and Podo, than follow me on such a treacherous journey. I've lost enough already. I will not lose the rest of you . . ."

"I won't leave you!" shouted Jalan.

"Nor I, now that I've just found you again," added Tara, daring him with her deep eyes to deny her right.

Sharak voiced his disapproval with Dar for suggesting that he stay behind. Even Seto added his vote, imitating Jalan's voice perfectly.

This unanimous choice by Dar's companions made the oracle laugh heartily. "Though I foresaw this moment, it still fills me with delight. He who has loyal friends is strong in the soul, Dar of Emur . . ."

"I will not set them into danger—"

"All Ancor is filled with danger now. Better they be allowed to choose which danger to face."

That was the end of it, Dar saw. He would convince no one to stay and, well aware of the young woman's skills, knew Tara would surely follow . . . and if she did, so would Jalan.

"Very well," he said. "We all go . . ."

"As it was meant to be. You'll see that, Dar of Emur. All will be as it was meant to be." But although Brother Ontas was smiling as he bent down to pour his guests more to drink, Dar's sharp eyes spotted an ever-so-brief change in the oracle's expression. A grimness that vanished as quickly as it had appeared.

A grimness that warned the Beastmaster that Ontas had not told them everything he knew.

RUH STIRRED, ONLY to find himself bound by thin strands that refused to break despite his powerful twisting. The tiger's mouth was bound tight and when he tried to at least growl, it came out so muted that even he could barely hear it, much less Dar . . . should his two-legged brother even be nearby.

The cat was aware that he was still in the jungle, but not the same place where he last recalled being. There were several scents around him, most unfamiliar and disturbing, but two very much familiar. One was the object of his hunt, the male ferret, Kodo.

The other . . . the other smelled like Podo . . .

Then one of the disturbing scents swelled in intensity. Despite the darkness, Ruh had no trouble seeing the figure approach. That scent had been near the moment of his capture, a knowledge that made the tiger try to growl loudly again.

The creature laughed, the sound more like a hiss. He stood as Dar and other humans did, but was scaled like a serpent. He also had no nose to speak of and a crest running from his head down his spine. Next to him floated what looked like a huge, downturned hand made of metal, the thing, the cat innately knew, that had seized him without warning.

"Poor little animal . . ." the hunter mocked and although Ruh did not understand the creature's words, he sensed the tone. The tiger struggled anew, but to no avail.

A second, equally grotesque figure joined the first. "The sorcerer comes soon, Drayz . . ."

"Good! Then, we can be done with this hunt!" responded the first. "Thisss beassst, he wasss amusssing to trap, but we should be doing more!" He pointed a fist at Ruh and although that fist was empty, the tiger sensed the danger hidden in it. "We should just sss-laughter thessse and leave their carcassssesss . . ."

"And suffer the wrath of Vorannos," interjected a third voice that, despite speaking more as Dar might have, made the great cat desire to arch his back in anxiousness. No scent came from this new being, though he now stood nearly as close as the tiger's two captors. "Fire, then, if you will, Drayz . . . and be damned for it . . ."

A sudden scent of fear emanated from the first of the reptilian beings. He shook his head. "Nay, Kyrik! We mean no harm to the beassstsss! Wasss jussst idle talk! Impatience! We be merely eager to ssserve our lord better . . ."

There came an angry hiss from Kuln, his companion the focus of his anger. "'We?' Don't share your troubles with me, fool!'"

The shadowy form chuckled, a sound that added to Ruh's anxiety. This creature was like none the tiger had ever come across. The wrongness was highly disturbing. "Of course you do, Drayz! Do not all of us?"

The first hunter quickly indicated the bound tiger. "Look! He'sss well! Untouched asss commanded! The sssmall onesss are, too," Drayz gestured off to the side, where Kodo and Podo lay as still as if dead, though their chests rose and fell. Their eyes stared sightlessly. "Including the one sssent to usss by you . . ."

"As they should be," the sorcerer reprimanded. He drifted like a ghost over to Ruh, studying the cat. "Such unbridled might. Such perfection of a predator . . . yes, they'll play their part well, won't they?"

Ruh wanted to lunge but naturally could not. The bound cat rolled toward the cloaked specter.

Kyrik's eyes filled the animal's view. Ruh could not look away. The dark eyes snared him as completely as the hunter's claw had, more so, even.

"Your task is done here," Kyrik murmured to the watching pair. "Leave."

The reptilian figures gladly muttered to the air, vanishing a moment later in a haze of gold. Ruh noticed none of this, though, unable to see anything but the ghostly figure's piercing orbs.

"It is time," whispered Kyrik to the mesmerized cat. "It is time . . ."

12

THE HORN SHOOK LEARDIUS TO THE CORE, FOR HE KNEW ITS meaning. For one reason only was such a long, strident signal to be blown . . . and that was if Edurac was under siege again.

Xorot of the Claw had returned.

It mattered not that it was in the middle of the night. War cared nothing for proprieties or the time of day. But Leardius had not survived so many years as a king surrounded by covetous neighbors to not have expected such an attack by the Vorundite warlord. The king rose from his round, voluminous bed already clad in his armor, only his helmet off to the side on the marble stand next to him. His sword he already clutched, for it lay with him night upon night as if one of his wives . . . they themselves not having shared his bed much these past several tense weeks.

Indeed, even now guards were ushering them and his children to a place of safety. Leardius had not spoken to Dar of his children, not dared even think of them much. None were even as old as the boy Jalan, for Leardius's eldest son and intended heir had died of plague some years back. The king's three remaining sons were too young to rule should he die, but the eldest, Loranius, would become ruler nonetheless. He would have to command with guidance from his father's most trusted generals . . . assuming that at least one of them would still be alive.

The lord of Edurac let out a growl at such morbid thoughts. Thinking of one's own death and what would happen afterward was inviting defeat. Leardius had no intention of surrendering that easily.

Outside of his chambers he was met by a score of guards who took up positions surrounding their beloved monarch. Beyond the palace walls, an aide handed him the reins of his horse. By the time the horn blared a fourth warning, Leardius had reached the nearest wall.

Once atop, there he beheld a sight that dredged up again the fears for his wives and children . . . and all others. The landscape beyond was filled with torchlight, and in that torchlight a sea of fearsome shapes marched upon Edurac. There were far more than even Leardius had anticipated, even including those treacherous kings joining Xorot's banner.

He was met on the wall by Heratos, whose grim aspect no doubt mirrored his own. The other monarch thrust a hand toward the thick of the enemy. "By the Skull of Ramu! Do you see them?"

"There are many," Leardius admitted, his voice steely. "But they are men and will die at the base of our walls as such."

"Men? Have you looked closely? Have you looked up into the sky, too?"

"The sky?" Leardius followed Heratos's gaze.

And there the king of Edurac saw things in the air, things that in some manner resembled men, in others not in the least. They moved in advance of the horde, and Leardius had no doubt that they were to soften the defenders up for the Xorot's main force . . . if that force would even be needed once these fiends were through.

But Leardius, who had made as careful a study of the invaders as anyone could, had considered the terrifying fact that they had come from the sky in the first place. Would they not, therefore, in all logic also attack from there?

Despite the ominous sight, he kept some hope. Leardius felt certain that Xorot's master still wished to take the kingdom intact. The key to the mystery of the Fountain might yet exist in the kingdom's libraries, and to the invaders, this could prove invaluable to their mission.

"Sound the battle horns!" Leardius shouted to a waiting warrior. "Give the fourth signal first!"

He had planned for this moment; now it was time to see if his defense arrangements would prove sufficient against the flyers.

The series of notes blared across the city and was countered by the same notes repeated from the other side. Above, the sinister shapes started to descend. Below, the horde pressed eagerly toward the walls.

Xorot's front lines were the first to discover that Leardius and his allies had been busy in their absence. The ground suddenly gave way before them, and, pushed on by those behind, score upon score fell helplessly into the deep, long pits dug in the dark of night by the defenders. Men fell screaming on sharp stakes set at a steep, upward angle.

At the same time, legions of archers summoned by the king's signal set themselves into position for the flyers. Some had simple, strong arrows, but others had bolts equipped with small pouches near the head and short, flammable strands dangling from those pouches. Men racing along the ranks lit the strands with their torches.

"Give the signal to fire!" Heratos shouted.

Well aware of how quickly those strands burned, Leardius nevertheless waited for the most opportune moment allowable. The sinister shapes began to coalesce into distinct, disturbing figures.

"Now!" Leardius shouted.

The horns sounded. A flight of arrows lit up the darkness.

The chosen archers were all highly skilled. Few bolts in the huge flight flew awry.

But the first ones to strike in great part bounced off of what the king knew to be metal. The invaders were surely confident in themselves, for they were far more advanced in their armor and weaponry than most of Edurac.

Yet the sight that followed proved that even "primitive" warriors such as his could come up with strong defenses.

The small sacks exploded with a terrible vigor that stunned even Leardius, who knew their contents. White fire spread through the heavens and for a moment it seemed as if the long-absent sun had returned.

The sky was filled with burning forms, but whether that meant success, the king did not yet know. Many of the flying fiends appeared to still press on toward the walls, which they would reach any second.

But then a few faltered. They suddenly spiraled to the ground, crashing among the attackers there. With them also came a torrent of white flame that swept down over Xorot and his allies. More screams filled Leardius's ears, and even though they were enemies, a part of him could not help feeling some regret.

"It works!" called Heratos to him. "It works!"

Orestian—who was oddly absent—was not the only sorcerer or alchemist to which the defenders could turn. Indeed, the white fire was an ancient chemical rediscovered only a short time back by one of his men and, despite some disparaging remarks by Orestian, the king had determined to make good use of it. That choice was proving a good one.

But for every flyer that dropped, several more continued on. Many flew as if the scorching chemicals had no effect on them whatsoever. Leardius had feared this.

Yet just before the first fell upon the defenders, a new, startling force struck at them.

Birds. Countless birds. They darted in among the fiends, alighting wherever the flames were not. Claws and talons ripped at cords, tore at any place that seemed vulnerable.

The battle was near enough for Leardius to watch in dismay as some of the avians were torn apart by metallic claws, others scorched by the sinister lightning weapons so favored by the invaders. Yet the birds gave as good as their own. Several of the flyers crashed into Edurac's outer walls, and though they did some damage in that, it was far less than they would have if unchecked. The explosions rocked the defenders but gave them heart.

The birds proved a weapon well matched with the fire, for they were nimble and used it well to protect themselves. Leardius marveled how man and animal were indeed fighting alongside one another as partners, though he wondered if it would be enough.

The first of the invaders crossed the walls. Leardius swung at it as it passed, but his sword only produced sparks as it sliced against metal. The armored creature, a four-armed demon with a wide, visored helmet from which two hoses descended to the throat, fired one of the tube weapons.

A warrior next to the king burst into flames. The man screamed, then fell over the side.

Heratos leaped up and, with better aim than Leardius had managed, cut through the hoses. The abomination struggled for a moment with the severed pieces, then collapsed dead.

Heratos kicked it over to an area where it could burn without being a threat to anyone. He looked up, his expression dismayed.

"There are more coming!" he shouted.

Yes, despite the birds' formidable effort, the sky above Edurac was now alive with ominous shapes shooting forth lightning. The top of a tower exploded, sending not only huge chunks of stone raining down on warriors rushing below, but also tossing the men who happened to be inside down to their doom. At locations all along the wall, fire enveloped good men, creating horrific beacons that seemed to Leardius to invite Xorot's horde.

In fact, the attackers had gotten past the pits at last, clambering over the dead in some places, crossing on long, metal planks in others. Even as he fought against another flyer, Leardius saw the first of the lines reach the base of the wall.

Another horn sounded, the one for which the desperate king had been waiting. He thrust his blade through the throat of his latest foe, then peered down.

From slots in the lower part of the wall, men began pouring boiling oil down. Caught off-guard, the attackers initially suffered terrible losses. However, streaks of lightning shot forth from the invaders' midst, ripping apart two of the slotted windows and slaying the brave defenders there.

But the oil was not all. Leardius saw two of Xorot's people ripped apart by a pair of bears that had come out of nowhere. A massive stag ran down another fighter. The king nodded grimly. Dar had kept his promise. Still, as grateful as he was, Leardius wished that the Beastmaster could have been in two places at once, for then the animals could have been used for better effectiveness. They fought well, but they fought only as instinct demanded, with no calculation.

Another flyer dropped upon the king. Before it could fire its lightning weapon at Leardius, the lord of Edurac managed to grapple with his attacker. The invader was shorter than the king, yet far brawnier. Leardius was pressed against the battlements as his foe tried to push him over.

But then a huge bird, a hawk, landed atop the creature. It tore at the hoses.

The helmed creature twisted its weapon around and fired at the bird.

Using the distraction, Leardius seized the invader by the throat and shoved his blade up under the helmet. A greenish liquid poured over his blade. With a harsh, gurgling sound, the creature fell into him.

Choking from the sudden stench, Leardius pushed his dying adversary to the side. As the abomination crumpled, Leardius glanced past . . . and saw that the hawk who had come to his aid had been incinerated so thoroughly that its remains were nearly unrecognizable.

The king uttered a short oath for the hawk, then thought of the Beastmaster again. *May you find the Fountain and quickly, Dar . . . for even with all we have, with all that the animals have added to our ranks . . . we may not last long . . .*

More horns sounded. Their shrill notes made Leardius forget all else. He looked to where Heratos was pointing.

"Look there!" the other king roared. "Look there!"

Leardius did, but the new sight only filled him with more misery. The far flank of the invaders was shifting as a vast swarm of new additions spilled toward them. The newcomers more than erased any gains made by the defenders. The lord of Edurac cursed under his breath.

But . . . rather than blend into the horde, the reinforcements were cutting through it as if so eager to be the first to breach Edurac's defenses that they did not care about their comrades. They poured through the others, closing on those nearest the gates with tremendous speed and ferocity.

Only then did Leardius realize they were not joining the horde; they were *fighting* it.

LET YOUR ANIMAL *instincts guide you,* Brother Ontas had said and Dar had done just that. *Let the chakra's full potential come to pass . . .*

Dar had stepped out of Edurac and immediately scents and smells had touched him that he had never noticed before. Yet they were different than what he expected, for they did not identify for him a particular animal, plant, or person, but seemed to mark a *way*. He smelled the bend of a branch, the slight crushing of grass . . . all as if someone had walked the path before Dar's coming just so he would know where to head.

"That way," the Beastmaster said to the others, pointing into the thick jungle. He smelled the air again. "It has to be." Dar headed off where he indicated, the others following faithfully behind. The Beastmaster was absolutely confident of his path, so confident that it amazed him.

That was not to say that the path was an easy one. More than ever, he and the others had to climb uneven terrain, struggle through densely packed underbrush, and avoid precarious rock falls. They also moved at as swift a clip as they could, aware every moment that the invaders were near. Though this day they saw no sign, more than once the Beastmaster was certain that someone—or something—was watching.

As they journeyed, Dar gently fingered the stone dangling over his chest, the one Baraji had given to him at the time of his departure. More than ever, the Beastmaster wished for the sage's presence and guidance. So many questions raced through his head. How would he approach those who guarded the mandalas? What should he say to them? Would they find him worthy enough?

Brother Ontas gave him encouragement, but the oracle could not—or perhaps simply *would* not—help him with those specific questions. Dar had grown increasingly frustrated as the day's journey ended, despite a strange certainty that they were still on course toward the first guardian.

That night he dreamed, not of the chaos overtaking Ancor, but rather of his missing friends. In his dreams, Dar tearfully reunited with each. Their familiar scents wrapped around him like a comfortable blanket, so strong that, when he suddenly woke, the Beastmaster expected to see Ruh and the ferrets right next to him.

They were not, of course . . . and yet . . . when Dar sniffed the air, he swore that he smelled Kodo and Podo and even Ruh.

He felt so strongly that they had been there, in fact, that finally the Beastmaster quietly rose from his slumbering companions and peered into the shadows. The dreams had been so vivid that he could not immediately surrender to reality, even though he knew that the animals could not possibly be in the vicinity.

He smelled the air. And yet . . .

Dar suddenly slipped away from the others. It had been faint, but he could swear that he had once more smelled Podo. That seemed the most unlikely, so long had she been missing, but Dar continued toward where he believed the scent had originated.

As he stepped from sight of his companions, the Beastmaster considered the folly of his act. *All a dream,* he told himself. *Turn around . . . turn around . . . it is only the scent of some other animal mixing with your desire to find her . . .*

But still he pursued the ghostly scent. Perhaps . . . perhaps Podo had escaped and had been following him all this time. Perhaps she could lead him back to Kodo and Ruh—

The underbrush ahead rustled.

Hopeful as he was, Dar was still no fool. He did not have his sword, but he did have his dagger. Pulling it free, he approached the area.

A small head poked out of the underbrush.

There was no mistaking that face, for it was one of the most cherished in his life. Dar lowered the dagger, his joy almost childlike.

"Podo?" he whispered. "Podo? Is it truly you?"

The female ferret wriggled her nose as she neared. Dar put away the weapon as he reached out with his thoughts to her.

Only . . . there were no thoughts to touch. His mind collided with an invisible barrier surrounding hers.

Podo leaped at his outstretched hand. The ferret tried to clamp down with her sharp teeth, but some instinct enabled a stunned Dar to jerk his hand away before his fingers could be bitten off.

"Podo!" the Beastmaster now shouted. "Podo! You know me!"

However, the ferret showed no signs of recognition. She spat and hissed, trying again to either bite or claw Dar and while neither would have caused him any mortal injury, the Beastmaster chose to remain far enough from her while he desperately tried to think of what to do and why Podo would even attack him in the first place.

From back in the camp, Jalan cried out.

Despite his own concerns, Dar turned at the sound. However, just as the Beastmaster did so, his instincts warned him of imminent threat to himself.

He threw himself to the ground at his left. Podo barely missed tearing the flesh on his leg. As Dar kicked at her, a new threat suddenly rose up next to his face. Kodo, as invisible in thought to the Beastmaster as his female counterpart, darted at the human.

With a desperate grab, Dar managed to catch the male ferret just under the jaw. Kodo wriggled like an adder. His claws raked Dar's arm, but not enough to draw blood.

At the same time, another sound arose from the camp. A large cat's roar.

Ruh's roar.

Fear ran through the Beastmaster, but not for himself. If Ruh had become like the ferrets, he would be a horrible danger. Dar could no longer worry about himself or Kodo and Podo. He had to save the others . . . even it meant slaying the animals.

Sensing Podo coming at him again, Dar threw the male at her. The two ferrets collided hard.

The Beastmaster did not bother to see what happened to them. Leaping up, he raced to Jalan and the rest.

As he feared, it was indeed Ruh that threatened the party. The tiger confronted Tara, who stood protecting Jalan and Brother Ontas—the latter oddly calm and still. The Touargang thrust over and over with her spear, but never toward a vital spot. She was, Dar knew, trying not to slay or even wound one she considered an old friend . . . even though that concern would eventually get her ripped to pieces.

Ruh reared up. Dar, aware of the tiger's methods of attack, knew that Ruh was about to bring Tara down.

Letting out a wild cry, Dar leaped at the great cat.

Predictably, Ruh turned to this new threat. Yet the tiger was slower to react than the Beastmaster assumed he would be, and Dar managed to get between the predator and Tara without trouble.

Seeming to recover from his hesitation, the cat reared up—but instead of attacking Dar, again he tried to lunge past him at Tara. However, the Beastmaster shifted position and caught the great beast's powerful limbs from underneath. Straining with all his might, he held Ruh at bay.

"Run!" Dar demanded of the others. "Go!"

But instead of listening to sense, Tara stepped up next to him and tried to force Ruh back with her spear. The tiger, though, appeared to care not a whit for her weapon and did all he could to twist toward the Touargang.

"Dar! You run!" she shouted in turn to him. "There's something wrong here! I don't know what it is—"

Dar ignored her warning, not at all concerned about himself. He had already noticed that Ruh seemed determined to reach the others, not him, and he had to prevent that from happening. Yet the Beastmaster knew that he could not long keep Ruh so. The cat not only outweighed him but was far more powerful. Only the Beastmaster's agility and sense of balance enabled him to briefly frustrate the possessed cat.

He tried in vain to discover from Ruh the cause of his bloodlust, but could not. As with the ferrets, the tiger's mind was closed to him. Still, the Beastmaster had to assume that it was a spell. There was no other reason for Ruh to turn on those he cared for the most.

"Dar!" Tara called again. "When I lunge again, let go and run! I'll do what I can!"

"No! Do—do what I said! Ruh must be under the mastery of some foul magic! I have the best hope against him!" That as much included luck as it did skill, for Dar noticed at least one time when Ruh could have severely injured the Beastmaster's arm, yet had avoided doing so. The cat had far more an interest in crushing Tara than his human brother despite the latter being a much easier target at the moment.

Why? Why would he be hesitant to kill or even wound me when he would harm the others? The Beastmaster hoped he could uncover the answer to that quickly, for his strength was waning. Once he failed, there would be no one to stop Ruh.

Jalan called out something, but Dar could not pay attention to what it was.

Sharp teeth bit into his calf.

Dar's leg collapsed from the shock. Ruh pulled free. The tiger leaped out of the Beastmaster's view, headed, he knew, for the female warrior.

The source of his bleeding injury was none other than Kodo. Yet the male ferret did not follow up on his bite even though Dar was momentarily vulnerable. Instead, Kodo—and Podo, Dar saw—scurried after the boy.

Ruh slapped a paw at Tara's spear and this time knocked it free. The tiger moved in for the kill.

Ignoring his pain, Dar threw himself atop Ruh's back. He wrapped his arms around the great cat's thick throat and squeezed as hard as he could.

The tiger let out a rasping sound. He shook back and forth,

seeking to remove the pressure from his throat. Dar did not celebrate his success; sooner or later Ruh would realize that all he had to do was roll over to crush his attacker and that would be the end of the problem.

Dar prayed that at last his human friends would see reason, but none of them had fled. Jalan sought only to keep the ferrets at bay, Sharak aiding him by trying to pluck one or the other up. He thus far had failed, but at least kept Podo and Kodo from doing any harm to the boy. The ferrets spit and slashed at the eagle, who tried his best not to do them harm despite their obvious desire to rend him to pieces. Already several feathers lay scattered around.

Ruh twisted and turned, almost managing to free himself. Dar strained, already exhausted from his first struggle with the striped titan.

Brother Ontas stood silent and still. Yet his expression was one of intense concentration. He looked as though he struggled the most out of all of them, though Dar could not imagine how that might be.

Then, without warning, Ruh stilled. Daring to glance at the ferrets, the Beastmaster saw that they, too, had ceased their attack. All three stood as if just awaking.

However, before Dar could breathe a sigh of relief, another animalistic howl shattered the night.

A howl erupting from Brother Ontas.

The oracle shook. His body twisted and his expression was one of tremendous torture.

Ontas suddenly crouched. His nose twitched and his head shifted left and right. As Dar dared release his hold on Ruh, it occurred to him that the oracle reminded him of nothing less than Podo or Kodo. Each movement was like that of a ferret.

The two small animals suddenly imitated his movements, as if invisible strings bound the movements of all. As he hissed, they hissed. As he snarled, they snarled.

And then, Kodo and Podo stilled once more. They looked around, eyes full of innocence and curiosity.

Again, Brother Ontas's demeanor changed. He bared his teeth and hissed. One hand slapped out, the fingers bared like claws . . . as if he were now a great cat, a tiger.

As the ferrets had, now Ruh moved in concert with the oracle. Ontas growled. Ruh growled. Ontas scraped the ground with his hands. Ruh did the same.

Then, like Podo and Kodo, the tiger, too, looked around as if seeing the world for the first time.

But the oracle still acted like a tiger . . .

"Brother Ontas?" Tara called cautiously.

He snarled at her. Dar, ignoring his own injury, approached the man.

The robed figure turned on him. Brother Ontas looked ready to lunge . . . but then, without warning, curled up on the ground. His breathing went from rapid panting to a barely perceptible rise in his chest every few moments.

Crouching at the man's side, the Beastmaster hurriedly checked Ontas's condition. The oracle had obviously somehow taken in the evil that had possessed the animals, but at what cost?

To his surprise, the oracle looked up at him with a weak smile. "I will . . . I'll be all right, Dar of . . . of Emur. Give me . . . give me time, that's all. The spell was potent. It took much for me . . . for me to engulf it in myself."

Dar shook his head, stunned. Brother Ontas had saved them all and there seemed nothing that the Beastmaster could do for him. "Can I—can I at least give you water?"

"Nothing. How are . . . how are the animals?"

"They are well. They are themselves again."

The oracle nodded, then shut his eyes.

The others swarmed around the resting figure. Podo gently

licked Ontas's face in gratitude. The ferrets and Ruh sat around the oracle as if to guard him. Jalan joined them, staring at Ontas in awe.

Tara leaned over Dar and the oracle. With wide, wondering eyes, she asked, "Will he recover?"

"He says he will." Pain wracked his leg, causing Dar to wince.

"Your wound!" Tara made him sit. "Let me see to that."

Her touch was gentle as she first inspected the gap, then reached for the water sack to clean the wound. At the same time, Ruh and the other animals came to Dar. The ferrets and the tiger rubbed their noses against him, seeking to apologize in their way for the terrible confrontation. Kodo especially tried hard to make up for having harmed his human brother.

"It is all right," Dar repeated over and over to the three as he nuzzled their faces. "It was not your doing . . ."

Sharak landed near, even the eagle apparently feeling some guilt for not having done more.

"You did well, my friend," the Beastmaster told him. "You tried to help us while also trying not to hurt these three." He smiled at all four creatures. "I have no anger with any of you. We are all family . . ."

They accepted his word, then moved back so that Tara could finish with Dar. Jalan sat a short distance away, watching the Touar-gang's work with interest. He looked up at Dar, who winked at him. Jalan looked relieved.

"They love you so much," Tara murmured, leaning so close that their faces were mere inches from each other. "Even I could see their pain . . . and feel it, too."

He met her gaze. "Thank you for trying to save my life."

"Ha! Thank you for saving mine, Dar." She smiled, a sight that for some reason made his heart pound faster. "For saving all our lives, I mean . . ."

"You should have run when I said, though," he halfheartedly reprimanded her.

She tightened the tourniquet she had created from a strip torn from an empty sack. "There's little blood. It should heal quickly. How does it feel?"

"It throbs now, but not terribly." Tara had purposely avoided arguing with Dar and he saw no good point in continuing, either. None of his companions would have abandoned him any more than he would have them.

"Can you stand?"

"I think so." With her help, he rose to his feet. His leg proved momentarily unsteady and the pair had to hold one another more tightly until the leg improved. Dar found he did not mind the nearness in the least.

Tara's face suddenly flushed. She moved from Dar back to Brother Ontas, who had remained in a still position all this time. His face was pale, but otherwise he looked unharmed. "Do you think he's truly all right?"

The oracle chose that moment to let loose with a loud snore. As he did, some color returned to his face.

Dar grinned, grateful for such a healthy sign. "I think so. I think he really only needs sleep now."

Despite the terrible struggle, the Beastmaster's heart felt considerably lighter. His family had been returned to him, safe and sound. Whatever sinister ploy had been intended had failed. Not only had their unseen foe underestimated the party—especially Brother Ontas, it seemed—but the animals themselves had surely proven stronger of will than imagined. How else to describe their reluctance to do terrible harm to Dar, who obviously had been their main target? Even under the spell, they had held back. Ruh had scarred him on the chest and arm, but none of those cuts had even been as harsh as Kodo's bite which, while drawing blood, had done little harm.

He watched as Tara did her best to adjust Brother Ontas's robes so that they protected him. Following her lead, the animals also pressed closer, giving the oracle some of their body heat. The Touargang petted each of them, reassuring them that there was no reason for any to feel guilty for the earlier attack.

In addition to the safe return of his friends, Tara was another reason for Dar's improved mood. Not just that she had saved his life . . . but merely because she was near. There was something he found refreshing about having her around.

And with such thoughts to cheer him, the Beastmaster could not help but think that there was hope for the quest as well. He sat down to meditate, feeling confident that by the time he stirred he would know exactly what path next to take. There was no doubt in his mind that they were not far from their next goal. The Beastmaster would quickly attain that mandala, then move on to the succeeding ones.

Dar absently fingered the stone from Baraji. In his mind formed a mandala like the one that he had been given by the sage in the pit. Overall, it had an emerald hue to it, yet included many other colors within its intricate design. The Beastmaster used it and the chakra it opened to begin his search for the way.

And as Dar meditated, that mandala also formed in reality, on his chest, as a tattoo . . .

KYRIK SHIVERED AS he awaited contact with his master. He was not certain how Vorannos would react to the negative results of the sorcerer's work. Ancor was proving a far more treacherous place with which to deal, almost as if the planet itself were trying to manipulate matters for its survival.

But that was not possible, of course. Worlds had no sentience, so Vorannos had decreed. The master had proven that time and time again, raping one after another on his quest to reach this particular piece of mud.

Kyrik cursed the oracle's surprising skills. If not for the man's risky spell, all would have gone exactly as planned, exactly as dictated. But Lord Vorannos only liked absolute certainty, which his sorcerer could not promise him.

"Well, Kyrik?"

The ghostly sorcerer fought back his surprise. Only Vorannos could come to him so unexpectedly. Keeping his head bowed, he said, "Most benevolent one, the deed's been done as desired! The first step has been taken toward ultimate triumph!"

"Look up at me, dog." When Kyrik had, Vorannos smiled darkly. The lord of Ishram appeared unarmed, but, even more than his hunters, the giant wielded a vast variety of hidden and vicious weapons. Kyrik had lost one of his duplicate bodies; he did not wish to lose another.

"My lord—"

"The Beastmaster is important to me, but tell me why the others *with* him still live, you pathetic cur. They have no true value. I would be rid of them. Tell my why I shouldn't scatter your miserable self over the length and breadth of this jungle for this failure in something so simple . . ."

Kyrik spread his hands as he sought to explain. "The oracle, the prophet, he is more than imagined! A guardian as well as a soothsayer! We did not anticipate that he would have the means to rip the spell from the animals before the feline had done his work . . . and with the feline not permitted to rend the Beastmaster to shreds, that put our own plan at a disadvantage from the start—"

Before Kyrik knew what was happening, Vorannos slapped a hand on his shoulder. The sorcerer immediately screamed. His body shook, and suddenly the ethereal image of Kyrik separated from his body. The body, in turn, became like one of the three figures that had stood in Vorannos's chamber.

The lord of Ishram released his hold. The two parts of Kyrik immediately bonded together again. The sorcerer fell to his hands and knees, panting.

"Any failure is yours, dog, recall that ever . . ."

"Y-yes, my lord . . ."

The mirror eyes looked into the black jungle. Vorannos saw none of the beauty, only the disorder. When he was done, this mess of a world would be a perfect, beautiful replica of his Ishram. The glorious smoke would fill the entire sky. His brilliant machines would work constantly to strip the land of all pitiful human resources. The inhabitants—those worth keeping alive—would be redesigned. He could already hear their screams slowly turn into cries of joy as he brought them their destiny.

"It is the Beastmaster alone whom I need, Kyrik. He is the key; the rest are nothing. Strip their living flesh from their bones, roast them in fire, or drive them to glorious madness, but see to it that they die. The Beastmaster's mind must be beaten down, made malleable, either to bring him to serve me or prepare him for death once he is of no more need."

"I will follow through and make him ready! I swear . . ."

The lord of Ishram raised his hand, causing the sorcerer to cringe. However, instead of harming Kyrik, Vorannos proved only to be signaling to other shadows in the dark. Kyrik knew them for what they were: Vorannos's favored hunters. There were other reptile men here, but also a good number of Pygmesians. These Pygmesians had been on Ancor longer than most and knew the lay of the land better because of it. They had, in fact, scouted Ancor before the first of the drills had descended like fiery gods upon the world.

"Think not that I rely only on you, dog," Vorannos concluded. "Yours is but one way to force the so-called champion of this pathetic world to bring to me the Fountain. Zorena delves in another. I go now to continue a third avenue that may make the Beastmaster of no need after all . . ."

"No greater wisdom is there than yours, benevolent one," Kyrik murmured. "But if it proves to be the human you need, it will be Kyrik who presents him to you for your pleasure . . ."

Vorannos did not reply, for Vorannos was no longer there. Neither was his band of hunters.

The sorcerer straightened. A hint of malice touched his cadaverous features, but not malice toward his master. Kyrik knew better than that. Vorannos could smell betraying thoughts from a world away. Kyrik was no fool there.

"I shall deliver unto you the Beastmaster," the hooded spellcaster muttered. "Mayhaps a bit beaten or burnt, but he will bow to you as master . . ." Kyrik silently swore. "And the prophet, the female, and the boy . . . they will be my pleasure to slay . . . slowly . . . even if it is the hand of the Beastmaster that does the bloody task."

13

As the unexpected reinforcements neared Edurac, Leardius braced himself for what might be the most risky command of his reign. He could not leave the daring fighters outside.

"Open the gates the moment they reach them!" he ordered the nearest warriors. "Get every available man to defend the way until they're all inside!"

"Is that wise?" shouted one of the other kings. "Open the gates and Xorot's vermin will folllow right in!"

"We're leaving no brave men out there!" countered Heratos impatiently. "Suppose it was yourself out there, Galain, eh? Consider that!"

There was no more protest, for which Leardius was grateful. He peered close, estimating just when the critical moment would come.

"On my signal!" he shouted.

The pace of the newcomers slowed as they neared, the horde becoming more and more aware of the enemy in their midst. Leardius swore under his breath; he knew not all these good men would make it, but he prayed that most would.

Chaos reigned. The many fires made the scene horrendous to behold. Riders in the column finally became distinct figures.

And in the fiery light, the king of Edurac beheld the reinforcement's leader.

"It's Tal of Aruk!" he shouted. "Ha! Who else, naturally?"

"They're nearing the gates!" Heratos said. "Open the way!"

"Not yet!" The men he had ordered up front were just getting into position. They were not as many as he would have liked, but Edurac was still under attack by the flyers. The defenders were holding their own, but too many of the fiends were above the city.

Flights of arrows rained down on Xorot's men. Leardius estimated the distance and time.

"Now! Open the gates now!"

The horns blared. With a thundering creak, the gates moved.

Some of the enemy immediately charged in but were met by a phalanx of spearmen who quickly decimated their numbers.

The head of the column entered, fighting all the way. "Keep enough men at the gates!" King Leardius cried. "We need to shut the way immediately when the last are through!"

Leardius all but leaped down the steps to the ground as Tal's column poured into Edurac. As the guards tried to shut the gates behind them, shouts arose and there was heavy pounding and the clash of arms. Leardius swore and joined the others rushing to Edurac's entrance.

There, Xorot's followers were seeking to keep open the way. Fearsome, hairy faces snarled at the defenders. Dark men in round helmets stood with them, warriors of one of the other traitorous kings. They wielded long, curved spears with which they sought to impale those in the front ranks of Edurac. Behind them, something large, multilegged, and shaped like a sphere began to advance.

The defenders forced the invaders back, but the giant sphere was closing in. Leardius had no notion as to its abilities and did not want to find out.

Then . . . the behemoth began to tilt to the side. There was a cracking sound and the tilt became even more severe.

He shouted up to Heratos, who could see better from his position. "What's happening to that thing?"

"The ground! The ground is giving way on its left!"

Leardius's men had not dug any hidden pits there. The king was baffled.

"The Beastmaster . . ." Heratos declared. "The voles and other underdwellers, he must have given them instructions to weaken the way . . ."

Dar's tactics, Leardius thought to himself. *Brilliant.*

The giant sphere attempted to right itself . . . and failed. It fell upon those nearest it, and as it struck the imploding ground, the cries of the dying beneath it startled those seeking to keep the gates open.

"This is our chance!" King Leardius roared. "Push them back while they're in chaos!" Edurac's protectors shoved forward. The invaders were pushed from the gates, and the gates were finally shut.

As his warriors bolted things tight, Leardius let out a sigh. "Praise the gods!" The king searched the riders and warriors all around him until he spotted the one he sought.

"My lord Tal!"

"King Leardius!" The younger monarch leaped down as his men converged to fight off the invaders. Behind him, a dwarf also descended. The lord of Edurac only momentarily started at this sight. He knew of General Om, though he had not met him previously.

The dwarf bowed his head, then kept a step behind his own monarch.

"Praise be that you're here!"

"Nearly too late!" Tal glanced at his men. He shook his head. "Too many good men lost, but more would have been if you hadn't opened the way so quickly, my lord!"

"And no one was more daring than you, to ride through the enemy so! You've put them in utter confusion, which will surely buy Edurac needed time!" Leardius shook his head grimly. "And I pray Dar will use the time well . . ."

"My brother will succeed! He must!"

"Brother?"

Tal quickly explained his tie to the Beastmaster and also the encounter. Leardius exhaled.

"Good news to hear," he finally replied to Tal. "Though I wish he were here, also. The animals, they fight well, but they fight on their own. The birds are the most organized. Even still, we lack proper coordination with them, for none can speak their tongue."

"Yes, I saw bears and lions, among others, tearing into the enemy as we approached. Still, I understand the quandary, Leardius, though I can't help."

"If I may," Om quietly interjected. "Though I could never claim the skills of the Beastmaster, I do have some affinity for animals. Perhaps I may be able to help."

Leardius looked doubtful, but he saw from Tal's face that the other king seriously pondered what the general suggested.

Tal finally nodded, his trust in the dwarf clear.

"Very well, then—"

"Listen!" Tal called.

The bearded monarch did . . . and realized only then that an odd lull had swept over the area beyond the walls. It was Heratos who told him what that meant.

"They're pulling back, Leardius!"

Indeed, for the first time the lord of Edurac noticed that even the skies were no longer infested with flyers. Either Xorot or his unseen master had decided to call a temporary end to the struggle. While everyone felt some relief at this turn of events, they also could not help sharing a sense of uncertainty as to the true cause of the reprieve.

Om it was who voiced what they feared. "They will adapt. The animals, they are something new, something surprising—even more than our arrival—but something that the invaders will come to believe can be crushed eventually."

Tal was in utter agreement. "When they come, they'll do so more deadly than ever."

Leardius nodded. "And we've no choice but to meet them the same way."

The general bowed his bald head. "I will see what I can do in establishing a rapport with the animals . . ."

The king of Edurac agreed, adding, "We need also to shore up our defenses against another assault from the sky. They'll surely try harder there."

"The fighters on the western flank need rest and reinforcements," Tal noted. "They were the hardest pressed of those beyond the walls . . ."

The comparative normalcy of battle strategy discussions helped set the men's minds more at ease. They were at least able to pretend that this was once again simply a struggle between two armies, not a stand against a power in many ways beyond their ken.

But all were still very much aware, though none showed it, that, come the next attack, that pretense would quickly be shattered . . .

ALTHOUGH BROTHER ONTAS showed some lingering signs of exhaustion, he did not appear otherwise to suffer from his desperate spellwork. In fact, his mood was quite cheerful, considering. Dar studied the oracle carefully and determined that the cheerfulness was no pretense. Ontas was truly a man who had learned to look within himself for peace, the very thing that the Beastmaster had spent years seeking to achieve.

He marveled at the oracle's swift recovery and questioned Ontas how he had learned to perform such a miracle as he had last night. The Beastmaster wondered if it was something he could learn as he moved along his own path.

"All paths are the same as much as they are different," Brother Ontas replied. "Yours will reveal miracles of which I cannot even dream. How you are shaped by those miracles will be unique to you, as they would be to others . . ."

Dar nodded, although he did not quite understand. Still, Ontas's bravery was definitely something which the Beastmaster would use as an example of what he hoped he would do if given a choice between his own life and that of his friends.

They moved at a fast clip, the failed attack having made them more aware than ever of the imminent threat surrounding them. Every shadow in the jungle made Dar wary of attackers. His senses remained heightened as he sought for even the slightest hint of either their goal or any possible menace, especially related to the invaders. Aware that the latter danger could come in elements of which he might not even be able to conceive, the Beastmaster noted every slight movement, every odd twist of a leaf or branch. At the same time, he looked within himself, focusing on the mandala and the chakra to guide him, to open his mind and his soul to whichever direction he needed the party to turn.

"Trust in yourself and your most basic truths," Ontas encouraged him at one point. "Those truths are the essence of all chakras . . ."

The party paused at a small open area in the jungle. While his companions rested, Dar—accompanied by the ferrets in their pouch and Sharak in the air—went in search of water. It took him only minutes to sense a possible source. The faint gurgling of a stream reached his ears. When the Beastmaster finally came across the focus of his search, he could only stare at it in wonder.

The stream flowed *uphill.*

The flow went against all that was natural, and at first Dar wondered if another water spirit or elemental dwelled there. He started to follow the stream, the sense growing that it had relevance to his quest. He immediately sent Sharak back to guide the others to him while he did a careful survey of his present surroundings.

The rest arrived but a minute later. Like him, they first stared in awe at the sight. Tara and Jalan were eager to follow the stream, and the animals, of course, went wherever Dar did. Brother Ontas said nothing, but his eyes glittered with interest.

A mist arose as they tracked the odd flow. Dar smelled the air, which was filled with scents to which he was not accustomed. Ruh offered to fall back just in case, but Dar wanted the tiger and everyone else nearby. Even Sharak he would not permit more than a short distance and, for once, Seto appeared content to perch on Jalan's shoulder and keep his beak tightly shut. The ferrets, meanwhile, seemed quite happy to remain in their pouch.

From somewhere ahead, the trickle of water suddenly became a loud gush. Dar waved the others to a halt, then, sword at the ready, approached the sound.

In the mist, a high ridge coalesced. That, though, was not the source of the gushing. The honor for that belonged to a tall, raging waterfall running the height of the ridge, whose presence gave the Beastmaster pause. However, it was not the natural beauty of the sight, though the falls were certainly striking, but rather a now familiar oddity that caused Dar to stare in awe.

The waters were *rising,* not falling. The stream that they had been following was one of several that fed the waterfall—or perhaps *waterrise* would have made more sense—and sent the fearsome torrent up and over the ridge, where it vanished from sight.

He started to turn back, only to discover that his companions had disobeyed his order to remain where they were.

"Did you think we'd take the chance of losing you?" Tara defiantly answered to his raised brow. "You've already wandered off once. We'll not accept twice." She gripped her spear tightly. Next to her stood Jalan, a stout stick in his hand.

Dar led them toward the rush of water, his gaze drinking in everything visible and his nose constantly testing the air. Something within him stirred. More and more, Dar felt the pattern of the first mandala form in his mind and at the same time sensed how it coincided with his surroundings. The flora, the rocks, even a bird in one tree—they were all elements creating the points of the design. Nothing around him was positioned randomly; it was all there for a purpose . . . part of which was to guide him.

Then, behind the falls, he saw a cave. More to the point, he also caught a glimpse of a comely, middle-aged woman in profile. She had long, dark hair just turning gray in some places. The woman stared back at him out of the corner of her eye, seeming to appraise him.

But as quickly as she had stepped into view, she vanished again, returning to the shadows of the cave.

"What is it?" asked Tara.

"I do not know . . ." But deep inside, the Beastmaster pondered the possibilities. Was it the sage he sought? Some demon? Evil could wear the most innocent or seductive of guises.

There was really only one way to discover the truth. Dar had to pursue the ghostly figure. He informed the others of that decision.

The Touargang nodded. Hefting her spear, she said, "I'll follow a few paces behind . . . just in case."

"The shortest path is not necessarily the best path," Brother Ontas suddenly interjected, "and oft it's only the *one* who may enter freely and unafraid. Those who are not meant to enter may find themselves swept up in their own illusions or base impulses . . ."

Dar did not understand what Ontas meant by his warning save that the Beastmaster should continue on to investigate the vision. With that, he could agree.

"I want you all to wait here. I must do this alone." Handing the pouch with the ferrets to Tara, he stepped up to the raging water. Ontas's words came back to him. *Swept up . . . swept up . . .*

On a hunch, the Beastmaster picked up a loose branch and threw it into the water.

The moment the branch touched, it was dragged up with frightening swiftness, vanishing with the water over the top of the ridge.

For good measure, Dar tossed a large rock in . . . with the same dread results. The rock battered again and again against the ridge until it disappeared. Whatever entered this reversed waterfall, no matter how heavy, was condemned to be dragged up and out of sight with horrifying speed and violence.

Suddenly, he felt as if he were being watched. Sure enough, within the cave, a man with long, brown, slightly graying hair leaned against a rock. As with the woman, the man was only seen in profile, but Dar knew that one visible eye was certainly on him.

Perhaps he had been wrong to think the woman the sage for whom he was searching. She might be another seeker of enlightenment who had nothing to do with his quest. The man might even have no tie to it.

It was possible that both were also not even human and that this was a trap, either one by the invaders or simply by some dark, supernatural being who liked to prey on innocents.

There was only one way to find the truth. Grip tightening on his sword, the Beastmaster warily approached. He leaned as close as he could to the water and shouted, "I come to speak with the guardian of the mandala! Are you he?"

Without turning, the man slipped into the cave.

Dar nearly followed, but then he feared what would happen if he entered the falls. Seeing the rapid pace of the water, he felt certain that any journey up it would end with his bones broken all over the rocky ridge.

But the falls covered the entire path. There was no other means by which to reach the cave, at least not without climbing up and over the ridge and searching for an alternative path, also a daunting prospect.

Dar sheathed his sword, useless here. He then considered his studies with Baraji and what Brother Ontas had said about the first mandala he had received. It had opened the chakra that had helped the Beastmaster to come this far. Surely, then, he was meant to reach this destination . . . but only if he had the will.

Slowing his breathing, Dar reached into himself, imagining the mandala he had received for his compassion for the beast. He instinctively recalled its multitude of round edges surrounding the crescent moons and more minute designs. This time, though, the mandala as he saw it had a soft, emerald hue.

It continued to take shape within his mind, turning and vibrating with a life at which he could only marvel. Yet, it was alone. Unbidden, there came a second vision in his thoughts, a bright, purple light before which the mandala moved.

Baraji had spoken to him more than once of something called the Third Eye, which existed in all but would only awaken when one reached a certain level of understanding. The Third Eye saw what the physical ones could not. Indeed, even as the Beastmaster came to grips with this new and wondrous revelation, he also realized that he saw the area around him with an entirely different perspective. The trees, the lush plants—the entire landscape was a cornucopia of colors and energies all interacting, all bound together by one grand design.

The more he concentrated, the more the vision grew so distinct that Dar could finally see it before his very eyes. Thinking of Baraji, the Beastmaster's hand touched the bronze stone his teacher had given him. It felt warm and gave him confidence. Using the Third Eye as his guide, Dar finally reached his hand toward the mandala, drawing comfort from it—

And only when it was too late did the Beastmaster notice that his hand now extended into the falls.

Yet, unlike with the rock or the branch, he was not dragged upward to his doom. Instead, it was as if a slight cushion of air surrounded his hand, protecting it from harm. That cushion extended down his arm as he dared move forward.

"Dar!" Tara called.

"No one follows him!" Brother Ontas suddenly warned, putting one arm before the Touargang. "He must do this alone!"

With more confident steps, he pushed on into the water. Although his ears filled with its rumble, nothing else happened. Keeping his breathing even, the Beastmaster continued.

And before Dar knew it, he crossed underneath. Although the rocks around him were soaked, his footing was dry and solid.

As Dar took a moment to refocus, he felt someone watching him again. At the right side of the cave mouth, the woman once more stood in profile. She was dressed in a gauzy orange robe so transparent that Dar was grateful she stood sideways to him.

"The master of beasts has come. I greet you," she said in a musical voice.

"You are the guardian of the mandala?"

"We are the guides to awakening its chakra, yes."

He frowned at her odd use of pronouns. We? Dar looked around for the man, but he was nowhere to be seen.

She started to turn toward him. As she did, her voice took on an oddly masculine quality. "We are who we are . . ." There was a pause. "And you . . . who are *you*? Do *you* know?"

The Beastmaster gaped. Seen now, her other side was entirely different. While her left was utterly female, her right was the *male* figure that he had also noticed. Yet, despite so many differences in build and face, the two opposing sides blended perfectly in the very middle, so much so that Dar found it hard not to think of her/his appearance as anything other than natural. A slight smile played across the face, which put Dar more at ease.

The robes, too, differed on the male side, for although they were of the same color, they were thicker, more strict. The male's chest was wider on his side, while the female's was more elegant and feminine.

"We are the Shagane, also named Saru/Sarin, and it is our place to be the guides here . . ." The sage continued to turn. The voice was completely masculine now. "If you will choose to be guided—"

"I have come this far."

"A quick answer is a determined answer," the male, Sarin, responded with a smile.

But then the female face turned into view. "Yet a quick answer is also one often without thought and, thus, full of regrets." The Shagane's hands spread apart. "For instance, where do you wish to be guided to? There are many possibilities."

"The Fountain," the Beastmaster replied.

Now Saru also smiled, if sadly. "So it must be."

Sarin's face returned. "If it is to be at all."

From within the cave, fire arose. As Dar's eyes accustomed themselves to the sudden illumination, he saw that the fire originated from four strong torches that gave him a view of the entire cave.

Such a view might have interested him more if there had been *anything* to see. The walls were bare and the floor contained only a single mat weaved from yellowed river grass.

There were no mandalas and nothing that laid hint of where Dar should look for any.

"Where is it?" he finally asked. "Time is precious. Ancor is in terrible danger . . ."

The split face turned to him again. Now the voice was both male and female. "Think not because we dwell here that Ancor's health is not known to us, master of beasts. Here, we feel the deaths that have been"—the profile of Sarin took over—"the many brave warriors"—the head shifted so Saru now looked at him out of her eye—"and the poor children, mothers, and infirm. The farmers and the artisans . . ." A tear ran down her cheek. "All of them."

"Then, guide me . . ."

"Where do you wish to be guided?" The female asked again.

This time, Dar hesitated. He was not certain that merely saying "the Fountain" was correct. The Beastmaster thought hard, then answered, "Guide me . . . to what will help prevent more from perishing . . ."

Saru/Sarin nodded. "The mandala will guide you."

"Where is it?"

"The mandala is not far," they answered together. The Shagane kept turning so that within seconds their back took precedence. "Not far at all . . ."

Dar gaped again. The robes of both halves separated in the back, revealing the soft curve of Saru and the hairy side of Sarin. Yet that was not what made the Beastmaster take a step back in dismay.

In the small of the duo's back, perfectly centered, was a small hole not quite wide enough for either Podo or Kodo to have fit through. Within that hole, Dar made out the bones of the spine and all the muscles, tendons, veins, and more that he knew from terrible existence could be found within the bodies of all higher creatures.

But to see within . . .

Then Dar noticed that the sage was not pointing or looking any-where. Instead, Saru/Sarin seemed to be patiently waiting.

The Beastmaster understood then where the mandala had to be and the very notion of what he might have to do took him aback. How could they ask something like this of him? Dar shook his head in dismay. In what way could this help him . . . or help Ancor, for that matter?

"We have been honored to bear it for these many lifetimes," the twin voice humbly said. "And we are honored to have Ancor's child now receive it from us."

"You wish—you wish me to—to—"

Though the sage continued to face away, he/she nodded. "It is as it is. It is as it must be."

Dar took a step forward, then hesitated. "There will be no pain, will there? For you, I mean?"

"Is there any true reward without some pain, some suffering?" And it seemed that the Shagane's question more addressed the Beastmaster's situation than the sage's own.

It was not the answer that Dar wanted to hear. Yet he seemed to have no choice if he wanted the mandala. Teeth bared, the Beast-master thrust his hand toward the hole.

But although he should have been able to put his fingers right in, it was as if some invisible barrier blocked his way. Worse, the sage let out a moan of terrible agony, and Dar's hand felt as if he had just tried to thrust it into a fire.

"Why can I not reach it?"

"Where do you—where do you wish to be guided?" the Shagane managed after a moment.

The question again. Dar desperately thought. "To the path that will save Ancor!"

Again, he tried to put his hand in and again he met the barrier.

Saru/Sarin all but doubled over in pain. Dar's hand felt as if the skin should be blackening from heat. Sweat dripped down his body.

"What am I doing wrong?"

But the sage only replied with the same question. "Where do you wish to be guided?"

The fire in his hand would not let up. He tried pushing the fingers inside without answering, but that only served to put his companion into even worse throes of agony.

Visions began to race through the Beastmaster's mind. He saw time speeding by. He saw his failure bringing cataclysm to his world, people dying everywhere and the sky filled with black smoke. Those visions mixed with the past—battles against priests and sorcerers, moments of peace with his adopted father, friends found and lost . . . and brief respites that might have led to love. Dar saw his past, present, and future and knew that if he did not succeed, than all that he had done previously meant nothing.

Where do you wish to be guided? What was the answer to that? Dar concentrated, aware that each time he failed, it made it worse not only for him, but the Shagane.

Where . . . where . . . The Beastmaster focused on the mandala within him, seeking the answer there.

And just as suddenly, he had the answer.

"Where do you wish to be guided?" Saru/Sarin asked again.

"Within . . ." Confident in his answer, Dar thrust the hand toward the hole.

It went in without the least obstruction. He instinctively sensed the vibrations of the mandala inside and reached for it. He recognized that his own quest of self-discovery, and not the location of the mandala, was the answer. Those two parts were bound not only to one another, but to everything else involved in his existence. Indeed, in all existence.

That was why both male and female were also combined in the

form of the Shagane. They were a symbol of the *oneness* of creation, of the serenity and the pain of life, the perfect vessel to contain this mandala.

But a sudden concern swept over the Beastmaster before he dared pull it out.

"What will happen when I remove this?"

The sage said nothing. The choice, it seemed, was Dar's to make on his own.

Tears of joy at what he had beheld mixed with those regretting the suffering he caused the Shagane. Body covered in sweat, Dar braced himself . . . then stepped back.

His fist came free.

Saru/Sarin shrieked, the double-voiced cry monstrous to hear. The sage fell forward, sprawling on the cave floor.

Dar nearly opened his fist, then feared that somehow that would let the mandala escape. After all he had done to the Shagane, that would have been the final torture.

The Beastmaster knelt over Saru/Sarin. His body convulsed as his distraught emotions finally took full mastery over him. He shut his eyes in a futile attempt to stem the tears.

A gentle hand touched the back of his neck. Dar ignored it, too caught up in his heinous deeds.

"Be not so condemning of yourself," came Saru's voice from behind. "Choices must be made that go against our beliefs, our very soul. You did what you must . . ."

Dar blinked away the tears. The sage no longer lay sprawled on the ground. Choking back his bitterness at himself, the Beastmaster looked up.

Saru/Sarin gazed down at him, the guardian's face serenely calm. The Shagane aided a shaking Dar to his feet, then guided his fist between them.

"It is earned," the double voice said quietly.

The female hand unfolded Dar's fingers. In it, the hard-won mandala gently vibrated.

A bright, orange pattern rose just above his palm. Within it were spirals upon spirals and within them diamonds and stars. At the center, what appeared to be a sun glowed the brightest. Each of the designs also included fine scrollwork within, the latter layered minutely until the detail became too tiny for even the Beastmaster's sharp eyes to make out.

The mandala flew from his palm to a spot just above the nose and in the middle of the brow. There, so Baraji had taught him, was the unseen location of the Third Eye. Dar, still shaking, did nothing as the mandala sank into his body. On his chest formed a tattoo of the intricate pattern.

As that happened, he felt something else awaken in him, and a sense of wonder mixed with his shattered emotions. Dar felt what he could only describe as a growing sense of wisdom or perhaps greater insight into guiding his own future.

"It is time you returned to your friends. Your path still has long to go."

Saru/Sarin led him toward the waterfall. For the first time, the Beastmaster saw the beauty of the rising water. He also saw in it the answer he should have known in the first place.

"What do you wish to be guided to?" Saru/Sarin asked, still smiling serenely.

"Within," he immediately replied. Only by following the path within himself could he ever hope to save Ancor.

At that moment, Dar heard a very welcome voice.

"Dar!" Tara wrapped her arms around him. "Dar! You've been gone an entire day! Are you all right?"

He tried to understand her. "A . . . day?"

"Time is an inaccurate measurement," Brother Ontas remarked from behind her. He glanced at Dar, then behind him.

"He has made hard choices," Saru/Sarin said to the astonished party. The Shagane backed up to the reversed waterfall. "He may have to make harder ones yet." The sage bowed to the Beastmaster. "We do not envy you . . ."

The figure stepped into the raging water. There Saru/Sarin suddenly glowed white.

The two halves peeled away in opposite directions . . . and, as they did, two fully formed figures came into being. Now Saru and Sarin were separate.

They looked into one another's tearful eyes, their love obvious. Smiles graced their handsome faces. The pair touched hands together and leaned in to kiss.

But as they did, their bodies washed away in the upward flow, dissipating as if the pair were only made of simple foam. Their lips touched just as the last of Saru and Sarin vanished.

Dar's legs buckled. He went to his knees and said a prayer of thanks to and for the saints.

It proved difficult to rise afterward, but with assistance from Tara and Jalan, he kept on his feet long enough to reach a rock near the original stream. There, Dar quickly sat.

"What happened in there?" Tara asked. "What did you have to do?"

He told them. Jalan gaped and Tara shivered. The oracle nodded, his face an emotionless mask. The animals, attuned to Dar's emotions, whimpered, then rubbed their noses—or, in the case of Sharak, beak—against his legs and arms.

The Touargang hugged him tightly, her eyes shut, as she seemed to Dar to be sharing his trials . . . and, he hoped, the deep energies that the opening chakras released throughout him. Tara's arms also helped ease his tensions. He was grateful to all his companions, but somehow her touch meant more to him at the moment than anyone else's.

And that suddenly stirred another concern within him. Saru and Sarin had hinted that there might be other, bitter choices ahead. He had already made several, leaving his animal family behind and now putting the guardians through such torture, something he had never thought himself capable of doing.

What might Dar have to do next . . . and would it mean willingly letting *Tara* suffer even something far *worse* than the rest?

14

As Dar turned his gaze inward, another pair of eyes kept focus on him . . . as they had during and even before the Beastmaster's encounter with the sage.

Zorena watched the would-be champion of Ancor from a distance, the huntress as silent and still as death as she studied the Beastmaster not for the first time. Unlike Kyrik, she liked to know her prey well before striking.

This Dar was a complex creature. His skills and natural instincts as a warrior were impressive, so much so that she dreamed of a moment when she would face him in combat and thus compare their abilities.

But that was not all. His initial reaction to what he had needed to do to earn the mandala had at first struck her as weak, but she began to see that his concern also served to strengthen him. He was not reckless, a fault among many of Vorannos's hunters.

A slight breeze arose, one which nonetheless forced the huntress to depart her hiding place. The breeze also brought to her sharp nose unique scents. Ancor was filled with unique scents, unique sensations, but so had other worlds Vorannos had conquered. No, what was so astounding about her time here was that Zorena had *noticed* all those things, noticed them as she had on no other world. There was a primal sense of life here—a young and wild sense of life—that called to her.

But the fiery-haired huntress quickly buried such thoughts, both because of their treasonous nature and the fact that, as with all else, those aspects of Ancor would soon cease to be. All would be transformed once Vorannos had the Fountain. Ancor would again match her twin, but this time wearing Ishram's face, not the other way around. As it should be.

Still . . . as Zorena maneuvered around to make certain that she could remain near without either the champion or his animals detecting her, she continued to take in Ancor's bounty. After all, what harm was there? The better she knew her surroundings, the better she could serve her master.

And to serve Vorannos was her only reason for existing. So it had always been, so it would always be.

Always . . .

THE WIZENED MAN sat beneath the shade of a huge rock teetering atop a tall, gangly stone. Each time the wind blew, the larger rock shifted dangerously above the elderly figure. Yet he made no move away from the threat, instead seeming quite satisfied to live so precariously.

Eyes nearly blind from cataracts blinked once. The concave chest rose and fell only twice each minute. The next gust of wind not only shook the rock, but sent the man's wispy white beard and equally thin, shoulder-length hair fluttering.

The sage—for he could be nothing else—was naked of clothing, but well clad of tattoo. A great one spread across his chest, around his sides, and finished at the center of his back. An array of decorated leaves filled the pattern, some of them red, others green, yellow, and more. The mandala was the visual essence of the sage's decades-long search into himself, a search with some failure, but more success.

A shadow crossed his lined countenance, one with no link to the rock above. The eyes blinked once and the head slowly turned to the source of that shadow . . . and the ones that now joined it.

The Pygmesian's oversized helmet filled his view, the ancient's face reflected in the thick, glass lenses. The toadlike creature uttered several clacking sounds.

"I am testing a theory," came a voice that for the first time caused the sage to shift, if even only a little. "You are to be the culmination of it."

The monstrous hunters moved aside to open the way for Vorannos. The elder's eyes blinked twice as the lord of Ishram approached him. Vorannos's eyes gazed avariciously at the mandala the other wore.

"I have such patterns myself now," he informed the wizened figure.

In truth, Vorannos had *many* mandalas now tattooed over his torso and his arms. Six they were, each distinct from the other.

The sage said nothing, though his weak eyes lingered on the mandalas.

"I need but one more . . . and that would be yours, I think."

A pair of Pygmesians rushed up and seized the sage under the arms. They dragged him to Vorannos, for the ancient's legs appeared no longer strong enough for standing.

Vorannos's mirror eyes came close to the elder's.

The path to understanding requires introspection and cannot be bought or stolen . . .

The sage's reply had been quick and direct . . . and had emerged not from his closed lips but seemingly formed as misty silver words in the air before the conqueror's glittering gaze. Yet this astounding act did nothing to impress Vorannos and, indeed, his *words* only made the lord of Ishram grin more darkly.

"There is nothing, fool, that cannot be taken, one way or another."

Vorannos seized the ancient by the throat. The two Pygmesians retreated. The lord of Ishram raised the sage up as if he were nothing.

"Nothing . . ." he repeated.

From Vorannos's hand, a black force enshrouded the sage. The elder's eyes focused on Vorannos as they thus far had not.

"And that is all that can be taken into the soul through evil," the wizened man intoned. "Nothing."

His body jerked as the black aura enveloped him. The ancient let out a gasp and his mouth gaped.

Vorannos grinned wider, drinking in the sight of his terrifying power at work. The sage's arms and legs began flailing of their own volition. The skin sagged, and within, it was as if the bones and sinews were suddenly turned into liquid. The body lost all shape, even the head, which flopped back like an empty sack.

The eyes rolled in on themselves, then vanished utterly. A terrible moistness formed below the sacklike corpse. It spilled over the ground and rolled away.

The lord of Ishram surveyed his foul work with great pleasure and satisfaction. He shook the macabre sack of flesh, then turned it so that the mandala was most prominent.

Mechanisms within his other hand went to work as soon as Vorannos pointed his finger at the pattern's edge. With grotesque efficiency, a small, crimson light from the fingertips precisely *cut* the skin containing the mandala from the rest.

The hunters watched with morbid fascination and complete obedience. If any had the capacity to be at all repelled by the evil deeds before them, they were wise enough not to show even the slightest hint.

Like a seamstress, Vorannos carefully turned the loose flesh as necessity dictated. Within a few minutes, he had the mandala perfectly removed.

Tossing the rest of the gnarled remains contemptuously away, the lord of Ishram eyed his prize. He looked down upon his bare chest, eyeing the largest empty space.

Vorannos clasped the skin to his own body as if he hugged tight a lover. Within him, more tiny mechanisms awoke. They sought out the skin of the sage and began redesigning it. As they did, the skin not only adhered to his chest, but began to become *part* of it.

Other areas of Vorannos's flesh also changed, as his body made room for his latest and largest prize. The lord of Ishram gritted his teeth, the only sign of discomfort. Yet he still bore traces of his smile, his pleasure outweighing all else.

The alteration was done in only the space of a few breaths. Vorannos stepped back and gazed down upon his chest.

"It is done," he said to himself, none of his servants meaning a thing to him. They only existed to fulfill his will.

Seven mandalas he wore. Seven, as decreed in the prophecy. Seven lives slaughtered in the process.

As Dar followed trails, so, too, had Vorannos. Each tattoo he wore marked also a delicious hunt. There had been the young, pale woman with the eyes sewn shut who had lived in a cave of utter darkness. Following the bats who brought her sustenance in the cave, Vorannos had granted her through his mechanisms a visual image in her head of his glory before summoning a blade from his wrist to slice off first her head and then the tattoo on her back.

He had followed that with tracking the second by means of

Pygmesians beating the brush to raise the seeds and pollen of the wildflowers and plants and watching where the wind took them. Gliding along those same winds, he had come to the gentle giant seated atop a mountain, a figure with childlike features and personality but whose touch on the ground beneath him caused those seeds to sprout into plants that fed the goats and other animals existing in the area. For him, Vorannos had granted a special favor: he had cut the tattoo from the still living body, then let the sage enjoy the spectacle of flying among the peaks—for a few amusing seconds before the laws of nature sent the still-smiling giant plummeting.

Torturing a few mountain folk by means of extracting their limbs had given him the clues to the third, a pious monk with a shaven head who twice in an hour would rise and beat upon a huge bronze gong set in the middle of a crumbling monastery. Despite the fact that striking the gong made no sound, the monk had seemed quite dedicated to his task, so Vorannos had left his body—minus the area of the tattoo—so that the wind would now and then let it swing hard against the gong.

For the fourth and fifth, he had gone to the sea, where one had been located by his pipe playing, sounds that caused calm where there should have been storm. Breaking the pipe had caused a maelstrom to form and Vorannos had used terrible force to batter off what he did not need of the sage's flesh, finally adding the patch to those already on his body. The fifth had actually been only a short distance from that one, for the two had been brothers. Vorannos had followed the ruined corpse along the flow of the storm, where it had gone to its sibling.

And as for the one previous to the latest of Vorannos's victims, she had been an elderly woman whom he had located through the horath. They had found her sitting in the midst of a constant flow of lava, which missed her only because of a delicate wall of flowers that she had built. Unimpressed, the lord of Ishram had dropped from the sky with the horath and seized her by her right leg, where the tattoo was. With a wave of his hand, he toppled the wall of flowers and let the flow cover all but the leg, from which he afterward removed his prize.

And that none had shown any fear or even concern had only briefly annoyed Vorannos each time, but no more so than their supposed words of wisdom, which had always concerned true seeking and the earning of enlightenment. Vorannos had lived longer than any of them and he had learned in that time that *everything* could be taken. He earned by right of utter dominance, the only true path.

Smiling at both the successful end to his grand hunt and the glory that would now be his, Vorannos looked to the shrouded sky and called out, "I have done it! I hold the key! Show me now that which is mine! Show me the Fountain!"

The wind swept up around him. Vorannos stretched forth his hands.

But the wind passed without any revelation.

A couple of the Pygmesians stirred, all the hunters suddenly uneasy.

Vorannos thrust one hand toward those that had moved. With a shout of rage, he reduced them to burning cinders.

The rest of his servants remained as motionless as statues. Still roaring his fury, the lord of Ishram peered up at the delicately balanced rock.

Now there was a response, albeit not as Vorannos desired. The sky suddenly crackled with lightning and thunder even though there were no clouds. A burst of wind as powerful as a tornado ripped through the area, carrying with it the lord of Ishram's fury.

Vorannos continued to shout. He sought out something upon which to vent his rage. With but a gaze, he shattered the balancing rock to rubble, which then rained down on his remaining servants.

The rubble should also have fallen upon the unfortunate sage's remains, but those were no longer to be found. Instead, as the bits of rock fell, they were met by a flurry of small, airborne seeds such as might have blown from a wildflower. Those seeds, though, all but went unnoticed by Vorannos in his wild anger . . . just as had the similarly astounding and mysterious vanishing of the other bodies during his incessant hunt.

AND FAR AWAY, others caught some hint of that terrible response. Dar stirred from meditating to see the flashes in the distance and, moments later, the pale, almost foglike sheet that flew upon the wind. Oddly, although the wind rushed to where he and his party camped, it only caressed the Beastmaster and his friends.

Brother Ontas stirred just long enough to gaze up and quietly say, "The souls of many sages have passed from this plane. They go to the Valley of Flowers, having earned their places in the next existence . . ."

Baraji had once mentioned such a place, a peaceful valley where all the colors of Creation existed in beautiful, ever-blossoming flowers and those who had persevered would learn their true place in all things. Dar had briefly expected to find that the Fountain would be located there, but that notion had quickly proven wrong.

The sky grew calm again. The Beastmaster returned to his meditations . . . and tried not to think of why so many sages would have perished . . .

SEVEN HAD DIED for the tattoos he wore, the mandalas that he thought would make dealing with the Beastmaster unnecessary. But though he felt something, it was an unfamiliar sensation that absolutely repulsed him. In no way did it open his mind to the Fountain, and so he utterly rejected it.

As if he were a hound shaking off water from his coat, Vorannos now shook free any interest in his failed hunt. There was only one thing that mattered to him . . . and it appeared that he would need it from the Beastmaster.

The very thought resurrected his rage, made Vorannos curse the sky and briefly cause anew the thunder and lightning.

Vorannos would have what he desired . . . no matter the terrible cost to all else, especially the Beastmaster.

THERE WAS NO time for Dar to truly rest. He had but two of the mandalas; five more were needed. The shroud from the south now extended well over the jungle through which they rushed, and those animals he met along the way—and immediately sent toward Edurac—informed him of dire things moving through the area. Worse, there were times when the wind blowing from the south, or even the west, hinted of the unnatural scents the invaders emanated.

"Are we near the next of the mandalas?" Tara asked, her tone tense. They had all grown more tense over the past few hours, all save Brother Ontas. The oracle carried about himself an aura of sublime calm, as if he awaited something he had expected his entire life. What it was, the man gave no hint at, but Dar hoped that the oracle's mood marked a kind of hope that he himself did not feel.

What he did feel was that he was indeed on the correct path. With each step, Dar felt certain that he was nearly upon the guardian of the next mandala he needed. At times, Dar even found himself moving along with his eyes closed, his Third Eye instinctively taking over now that they were so close.

"Why only particular mandalas?" he had asked Brother Ontas earlier. "Will not any do, so long as they open the chakras?"

"But they must open the right chakras, in the right order, and for the right purpose. Let not fear or doubt ensnare you now. Follow as you have followed."

Dar would have preferred a more definite comment than the last, but he knew better than to seek one from the robed man.

Sharak and Ruh kept watch on the path for any signs—such as the odd turn of a tree or the reversed flow of a river—that might hint of the mandalas or even the Fountain. The eagle covered the sky with a little assistance from Seto. Although Dar did not have the greatest faith in the parrot, for once Seto appeared to take matters seriously. It was possible much of that had to do with Jalan, who had taken a stand against the bird's antics after seeing how shaken the Beastmaster had been.

"You've got to be really good for Dar," he had caught the boy saying just before they had left the waterfall. "He needs to concentrate hard, so we all have to watch out for any monsters, you understand?"

"Jalan!" Seto had merrily responded and although Dar had not taken this as anything positive, Jalan had nodded as if the parrot had sworn a blood oath to protect the Beastmaster.

But Seto was hardly a concern at the moment. Dar cared only for his goal. He glanced down at his body, now tattooed with both mandalas he had gained. Running a hand over one of the mandalas, Dar prayed that he would find the other five and find them quickly.

The Beastmaster had come to a realization about the years during which he had studied with Baraji. The sage had not been trying to teach Dar enlightenment; rather, he had been preparing him for the journey through life he would need to achieve it. Only through experience and strong belief could Dar actually gain the understanding for which he strived.

They continued to cross paths with animals heading away from the ruined lands, and these beasts Dar immediately sent to Edurac. It mattered not if it was a herd of antelope, serpents crawling through the brush, or wild boars . . . they all listened.

Tara marveled at his constant communication with the various animals and how they all did as he asked of them. "Only you could manage this, Dar! So many! Surely they'll be of help to the defenders . . ."

"I can only hope so." But he knew that they would not be enough. He had to reach the Fountain before the invaders . . . if he could.

The stench that accompanied the black smoke grew stronger, indication that they more and more skirted the lands razed by the invaders. The crimson aura rose briefly to the south, then faded again. The Beastmaster could only assume that more of the fireballs had fallen from the sky on that distant location. He prayed that the people and animals had already fled.

Despite the fact that Sharak now flew farther ahead again, the eagle discovered nothing that hinted of their goal. Yet, late in the day, even as the bird again circled back, Dar thought that he heard something. At first he imagined it rushing water, but then it sounded more like a crackling fire.

He sent Sharak in that direction, but the avian again came up empty. Dar frowned.

"What is it?" Tara asked him.

"That noise . . . it's close, but Sharak can't find the location."

"What sound?" Jalan interrupted.

Tara glanced at the boy, then nodded. "What sound do you mean, Dar?"

He looked at the other three in confusion. Brother Ontas looked interested but clearly did not know what he meant, either.

"Raging water . . . like the waterfall, but also fire, as if the jungle itself were on fire." Clearly that was not the case. Not only would the smoke and burning scent be evident to everyone, but this close they would surely have seen the flames.

The others shook their heads. Even the animals indicated that they heard nothing. Yet the Beastmaster continued on in that direction, the sounds strong in his ears.

The others' reactions did not disturb Dar but rather made him hopeful. He picked up the pace, leading the party to where he thought the sounds originated. Yet, even despite his certainty that he was so close, Dar still took the time to speak with whatever animals were near, in this case a band of chimpanzees moving among the treetops. Like the other creatures, they agreed to head to Edurac.

With some hope, he also asked them if they knew the source of the sounds, but only a younger male showed any hint at all of possibly understanding. Dar eyed the direction the male indicated and felt deep within himself a swelling confidence.

The jungle landscape rose just ahead, culminating in a steep hill. Dar had to help Brother Ontas with the climb up, but otherwise the party did not need to slow. Still, the Beastmaster wondered if both he and the chimpanzee were wrong. The jungle on the other side grew thicker, not clearer, and the sounds of water and fire had become fainter with each step.

But no sooner did they reach the top than Dar was assailed once more by the odd sounds. This time they were so loud that he nearly had to cover his ears. The others, too, finally heard as he did.

"Where does the noise come from?" Tara shouted.

Dar surveyed the land below . . . and suddenly the trees before him opened up as if gaining feet. A narrow clearing greeted his eyes . . . and within it he sighted the guardian of the next mandala.

The sage was an older man with a beard reaching his chest. He sat cross-legged in the center of the clearing. Even from where he stood, Dar thought that the man looked extremely hungry and he certainly was parched. His lips were wrinkled and flakes of skin hung from them.

Yet Dar did not look so long at the man's face, for the latter's body demanded more attention. Wrapped around the figure's torso was a tattoo of a vast yellow-tinted mandala. Within it, Dar saw images of bodies of water—rivers, lakes, and seas—intertwining with symbols representing various aspects of fire, such as a torch and the sun.

But even that sight was not what the Beastmaster stared at longest. Rather, it was what flanked the obviously hungry and thirsty sage.

Towering over the bearded man's left was a high wall of rushing water that began and ended abruptly in thin air. Unlike the waterfall, the flow of the wall was downward. There was also a clarity to it, as if there was not even the slightest bit of dirt or other grit. As Dar looked close, he also saw that this astounding vision seemed to be trying to float toward the seated figure.

As if that was not amazing enough, on the opposing side was the source of the other sound. An equally unsettling wall of flame tormented the sage there and, like the water, appeared eager to come nearer yet.

Dar approached alone. Up close, he saw that the naked figure sat on a small path of dried coals.

The sage turned his pale, brown eyes to him.

"You are the seeker," the seated figure croaked. "I am Nanda. I have been waiting for you so long . . . so very, very long." However, as an amazed Dar silently took a step toward him, Nanda ever so slightly shook his head. "Come no closer, for the balance must not be upset."

"What—what are these two walls? What is their purpose?"

"They are fire and water. They are life and death. The twin sides of purity, for what cleanses the world more than they? They are brothers but mortal enemies, always seeking to quench or scorch one another."

"Why do you not let them?"

The sage barely shook his head. "If they were to have their way, they would take all Ancor with them. That is why I sit here, acting as a buffer to their hunger for one another's destruction."

Dar could not imagine such a task. He eyed the unfortunate sage. "Why you?"

"Before I saw the truth of everything, I was as they. I seek to make amends for that life."

Just a little out of reach of the sage was a weathered bowl filled with water. Dar suspected that even if Nanda tried to snatch it up quickly, it would take him from his position too long. "Can I—may I give you something to drink?"

The naked man shook his head. "Were I to take a sip first, it would mean that I favor water. Were I to eat a crumb first, it would mean I favor fire, for what is food but fuel for our own fire? I must remain in balance or else I cannot keep them in balance."

Grimacing at such a fate, Dar decided that he could do nothing for the sage. That left him only the reason for his being here, though he felt guilt at even asking for anything.

"You called me a seeker. Do you know what I seek?"

Nanda opened his mouth, then shut it. At first, the Beastmaster thought that the sage did not know how to answer . . . but then he looked deeper into the bearded figure's eyes.

In them, Dar suddenly beheld a warning.

At the same time, the ground began to shake.

From behind him, Tara cried, "Dar! It's opening up behind you!"

He thought at first she meant that the trees were moving farther apart, but then came the savage, cracking sound. Aware of what it presaged, the Beastmaster tried to leap to safety—

The chasm that opened beneath him proved much wider than he had calculated. Instead of landing safely on one side, Dar had to grasp for the very edge.

He failed.

He slid down the chasm a short distance before managing to

find some handhold. Unfortunately, Dar could feel that the rock to which he so desperately clung was quickly loosening. Worse, there was nowhere else he could reach.

Some distance away, he heard his friends shouting, but they were too far.

From his pouch, the ferrets emerged. In his eagerness to reach the sage, the Beastmaster had this time forgotten to hand the pouch to Tara. Now Kodo and Podo scurried up past Dar, using their claws to find hold where the human could not.

The pair was not abandoning Dar. Rather, they rushed up to the top and began seeking something with which to help him climb to freedom. Through his link with their minds, Dar knew immediately that the ferrets could not find anything of use. Above dangled strong creeper vines, but by the time either Kodo or Podo could climb high enough and gnaw through the thick vegetation, their human brother would be long dead.

Indeed, the Beastmaster could already feel the rock shifting. Although well aware of the futility of it, Dar looked to the distant treetops. If only Tara or Brother Ontas were nearby, one of them might be able to pull a vine free—

But while neither of his companions was near, Dar found himself staring into the eyes of an unexpected figure. Perched atop a thick branch, the young male chimpanzee with whom he had communed earlier eyed the Beastmaster with thoughtful eyes, then reached for the nearest vine.

With a powerful tug, the primate freed the vine. He tossed it unerringly to the ferrets, who immediately nudged one end over to Dar.

At first, the Beastmaster thought the vine too short, but at the last moment it seemed to extend just enough. Dar grabbed hold of the vine just as the rock gave way, wondering if doing so would do him any better. Kodo and Podo were not in themselves strong enough to do more than slow his fall.

Yet the vine not only held, but it began drawing Dar up. He held tight, watching for any chance to grab hold of something more secure.

A hand thrust out to him. Tara's. Dar gladly seized it. As the Touargang pulled him to safety, the Beastmaster also saw that the ferrets had not been alone after all. Ruh stood behind them, the end of the vine in his great maw.

Brother Ontas also stood there, and from his look of concentration, Dar suspected that the oracle was the reason the vine had suddenly seemed longer than at first.

Dar's nostrils flared as a monstrous scent filled them.

"Beware!" he warned the others.

From the jungle burst several Pygmesians. The toadlike villains pointed their tube weapons at the party.

Muttering, Brother Ontas waved his left hand to the side.

The first of the tubes fired . . . but the bolts flew astray, just missing their targets.

Dar had no time to admire the oracle's power, for out of the corner of his eye, other figures were approaching not his party, but rather the seated sage. Sword unsheathed, he spun to face the first, a brawny creature shaped like a man but scaled like a reptile. The fearsome figure wielded a deadly, curved blade in one hand and some larger version of a tube weapon in the other.

Their swords clashed. The lizard man pointed the other weapon at Dar—and a wild-maned woman with hair like fire broke between them. Her exotic beauty was only marred by the devilish pleasure she radiated as she attacked the Beastmaster. Dar was pressed back by a flourish of strikes that put his natural agility and skill to their greatest test.

"Fight me . . ." she cooed, almost as if speaking words of adoration to her lover. "Fight me . . ."

Dar did, of course. Fearful of what might be happening to Nanda and his friends, he tried to look past the woman as they battled . . . and for his inattention received a light slash across his left cheek.

"There is only me for you," the warrior woman purred.

Dar grew furious. He had no time for games, however deadly. So many lives, not just those of Tara, Dar, Ruh, and the rest, depended on his meager self.

His sword flashed left, right, left, under, over. Her expression shifted from eagerness to fear . . . and then, perversely, admiration. She pressed her own attack and momentarily held him from further advantage, but Dar adjusted, his instincts telling him where and when she would move her sword just before she did.

He finally struck the weapon from her grip and as she grabbed for it, hit her hard across her chin. Dar waited only long enough to watch her fall stunned before he turned to the others.

But the awful tableau that he had expected had not come to pass, though the situation was still a desperate one. Tara and Ruh stood at the forefront of a battle with Pygmesians and the reptiles and the bodies on the ground gave evidence of the combined might of the Touargang princess and the tiger. The ferrets aided in the struggle, slipping among the squat, demonic fighters and biting at hoses and other vulnerable connections. Sharak and Seto dove, blinding those that Tara had cut down.

Jalan stood guard by Brother Ontas, who at first glance appeared asleep. In truth, though, the oracle protected the boy, for Dar saw one villain after another somehow miss their presence. Yet that was not likely all the robed figure did, for Dar saw more than one attacker stumble badly as they tried to aim at or attack Tara and Ruh.

The party had one unexpected ally: the chimpanzee that had tossed the vine down earlier now hovered over Tara's location. He threw branches and other objects at any of the attackers who drew near her.

Then Dar looked to Nanda. The reptilian hunters stood before and behind the bearded man, eyeing the sage's position—and especially the two astounding walls—with wariness.

One finally reached for the motionless sage.

The walls of fire and water shifted, spinning around so that they now blocked the paths of both creatures. The one reaching for Nanda pulled back a hand whose fingers were singed. Whether it was by the sage's will or that of the water and fire, Nanda appeared protected.

Before that could change, Dar threw himself at the nearest reptile, who turned too late. Dar punched him hard in the chest, then threw him over his shoulder.

The second met him even as the first tumbled away. Fetid breath assailed the Beastmaster. One scaled hand turned a tube weapon toward Dar's face.

The Beastmaster twisted the hand backward just as his adversary fired. Rather than stop firing, the reptile set off several wild shots. He grinned, though Dar knew no reason why. Still, that grin suddenly invoked within the Beastmaster a fury such as he had never felt. He had no greater desire than to rip his foe limb from limb.

The reptile's grin did not falter despite Dar's clear vehemence. Instead, he whispered in a tongue Dar did not understand, almost as if speaking with someone unseen.

The scaled killer vanished in a golden glow that momentarily blinded Dar. The Beastmaster swung wildly, certain that his foe was still somewhere near. Yet as his eyes cleared, he saw no sign whatsoever of the foul creature.

But what he did see horrified him.

Nanda lay slumped on the coals, his body as white as ice. Two retreating Pygmesians sought to drag the still figure away and this time the water and fire walls did nothing to stop them. With Nanda no longer there to keep them in balance, the elemental forces converged slowly but determinedly on each other.

Dar leaped at one of the Pygmesians, striking through the hose at the front of the helmet. As that foe collapsed, he drove his sword through the second.

The second Pygmesian sprawled lifeless. Ignoring all else, Dar went to the sage's side and touched Nanda's arm in the hope that he might yet find life within. All thought of the hunt for the mandala had fled the Beastmaster's mind.

He recoiled, his horror magnified a thousand times. Nanda did not just look as white as ice . . . he was ice.

Dar had no idea what sort of dark sorcery or alchemy had caused it, but he knew that the reptile's tube weapon had been the source of the tiny needles sticking out of the sage's body. Perhaps that had been why the creature had grinned. He had intended for his confederates to steal away Nanda's body while the Beastmaster had been occupied. If not for the sudden, almost uncontrollable moment of rage—

But Dar suddenly had no time to concern himself with that brief, unsettling moment, for then he became aware that the two walls were moving in on one another. Thrusting away retreating Pygmesians, Dar glanced down at Nanda . . . then rolled over to the path of coals. He sat himself down in a cross-legged position as Nanda had, then tried to draw from the chakras and his learning a sense of peace despite the looming presence of the two powerful forces.

The walls ceased moving. More important, they moved back to their previous positions. However, Dar could now sense their hunger for one another, their desire to quench or burn their opposite. It would always be there, just as he sensed also that there would always be a serene balance between them, as Creation demanded.

As the walls stilled, the crevasse closed, allowing Dar's companions to reach him. Brother Ontas stepped up next to the

Beastmaster. The oracle gazed down at him with a brooding expression.

Jalan, Tara, and the animals, including even the chimpanzee, joined him. The Touargang reached out a hand—

The water and fire started to shift.

"No!" commanded Dar. "No one comes near!"

"Dar!" she anxiously called. "Get away from there!"

"I cannot. If I do, Ancor will see destruction as terrible as that by the invaders . . ." He quietly told them what Nanda had said.

They were horrified. Tara looked to Ontas for help, but the oracle shook his head.

"The choice was Dar's. He is able to take this one's place. I would take it for him in turn, but that is not to be my fate." Before Tara could answer back, Brother Ontas added, "And nor is it yours or the boy's. Were any of us to attempt it, these elemental forces would finally clash." The oracle glanced at the Beastmaster again. "It is Dar's quest and Dar's alone. Only he can make the choices."

"You must go on without me," the Beastmaster urged, resolute in his decision. "It seems my part in the prophecy is ended, Brother Ontas. It is up to you, Tara . . . and you, too, Jalan," he added with a sad smile to the boy. "You must succeed."

He settled into his meditation, seeking to attain the level he had atop the glacier. Some doubts briefly assailed him, doubts about whether he was making the right decision, whether or not he had failed his quest, and whether he had abandoned his friends. Yet the Beastmaster fought down those doubts, recalling that if he had decided not to take up Nanda's arduous task, there would not even be an Ancor left to protect, anyway. Now at least there was still hope, even if he was no longer a part of it. He also considered his decision justice for not having strived harder in the first place . . . and for letting Nanda perish.

His eyes closed. The physical world began to retreat.

. . .

"DAR!" TARA CALLED from what to the Beastmaster suddenly felt so far, far away.

Brother Ontas tried to make Tara leave, but she would not have it. "There must be more to this!" She went to the sage's frozen body, leaning close. "The mandala is right here and you have the others, Dar!" The Touargang focused her distress on the mandala itself, as if it were a living thing. "This wasn't Dar's fault! He earned you as he did the others . . ."

Without at first realizing it, the female warrior began a prayer of hope that she had known as a child. As she spoke, the Touargang's fingers softly touched the pattern.

Tara let out a gasp that was echoed by the other humans. Almost as if it were awakening, the tattoo vibrated gently. As she bent back in surprise, the pattern rose above Nanda's body, growing smaller as it did. It then floated to Dar as he sat in a deep trance.

But that was not all. Nanda suddenly opened his eyes wide and looked at Dar.

"Your choice came from your heart," he said, answering the Beastmaster's doubts. "And so she will not let you suffer them anymore. She is yours."

It was apparent to Dar that the "she" was the mandala. Even as Nanda spoke, the pattern took up a place over the Beastmaster's heart.

"So it is done," the sage said, closing his eyes again.

His body melted then, becoming both flame and water that poured into a small pit where he had lain. The fire and liquid intermingled but did not destroy each other. They then spread around the vicinity of the pit. Wherever the water spilled, green life grew. The flames caressed the coals, warming them just enough to help that life flourish. The path of coals was now one of grass and flowers, flowers that unleashed pollen into a sudden breeze . . .

Yet, though his body was no more, the sage's spirit still existed. The pollen shaped itself into Nanda's form, hovering over and *through* Dar.

"You sacrificed yourself," it intoned. "You sought atonement. That was the only way for you to earn the mandala . . . and open the chakra it represents."

Dar sensed the new chakra, and though it filled him with more understanding, he still tasted bile in his mouth at the thought of Nanda having to die for it.

The spirit shook his head. "Be not ill for me. Now I may fulfill my duty without hunger, without thirst. I am happy in this and you may rejoice for me . . ."

"Dar—Dar can go?" Tara dared ask.

"He may."

The Beastmaster warily slipped from between the water and fire. Nothing happened. He stood, staring at the sage.

"Nanda—"

"There is much left in your journey, seeker," the sage continued, fading again. His voice now seemed to come not from one place but all around Dar . . . *wherever* the pollen still drifted. "And not all of it will be as simple as this was."

The two elemental walls also vanished. Only the wondrous patch of ground remained . . . that, and the gentle, serene sound of water and fire ever intermingling together.

Brother Ontas put a hand on Dar's shoulder. "We'd best move on, my friend."

Dar frowned . . . then realized that the oracle was correct. The invaders had nearly stolen hope from them this time. They had to move on and on, no matter what the obstacles.

And no matter how much each of the confrontations seemed to try harder to strip the Beastmaster of the very core of his soul.

15

KYRIK EYED THE HUNTRESS AS SHE POLISHED HER BLADE, AND although Zorena pretended his gaze disturbed her not in the least, inside she wanted to swing the sword around and cut off the sorcerer's head.

Which was probably why Kyrik stood just out of reach of such an act.

"Ancor's would-be champion is quite formidable, would you not say, my dear Zorena?"

She did not look up. "Would you expect anything less? It is fated that he fall to our lord, it seems."

"Mayhaps . . . though the failure on your part may not enable you to live to enjoy that spectacle."

Zorena could ignore everything except the word "failure." She leaped to her feet, the point of her blade aimed for where Kyrik's heart should have been . . . had he one in the first place.

"If there was failure, it was due to your decision to attempt this plan in the first place! What a fool's quest I agreed to partake in! We are fortunate that it still served to urge the champion to greater haste in recovering the other necessary mandalas! Vorannos may let us both live because of that!" She sneered. "Ha! To think that you believed we could take not only the one from the sage, but strip those already worn by the Beastmaster!"

The cowled figure chuckled. "Oh, I never truly believed that . . . but convincing you that it was possible was necessary, otherwise I could not have tested this Dar of Emur properly. You needed to believe so that he, in turn, would not suspect anything other than what he saw happening . . ."

" 'Tested?' 'Never truly believed?'" Zorena lunged at him, but, like the specter he so resembled, Kyrik proved elusive. "What do you mean?"

"I mean that the primitive will be made to serve our lord Vorannos willingly and so bring a swift end to this charade. Lord Vorannos wishes the Fountain, and he who provides him with the means to do it quickly will be most favored."

Zorena was not impressed by the sorcerer's statement. She already knew all that. "Obviously."

Kyrik drifted further back. His smile was like that of a hungry wolf. "It would be interesting to see this world's only hope fighting alongside us, don't you think? I believe you would especially find that amusing, my dear Zorena."

"What do you infer?"

He shrugged. "Only that he and you would make a formidable pair . . . in combat."

The huntress snorted. Turning from him, she began to work on her weapon again. Kyrik hovered near her for a moment longer, then, with another chuckle, gave a mock bow.

"I go to serve our great and magnanimous lord. I shall keep you informed of my success, my dear Zorena . . . and, if you like, bring the Beastmaster to you when I am done."

She gave another snort. After a moment, her highly attuned senses marked his vanishing.

Zorena exhaled. She was grateful for the solitude of the jungle. Kyrik's hints had struck closer to home than she liked. Her confrontation with Ancor's champion had left her confused, something she did not like . . . and yet found enticing. The Beastmaster—Dar—had not only impressed her further with his magnificent fighting skills, but his very demeanor, his very bearing, had struck some long-buried part of her.

It was this world, she tried to convince herself. It was infecting her somehow. Zorena had found herself pausing to savor a breeze, feel the coolness of its night . . . and admire the one who stood against her master.

Kyrik suspected that there was something amiss with her, but Zorena knew that he could prove nothing. She had not betrayed Lord Vorannos in any manner and never would. The huntress would applaud Kyrik if he succeeded in turning Dar to their side, for it would please their master and that was all that mattered. Ancor would then give up the Fountain to Vorannos.

All would be as it should and, assuming he lived, the Beastmaster would become one more warrior to serve their lord's glory.

One more.

Zorena frowned.

SHARAK WARNED THEM of the horrific tableau ahead just before the first stench wafted past Dar's nostrils. Ruh let out a growl of distaste and the ferrets hid in their pouch. Tara, also smelling what lay ahead, clutched Jalan tightly.

Brother Ontas muttered what Dar realized was a prayer. How useful that would be, the Beastmaster did not know, but he was glad to hear it, if only for himself.

Though the jungle stood all around them, they had found little food in the last two days with which to supplement their shrinking supplies. The rivers and streams had been oddly empty of fish and none of the trees or bushes had borne any fruit or berries. Dar had been forced to ration what they had left, leaving more for young Jalan than himself. Even the animals had failed to find sustenance, the ferrets not even finding grubs or other insects.

But all that was momentarily forgotten with this new and awful discovery. Even though Sharak enabled Dar to make out that to which they were heading long before they would arrive, seeing it truly with his own eyes struck Dar just as if it were all new again.

The village before them had been razed to the ground, but not with the monstrous effectiveness of those he had seen in the recent past. The bodies of the dead lay strewn all over, the first at the very entrance to the village.

"This is not the work of the invaders, not directly," Dar commented as he studied the ground for footprints and sniffed the air for questionable scents, "but it is the result of their coming to Ancor . . ."

"Xorot of the Claw," Tara muttered.

"Or one of those others who seek to curry favor with the invaders." Rising, Dar cautiously led the party into the village. He was wary not only of possible looters but also of plague or some other deadly disease that flourished among the rotting dead. Most of all, after previous events, he was wary of traps.

Most of the wooden homes had been burnt to the ground, and those that had not often contained ghoulish sights. Dar estimated that it had been nearly two weeks since these people had been slaughtered.

"Swords, spears, and arrows," he noted. "Yes, those that slew them were of Ancor, which makes it all the more monstrous."

"Should we bury them?" Tara asked.

Dar shook his head. He would have liked to, but they did not have the time. They could not even gather the bodies and burn them.

A continued search revealed no edible food nor even drinkable water. Dar was reminded of Nanda's situation.

Then the Beastmaster paused. He sensed something close by.

"That way," he suddenly announced, pointing to the southern edge of the village.

A river flowed next to the settlement, but not one in which any of them thought to satiate their thirst or wash the dust and sweat from their bodies. Either desire could have quickly led to disaster, as at least two *dozen* torn bodies attested.

Crocodiles rested on the banks. Others swam along the river, their routes veering toward where the party stood. Dar counted more than fifteen and knew that this particular predator might exist here in double that number.

He sought to speak with them, but though he could touch their minds, they were oddly hostile. None would listen.

"There is something wrong here," he whispered to the others. "They act as if—"

Someone was singing. He, Tara, and the others paused to listen. The song had no rhyme or reason, sometimes rising or falling unexpectedly, and with no seeming end.

"Who would sing among such carnage as this?" Tara asked disbelievingly. "I walked among the dead of my people for a whole day! I had no voice with which to cry, much less sing . . ."

"Grief comes in many forms," Ontas suggested. "When my father, my mother, and my sister perished from plague, I laughed madly for more than an hour at life's cruel jest . . . and only ceased when I realized that I was laying blame where it did not belong." He smiled. "And then it was that I first began my own quest to find enlightenment—"

"Listen!" the Beastmaster told them. "It is not just singing. He speaks, too."

Indeed, on random occasion, the singing was punctuated by

sudden muttering, as if the singer had conversation with himself. Then the song would go on from where it had last been interrupted.

And then, there among the dead, Dar spotted a ragged figure in a soiled loincloth, an old man with wild hair and wilder eyes who looked to be covered in filth. His dirty hair thrust out madly and the Beastmaster swore that he saw small plants growing out of it. The hair all but enveloped the small head, whose most prominent feature was the two wide, round eyes almost bulging out of their sockets. The eyes were all white save for the pupils, which were gray. The man was not blind, though, as evidenced by his agile avoidance of any obstacle in his path.

He waved his hands around as if bidding both hello and farewell to unseen folk. His nails were long, in some cases nearly a foot, and gnarled toward the ends. The man danced at the edge of the water like a long-legged bird regardless of the many crocodiles nearby.

Tara clutched Dar's arm. "A survivor!"

But the Beastmaster doubted that the man would survive long. He had to be mad, for, with astounding agility for one his obvious age, he leaped barefooted between one resting crocodile after another. None of the reptiles snapped at him, though that was likely due to the fact that they had no doubt been feasting on the dead. Still, his luck would soon run out unless they did something.

The Touargang already had a rescue in mind. Tara cautiously strode toward the madman, but the first crocodile she neared took a sudden, intense interest in her. It snapped at the female warrior, who at first tried to prod it with her spear until a second and third crocodile joined in.

The Beastmaster quickly retrieved her. The crocodiles backed up a little but did not retreat. They also refused to listen to Dar's entreaties.

Still, he would not let Tara or anyone else try again. He had the best hope of all of them of reaching the survivor.

"I will get him, Tara," the Beastmaster promised. "Warn me if any of them move behind me." Normally, Dar would not have had to worry so, but with the crocodiles behaving oddly, he was not certain just what to expect. "I think I see a path to take."

The reptiles stirred as he approached, finding far more interest in him than the old man in their midst. The Beastmaster sought again to reach their thoughts, but again they refused. However, unlike when he had gone after Tara, this time the crocodiles did nothing more than watch.

When Dar was near enough, he reached a hand to the mad figure. "Come to me. Can you not see you are in danger?"

Still dancing, the figure replied with some irritation, "Who says I am supposed to see?"

His words made no sense to Dar. The Beastmaster tried again. "You are in danger. Come to me carefully."

The wild-maned elder paused in midstep. Arms bent in imitation of a bird's wings, he snapped, "Whatever for? I don't think we've met!" Raising his voice, the figure shouted, "Leave me alone! You are intruding on my precious work!"

At this outburst, Ruh growled and Tara started forward, only to have Brother Ontas take her by the shoulder and gently pull her back.

Dar indicated both the reptiles and the many dead bodies. "You must beware the crocodiles! They may be full, but one might still decide to add you to their larder . . ."

"These little ones? But my friends wouldn't harm me! They're far too busy . . . and at least they've the politeness to leave me alone!" He turned his gaze from the Beastmaster and began his peculiar song again. Many of the words seemed randomly drawn and some of the changes in pitch and tone caused Ruh and the other animals to twitch their ears or duck their heads at their harshness.

From above, Sharak suddenly called to Dar. Though Tara and

the others could not see what was happening yet, the eagle had spotted several of the reptiles heading toward the shore where Dar and the man stood.

"Your . . . friends?" the Beastmaster cautiously asked, keeping a wary eye on the oncoming creatures.

The dancing figure put down his other foot. He grinned wider. "Yes, I said my friends! Goodness! Do you have trouble with your hearing?"

The Beastmaster grew more and more frustrated but also intrigued. This might be a simple lunatic, but also could very well be the sage for whom he had been looking.

But what if he is not? Dar suddenly thought. *If he is simply mad, I should leave him alone . . . and if he is a demon, I should beware . . .*

His gaze suddenly narrowed as the wild man looked directly at him. The Beastmaster noticed something on the other's face that he could not recall seeing before, right above his eyes. Two tiny wounds above each lid, one a wavy line colored yellow, the other a straight red line with a single dot—also red—above that. They were so subtle that Dar had at first mistaken them for discoloration of the skin, but now he knew them to be far more.

He noticed that his hand had started to raise up toward the wounds as if of its own volition. Lowering it again, the Beastmaster considered the situation carefully. On a hunch, Dar bent down toward the nearest crocodile.

Tara gasped but did not otherwise speak. Ruh let out a warning rumble.

Paying them no mind, the Beastmaster reached his hand to the huge creature's head. The crocodile hissed and the mouth opened slightly.

Dar did not pause even then. He set his hand atop the reptile, then gently patted it as he might have Ruh, the ferrets, or Sharak. The crocodile did not react even when the Beastmaster bent closer.

And there, above the inhuman eyes, Dar suddenly saw the same scars. He leaned back, blinking in surprise.

But with the blinking, the scars suddenly vanished . . . and Dar had to wonder if they had been there at all.

"Ah, they like you . . ." the old man abruptly said, his tone much more cordial than prior. That said, the wild figure turned back to his singing.

"Who are you?" Dar asked. If this were truly the sage, how could the man sing when such despair surrounded him? Had his path somehow caused him to turn his heart from others? How could that be? It went against everything Baraji had taught Dar.

"I am Vaish and you are not! None of you are!" the filthy elder snapped, suddenly impatient with Dar again. Yet there also was a hint of amusement in his tone, as if he enjoyed teasing the stranger before him.

Dar was mindful of some sort of test. He had to trust that this man—if he was the sage—would lead him where he needed to be led. "No," the Beastmaster finaly replied. "We are not Vaish."

With a comic frown, Vaish rubbed his stomach. The sage was even more emaciated than Nanda and looked like nothing more than skin and bones. "I am hungry! Are you hungry, Master of Beasts?"

He knows who I am! Dar was more certain than ever that this was the sage . . . and, if so, then surely everything was part of some test.

Hoping that this would lead to better communications with the apparent sage and thus ease the way to learning about the mandala, Dar nodded. "We are hungry, too, my friends and I. Would you like to eat with us?"

"You are hungry, too? We shall share, then, my young friends . . . but only if you show me your bounty first."

In truth, Dar and his companions had little enough, but when the Beastmaster dug into his pouch for what he carried . . . he found a rip in the bottom through which most of the few remaining nuts and berries had evidently fallen. All that was left was one very dried fig, which he produced nonetheless.

"Oh, we should have a better feast than that!" proclaimed Vaish with more than a hint of amusement at Dar's meager offering. "Let me see . . ." He looked around eagerly, though for what, Dar could not say. "Ah! That looks very delicious! Would you mind bringing it to me?"

Dar glanced over his shoulder to where the sage was pointing . . . and revulsion struck him. There was only one object that Vaish could have meant.

A man's severed and rotting arm lay where the madman had indicated. Dar fixed his unbelieving gaze on Vaish again.

The elder looked impatient. "Do hurry! I am famished!"

"You must be . . . you must be insane!"

"Of course I am!" Vaish went into a fit of anger. He started shouting nonsense words to the jungle, then called Dar and the others—even the animals—a variety of names and insults that had Tara glaring, Jalan red-faced, and even Ruh, Sharak, and the ferrets shocked. Only Ontas remained serene in the face of the verbal onslaught.

At last, apparently running out of breath, Vaish shrugged his bony shoulders. "Very well! If such fare makes you queasy, you may be on your way!" He waved the Beastmaster off. "Be gone! Be gone! I've so much to do and no time to waste on those so unappreciative!"

Dar was very much tempted to leave, despite his need for the mandala. However, he was still suspicious that Vaish was doing all this for his benefit. Still, the Beastmaster wondered what sort of ghoul he faced, and what did that say for the mandala the man guarded? How could any sage suggest such a grotesque feast?

Dar steeled himself. There had to be a point to this and he would find it.

Then, without warning, Sharak dropped down from his high perch in the trees. To Dar's surprise, the eagle landed atop the grisly morsel Vaish desired. The bird eyed Dar.

Although Sharak did not make clear why, the Beastmaster sensed that the avian wanted him to give the arm to the sage. Dar, trusting in the eagle's wisdom, bent down and gingerly plucked the horrific limb from the moist ground. It came away with a sucking sound that nearly made Dar drop it.

Vaish clapped his hands in eagerness as the Beastmaster turned to give him the severed arm. "Wonderful! Doesn't it look enticing?"

The madman held the green and gray arm up to his nose, smelling it as if it were a fine, seasoned roast. He then turned and headed for a small fire near the river that Dar could not recall seeing earlier. Next to the crackling flames sat a wide, iron pan with two handles. Vaish set the limb on the pan, then, cheerfully humming, arranged the pan over the fire.

"By the gods!" Tara blurted from a few yards back. She looked away. Ruh sniffed in disdain, carrion far beneath him even in times of starvation. Brother Ontas wisely obscured Jalan's view. The oracle left the Beastmaster to deal with the horrific meal himself.

Dar could not hide his disgust as the scent of human flesh beginning to cook overwhelmed him. "How can you eat such?" he finally blurted. "How can you even in madness eat it?"

Vaish's expression tightened. Ice-blue eyes silenced Dar. "If there were nothing left to eat, no hope of finding anything to eat, would you then find this morsel more appetizing, Master of Beasts?"

"I . . ." Dar could not answer with certainty what he would do. With starvation imminent, would he do as Vaish suggested?

The sage would not let him rest with even that, adding, "Would you, if must, devour your friends or they you?"

There was one part to that question that he could, in all honesty and despite his disgust, answer. "If it would save their lives and I was dead, I would hope that they would."

"And you, them?"

"I . . . would hope not."

"Fair enough, fair enough." Vaish eyed the sizzling flesh. "Ah! Almost done!" He peered at Dar once more. "And if you had the choice of saving them, saving yourself, by dining on this such fare, would that not be far more appetizing?"

Dar was silent but deep in thought. Consuming carrion, assuming it did not sicken or kill one, was far better than the alternative. "Yes," he finally answered. "It would be."

Indicating the ground next to him, the wild-maned figure said, "Sit and sup! If you find the meal to your liking, then we shall call your friends and all of us will have a merry feast!"

Although doubting that his companions were quite ready for rotting flesh—even the animals—Dar nevertheless seated himself. There was a point to this and he had to have faith. Faith was the key. Besides, if this somehow proved a manner by which to feed the others, that would make it all the worthwhile.

So he hoped . . .

"It may help," Vaish commmented blithely, "if you imagine it instead something better." From behind him he drew a long knife, which he then used to cut a piece for the Beastmaster.

Dar almost lost what little he had left in his stomach but somehow managed to accept the morbid fare. The flesh was hot, but not enough to burn his hands.

"I find," the sage went on, "if you imagine it a soup, for instance, with potatoes, carrots, onions, and other vegetables, it proves quite palatable, Master of Beasts! Go ahead! Think of it as such! It'll do you good, believe me! Look into yourself and think so . . ."

Dar considered the man before him. The sage knew so much

and surely would not lead him astray. If Vaish thought that this would help Dar, then the Beastmaster would try his best.

Belief beyond doubt is the real truth, Baraji had taught him. Dar had practiced long and hard with his mentor in this respect; he prayed that all his practice would help him now.

The Beastmaster shut his eyes, at the same time trying not to inhale through his nose the awful scent. Soup. A fine soup with potatoes . . . carrots . . . onions. Dar had liked onions since he was a small child. He pictured the soups the farmer had made for them, rich in texture, rich in taste. He could almost smell his favorite, one with the spices only his father had known how to add.

Dar opened his eyes and, gritting his teeth, prepared to eat.

Only . . . there was now a small, clay bowl in his palms. The familiar and enticing scent of onions arose from it and the Beastmaster saw several different vegetables floating in the broth.

"Oh, quite delicious!" Vaish exclaimed and when Dar looked to him, he saw that the sage had a similar soup in his bowl. The elder used a wooden spoon to eat. "My compliments on the herbs!"

Over the fire, there now sat a huge pot brimming with more soup. Dar sat there, astounded, then, instead of eating his meal, he asked, "My friends! Can they eat, also?"

"Take it to them! Why else is it all there? Why are there bowls by your side? What a fool question!"

Setting down his bowl, the Beastmaster seized the pot by its handle. He then retrieved the other bowls and spoons—none of which had sat beside him earlier—and carried everything toward Tara, Jalan, and the rest.

And only as he neared them did Dar register the fact that there were *no* bodies anymore. The entire village was empty.

"When did they disappear?" he asked Tara as he handed her the pot and Brother Ontas the bowls.

The Touargang blinked. Even the oracle looked aghast. They had not even noticed the change.

The Beastmaster quickly returned to Vaish. Thus far, they had not even spoken of the mandala, the true reason for this unsettling encounter. Seating himself before the sage, Dar took a bite, then had to ask, "The bodies . . . were they ever there?"

"A very delicious soup!" the ragged figure replied obliviously. "Very delicious!"

Dar tried a more relevant question. "The mandala? Have I earned it? Will you give it to me?"

Vaish leaned close, his eyes hinting again at a sanity he generally did not show. "You understand now, don't you, Master of Beasts? There comes a time when we must make harsh decisions that twist our cherished values to the extreme. We are repulsed by them, but they must be made."

It was true. Never in his life had Dar thought that he would choose to dine as he thought that he would have to. The Beastmaster also understood that this was one of the simplest of such decisions, that there might come other times in his life when he would beg for such an easy choice . . . and yet would still make those other harsh ones that confronted him.

"I understand," he agreed. "Does this mean that you will give me the mandala, or is there more for me to learn?"

Vaish abruptly grew impatient. "Mandala, mandala, mandala! All this talk of giving you a mandala! Why? You already have it, so why do you keep asking such a silly question!" Bowl in hand, the cadaverous man rose. "Go! Eat with your friends! Too much talk here for me! I will go eat with my friends!"

He strode off, still talking to himself about foolish questions . . . and in his wake, the crocodiles one by one turned and followed.

And then it struck Dar like a thunderbolt. In standing, Vaish had revealed something to which the Beastmaster had paid no mind. The colored wounds were no longer visible over the sage's eyes.

No longer concerned about crocodiles, Dar rushed to the river and looked at his reflection as best as the shadowed sky allowed. There, over his eyes, the tiny wounds glistened.

As Dar stared, he saw that the other tattoos had shifted. The emerald-tinted one he had first received for his compassion to the reptile in the pit was now centered on his chest. The orange-tinted mandala obtained from the Shagane now rested on his lower belly. Nanda's tattoo, the reward for Dar's determination to do what he must even if that choice meant other potential troubles, was now set on the mouth of the stomach.

And as he watched, the markings over his eyes faded and on his throat an indigo pattern of triangles ringed with two circles formed. It was the mark of Dar's faith, his intuition, that if he followed Vaish's suggestions, all would go as it must.

He returned to the others, who stared at him in wonder.

"You have it!" Jalan cried.

"Praise be," Tara added. She looked at Dar in concern. "Are you all right?"

"Yes . . . I am just . . . just weary."

And he was. Terribly so. Dar had not realized how much this last test had taken out of him until this very minute.

"You need rest," the Touargang worriedly said, moving toward him. "You look as if you're about to—"

Dar's knees collapsed. The world spun around . . . then turned black.

16

"They're on the move again," Heratos warned.

Leardius and Tal immediately stirred. The three of them had taken up positions near the front wall the night before, then traded turns throughout the next day watching for some sign of movement by the enemy. Since Tal's arrival, the horde had attacked only once . . . and that more of a feint than a true rush.

But now they were at last coming in earnest . . . and the kings all understood that this was to be the great assault. Xorot and his dark master would not be pulling back. They would pound and pound at Edurac until it fell.

Or, if by some miracle, the defenders triumphed.

But thus far, there was no other miracle save the animals, avians, and insects that Dar had sent to them. No hint of the Beastmaster's own return had thus far come, though the continued inflow of Ancor's fauna gave them some little hope, at least. Still, none expected that the Beastmaster's quest would be simple—if even possible.

Yet they had no other choice but to hope, though from what Tal could see before them, that hope was shrinking.

"They will still want the libraries intact," Leardius said as encouragement. "That will slow them. And the animals will slow them, too."

A roar erupted from the horde, some of it from human mouths, some of it not.

"Sound the battle horns!" Leardius shouted. As the trumpeters obeyed, he and Tal left Horatos for their own positions.

Dar's brother leaped down to where a massive band of riders waited. They were all part of the column he had led into Edurac and now they prepared to leave its safety to confront the enemy again. Tal regretted the deaths to come, the brave men who would perish.

But he did not regret that he would lead them.

"Ready for the gates!" he shouted. They were to ride out before Xorot could reach the walls and meet the enemy as hard as they could. Then, when Leardius gave the signal, another force would come to fill the gaps and those left from Tal's would retreat to rest. It was a plan by which the defenders hoped to constantly keep a solid front.

Let us pray it works, Tal thought as he drew his sword. *Let us pray . . .*

The next horn sounded . . . and the gates opened.

With a roar, Dar's brother led the riders through. As he caught sight of the approaching enemy, it was all Tal could do to keep from turning his mount around.

Not just the land, but the dark sky above was *filled* with threat. Metal behemoths of all shapes and sizes flew toward Edurac.

"We're doomed!" someone near him gasped. "We cannot fight that!"

"Silence!" the king warned. "There is nothing we cannot fight and defeat, for we have justice and right behind us! We fight for our people, our loved ones! We fight for all that we hold dear! We fight for all Ancor!"

And to ensure that they understood how much he meant what he said, Tal spurred his steed on. He did not look back, but assumed that the others were close behind. If not, his charge was going to prove as foolish looking as it would be short.

Vorundite faces filled his view. Xorot's warriors wanted their share of the blood.

With a cry worthy of Ruh, Tal swung at the first foe. As his blade sank through the wooden breastplate, he heard his men also close with the enemy. The horde's progress came to a stunning halt as men from both sides traded deadly blows.

But "men" was a loose term with what mixed with the Vorundites. More and more grotesque forms pushed to the forefront, many of them the helmed fighters with which Tal was most familiar, but behind them were giant figures that resembled spiders who had mated with men, batlike forms with only vestigial wings and faces that reminded Tal too much of human faces, and many other monstrosities. As he cut down a second of Xorot's people, Tal wondered how long he and his riders could hold against such.

Above them arose a tremendous humming. Tal thought it some of the sinister flying vessels, but instead swarms and swarms of bees, wasps, and other powerful insects covered the sky above, a cape as vast as that coming from the invaders' side. Dar's brother watched with hope, knowing that the insects had ways of infiltrating anything.

The insects moved with more precision than natural, and there was only one reason for that. Om—situated near the city walls—had managed some sort of communication with them, just as the dwarf had hoped. When Tal had first met Om, he had seen in the dwarf some of the tendencies of his brother. That observation had proven a fortuitous one, Om revealing over the years abilities that had made him invaluable to Tal and Aruk. When the general had suggested to the others that he might in some small way be able to guide the creatures Dar had sent, Tal had not for a moment doubted him.

Yet Om was not the Beastmaster, as he himself had said. Tal knew enough to understand that Om had methods by which to influence even the insects, but he could not speak with them, guide them, with the precision that Dar could.

But it would have to do. Tal *prayed* that it would do until Dar returned.

Then he had no more time to concern himself with anything but keeping alive. He thrust at any vulnerable spot that opened in front of him, well aware that those fighting him were doing the same. Tal thrust again and again, not caring whether his foe was human or, as the lines shifted, things out of his nightmares.

And around him, he knew, the other desperate defenders did the same.

DAR WENT IN and out of consciousness. He was aware of his surroundings at times, but only enough to know that they were no longer the razed village. Tara's worried face appeared several times during his moments of waking and even more often during his long periods of troubled slumber.

Then something dread began to encroach on Dar from the black void in which his mind floated. It touched him in his leg first, creating a numbness that slowly turned into a burning sensation. That burning sensation spread throughout his body and deep into his mind. It grew more terrible, finally causing the Beastmaster to scream.

And, in screaming, finally wake up.

"It's all right, Dar!" Tara's voice cried in his ear. "It's all right!"

He blinked. The world coalesced.

Dar lay on the ground in the middle of the jungle. A small fire had been built to his right and by it sat a concerned Jalan and a strangely serene Brother Ontas. Seto, a piece of dried fruit in his beak, perched on the boy's shoulder, eyeing Dar as if wondering whether the Beastmaster had another treat for him.

Near Dar's feet, Ruh and the ferrets lay watching their human brother, their love and fear for him obvious. Sharak perched in a tree above, the eagle squawking his pleasure at Dar waking.

An intense chill ran through the Beastmaster. Tara held him tight, but even that did not make it go away.

"Brother Ontas made us a broth from some of the plants nearby," Tara murmured to him. "Let me get some for you."

Dar did feel hungry, which made him wonder why she had not already had a bowl waiting. Did she not care that he needed sustenance? Was she that blind?

Ruh let out a rumble. Dar started, surprised by his own anger. How *could* Tara be expected to do something like that and how could Dar grow furious for it?

The Touargang returned with the broth, the bowl she used one of those Dar remembered from Vaish's village. Dar again grew angry, but this time at the sage. The Beastmaster's illness was likely the old man's fault. After all, it had not started until after he had eaten with the madman.

"Dar—what's wrong?"

"What do you mean?" he snapped at her. "Why are you always accusing me of doing something wrong?"

Tara pulled back in shock. Kodo and Podo, also startled, scurried behind Ruh. The tiger looked alert.

"She means nothing but good for you, Dar," Ontas calmly interjected. "You know that. We are all concerned for you."

"Concerned I won't save your miserable lives?" the Beastmaster growled. Then, looking aghast, he added, "I did not mean that! I—"

Why are you apologizing to these fools? he thought to himself suddenly. *What you said was true! They only care that you save them, since they cannot save themselves! How weak they are! How weak they all are!*

Something in his expression must have changed for the worse, for Tara retreated from him and Jalan shifted closer to Brother Ontas. Sharak screeched at Dar, which only served to infuriate the Beastmaster more.

Leaping to his feet, he threw the bowl and its contents aside. "You all make me sick!" Dar snarled. Hands twisted into claws, he stalked toward Tara. "I nearly die more than once while all of you stand back and watch!"

The oracle stood up. "Dar. Look into your self. You don't mean what you say—"

"I mean everything I say, which is far more than you can proclaim!" The Beastmaster spat at the robed figure. "You spout words you claim could save Ancor, but you do nothing else!"

More and more, Dar could not believe that he had traveled so long with this worthless band. He wanted them gone. They were a tremendous burden, helpless in every way. Certainly not fit to survive. With such as these as allies, Dar was better off siding with the invaders.

Why not? he asked himself bluntly. *They will conquer Ancor, anyway! Better I find the Fountain for them and be rewarded!*

"Dar!" Fear filled Tara's voice. "What's happening to you?"

"Nothing!" he responded . . . or at least tried to respond. The word came out as an inarticulate roar. However, Dar was not bothered in the least by his inability to speak. The world around him had become one of pure fury. He desired nothing more than to tear them limb from limb . . .

Why not? Dar grinned . . . and did not notice in the least that his grin stretched far wider than humanly possible. Nor did he notice that his nails had grown several times their original length and were now as sharp as blades. He also did not pay any heed to the fact that he now crouched rather than stood straight and that thick brown hair—fur—covered his arms, legs, his entire body. Nor could he see that his eyes were wider and slanted and that his face was now more that of some monstrous feline than a man.

But the others saw. Yet the horror on their faces only served to fill him with eagerness for the kill. He stepped toward Tara, smelling her uncertainty and savoring it. She raised a hand toward him, a pathetic, futile gesture to his mind. Dar stared at her unprotected throat, estimating the distance he needed to jump.

Then, in her other hand, her spear suddenly appeared—she had used the first hand to distract Dar while seizing the weapon. Her duplicitous action only made the Beastmaster more enraged and he was determined to rip open her throat.

Ruh roared a challenge from behind him. Dar whirled and greeted that challenge with a snarl that echoed through the jungle. The tiger bared his teeth, but Dar sensed that, like Tara, Ruh was actually reluctant to attack.

And so, Dar attacked instead.

The tiger was taken completely off guard by the foul deed. Only a last-minute twist of his body saved Ruh from having the Beastmaster's monstrous teeth sink into the side of his neck.

Spitting out fur, Dar slashed with his claws. Ruh stumbled back, his shoulder bleeding. The tiger hissed but did not counterattack.

They are all like cowering fawns before me, Dar thought. *I will slay them all, then hunt the remaining sages I need! I will rend from them the mandalas and wear their power . . .*

He did not question these thoughts, though if his mind had been whole, Dar might have wondered why some of them sounded like another's, not his. All that was paramount was to do as the thoughts indicated. The tiger was wounded and clearly would not fight, for he kept backing away from the Beastmaster. The ferrets hid behind the bushes; they were certainly no threat to him. Of the eagle, there was no sign. That meant Dar could concentrate on the female again and her soft, easy-to-rend flesh.

"Stay back!" she pleaded, the spear up again. "I don't want to kill you, Dar . . . but I will if I must—"

He let out a mocking howl at her suggestion that she might be able to do anything against him. The puny weapon was hardly a match for his savage might.

But as Dar reached for Tara, Kodo and Podo got under his feet, both biting and seeking to trip him up. Sharak flew into his face and even Seto attempted to blind him.

With rising fury, Dar kicked and slashed at the animals, aware that their interference might enable the warrior woman to actually injure him. He felt some satisfaction as the ferrets went tumbling away and Seto, caught by a glancing blow by the back of one hand, sprawled stunned on the ground.

Dar's vision cleared . . . just in time to see Tara thrusting the spear at his chest.

"No!"

Jalan lunged between the two of them, Seto in his hands. With a curse, Tara managed to steer her spear to the side.

Dar wanted the female, but the boy was in the way. Mouth wide, claws raised, he looked down at Jalan. It would only take a second to remove this obstacle—

Their eyes met. Dar saw the pure innocence within Jalan. The boy stood unwavering as the Beastmaster loomed over him.

"No, Dar . . . please don't . . . you know you don't want to . . ."

The claws started down . . . then hesitated. Dar could not look away. In those eyes he was reminded of someone else, someone he had known so long ago.

Himself . . . Dar saw in Jalan's pupils a little boy playing with a bear while in the background his father played the flute. It was as if time had utterly stopped. The animal within Dar was transfixed.

"Jalan!" snapped Tara. "Out of the way!"

"No! Dar wouldn't hurt me! He doesn't want to hurt anyone! He's just a little . . . a little lost."

Tear him to shreds! the voice in the Beastmaster's head shouted . . . only, it no longer sounded like Dar. It seemed more an intruder.

"Dar . . ." continued Jalan. "Dar . . . you don't want to hurt anybody—you only want to help people . . ." The boy talked as if to someone of his own age, using the simple but irrefutable logic of youth. As he spoke, the child that Dar saw in his eyes seemed to look at the transformed warrior, calling him to return to himself.

The Beastmaster stepped back, his mind in turmoil. One part of him wanted to slaughter these people, but another—a growing part—understood that this was wrong and struggled to remind him just who he truly was.

The voice kept urging him to bloodshed, but Dar finally stopped listening. As it pressed its will on him, he fought back. Jalan, Tara, and the others were among those closest to him; he could not hurt them. That would be like hurting himself. Even worse.

His head throbbed. Dar went down on one knee as he battled the inner voice's murderous suggestions. He rolled on the ground, ripping at his fur, tearing at his chest. Like a mortally wounded wild animal, he snapped and bit at the darkness within him, heedless of the blood and dirt quickly caking his writhing body.

No! he finally insisted. *That is not me! I will not do it! I will not harm them!*

You will! You must! You serve only the will of Lord Vorannos!

It was a spell, Dar thought as he seized his head, which felt as if it were about to explode. Ignoring the others' horrified looks, the Beastmaster threw himself against a tree. He had fought spells before. *Look within,* Baraji had taught him. He silently repeated that mantra. *Within . . . within . . .*

At the same time, he physically struggled to find Jalan again. Dar refocused on Jalan's eyes, staring deeper than ever. In them, there was the hope. As he stared, his rage diminished . . . and, conversely, his ability to fight off the darkness grew. A light seemed to call him back to life. As his mind strived to reach it, the Beastmaster felt as if he suddenly sped swifter than the fleetest cheetah toward it—

Dar let out a roar . . . but a very human roar. He thrust the last of the darkness from him, sending it back to where it had come and sending with it that part of him that had proven so willing to embrace it.

Sweat dripping all over him, the Beastmaster fell down on all fours. He felt a small, soft hand touch his shoulder and knew it to be Jalan's.

"Dar? You're all right now, aren't you?"

The aching, exhausted Beastmaster did not answer at first, in great part out of fear that he would be wrong. Only after a swift but thorough investigation of his own thoughts did he finally gasp out a reply.

"Yes . . . Jalan . . . I am . . ." Dar looked up, not only at the boy, but a horrified Tara. He understood immediately that her horror was not aimed at him, but at herself. She had been willing to slay him in defense of the others.

He nodded in order to let her know that he understood, that he would have done the same in her position.

She gave him a tentative smile, then rushed to his side. Her smooth skin felt good against his and further eased his troubled mind. Brother Ontas and the animals joined them, though the oracle seemed to hold back more than the others. Dar thought his smile sad, though he could not say why.

"What could have caused that?" the Touargang asked. "It was so awful!"

"A spell," Dar replied simply.

"More than just a spell," Ontas interjected. "And I fear that I failed you in that respect. Recall you the bite you received?"

"The bite?" The Beastmaster rubbed his leg. "From Kodo?" The ferret squeaked apologetically. "You meant me no harm, Kodo; I know that."

"No, but whoever controlled him and the others did, and more than I imagined. I see it now; you were never in danger of death, although the rest of us were. That was why Ruh did not bite or truly attack you as he could have. The ferrets were the true instruments of what was desired. One of them had to bite you, so as to help infect you with whatever magical poison their unseen master needed to touch you with his evil. I don't doubt that he reached into your mind and began the change, slowly at first, then culminating tonight. A very intricate spell and one I suspect most could not have overcome."

"It was Jalan more than me," Dar told him, looking at the boy. "He helped me remember myself." The boy beamed at being so important. Indeed, without his innocent trust, the Beastmaster wondered if anything else could have possibly saved him. "I only hope I will not fall victim to it again . . . for all your sakes."

The oracle shook his head. "You're cleansed of it. I made certain. You not only overcame the spell, but you cast it out utterly. We have nothing more to fear from it . . ."

And then a howl filled the jungle.

THE MUTATES SERVING Kyrik had watched anxiously as he had cast the spell, but the sorcerer had not had any concerns himself. The

Beastmaster had been in a perfect state of mind for the spell to overwhelm him.

The initial elements of the spell—a magical poison, just as Ontas had surmised—had indeed been passed on into the Beastmaster through Kodo's bite. Kyrik had planned it that way all the time. The small creatures were the perfect vessels, quick, sinewy, and not too large. The tiger might have accidentally slain the Beastmaster and therefore had been reserved for a distraction and the possible removal of some of the unnecessary members of Dar's party.

Though that last had failed to happen, the sorcerer had not cared. In fact, the temporary survival of the Beastmaster's human companions had proven a boon. They were to become the means by which any decency, any humanity, was ultimately stripped from Ancor's champion.

Kyrik had had it all plotted out to the finest point. Under the influence of the sorcerer's foul work, the Beastmaster would be driven to slay his companions, that dark act forever sealing him to Lord Vorannos's servitude. Then, even if other avenues of search failed, they would be assured that Ancor's supposed savior would willingly retrieve the rest of the *proper* mandalas—the ones that Kyrik expected *would work*—for the master of Ishram.

Whether or not Vorannos deigned to let the Beastmaster live afterward had been a moot point to Kyrik, who suspected he knew the dark answer. Unlike Zorena, the sorcerer had no fascination for these primitives.

The overall spell had progressed even better than Kyrik had imagined. Already weary from his trials and with the magical poison spread throughout his system, Dar's mind had readily opened up to the sorcerer, and Kyrik, intent on also gaining all information he could, had delved deep into the Beastmaster, their thoughts intertwining until Dar could not tell which were his and which were not. The result had been that Kyrik knew as much as the Beastmaster.

Then . . . the unthinkable had happened.

Kyrik had thought nothing of the child, a mere speck that his puppet should have easily swatted aside. Only the female had concerned him, she the one in the party who had been realistic enough to know that only death would save them from Dar.

But the boy had touched something within the Beastmaster and, despite the sorcerer's powerful will, his puppet's desire to throw off the murderous rage had proven greater.

For Kyrik, so bound to Dar, that had proven a monstrous catastrophe. The full force of not only his spell, but the Beastmaster's very rejection of what little darkness his own mind had held, struck the sorcerer like lightning.

Kyrik had been engulfed by his own evil work. Unlike his intended victim, he could not stand against it. The primal forces had twisted his mind, brought it to depths even the Beastmaster's had not suffered.

And worse, Kyrik was a thing of no true body. He had forsaken it for pure magic. The artificial hosts he had created had in the past served him well, but they were far more malleable than a human form. Where Dar had gone through some physical transformation, Kyrik went through far more.

His last coherent thoughts vanished with what remained of his original form. Rage filled him and one face became his fixation. The Beastmaster. Kyrik knew only hatred for the Beastmaster.

A Pygmesian stepped in front of him, its infernal clacking driving Kyrik to greater rage. With a single stroke of his long claws, he not only severed the breathing hose, but much of the throat area as well.

The other mutates flew into a panic. Kyrik was one of the master's highest servants and so they hesitated to fire upon him.

That hesitation cost them their lives. Even in such a bestial state, he knew their greatest weaknesses and swiftly took advantage. The half dozen mutates perished in less than a minute, still more time than Kyrik desired. He wanted only one thing.

With a howl, the transformed sorcerer plunged into the jungle. The prey was not far. Kyrik needed to be near enough to make certain of his work.

He ran on two legs at first, then loped on four for the most part. As he picked up the scent, he began to slaver. So near . . . the prey was so near . . .

Already he savored sinking his fangs into him.

"MOVE!" DAR COMMANDED the others. He helped Jalan to his feet and guided the boy to Tara. The Beastmaster then turned to Ruh, wounded earlier by him. He feared that the tiger would be unable to move quickly, but Ruh immediately quelled any concern. Dar's strike had been painful, but not so much that it would slow the cat in any way. Still, Dar wanted Ruh to go on with the others.

Brother Ontas proved the largest obstacle to Dar's plans, the oracle stumbling and moving more slowly than anyone else. Dar finally asked Ruh to help guide Ontas on his way, though the tiger agreed to do so with a reluctant roar.

The Beastmaster took up the rear, praying that the party would be gone before—

A scent that raised the hair on his back made Dar swerve to the side.

The monstrous creature dropped down on the very spot he had just vacated. Dar locked eyes with a thing vaguely human, but overall far more akin to some demonic feline. It spat at him, revealing in the process fangs longer than the Beastmaster's fingers.

Dar brought his blade around—and suddenly it felt as if it

weighed twice as much as him. The tip of the sword sank into the ground.

His confusion nearly got him slaughtered. The cat creature lunged at Dar, and only by releasing the sword did the Beastmaster escape disemboweling. He rolled back, still trying to comprehend what had happened to his weapon.

Then, to Dar's further shock, small tendrils of grass under his feet sprouted up, growing more than a yard in less than the blink of an eye. They wrapped around his ankles like constricting serpents, pinning him in place.

As he struggled to free himself, Dar stared into the slanted, yellow orbs of the cat creature . . . and knew that it was the source of the magic that had both weighed down his blade and now doomed him. It perfectly mirrored his own transformation and, seeing it face-to-face, Dar marveled that his friends had survived unscathed.

One paw thrust at him. But the claws that intended to rend him to bloody gobbets stopped a few inches short as if some invisible wall now protected the Beastmaster. With a furious snarl, the monster whirled to its right.

"You must run, Dar!" Brother Ontas shouted. "Follow the others!"

The grass securing the Beastmaster shriveled. Dar glanced at the oracle, whose eyes glowed bright. A black aura surrounded the robed figure. Ontas shook in pain, then gritted his teeth. The aura vanished.

"It will be more than that which takes me down," he said in what almost sounded like resignation.

The cat creature leaped. Ontas stretched his hands forth and in them a staff of silver materialized. With it, he blocked the abomination's path. When the fiend sought to tear the staff away, its black paws burned.

Despite Brother Ontas's insistence that he leave, Dar had no such intention. He retrieved his sword, now once again its normal weight. Taking advantage of the cat creature's distraction, the Beastmaster swung at its back.

The blade cut deep—but no blood spewed forth. Rather, it was as if soft ice, but ice that sealed itself almost immediately.

"You can't kill him in that manner, Dar, for his body is but a shell! It is the spirit within that must be slain and that can only be done by piercing its Third Eye!"

"I see but two!" the Beastmaster shouted as the cat creature again turned to him. Each time he looked into its inhuman face, Dar nevertheless thought that he should recognize who it had been.

With a growl worthy of the creature, the oracle thrust a finger forward. Leaves began spilling in front of the feline eyes, blinding it. "The Third Eye is no mortal orb, my friend! It is a mystic region hidden from normal sight!"

While Ontas had been talking, Dar had used the blinding by the leaves to plunge his sword into his foe. Unfortunately, the wound sealed the instant that he withdrew the blade.

"How do we find it?" he asked in desperation.

"We do not! I do! Go! Run! It is not your fate to perish here!"

Dar ignored him. This creature was tied to his own earlier transformation and all this talk of magic had finally made him hazard a guess as to what he fought. The earlier spell had been cast on him by some sorcerer and, somehow that spell had seized its creator. Still, while Dar now understood his foe, he did not yet understand why he could not slay him. The Beastmaster had confronted priests and sorcerers in the past, and few there were he could recall able to resist the clean cut of a sword.

The leaves abruptly blew away. The cat creature slashed at Dar, almost taking out his sword arm. The Beastmaster retreated, seeking this Third Eye that Ontas had already told him he would not find.

"So it must be, then," he heard the oracle suddenly say. Out of the corner of his eye, Dar saw Brother Ontas clasp his hands together and begin murmuring under his breath.

A silver glow enveloped the monstrous feline. Still continuing to mutter, Ontas stared intently at the creature's back, then nodded.

"I know your weakness!" he shouted. "Just as I know the name you once bore! You are Kyrik of Ishram, and your eye is open to me!"

To Dar's astonishment, the cat creature abandoned him immediately for the oracle. Brother Ontas kept his gaze on the fanged fiend but did nothing to defend himself as it went for his throat.

But he did not remain silent. "See it, Dar! Know where to strike! I can't keep it visible for much longer—"

On the back of the abomination's head and just barely seen through his fur, a crimson point momentarily flared into existence.

With a shout, Dar pulled back the sword with both hands, then dove after the cat. He shouted long and hard, hoping that by doing so not only would he find the strength to pierce the mystic mark, but also distract the monster from the helpless oracle.

The cat creature hesitated. It started to turn, but too late.

The Beastmaster's sword sank deep . . . so deep, in fact, that he expected the point to come crashing through the front of his adversary's skull. Yet even though more than half the blade vanished within, nothing happened on the other side.

But something happened at the point in which the crimson blade glowed. The area expanded, and at first Dar thought that he had done something wrong. His sword was suddenly thrust out, tossing him back in the process.

As Dar fell, he heard the cat creature howl. Yet this howl was one of utter agony. The crimson now completely covered the furred body.

Then the Beastmaster's fiendish adversary split in two. The more substantial part became a blocky, incomplete statue that stumbled a few steps before freezing in place. A thick, purple fluid spilled out of where the Third Eye had been, quickly covering the statue.

It tipped over, cracking in half. The body dissolved into sand, which sank into the jungle soil.

The second and even more astounding part was like a ghost in both appearance and intangibility. Under a voluminous hood, Dar caught glimpses of a man with harsh, birdlike features.

Briefly the howl became words. "Foul primitive! Foul primitive! This cannot be! I am Kyrik! You are nothing! Nothi–"

The last became garbled as the howl rose in intensity. The shrouded sorcerer grew less distinct. The ethereal figure twisted and turned, disappearing more with each moment. The aura changed from crimson to the same deep purple as the fluid and, as it did, it swallowed up what remained of the sorcerer.

At last, even the purple aura faded . . . and with it went the hooded phantasm. His desperate howl cut off just a second later.

Gasping for breath, Dar turned a grateful smile to Brother Ontas.

The oracle lay sprawled on his back, his chest soaked in red.

As the Beastmaster rushed to Ontas's side, he saw that the deep wounds had been caused by the cat creature's claws. It could only have happened at the same time as the Beastmaster's strike. Dar cursed himself for being too slow.

The oracle opened his eyes. Although his breathing was ragged and he was clearly in pain, he smiled peacefully at the figure above him.

"Weep not for me, Dar of Emur," he murmured. "This was destined . . ."

An exclamation from further on presaged Tara and Jalan's return. They and the animals gathered around as Dar tried to bind the wounds.

"It is far . . . far too late," Ontas insisted, even managing to slap the Beastmaster's hand away. "You have better concerns to deal with than me . . ."

"I will not let you die!"

"That—that is not your d-decision . . ." The oracle coughed harshly. "I foresaw this . . . this point and although . . . although human frailty did cause me to . . . to attempt to avoid it." Ontas inhaled and as he did, he seemed to gain strength. "But now I see where I am to go, what I am to do, and it gladdens my heart to be so honored . . ."

Tara put a hand on the Beastmaster's shoulder. "Dar . . . is there nothing—"

"There is nothing any of you can do but go on with the quest," the oracle managed. "The quest is what matters most, for without it, there may be no Ancor, merely another Ishram . . ."

"Ishram . . ." How Dar hated that name, though he had heard it only a few times.

Brother Ontas reached out to the Beastmaster. With a gentle smile, he added, "I go to begin my next life quest. Remember, let the mandalas and the chakras they have opened guide you, my friend . . . and trust in who you are . . ."

Dar blinked. "Ontas! What is happening to you?"

The oracle looked at his hands. All around him there formed a delicate silver glow.

"It's only time," he remarked cheerfully.

There was an explosion of light . . . and from where the oracle's body lay, countless tiny butterflies—all bright silver—fluttered off in different directions. Yet, as Dar watched open-mouthed, he could not help but think that they flew with purpose.

Jalan gaped, fascinated by the magical sight. The others, even the animals, watched in silence, so awed that they did not move even long after the last butterfly had vanished into the night.

Although the vision gladdened Dar's heart, he also felt bitterness at what had happened. It reminded him again how so many lives had been lost and how many more would be lost while he continued his search.

The death of the dark sorcerer, while obviously a victory for the Beastmaster and Ancor, would surely also make the villain's dread master more eager than ever to claim his prize . . . which meant that Brother Ontas might not be the last one of Dar's companions to perish.

17

THE HOWL FILLED THE LORD OF ISHRAM'S HEAD, FOR THE master had been bound to the sorcerer in so many ways. The utter intensity of that howl momentarily startled Vorannos, who was simultaneously coordinating the movements of his legions while still trying to divine why the Beastmaster's mandalas could be used while his own stolen ones were of no value. The Lord of Ishram focused his thoughts on the reason for the sorcerer's anguish and felt Kyrik's brutal death as it happened.

The sorcerer had failed him. Although Vorannos would have inflicted a far more terrible punishment for Kyrik's failure, the lord of Ishram was angered at those who had caused Kyrik's death. Vorannos reserved such punishments for his own dispensing alone. It was just one more on the list of crimes for which this world would suffer.

But, for now, all that mattered was that He Who Must Be Faced, this Beastmaster, continued the hunt for the mandalas. In fact, it was the *only* thing of importance to Vorannos, for, while Kyrik had been foolish enough to fall victim to his own cleverness, the sorcerer *had* done one thing right. Kyrik had drawn from the mind of Dar of Emur the full details of what the would-be champion of Ancor hoped to do, and through those details Vorannos understood one matter . . . and that made him turn to Edurac to face his human allies.

It was a simple matter to transmit his image to the vermin who led the horde, the insipid Xorot. The barbarian jumped like a scared rabbit at the sight of the imposing giant, as did the other buffoons with him.

"You know me," Vorannos intoned.

They did, all falling to one knee simultaneously.

"Great lord—" Xorot began, but the mirror eyes cut the warlord off.

"I give you Edurac without any restraints to your desires," he informed them. "Do with it and all within as you will, so long as the libraries remain intact and the secrets they contain about the Fountain—be they maps, words, or whatever else—are brought to me immediately!" Vorannos surveyed his pack of human jackals. "But if the libraries are lost, be warned that *your* blood will flow as rivers with those of the fools defending the city . . ."

A startled Xorot could only mumble at first. "Done it shall be . . ." he said in his broken version of Ancor's most common tongue. Then, recovering, the warlord raised his ax and shouted, "And all the blood will honor Vorannos!"

They started to cheer him, but he was already gone. Edurac forgotten, Vorannos appeared before Zorena. The huntress, bent low so as to study the ground, started when she realized that he was near, a rare show of uncertainty from her. Two Pygmesians standing nearby quickly fell to their knees and bowed their oversized heads.

"My Zorena . . . you are frightened to see me?"

"No, my lord. Kyrik's death was on my mind and how he failed you so utterly that I wish I could draw him back to life so that you could properly execute him."

He nodded at her thoughtfulness. "So loyal you are, my dear Zorena . . . and such loyalty I always reward . . ." He peered into the jungle in the direction he knew the Beastmaster journeyed. "Where is he?"

She did not have to ask who her lord meant. "The Beastmaster and his friends are about an hour ahead that way." Zorena thrust her finger eastward. "It is my judgment that they are heading toward a wooded grove a horach spotted further on. I have several horach watching them every second, even with his eagle keeping a wary eye out for observers. I have not dared let anyone get any closer for the moment, for, due to Kyrik's bungling, they are much more wary. However, we watch for an opportunity! If we can take the mandala—"

"With less bungling than before," the lord of Ishram growled.

"The Beastmaster is a strong, daring foe, my lord. Like none I've faced! He is a skilled warrior, an adept hunter . . . but not so much as—" She stopped abruptly, as if she had said too much.

Vorannos observed her closely. He sensed her thoughts turning this direction and that, ever on the hunt or the invasion, but in manners that seemed most . . . distracting. It was almost as if there was something else she sought to hide behind them. Mirror eyes reflecting her face, he asked, "Would you like him, my Zorena . . . would you like me to save him for you . . . as a pet, perhaps?"

"There is nothing I desire but to serve you, my lord," she responded without hesitation.

"Nothing? As you like, then. The human's fate is sealed. Kyrik's abysmal failure to turn the Beastmaster's mind and soul to my cause now marks Ancor's would-be savior for death once he has retrieved all the proper mandalas."

"This I understand."

"But I grow impatient to embrace the power of the Fountain and so he must be made to hurry more! Can I rely on you for that while I prepare for the glory that shall be mine? Can I rely on you to obey me with complete adoration and so do exactly as I wish? Well, my dear Zorena?"

The huntress slapped her fist against her breast, at the same time hiding her concern. When Vorannos spoke so, almost flattering in his suggestion of his trust in one, it was a clear indication of his actual *distrust*. Even the smile now on his face meant nothing, for the lord of Ishram would have just as easily smiled if he decided to slay her.

Her expression showing nothing but loyalty, she crisply replied, "My life, my existence, is yours, my lord . . ."

The mirror eyes shone bright. "As are all else, my dear Zorena, as are all else . . . even the Beastmaster . . ." He peered east. "Go! I feel the culmination of everything imminent! Either seize for me the mandalas I need or see to it that *he* finds them for me! Go!"

The huntress and the Pygmesians rushed off as if their lives depended on their speed . . . which was not far from the truth. Vorannos watched them depart, then grinned.

One way or another, the Fountain would soon, very soon, be his . . .

DAR CUT THROUGH the thick underbrush without paying it much mind. His thoughts were still on Brother Ontas, who had sacrificed himself for him. Dar wanted no one to die for his sake and the oracle's loss renewed his fear for all his companions. He especially eyed Tara, who had grown to mean more to him in some ways than even any of his animal brothers. She represented something that the Beastmaster had never thought to have and it was clear that the Touaragang felt much the same way.

They had spoken alone after Ontas's death, spoken quietly, with Dar keeping one eye on Jalan, who most of all had been touched by the oracle's death. Even though they knew that Ontas had gone to a new, more miraculous existence, it had still been difficult to separate that from the fact that he was, by human standards, no more.

But where the Beastmaster had been concerned with Jalan, Tara was, in addition to the boy, worried about Dar.

"You're not to blame for Ontas," she had told him, not for the first time. "You've only done your utmost for him, for all of us . . ." He had not replied and so, in a greater attempt to bring him comfort, she drew up memories of him from her childhood. "Ancor already owes you so much for what you've done in the past . . . I remember when you saved my people from the bull elephant that rampaged through our holdings! Two men died trying to slay it, but you stood before it, soothed its anger, and sent it off to where it wouldn't harm anyone else . . ."

"But that was far in the past," the Beastmaster said, trying to smile and failing. "And in the end, none of that mattered. In the end, your people fell with all those others the invaders attacked." He shook his head. "Today is far different . . . and there is so much more facing us. . . ."

"You put too much on your shoulders, Dar. I saw that even as a child. I always felt sorry for all the burdens you carried. I wanted to help you carry them." She had put her hand on his cheek at that point. Her slim fingers trailed across to the side of his mouth. "I still want to. I know you went in search of answers about your place in the world; you were asking them even then." The princess looked away. "When you disappeared years ago, I—I was afraid that you'd died trying to find those answers. I even went in search of you for a time . . ."

Dar had been startled. "You did?" He had not expected that from her. Why would she risk herself so? She had only been a *child*.

The thought of her having endangered herself and being so concerned about his faith had made Dar look at her as he never had before. Her garments failed to hide her feminine shape. Her lips were full. She was truly no longer a child. Emotions swelled up that he could not control. On impulse, he had then reached out to Tara, setting his hand on hers.

There had been no words, then. Their eyes had met. Dar saw nothing but the dark-haired beauty before him. Their hands had taken hold—

At that moment, Jalan had stirred to waking. The moment had been broken . . . but the emotions behind it had remained, at least where Dar had been concerned. After Tara had seen to Jalan, they had all settled down to sleep, but the Beastmaster had remained awake for hours . . . and for the first time, his thoughts had not dwelled as much on the arduous quest they were on, but more personal matters.

As they continued their trek the next day and the next, the jungle grew more and more dense, so much so that they had to pause on occasion just so Dar could cut them a path. He might have led the party along a detour, but for some reason the Beastmaster sensed that it was important that he follow his instinct . . . and that said to keep going forward.

There was no outward sign of their pursuers, but Dar assumed them near. The death of the sorcerer might have cowed the others slightly, but Dar was certain that if they thought it advantageous to attack again, they would do so without hesitation.

He sensed first rather than saw the clearing where the sage surely had to be. When he and the others finally entered it, Dar immediately looked around, expecting to see the focus of his quest awaiting him.

But there was no one. Still, Dar was certain that he had found the location, not only because he felt so within, but because the clearing itself gave every indication. It was, first of all, perfectly circular, as if a master gardener had spent a lifetime cultivating the shape. A beautiful array of flowers lined the circle, the colors of the rainbow represented in their blossoms.

At the very center, a massive tree with broad, arching branches draped long, deep green fronds over the clearing. The trunk was nearly as wide in diameter as Tara was tall, but what marked the tree most in uniqueness was the lower third, which looked as if it had been formed from a thousand writhing roots.

"There's no one here," Tara whispered.

"There must be . . ."

Then, from the other side, there came a gentle snort. Dar sensed a presence that could not be the sage, but might have something to do with their elusive quarry.

A beautiful white steed appeared on the opposite edge of the clearing. It snorted again at the newcomers, this time in a soft manner that almost sounded like invitation.

"Look at him!" The Touargang stepped forward. "Isn't he wonderful?"

He was indeed, and as Tara reached out a hand, the horse—an unusually tall mustang—casually trotted toward her. A moment later, he was nuzzling her palm, as if seeking a treat. Tara wore an expression of awe so childlike that it reminded Dar of when he had first met her.

"He is a choosy one, that male," an elder, female voice remarked. "but you can trust his taste."

Dar whirled, only to find no one behind him. He quickly stepped around the vast, gnarled base of the tree but still came up empty.

"Seto!" the parrot suddenly fluttered up from Jalan's shoulder, alighting on a branch high up in the great tree. Once there, he began preening himself. It reminded Dar of when they had found Brother Ontas. The parrot acted as if he was very familiar with this place.

The tree was the focus of the clearing, so Dar wondered if it might hold a clue to the mysterious sage. With much more care, he slowly wended his way around the twisted roots.

On the side facing Tara and the white steed, Dar finally found something. He was not certain at first what it was, but by cautiously moving aside lesser roots, the Beastmaster managed to uncover an odd discovery.

It was a woman's face, carved with incredible skill into a knot in the tree. Created lifesized, its detail included individual hairs on the top and even lines of age in the round, pleasant face.

Dar felt more relaxed as he stared at the face. There were elements that reminded him of what he believed his mother would have looked like had she lived. The farmer who had raised him had never known how often, as a boy, Dar had wondered what it would be like if he and his unknown mother had shared a life together. It was not that Dar had not had any love for his foster father—far from it—but a mother was something he had always dreamed of having.

Jalan came to see what he had found. He giggled. "She looks like my grandmother!"

"I suppose she does," the Beastmaster replied. There were elements to her features that reminded Dar of many races. Again, he was awed by the handiwork of the artisan . . . very likely the sage.

His interest in the detail growing, Dar touched one side of the face.

The eyes opened, eyes a startling yet earthy brown.

"So pleasant to have company," the face said kindly. "I do so love company."

Dar pulled Jalan back, then felt a wave of shame wash over him. He could sense that this being meant no harm to them. After all, this was the very sage for which he had been looking.

"I am Sravasi," she added. Looking past Dar, the face suddenly called, "That's enough of you for now! Your time is coming!"

The white horse whinnied, then withdrew from Tara. As the steed departed, the Touargang looked to Sravasi with an expression of loss.

"He has been waiting long for his time. You must wait a little longer, too."

"I don't understand!"

"You will, Tara of the Touargang, when it is right that you do." Sravasi looked at Dar. "But your time is now, Dar of Emur, Beast-master, child of Ancor."

"I have come for the mandala in your charge. Tell me how I must earn it."

"But that would defeat the purpose." The brown eyes drank in the party. "Such a lovely group." Her gaze went back to Tara, then fixed on Dar. "Such a lovely couple."

The Beastmaster felt his face flush. He dared not look in Tara's direction and was grateful when Jalan became the focus of Sravasi's interest.

"And such a handsome child! I can't think how long it's been since I saw a child, much less one so handsome! I can smell the life and growth in you! You have so much to look forward to, so much to accomplish!"

Jalan gave her a big grin.

"And such beautiful animals! What a fine coat you have, tiger, and you, also, my little ferret friends!"

"Seto!"

The leaves of the tree shook, though Dar could feel no breeze.

"Yes, little one, you are handsome also, with your fine, colorful plumage, but so is your friend, the stalwart eagle here!"

Sharak let out an uncharacteristic squawk in which the Beast-master sensed the eagle's pleasure at this compliment. No one doubted the truth of Sravasi's words to each of them, even if she had spoken well of all there.

"But come! I babble on! You must all be famished! Here! You must have sustenance!"

From the treetop there suddenly rained down fruit . . . but not just one kind. Dar found apples and bananas and exotic fruits he could not name. There were also nuts of many sorts.

The party gathered what they needed. Dar worried about the meat eaters of his band, but Ruh and Sharak seemed so interested in the nuts that he finally let them do as they pleased.

"Dar!" Jalan called. "Taste this!"

The Beastmaster took the pear that the boy offered him and bit into the side. Immediately, a sweet wondrous taste filled his mouth. It was the most delicious pear—the most delicious *fruit*—that Dar had ever eaten.

"They will provide what sustenance you need as all good food does provide," the face said. "Eat, my children! Eat! All things can wait long enough for a good, healthy meal . . ."

Dar would have protested, but his stomach growled too much. Sravasi was correct; they could do nothing more until their hunger was satiated. They needed their strength for the trials still to come.

Although she was stationary, Sravasi yet somehow seemed to hover over them like a good mother, asking each if they enjoyed their food, would they like some more, and would they also like something to drink. The drink came in the form of other fruits, large gourds that, when easily cracked open, gave the one holding them a slightly sweet, clear liquid that refreshed not only the body, but, at least for Dar, the soul, too.

The scene was an idyllic one, and for the first time since well before even Brother Ontas's death, Dar found himself able to breathe easy. He and Tara sat before Sravasi while Jalan played a game of chase with Seto. The other animals, filled well by the repast, rested.

"Great sage," Dar began delicately. "We must speak of the mandala . . ."

"So we must," agreed the face. "We must speak of compassion, well-being, perseverance, and intuition, some of the things that their chakras have opened for you. We must speak of you—"

A cry cut her off. Dar leaped to his feet.

"Jalan!"

JALAN LOVED SETO as much as he loved Dar or anyone else. The parrot, though, had a special place in the boy's heart because he always seemed to know what Jalan wanted or needed. They shared a communication that no adult, not even the Beastmaster, could comprehend. Seto saw with both a young and old mind and he saw in colors and flashing images that would have been maddening for anyone other than the boy to understand.

Jalan's uniqueness was something he also did not understand, and at the moment all he cared about was Seto's antics. That the bird might consciously be trying to keep the boy from thinking of Brother Ontas would not have occurred to Jalan. They were just two friends playing.

The boy dodged into and out of the flowers and bushes on the edge of the clearing, like all youths venturing out further than he should. The trials of Ancor were also momentarily forgotten as Jalan lunged again at where the parrot had last perched.

He missed, of course, the object not truly to catch Seto. With a laugh, Jalan tumbled into the jungle. Leaves in his hair, he rolled into a sitting position.

Seto landed on his knee, the parrot keeping his wings spread and hopping back and forth like a dancer. Jalan clapped his hands.

Then shadows spread over the pair. Jalan looked up.

Four Pygmesians stood over the duo.

Oddly, Jalan had no fear. That was perhaps due to the fact that

Seto seemed unconcerned. Indeed, the parrot turned to face the four creatures.

"Seto!" he merrily chirped, displaying his brilliant plumage to full effect.

The Pygmesians seemed entranced by the bird. Seto fluttered off Jalan and performed small circles before the monstrous foursome.

From the invaders there came a series of muted clacks. The oversized helmets clustered together, the glass lenses all fixated on the colorful, aerial display by Seto.

Then, slowly, the lead Pygmesian stretched forth a tentative hand toward the parrot. Jalan could see that there was no malice in the action. Almost like a child, the creature appeared to simply want to touch the brightly feathered avian.

Seto landed on the creature's hand, then peered into the lenses at his own image. The parrot cocked his head, then stretched his wings wide, displaying himself for both his image and the Pygmesian. The macabre warrior stood absolutely still.

Then . . . another figure suddenly stepped up behind the lead Pygmesian, a creature more like a man in shape, but flat of features and utterly scaled. Jalan recalled his kind from the struggle around the sage, Nanda.

There was no fascination in the deadly orbs, only malice and death.

"Jalan!" Seto suddenly called. The parrot flew up from the arm, then darted toward the reptilian hunter.

The helmeted creatures stirred as if from a deep sleep. They grasped for Seto, but missed. The parrot flew into the other invader's flat face.

A six-fingered hand rose up, a tube weapon in it.

Rising, Jalan let out a cry.

Somewhere in the distance, he heard Dar call his name. Although that should have made Jalan immediately turn and run, the boy's fears for the parrot kept him where he was. He charged into the Pygmesians and only because they were distracted did he not suffer instant capture or worse.

Jalan seized one hand wielding a tube and twisted it around as he had seen Dar do. The Pygmesian fired instinctively, the blast sending renewed confusion through the vicinity.

Calling Jalan's name, Seto flew past. The boy followed just as flame exploded near where he had stood.

And as he ran, Jalan saw Dar, Tara, and the other animals racing toward them. He also saw something else spilling into the clearing from other directions.

More Pygmesians.

SHARAK WARNED DAR of the other attackers, but the Beastmaster only cared about those who might have Jalan. Dar ran hard, fearing the boy already dead, but then the small but familiar form burst into sight in front of him. Seto flew around Jalan, both seeming to urge his friend on and watch behind.

Just after Jalan there came a snarling reptile man, and with him at least four Pygmesians, all of whom he clearly commanded.

Ruh raced again. The tiger reached Jalan but then continued on. Dar sensed that Ruh was especially eager to reach the reptile . . . whom the cat identified as one of his captors.

The reptile thrust a hand forward. Before Dar could warn Ruh, the tiger twisted to the side.

A black spray saturated the area where Ruh had been and smoke rose from the grass, which shriveled and died.

Despite the tiger's eagerness to do battle with his enemy, Dar demanded that Ruh pull back. At the same time, the Beastmaster raised his sword.

Sharak cried out.

Dar ducked as something metallic whizzed by his head. It flew across the rest of the clearing, finally striking an outer tree . . . and ripping into it.

The Beastmaster turned and slashed, his sword cutting into the source. The tall, metallic golem—like a scarecrow with too many arms and an overturned bucket for a head—let out a squeal as what appeared to Dar to be oil spilled from two severed hoses.

Tara speared a Pygmesian, then ducked as another fired. The ferrets scurried over other odd golems, chewing and biting with great effect. Dar marveled as lightning flashed from ruined connections and the metal men—if some could even remotely be called that—teetered and fell like statues.

Sharak provided Dar with warnings and attacked whatever prey looked vulnerable. The eagle also acted as distraction, confusing those that would fire upon his friends.

Ruh, meanwhile, tore into the attackers with his usual unstoppable ferocity. He moved far too quickly for most of the creatures, tossing them about like rag dolls. Still, Dar knew that the tiger wanted to slay the one reptile man in particular. Ruh fought his way toward his desired prey, but the heat of battle kept them apart nonetheless.

Then, Dar thought of Sravasi. He suddenly feared that, like Nanda, these attackers would go after her. As he kicked away the body of a Pygmesian, Dar glanced over his shoulder.

The great tree proved to be far from helpless. Each of the branches stretched down and, whenever a foe got too near, Sravasi would seize them and toss them into the jungle beyond. She did so with a reproving expression on her face. Violence was not something that would have appealed to any of the sages, but evidently Sravasi accepted the necessity.

Then another of the scaled assassins emerged behind the sage. However, his target did not appear to be Sravasi, but Tara.

Dar desperately hefted his sword, preparing to throw it like a missile. He could not hope to slay or even wound his foe, but he wanted to at least ruin the creature's aim.

But his target noted his intention and shifted, making even a distraction impossible for Dar. With a toothy grin, the scaled figure again took aim at Tara—

Then from the jungle leaped the red-haired woman warrior with whom Dar had previously battled. Eyes on the Beastmaster, she landed directly between the reptile and Tara. The would-be assassin hissed something at her, but the huntress kept her back to him, and although the reptile might have thought she had not heard, the telling glance she threw to Dar said otherwise.

But before he could comprehend why the woman would save Tara, the huntress was upon him. However, her attack was so simple, so slow, that he easily parried it. Her gaze smoldering, the woman smiled seductively.

"We are one and the same," she murmured as their blades clashed again. "I saved her not for you, but to show how akin you and I are! I might've sacrificed myself, all for you . . ."

"I do not understand . . ."

She laughed quietly. "Do you not?" Pressing their swords together, she came within inches of his face. "Zorena can give you so much more than her, and not just your life! So much more!"

The huntress suddenly leaned close. Her lips came near Dar's and it almost seemed that she invited his kiss. But Dar found nothing in the temptress that he desired. In fact, there was only guilt in his soul, guilt that Tara might see the two so close and misunderstand his feelings.

Shoving her back, he growled, "I want nothing of you! You are but a servant of an evil desecrating all Ancor!"

To his surprise, her expression turned troubled. Zorena looked as if she wanted to say something . . . but before a single sound could escape her lips, her head jerked slightly, as if some voice urgently whispered in her ear. Behind her, Dar saw the reptilian assassin taking aim at Tara again.

With inhuman swiftness, he shoved aside Zorena, who made no

move to strike at him though she had the opportunity. The warrior woman forgotten, Dar ran toward the scaled figure, although he already feared that he would be too late.

Without warning, a score of branches dropped down on the reptile. Though she faced away from the villain, Sravasi had apparently finally sensed his nearness.

But as the branches engulfed him, the reptile fired. Black lightning shot up.

The tree that was also Sravasi burst into flames.

Fire quickly engulfed the crown. Branches went flying. As if guided by an evil hand, the fire swept downward to devour the trunk.

A great cry arose, and it took a moment for Dar to realize that he himself was the source.

Yet, the carnage had a peculiar effect on the attackers. They first froze, then fled in what seemed distress. The creature who had fired on the sage gaped at the results of his act with open fear. Dar understood that he had not meant to destroy the tree, but that hardly made up for the catastrophe that he had caused.

Enraged, the Beastmaster raced after him . . . but then a desperate hope that he might still save Sravasi took over and he turned to the tree. He came around to where her face was—

A mass of fiery branches dropped down before him, obscuring the face from his sight. The heat beat Dar back.

Hands pulled him back. In his ear, Tara cried, "There's nothing that can be done! You need to step back! It's too dangerous!"

He knew she was right, but still he hesitated. There was no sound from the direction of the sage, no cry, no murmur. Dar could only pray that her spirit had somehow gone on the moment the tree had burst into flames.

"They're gone . . ." the Touargang added. "They just . . . left. As Sravasi's tree burst into flames, they just . . . they just froze. It was as if they . . . as if they saw or felt something in the fire and it touched them." Tara swallowed. "They *panicked,* Dar! In all the time that I've seen them, I never saw such a reaction. They panicked and ran . . ."

Trying to tear his mind from Sravasi's fate, Dar looked around. Only the bodies of the few slain remained. They were a small comfort to the Beastmaster. In the short time that he had known Sravasi, she had touched him like the mother that he had never known, the mother whose life had been so terribly destroyed when Dar was ripped from her womb by dark sorcery.

A tear slipped from one eye. It was followed by another. There were times when any person, be they a child or a full-grown, seasoned warrior, had to shed tears for those lost to them. Dar had shed them for his foster father.

A breeze arose. It caught the first tear and carried it to the dwindling fire and the ruined trunk. The other tears followed.

With only the first two, the last of the flames doused. The other tears, still somehow carried aloft, finally landed on the smoking stump.

And as they did, a mandala flashed into being, one golden yellow, with a single perfect triangle inside and petals like those of the surrounding flowers.

It lasted but a moment, yet in its wake a hint of green emerged from the charred area. That green became a small tendril, then two. The tendrils intertwined, in the process becoming a single sprig.

At the same time, new buds began appearing all over the remnants of Sravasi's ruined tree. The roots reformed, turning fresh and full.

And as a stunned Dar and his friends watched, from the ashes grew a *new* tree that enveloped what remained of the old until there was no telling that the first had ever even been there. Branches by the dozens burst forth, each blossoming with rich leaves and beautiful yellow flowers before they reached their full lengths. A fresh canopy developed in seconds, spreading nearly as wide as the previous.

The new, younger tree was a vibrant giant. Its roots stretched even further afield than the original. But Dar cared not so much about that as what began to form in the bark between those roots. It was vague of form at first—merely a pair of slits and a slight bump—but it quickly coalesced into a distinct, highly recognizable shape.

The face of Sravasi gently smiled at Dar.

"Your tears were of love, and so they began the rebirth of life," she said, "and rebirth of life is a thing for joy, the greatest of human emotions. Without joy, there can be no hope, no love . . ."

Dar only partially heard her. He was too grateful to know that Sravasi lived. Without caring how it looked, the Beastmaster embraced the trunk and kissed Sravasi on the cheek.

As he did, time seemed to momentarily stop for Dar. He saw the continual cycle of life and death and how he—and all people—had to carry on. Life would renew. As Sravasi was able to renew herself and her purpose, so, too, did all others in different ways.

Near his face, he suddenly saw another sprig growing. On its tip was a tiny flower that reminded him in the shaping of its petals of the mandala.

"This is the rarest fruit of all," Sravasi whispered in his ear, "for it is one not grown, but earned. Eat of it, Dar. Eat of it."

Plucking it, the Beastmaster thrust the sprig in his mouth and chewed. A sweet, calming flavor graced his tongue. He swallowed the chewed sprig.

And as it descended down his throat, Dar felt a warmth that seemed to increase as the sprig went lower. The warmth finally settled at the mouth of his stomach.

Glancing down, Dar saw that the tattoos had shifted position again so that now a new one—identical in pattern to that which he had seen before the tree's rebirth—was located there. At the same time, Dar felt something new within him awaken.

Yet, perversely, Dar also felt a new sadness, one that built upon the results of his previous quests. It seemed that he could gain nothing without harm coming to someone else. Worse, that this had not occurred to him immediately made the Beastmaster wonder if he was becoming more and more callous to that. Dar felt as if the chakras—even as they revealed to him new truths—were somehow turning him also into a thing almost as ghastly as what the sorcerer had become.

"We grow with each trial life gives us," Sravasi commented, as if reading his concerns, "and we have the final choice in what fruit our learning bears, good or ill."

"Sravasi—"

The sage's smile grew sad again. "It's been marvelous to have children about me . . ."

She was bidding them farewell. Dar knew they had to move on. The hunters were growing more bold, if also more reckless. It amazed him that he and his friends had survived and that he had managed to gain that for which he had come.

"Thank you for your kindness, Sravasi," he said with a bow.

"Thank you for you, Beastmaster." The sage closed her eyes and as she did, her face receded into the bark and roots. Within a heartbeat, her image was barely visible.

Dar stared for a moment . . . then, in silence, led the party out of the clearing.

18

THE BEASTMASTER AND HIS PARTY HAD NOT VENTURED FAR from Sravasi's clearing before the land suddenly grew more foreboding and the cataclysm facing Ancor became highly apparent. Dar had known that they would sooner or later delve deep into the ruined lands, but he had hoped it would still be a little longer.

The jungle here was dead, the trees long rotted even though many still stood hollow and dry. In some areas, the ground had been completely upturned, creating jagged hills or harsh ravines. As Tara put a hand on a branch to balance herself, it snapped easily, almost making her fall. The branch landed on the ash-ridden ground, raising up a dust cloud.

"This is a desert," the Touargang murmured, aghast at the horror through which they walked, "or a sea of desolation . . ."

"A desert or a sea, either teems with life, however hidden by the

earth or the depths," the Beastmaster replied. "They are both para-
dises compared to this place . . ."

The scents that filled the air reminded Dar of the village of
Vaish, but he doubted that this time it had anything to do with his
quest. No, these foul odors hinted at things all too terrible. That was
verified quickly by something large and metallic that darted through
the air some distance ahead of them before descending to the east.

And as it descended, the Beastmaster blinked and declared,
"That is where we must go."

Tara frowned. "There? Where that thing went?"

"Yes."

She did not argue and no one hesitated to follow him. They
knew that Dar would lead them where he had to, whether he liked
it or not.

The land grew more desolate and the stench marking the invaders' encroachment was so strong it burned Dar's nostrils. Kodo and
Podo hid in the pouch in an effort to escape the acrid odor and Ruh
constantly snuffled, as if by doing so he could somehow clear his
even sharper nose of it. Even Tara and Jalan sought to cover their
noses as much as possible.

In the distance, the thick plume that marked one of the gargantuan diggers came into sight. Although he desperately wanted to
find the sage, Dar was forced to slow the party down.

It proved a wise notion, too, for shortly after a giant form heading south passed nearby. The Beastmaster recognized one of the
three-legged, less humanoid golems.

He quickly surveyed the area for a hiding place. A shallow cave
to their right promised some protection. Dar hoped it would be
enough. He ushered the others to it, even Sharak. In this no-man's-
land, the invaders would not even suffer a lone eagle to live.

The golem hesitated. The round head swiveled, the one great
eye peering in the direction of the party.

The head suddenly split open at the top. Out of it emerged two small spheres that flew toward the Beastmaster's position.

Several yards from the hiding group, the small spheres—no larger than a human skull—suddenly hovered. From out of the bottom of each sprouted three limbs akin to those of the giant. The miniature versions of the huge golem stalked along the landscape, searching.

Jalan's foot shifted. A pebble rolled away.

The orbs of both golems turned toward the sound.

Dar gripped his blade, knowing that even if he was swift enough to deal with both, the giant would immediately pursue.

One of the three-legged hunters took a step closer. The second followed suit.

A brief, sharp noise—like a bee's buzz amplified—filled the air.

The heads of the two smaller golems swiveled around to face the larger. The huge orb of the giant changed color, turning red, blue, green, blue, then white.

The legs of the hunters withdrew into the heads. The two then flew back, re-entering the gap in the larger head. The gap sealed.

The huge golem turned its gaze to the south again. It moved on, its pace twice as quick as earlier.

Dar led the others out again. They watched as the golem vanished over the horizon.

"That was very close," the Touargang said.

Dar nodded. "Fortune was with us . . . this time. We will have to be more observant. The invaders are everywhere."

Keeping an even more wary eye open, they cautiously wended their way along the path Dar knew they had to take. Their surroundings turned even more bleak; in some places there were not even any burnt trees around which to hide. More than once, they also came across skeletons, most of them scorched and far too many of them human.

"This must stop," he murmured. "This must stop . . ."

Sharak suddenly gave warning. Dar waved the others flat to the ground.

In the dark sky, a thing with wings akin to a bat's soared on to the northeast, then descended. Dar was unable to determine whether it was animal, golem, or some grotesque combination of both. He was only thankful that it obviously had some other task in mind and thus did not notice them.

But barely had it left when the eagle alerted him again. This time the Beastmaster immediately linked to Sharak in order to see.

He beheld a force of Pygmesians and other mutates—Dar had never known what else to call the invaders before, but the word "mutate" had begun to pop up in his mind ever since the night of the sorcerer's foul spell—moving with dread purpose in the same direction as the bat-winged flyer. Sharak surreptitiously banked that direction, aware that Dar wished him to follow the invaders and see what they intended. They were suspiciously close to where the Beastmaster sensed he was heading . . . close to where the guardian of the mandala surely awaited him.

Moments later, the eagle sighted an odd lake. Its surface was a peculiar dull brown. Dotting the lake were large, broad, flat water lilies of varying size, a few of them so wide that Ruh could have easily slept on them—if they had been able to hold his weight—while others were smaller than Jalan's palm.

Dar frowned, wondering just what it was the invaders sought here. He asked Sharak to cautiously scout the lake. The eagle obeyed, circling around the shoreline, then turning more and more toward the center. Through Sharak's eyes, Dar viewed every-thing . . . or, in this case, very little. The lake seemed of no interest.

Then a small cluster of water lilies attracted his attention, in great part because they were a startling, unusual orange in color. In the center of the cluster was an indistinct shape. Dar asked Sharak to descend toward that shape, but only if the situation appeared safe. The eagle projected confidence, then did as requested.

And as Sharak closed, the shape coalesced into an astounding sight. There, sitting cross-legged atop what should not have been able to hold him, was a slim, bald figure. His eyes were closed and his hands, resting just above the knees, were turned palms upward. On his shoulders was the tattoo of a mandala, though Dar could not make out its details.

His momentary joy at locating the sage was quickly smothered by Sharak's swift veering as a shadow enveloped the water lilies. The eagle pulled away just as the bat-winged shape, now identified as a thing of metal, dropped to a height just above that of the seated elder.

From the underside, a monstrous, glittering tentacle with a three-clawed appendage shot forth to seize the sage. Dar bit back his anguish, aware that he could do nothing for the man.

But a pink aura surrounding both the sage and the lilies flared to life. As the claw touched it, a violent shaking overtook the hovering flyer. The tentacle waved wildly and the flyer tipped to the side, then flew in an erratic circle before suddenly diving for the lake.

And throughout it all, the figure on the lily pads did not even move . . .

VORANNOS OBSERVED FROM his flagship all that occurred at the odd lake. He had calculated with the utmost certainty that this was indeed one of the mandalas and, impatience growing rapidly, had decided to take it even though he was certain that the Beastmaster was near. *Very near.* But he could not wait. And he reveled in seeing his foe watch as all his arduous work proved for naught. How delicious to imagine the face of Ancor's savior when he realized he had wasted all his efforts, that the Fountain and all else belonged to the lord of Ishram.

Capturing the mandala's guardian could not be simple, of course. The flyer had been one of a series of preliminary attempts. Now Vorannos had other flyers in motion and one of his officers would guide the efforts from below while Vorannos kept command.

He was alerted that the flyers had reached the rendezvous point. The lord of Ishram grinned in anticipation . . .

DAR HAD NO time to witness the flyer's unexpected crash, for loud, grating sounds made him steer Sharak back to the shore.

A series of small, metal flying ships approached the lake, coming up short just over the shoreline. There, one by one, they took up positions leading toward the sage and began opening doors in their bellies.

Out of the open bellies descended metallic structures that expanded as they dropped. Long, sturdy legs thrust out.

"Are they more golems?" Tara asked him.

At first, Dar thought the same, but then he saw that the four legs of each were locked in place and much thicker. The top of the descending structures was long, wide, and flat—hardly like the golems.

As each reached the surface of the lake, the legs thrust into the odd waters. One by one, the structures settled in a line, reminding Dar more and more of one thing in particular.

A massive, armored figure—almost resembling a tortoise that walked like a man—roared something unintelligible. A mass of Pygmesians and other invaders rushed forth onto the structures.

Above, all but one of the small flyers soared off. The remaining one turned to better view the activities below and as Dar studied it, he could not help but feel that through it, the lord of Ishram monitored his servants' work.

"Nothing so deadly as a golem," he murmured to Tara. "But of threat to us, nevertheless. They are building a *bridge* to the sage . . ."

But what a bridge, for it extended segment by segment over the lake all the way to the center . . . and the seated figure. Dar marveled at the elaborate construction even as he feared that where the flyer had failed, this would surely succeed. The mutates worked hard and swiftly to secure one part to the next, moving ever closer to the still man.

They were obviously still intent on claiming the mandalas and, this time, they had actually located the prize first. Whether or not the invaders could gain from it what they desired was a moot point; if they kept Dar from succeeding, Ancor was doomed.

"Hurry!" he whispered, guiding the others toward another area of the lake. Sharak, careful to keep enough distance, watched the events at the bridge for him. Dar cursed as the eagle's view verified for the Beastmaster that the fantastic creation would reach the sage well before he could.

They reached the far shore in time to see the bridge already more than two-thirds secured. The sage continued to sit perfectly still, almost as if oblivious to his danger.

The observing flyer moved along with the workers. Dar watched the tortoise-shaped mutate beat at the others to finish their task faster. In one hand he held a box in which he occasionally spoke . . . and which apparently spoke back to him. Truly astounding were the ways of the invaders, astounding and monstrous.

Returning to his own task, the Beastmaster looked around for a boat or anything that might be strong enough to hold him, but the shoreline was absent of possibilities. There were no useful pieces of wood, all the trees charred.

"I will have to swim," he told the others. Seen up close, the water had a filmy, ashen look, almost as if it were land rather than a lake. Yet now and then it rippled, proving otherwise.

It suddenly reminded the Beastmaster of something else, but before he could put his finger on it, Tara excitedly murmured, "Dar! They're launching warriors toward him!"

A band of armed fighters were already striding across the bridge, which had almost been secured up to the sage himself. The invaders were mere moments from seizing their quarry . . . and possibly condemning Ancor.

But a startling turn of events suddenly left Dar and his companions gaping. The support legs began to sink. The scores of mutates did not immediately notice, driven on by their commander and the hovering flyer.

But as if with a mind of its own—which was certainly possible considering what Dar had seen of the invaders thus far—the bridge itself sought to compensate. With a loud whirring, the legs thrust higher. A few Pygmesians were tossed off in the process. They hardly had a chance to struggle before sinking under without a trace.

And still the legs sank faster than the bridge could offset.

"This is no lake . . ." Dar finally told the others. "This is more like quicksand . . ."

"CORRECT THE BALANCE!" roared Vorannos. "Correct the balance, you imbecilic cretin!"

The mutate commander clacked a response. The lord of Ishram did not bother to listen. With a single thought, he summoned a panel before him, a panel made only of light, no substance. Vorannos touched a series of lit buttons on it.

Back on Ancor, the unmanned flyer suddenly maneuvered over the sinking bridge.

THE BEASTMASTER GLANCED toward where the sage sat, recalling the flyer that had gone down near the seated figure. Dar had never seen it strike the surface, but he would have expected, had it been water, for some wreckage to be visible. There was nothing, though. Whatever fell into the brown mass was swiftly and completely engulfed.

A tremendous groan brought his attention back to the bridge. Tara gasped and Jalan gaped. Ruh growled, his fur bristling. The bridge had tipped to one side and now the edge of the walkway itself touched the surface. That seemed to accelerate whatever process by which the quicksand—for lack of a better word—swallowed its prey.

From the flyer above sprouted a series of long, metallic tendrils that quickly reached down and wrapped around the base of the section beneath it. A great groan arose as the flyer pulled up, raising the bridge straight in the process.

But just as quickly, the bridge shifted again. Several of the tendrils ripped off. The flyer spun around, out of control. It started to right itself—and crashed into the lake before it could finish.

As if a giant mouth swallowing a treat, the lake enveloped the vessel.

Atop the bridge, some of the invaders tried to back up, but the structure suddenly lurched once more. Scores were thrown over. They spilled into the "lake." A few tried to reach for the structure, then vanished with a frantic waving of arms.

Mass chaos ensued. However, it was already too late. The end of the bridge now dipped into the brown quagmire . . . and the moment it did, the entire construction sank with a rapidity that was breathtaking. Even the vast mechanism at the other end was not sufficient weight to prevent the destruction; it rose into the air as if nothing, then was dragged along into the vast body.

With it went the rest of the invaders left aboard. Despite the horrors their kind had created across Ancor, Dar could not help feeling for them, but there was nothing he or anyone could do.

Tara shared his dismay for their enemies. "By the gods! They can flee nowhere . . ."

In less than the shadow of a minute, the entire dread tableau had played itself out. The brown surface smoothed. There was not even the least hint that a massive assault had even taken place save for the handful of Ishramites on the shoreline. Some of them fired in the direction of the distant sage, but to no effect. At last, they retreated back into the jungle, perhaps to seek some new method to safely reach their target.

Realizing that, for the moment, they were the only ones nearby, the Beastmaster knew that his chance had come. Yet he still did not know what to do. That this was the sage, Dar was certain. Indeed, that gave him one hope. He shut his eyes and tried to send his thoughts toward the figure, literally asking the holy man for guidance.

But there was only silence. Deflated, Dar opened his eyes again . . . and saw through Sharak's own gaze that the distant figure now looked at the far-off Beastmaster.

To be where you wish to be, you must look to yourself as you are seen in the eyes of others, a voice in Dar's head abruptly said.

Dar's eyes widened. What did the sage mean?

To be where you wish to be, you must look to yourself as you are seen in the eyes of others, the voice repeated.

The Beastmaster frowned. To the sage, he thought, *I need the mandala and quickly! Tell me what you mean . . .*

There was no reply.

The Beastmaster gritted his teeth. It was obvious that the figure would say no more. Clearly, this statement was the only clue Dar would have as to how to reach the sage.

"To be where you wish to be, you must look to yourself as you are seen in the eyes of others," Dar repeated out loud.

"What did you say?" the Touargang asked in confusion.

But now it was Dar who did not reply, the Beastmaster furiously thinking. He had to find the answer to this riddle.

A thought occurred to him as to how he might discover it. Despite the urgency, he closed his eyes and looked into himself.

Through his learning, he reached into the chakras, letting them guide his thoughts.

His eyes opened wide. He looked to the sky. "Sharak, my winged brother . . . go to him . . ."

The eagle shrieked, then headed toward the sage, who all the while kept his gaze upon Dar and whose eyes in turn the Beastmaster met as much as possible to keep the mental connection between the two men strong.

Tara was concerned. "Dar! You saw what happened to whatever tries to reach him! If the lake doesn't take them, then that aura prevents anything from touching him! It might even cause Sharak to fall in!"

That was a danger of which the Beastmaster had already thought. But Dar continued to trust that which had awakened within him to help safely guide the bird.

As Sharak banked toward the sage, the seated figure, still staring deeply into Dar's own eyes, slowly raised the arm nearest to the eagle as if offering a perch. As Sharak headed toward it, the two men continued keeping their gazes locked.

The Beastmaster tensed. Tara shook her head in fear—

Sharak alighted on the arm without a threat. The aura did not appear.

Suddenly hopeful, Dar asked the eagle to look into the holy man's eyes. As Sharak did, the Beastmaster looked through the avian's gaze into the gray orbs of the sage. The silent sage finally shut his eyes, but only for a moment.

And when he opened them again . . . it was Dar who stood before him and Sharak who hovered near Tara at the shore.

But the Beastmaster had only a moment to grasp this impossibility before his weight caused the water lilies to sink. Worse, not only was Dar slipping into the quicksand, but, because of him, so, too was his silent companion.

Despite his predicament, the sage did nothing but continue to look at Dar. He seemed perfectly calm, almost satisfied, despite the moment. Ignoring his own peril, the Beastmaster seized the holy man and thrust him up as best he could. Try as he might, though, the dark sands continued to drag the sage down with him.

In desperation, Dar kicked with his legs, hoping that he could at least swim a few feet toward where several undisturbed water lilies still floated. The holy man had been able to sit upon them as if weighing nothing. If Dar could somehow reach them, then he might at least be able to save the sage.

"Put your hands on my shoulders!" the Beastmaster cried. "Hurry!"

With what Dar took for a grateful smile, the sage did as he bade. Dar inhaled and pushed for the nearest lilies.

Then, to his surprise, the plants to which he had been heading suddenly moved. They gathered around the Beastmaster and his burden as if more fish than flora. Summoning his strength, Dar pushed down on those before him. He prayed that if he was able to scramble over some of them, the sage could then climb atop him and onto others that would once again support him.

However, the lilies suddenly held Dar's weight. Encouraged, he dragged himself atop them. They were soft, yet stable.

A still-stunned Dar stiffened as he and the sage finished climbing atop with not even a trace of the brown substance clinging to their bodies.

The holy man silently adjusted himself back to his original position, then looked up at Dar with gratitude. His eyes held Dar's again and though he still did not speak, the Beastmaster understood that, as with the other sages, he had been tested . . . and had succeeded.

The mandala rose from his shoulders and back, then drifted to Dar. As the tattoo became a part of the Beastmaster, a brown aura enveloped him.

Dar felt the chakra open within him.

"Thank you," he murmured to the sage, who merely nodded.

There was nothing more to say. The Beastmaster glanced back at the shore, where his friends anxiously awaited, then into the sage's eyes.

But to the question he was about to ask, he suddenly knew the answer as if the holy man had spoken: *to be where we wish to be we must always think ahead.*

The lesson taught, the sage tilted his head down and went back to meditating.

With reluctance but also a sense of accomplishment, the Beastmaster turned to face his companions. He took one step forward, placing his sandaled foot on a water lily. Without hesitation, Dar put his weight on it.

The water lily held.

One step at a time, Dar went from water lily to water lily. Now and then, he feared that somewhere along the way the gap would be too great, but always there was one enabling the Beastmaster to continue.

When he reached the shore, his friends surrounded him.

"I thought you surely dead this time!" Tara exclaimed and a tearful Jalan echoed her feelings with an anxious nod of his head. The ferrets scampered up his back and nuzzled his neck.

"I thought much the same," he admitted.

"You have the sixth one! There is only one remaining to find!"

"Yes . . ." But, unlike after the previous successes, Dar did not sense where next he had to head. It was as if the trail had come to an utter end before it should.

Then he felt a warmth that touched both his chest and the fingers of his left hand. Dar belatedly discovered that he had reached up and touched the stone that Baraji had given to him. It was the stone emanating the warmth.

But there was more than just that. As he continued to play with the stone, it began to change form according to his manipulation. As it did that, images materialized in Dar's mind, foremost among them the image of a ruined city buried by the jungle.

He also knew where that city lay.

"I know where we must go," he quickly told the others. "To the city of Nadeesh."

"Nadeesh? The city of the holy temples? But it's long gone! There are only ruins—"

Dar nodded. "But those ruins have always been said to retain the holiness of its past and that the souls of many of its enlightened builders remain . . . I should have seen it from the beginning. It makes perfect sense that Nadeesh would be a part of this." He exhaled, aware that matters would not be as simple as finding the ancient city. "And though it is not far from this place, it is more obvious than ever that we must race there as quickly as we can."

Even as he said that, they heard again the war machines of the invaders soaring over Ancor's skies. Whether they hunted his band or sought other enemies, he did not know. What mattered was that time had run out. The fate of Ancor was imminent.

For . . . among the other images that had so briefly passed through his thoughts was one of Edurac.

Edurac . . . in flames.

VORANNOS TOOK OUT his rage on the remaining figures that the dead Kyrik had used to house his spirit. With a brief glare, he caused them to shatter to a million scant pieces.

In the midst of his tirade, the voice of Zorena touched his thoughts. She had news to report.

"This is the direction he goes, my lord," the huntress said, sending images of Dar's path. "There is a city that way, one long dead and buried by the jungle . . ."

"A city?" Vorannos forgot his anger. "A city . . ." The sorcerer Orestian had on previous occasions presented him with several old parchments from the libraries. While they had contained few items of interest, one name had caught Vorannos's attention.

The lord of Ishram grinned. Fate was truly his servant.

"Nadeesh . . ." he said with pleasure.

WE'VE DONE EVERYTHING *we could and it isn't enough!* Leardius thought in growing dismay as he watched his beloved kingdom struck again and again by waves of evil. On the ground, Xorot's horde pressed from all sides. In the air, demons—or things that could easily pass for such—continued to raze the city within. There was nowhere to hide, nowhere to run.

He knew nothing of his family's fate and could only pray that they lived. Yet how long would he wish that upon them, what with the defenders dying by the scores with each passing minute? Communication had broken down with most of his allies, too, but some dire messages had reached him.

King Akuran was dead, his head supposedly sent flying from his charging body by some foul disk racking through the air. Two of Leardius's other counterparts were nowhere to be found and their forces were in disarray.

Heratos lived, thankfully, but minus one arm. He was only that much whole thanks to the sacrifice of his mount, Baliphon, who had, despite his own mortal wounds, managed to return with his master before collapsing dead.

There are many to honor here this day and not all of them are human! Indeed, if not for the animals and insects that Dar had been able to send during his journey, Edurac might already have fallen. Leardius had no idea just how many of Ancor's fauna had perished, but the numbers had to be as great as that of Edurac's human losses, probably far more if the insects were counted individually.

Om had done his best to guide the creatures and although he had done as astounding job as far as the bearded monarch could see, there was no doubt that Dar would have far better organized them. Only the Beastmaster could truly communicate with the animals, but, through the deep meditations he had learned through his martial arts, the dwarf was at least able to influence some of the creatures to do certain tasks. However, without Dar, a true cohesive force was a concept beyond any of them, and so they perished by the hundreds.

Maintaining a cohesive force was also a concept quickly being lost by the human defenders as well. The various armies were splintering and the fires breaking out throughout the city were surely fueling their falling morale. Where could there be hope when there was nothing left to defend? Telling them over and over that the libraries needed to be preserved was not enough; most of the soldiers—and their leaders—had enough trouble thinking a cache of old parchments and the like were worth their lives . . .

"Something must be done," Leardius said to himself, a habit that had grown more frequent in the past few harrowing days, "even if it is only to show these damned fiends that we'll not simply set our heads to the chopping block for them! We'll make them know that they've been in a war . . . one they'll never forget . . ."

"What was that you said?" shouted Tal, marching up to him. The Beastmaster's brother was covered in blood, grime, and what passed for the life fluids of many an invader from the stars. Dar would have been proud of his younger sibling, Leardius thought.

"Edurac will fall," he told Tal bluntly.

The other king opened his mouth to protest, then nodded. "Unless my brother's return is imminent, you are right."

"There is a chance to save the weak for a time." Leardius looked to the front gate. "If we can gather every good man and horse left to us and pray that the animals at least charge in the same direction . . ."

"And the libraries?" Dar's brother was one of the few who truly grasped their possible importance.

"The invaders still think there's something—a map, a description—in that place that can lead them to this . . . this Fountain. I've set a small detachment of trusted men into the place. When the city's emptied—us charging the enemy and the unarmed fleeing the opposite direction—they'll wait until the last moment and set everything inside on fire at a prescribed time. And both the glory of Edurac's past and whatever they hope to find in the libraries will be gone forever . . . damn them . . ."

Tal immediately grasped what he intended, and approval—with resignation—crossed his features. He knew how hard it was for Leardius to destroy both his city and its legacy. "I'll give word immediately."

With every able fighter already prepared to give his life, it was not all that long before the force Leardius desired took shape. Messengers sent word to those outside the walls to be ready. A select guard—a weak and injured Heratos at its head—put together the most delicate part of the plan: the gathering of the innocents for escape.

"I should be with you, damn it!" the burly monarch growled to Leardius and Tal.

"There must be someone with a presence to lead them," the lord of Edurac returned. "If you can reach Harrath, it'll at least buy some lives for a time."

"Until Harrath is also swept under the shroud."

"The Beastmaster may yet come, even if not in time to save Edurac. I would that some of our loved ones survive."

With that, Heratos could not argue. He bowed his head and saluted the pair. "May you and the others mark Edurac's passing with the blood of many a foe."

With Heratos gone, Leardius and Tal returned to their own mounts. Outside, they knew, the other defenders had managed a strategic retreat. The invaders seemed willing to let them do so, since there was, in truth, nowhere to go that they would not soon be overwhelmed.

An explosion rocked Edurac. Tal and his host looked back.

"They're so anxious, they nearly hit the libraries themselves," Leardius commented bitterly. They both wondered whether it was a sign that Dar had failed and that the enemy's master had the mysterious Fountain, but neither had put that fear into words.

Another explosion struck one of the nearby sections of the great wall.

"Time's run out! Leardius shouted. "Sound the horns! Alert those at the back gates, too!"

The horns blared. The men at the front gates quickly worked to open them. Leardius nodded to Tal, who nodded back. Unlike previous forays by both of them, they had no illusions about returning. They would fight and fight until they could fight no more.

At the same time, through the lesser gates to the north, the kings knew that thousands of innocents were now fleeing with whatever they could carry toward the bitter land of Andereas and, beyond that, Harrath. Neither man suggested to the other that the refugees might not even make it. What mattered was to give them the chance.

"For Edurac!" shouted King Leardius, waving his sword. "For all Ancor!"

They burst out of the city with a combined roar so great it sounded like thunder. As they rode, they were joined not only by those defenders who had pulled back, but those few animals who had thus far survived. Leardius rode past lions and elks and rhinos and more. General Om appeared among the lead riders, his expression calm but his eyes burning.

Leardius knew exactly where he wanted the point of his force's spearhead to hit. Even from here, he could see the standards of the traitor kings . . . and, especially, Xorot.

"There!" he shouted. "There!"

Tal acknowledged his command, understanding that, if they were to perish, they could do so to best effect by trying to do damage to their villainous counterparts. Such a brash act would also hopefully startle their enemies, buying precious time for the escape of Heratos and his charges.

The land ahead filled with shouting, bloodthirsty faces. Above, monstrous things of metal, flesh, or both began to dive down upon them.

The front lines collided. Leardius struck down one Vorundite after another but could not get close to the standard he desired.

Instead, he was suddenly attacked by another helmeted figure familiar to him.

"Cassiun!" Leardius growled. "Surprised to see your cowardly Halcurian hide up in front!"

"Save your taunts, old one!" retorted the enemy king, a broad-shouldered warrior half Leardius's age and with long blond hair bound into a series of tails. Clad in a combination of leather and mail, he swung at the ruler of Edurac with a huge war mace.

The nailed head pounded against Leardius's round shield, nearly cracking it with the first blow. Leardius returned the favor with a quick slash at Cassiun.

"You're a fool, Cassiun!" Leardius shouted. "Think you'll get the rewards promised you? They won't need you or that lapdog Xorot once we've fallen!"

Cassiun did not answer, more interested in crushing his foe's skull or chest. The war mace pounded down again and again, pressing Leardius back.

"Your day's past, old one!" the Halcurian king mocked. "You

should've stayed with the women and children . . . and awaited our coming."

He raised his mace for one more powerful swing.

Leardius ran him through under his weapon arm.

The Halcurian's brow wrinkled in surprise. He started to shake his head—possibly in denial of being defeated by the much older king—then fell off his horse.

A panting Leardius tried to catch his breath. The battle had already taken more out of him than he had thought it would. There was some dreadful truth to Cassiun's words.

Someone struck him hard in the side. Although the breastplate took the brunt of the blow, it was still a heavy-enough hit to rattle his ribs and knock some of his regained breath from him.

He twisted to meet his new foe—and beheld Xorot of the Claw.

"Ha! Saw you with that pig of a Halcurian! Good strike, Leardius! Saves you for me!"

"You'll be . . . joining Cassiun soon!" The king of Edurac swung, but Xorot easily deflected his blow with his own wooden shield. Leardius barely parried a vicious strike by the warlord's battle-ax.

"Told him that you were mine, Leardius!" growled Xorot, grinning like a mad wolf. "Told all!"

They traded blows again. Leardius felt his strength failing. *Maybe Cassiun had been right,* he thought.

Then, with a roar of rage in great part focused on his own foolish thoughts, Leardius attacked in earnest. His blade bit at Xorot again and again. The warlord retreated as best as his horse would allow him.

Leardius's confidence rose. He darted in again. His blade left a small scar of blood on Xorot's left arm. Leardius had the Vorundite pressed. He watched for an opening, saw it, and lunged.

Xorot's shield easily knocked his sword to the side. The warlord's ax came at Leardius, who tried to move swiftly enough to deflect it but could not. His flurry of attacks had left him too weary and slow to protect himself now . . . just as he realized Xorot had intended.

The ax buried itself in the top of his breastplate near the collar bone. Leardius felt an agonizing shock of pain . . . then a numbness. His sword and shield dropped from his twitching hands. He wobbled in the saddle.

I am dead, the king of Edurac knew. *May my people at least be safe—*

He toppled lifeless from his mount, the last sound the wild, raucous laughter of Xorot.

19

THE HILLS WERE JAGGED AND STEEP, ALMOST LIKE SMALL mountains. Yet although they had to struggle with a trail that was often nearly vertical, Dar and his companions pushed forward, the sense that they were near to their goal growing with each step.

Sharak flew ahead, assisting the Beastmaster by seeking the best possible path based on Dar's desire. However, the eagle's work proved more and more difficult as mist began to drape over the vast region. Only the high peaks and the highest tree crowns were visible in the long valley. The mist continued on all the way to the horizon.

The Beastmaster gritted his teeth, certain that Nadeesh lay somewhere under that mist, but now wary that because of it he might yet lead the party astray. As they reached the summit of the highest of the mountainous formations—a place that made them feel as if they stood at the top of the world—Dar carefully surveyed the sea of fog below.

"Is it down there?" Tara asked, squinting.

"It must be . . . I feel it . . . but . . ." He would have liked some visible sign.

Sharak let out a screech. The magnificent eagle suddenly dove into the mist. Dar tried to make him stop, but the bird ignored his mental entreaties.

A moment later, Sharak's mind vanished from his. The Beastmaster started.

"What is it?"

"I can no longer feel him . . . it is not as if he's dead, just that . . . he's beyond my reach."

Before he could say more, the eagle suddenly rose up from the mist. With another screech, Sharak turned and headed back into the mist.

"He has found something!" Dar explained excitedly. "He won't say exactly what, but it must be Nadeesh!"

With growing eagerness, the Beastmaster led the others down the side of the imposing mountain. The mist enveloped them, and although Dar expected it to be cool and moist, it was slightly warm . . . and comforting.

He and Tara had been trying to keep an eye on Jalan's safety, but although the Beastmaster had made sure to have the boy follow directly behind him, Jalan somehow lost his footing.

The boy suddenly slid into Dar and Tara. The three humans went plunging down at a terrible pace, crashing through shrubs and rocky outcroppings that then joined them in their tumble. Behind them, Ruh rushed to keep up, while the ferrets, on Dar, scrambled up to his chest to avoid being injured.

With a swift grab at a solid-looking outcropping, the Beastmaster stopped his momentum. The Touargang snatched hold of his leg.

"Catch Jalan!" he called.

Tara seized the boy with ease. The three lay there panting.

"I—I'm sorry!" Jalan gasped.

The Beastmaster smiled. "Do not apologize. We are all right, even Kodo and Podo, see?"

The two ferrets jumped over to Jalan and began nuzzling and licking his face. The boy giggled and, now that it was safe, hugged the pair.

With a chuckle, Dar helped Tara to her feet. The two grinned at one another, but just as he was about to say something, a vision over her shoulder made him forget all else. She glanced behind her . . . and her amazement mirrored his.

"It's a city . . ." Tara declared. "It's Nadeesh . . ."

Nadeesh. Dar continued to stare, now aware that he still had quite a search to go. Yes, here could be found the next and final mandala, but, looking over the vastness of the ancient city, Dar had no idea where to begin.

Mist infiltrated the stone structures and surrounding growth, but enough was visible to give some hint of the city's former glory. Nadeesh spread as far as the eye could see. Tremendous overgrowth embraced the buildings, statues, and other structures as if lovers. Lush flowers covered much of the plant life—golden, tube-shaped flowers, red ones like stars, deep blue blossoms akin to faces, and so many more. Bees and other nectar-seeking insects fluttered docilely from flower to flower. Shimmering green and gold hummingbirds darted past the party as they strode toward the city. Butterflies were in abundance, sometimes seeming like flowers themselves, so great was their clustering and so varied in color were their wings. Nadeesh was truly a paradise . . . but one without people.

The Beastmaster was not heartened too much by the wondrous growth; the invaders would eventually raze even this area once their search and the eradication of Ancor's people was finished.

The bronze stone given to him by Baraji continued to grow warmer on his chest. Dar touched the stone, inspecting the gold striations, which to his eye seemed to glow. Yet, with all these signs, he had still seen no one other than his own party. Where was the sage?

They made their way among the ancient edifices, their attention ever shifting between the great task and marveling over the city itself. Around them, the evidence of what had once been a mighty kingdom continued to present itself. Great walls indicated construction of tremendous height. Traces of gold made the statues and structures glitter even in the mist. Intricate carvings covered everything. Stylized beasts that reminded him of tigers, horses, elephants, and more stood proudly as if as much a part of Nadeesh as the human characters beside them. There were images of dancing figures reminiscent of Om in look or even Baraji at times. Dar wondered if his former mentor had any tie to the city, as the stone perhaps indicated.

Along the remnants of a stone street wide enough to admit a herd of elephants, the party came across giant statues of what the Beastmaster could only believe were gods and goddesses, wise men and women. Some were absolutely human, others seemed to have the traits of animals, such as the eyes of cats and the hooves of antelopes. Each was carved with such accuracy that they were clearly individuals. They all wore flowing robes, but none exactly the same. Even their general features were distinct enough from one another that they appeared to be from many lands, many races. The only unifying factor was the look of immense understanding and calm on each face. The statues seemed to watch the intruders as the group passed, but, if so, not with enmity, Dar thought.

The stone grew hot. A vision flashed through his head. He saw the street new, the stones perfectly aligned as far as the eye could see and with not even a single weed poking out between them. The statues were perfectly preserved and now were painted and sculpted to look as if they were real people.

Dar blinked. Another memory came unbidden. Robed figures like monks drawing massive, highly intricate mandalas in pools of sand. With tiny, colored pieces, they created panoramas that made the Beastmaster's own previous drawings crude by comparison.

However, even more than their complexity, there was something about these mandalas that differed from the rest. These were being created with a definite and more immediate purpose in mind. The sages—Dar could think of them as nothing else—looked as if they were preparing to leave for somewhere.

The vision faded. Dar could only assume that he had somehow witnessed a scene out of the kingdom's abandonment, although why that should be significant, he could not say. He fingered the stone again, wondering what, if anything, he could do to hurry the search. Dar had no doubt that the earlier vision of Edurac had been a true one. They had to find the Fountain . . .

He focused inward, trying to combine the forces unleashed by the chakras and somehow use them in conjunction with the stone. The stone had to be part of the answer or else why would Baraji have given it to him? There was a point to its malleability—

Above, Sharak let loose with a warning screech. A strange, pale light illuminated the mist . . . followed by a blinding, gold glow that surrounded Dar and the others. Shielding his eyes, the Beastmaster stared through the slits between his fingers.

Shapes formed in the glow, shapes easily recognized by now.

The Pygmesians and the other mutates surrounded them. Among the latter, Dar sighted two of the scaled figures from Sravasi's clearing.

And, looming tall over the rest, was a brutally handsome giant in whose defining countenance the Beastmaster saw only evil. Dar did not have to see the fear in which the mutates held him to know that the Ishramites' dark lord was among them.

The materialization of the invaders took but a heartbeat, yet in that time Dar also acted. Even as he recognized who the giant must be, the Beastmaster had his sword out. He lunged among the nearest of the Pygmesians, cutting open a path.

But a cry from Jalan stopped him in his tracks. Dar whirled. The boy struggled with one of the chief reptiles as the ferrets sought to help him. Tara and Ruh were surrounded by Pygmesians.

A powerful fist struck a distracted Dar hard in the jaw, sending the Beastmaster flying to the ground.

The giant loomed over him, the eyes an inhuman mirror showing Dar his own battered face. Baraji's gift shimmered bright on his chest.

"I am Vorannos," the lord of Ishram declared, his voice booming. From where they were trapped by the mutates' deadly weapons, Tara stared open-mouthed at the invaders' leader and Ruh growled angrily. "Bow before me, kneel before me, and I will grant a painless death for you and yours . . ."

Dar did not move. He eyed the giant defiantly.

"And you are this mudhole's glorious savior?" Vorannos laughed. "Do you think to fight me? The only reason you are not dead already is by sheer whim on my part, Dar of Emur, so-called master of the beasts! There is only one thing I need of you, and you wear it on your skin . . ."

The tattoos scattered over the torso of the giant were evidence enough of what Vorannos desired. Dar mourned those sages who had suffered at the invader's hand and he determined to see that the suffering for *all* Ancor end here and now.

The Beastmaster jumped to his feet in a single movement so quick that it made Vorannos's momstrous underlings stiffen in surprise. But the lord of Ishram caught Dar by the throat in midleap.

He pulled the Beastmaster close, whispering for him alone, "We are bound together, you and I! From the first moment a breath was taken by life on Ishram and Ancor, our destiny was decided! The ancient script reads that one world was destined to become the Gate of Heaven while the other the Gate of Hell and each was to have its guardian!" Vorannos shook Dar. "But Ancor will be without its guardian and I shall make of it the Gate of Hell a thousand times over once the Fountain is mine . . ."

Dar did not answer, looking instead to the chakras and himself. He saw with their help where he needed to attack. Summoning his will and strength, he threw his efforts into one powerful strike.

The edge of his hand hit the base of Vorannos's neck.

A shock ran through Dar, but also his foe. Vorannos let out a howl of pain and threw the Beastmaster from him. Both warriors were surrounded by a static aura.

"You—have caused me—*discomfort*—little one," the lord of Ishram rumbled like thunder. His mirror eyes flashed and in them Dar saw his death reflected.

They lunged at one another, hands grappling, gazes locked. Dar did not fear death, only failure to Ancor and his companions. With his hands alone, he held the giant at bay.

"I have plotted this moment a thousand ways," Vorannos roared at him, "calculated if I could use any mandalas or only those you sought! I urged you on through pursuit and death, even tried turning you—"

"And lost your sorcerer because of it!"

"What is one less dog when one has an endless kennel of eager hunters?" The giant shifted his gaze. "See how easily they have dragged your friends to their knees . . ."

Dar could not help but look into the mirror eyes and see what was reflected from behind him. He saw Ruh struggling against Pygmesians and Tara on one knee battling others. The reptile that had earlier seized Jalan now grabbed for the boy again, while other servants of Vorannos pursued even Sharak and the ferrets. The mutates pressed his friends farther and farther back, finally vanishing among the ancient buildings. The sounds of struggle almost immediately faded.

With a shout, the Beastmaster pushed away from Vorannos. He turned to follow his besieged companions—

A fiery force beat him to the ground. He could not see what happened as he was thrown, nor could he hear the struggles of his friends. Whatever force Vorannos used continued to press him into the dirt, as if the lord of Ishram intended to crush his bones.

"Seven mandalas you were told to seek, but with the six you have, that stone on your chest now comes to blazing life," the giant's voice called through Dar's agony. "This is no coincidence! I believe I have seven now—"

The Beastmaster was turned over by Vorannos's power, but he did not land on the ground again. Instead, arms and legs splayed out, Dar floated a foot above.

"Such a short, disappointing battle. I hoped for more."

Vorannos tore the glowing stone free. He clutched it in one hand, while raising his other hand palm up.

A terrible heat washed over Dar's skin, as if a thousand suns beat down on it. He felt his flesh ripple, pull against his muscle and sinew.

Dar screamed as his skin pulled up as if hooks tore it away. A tear erupted near one tattooed area, then another. With each, the Beastmaster screamed anew.

" 'He Who Must Be Faced' . . . in some things, the prophecies have been very misleading. All this interest in you . . . and for nothing save the mandalas . . . you could have been any fool."

His open hand squeezed into a fist.

All over Dar's torso, wherever there was a mandala tattooed to him, the Beastmaster's skin ripped free. Blood poured from the open wounds and dribbled on the ground from the floating patches of flesh. The mandalas that Dar had struggled so hard to achieve now hovered over him . . . then flew to Vorannos.

As they neared, the lord of Ishram spread wide his arms as if ready to embrace them. His torso grew crimson.

The tattoos adhered themselves and, as those before them had, immediately melded into the flesh. Where they had once looked a part of Dar, now they appeared as if always having been of Vorannos.

Without ceremony, he let the Beastmaster's gore-soaked body drop. Dar struck with a sickening, moist sound. One hand briefly rose, then fell. Dar lay still.

Vorannos grinned. " 'Ancor's Savior' . . . his name will be cursed by those who believed in him as they die . . ."

THERE WAS NOTHING she could do for Dar or the others. Tara readied herself for death, only wishing that she could somehow yet save Jalan.

They had been herded into a part of the city just beyond sight of where she had last seen Dar struggling. The invaders looked ready to end their little entertainment with one final, deadly sweep.

Jalan threw himself by her side. The lead reptile raised his weapon, the others following suit. Tara had witnessed enough of the horrible power of the invaders to know that there would not be much left of either her, Jalan, or the animals.

She clutched the boy tightly as they fired.

A great warmth spread over her. Tara opened her mouth to scream—

"You are not worthy of him," said a voice that she at first thought her own.

The Touargang looked around. She and the others no longer stood in Nadeesh, but in a mist-covered area of the jungle nearby.

Somehow, instead of dying, they had been magically transported to safety.

Ruh growled. Spear at the ready, Tara spun about.

The crimson-haired huntress who had earlier fought Dar slipped out in front of her. It was clear that she had come alone.

"What do you want?" Tara challenged.

"To find out what it is that makes the difference," Zorena replied snidely. "I see nothing worth mentioning, yet this is his choice . . ."

Tara finally realized that the huntress was comparing the two of them by measure of their feminine charm. The Touargang blushed.

"Yes . . . perhaps that's part of it . . . part of this world, even . . ."

It finally dawned on Tara what had happened. "You saved us!"

"A moment's rebellion, and one for which you've no cause to be grateful. I did it"—Zorena shook her head—"for him. I already regret it." She paused again. "But it won't matter. This world belongs to Vorannos . . . and your Beastmaster is dead . . ." Her tone as she uttered the last held a hint of what might have been sadness.

But if so, Tara, stunned by the revelation, did not notice it. "You lie!" the Touargang shouted. "It's not true!"

The other female warrior shrugged. "If you wish to see his flayed corpse, it lies in Nadeesh. It'll only cost you the life I just spared, even if only until my lord finishes off this—this *unique* world!"

Tara hesitated. Jalan looked up to her, his eyes pleading that the crimson-haired figure was lying. However, the Touargang princess could not honestly tell him so.

"Take this one and these animals and run as hard and as far as you can!" Zorena ordered. "I won't risk my life for you or him again! I won't! Go back to Nadeesh and get caught—and I'll gladly be the one that burns all of you to ash!"

And, with that threat, the other woman turned and vanished into the jungle again.

Tara spun in a circle, the spearpoint before her. She waited, but there was no sudden rush of invaders.

Ruh sniffed the air, and from the sound he made, the Touargang understood that he did not smell anything, either. They were truly alone in the jungle.

Her thoughts immediately shifted to Dar and what the other woman had said. Tara imagined the grisly scene and did not doubt that her adversary had spoken the truth. She would not have bothered saving those Dar had most cared about, otherwise. The Beastmaster had touched this one invader in a manner of which the Touargang had some understanding.

"Ruh!" Tara's mind swirled as the great cat came to her. Ruh would understand her, even if she was not the Beastmaster. "Ruh . . . I must go see to Dar and . . . and after that try to stop the invaders from reaching the Fountain! But I need you to take Jalan and Kodo and Podo with you and find help!" She looked up to where Sharak circled, the bird clearly caught between watching over the others and returning to Dar. "Sharak!" Tara called. "Your sharp eye can aid them in locating any other defenders nearby, be they human or animal! You must do it!"

The eagle screeched in protest, but then reluctantly veered away from Nadeesh. Ruh rumbled something that she decided to take as agreement to the rest of her plan. At least he did not follow her.

But Jalan tried. "I'm going with you!"

"No! You stay with the animals!" Before he could argue, Tara turned and raced off. Jalan had come from a more civilized race; his people did not live side by side with the ways of the jungle as the Touargang did. He did not have the tracking skills that she had. His only choice now would be to do as she said and follow the tiger in search of help.

Although her concern should have been first and foremost to find Zorena's master, Tara could not keep herself from trying to discover any trace of hope for Dar. Not only because of his destiny, but because she could not bear the thought of his dying. She had only just found him again . . .

The edge of the ruins rose up. Forcing her feelings down, Tara the warrior took over. She skirted around the area where the party had been surprised, watching for sentries.

A Pygmesian fell to her spear, the point thrusting through the joint at its neck between the helmet and the rest of the armor. Minutes later, she slew a reptile man. Still, the number of guards she encountered were oddly slight.

No, not so odd. The invaders' master, the horrific Vorannos, had what he wanted. There was nothing to stop him now. Why be overly concerned about one female warrior, a child, and some animals?

I'll make him regret that lack of concern, Tara swore. Somehow, she would. Her people were exceptional trackers. Once she had dealt with Dar's fate, Tara would find Vorannos and avenge the Beastmaster . . .

She finally made it to the Street of the Wise Ones, as she had originally felt that part of the path should be called. Dar's body would not lay far ahead. There was still no sign of any of the invaders and while on the one hand Tara was uneasy by that, on the other she was pleased to have no delay before her. Despite the certainty of what their reluctant rescuer had said, there was still a desperate hope in Tara's mind that, no matter what the nightmarish tortures through which Dar had gone, he might still live. If so, and if Vorannos believed him of no more threat, then perhaps Tara could help. Perhaps there still might be a chance for Dar . . . and Ancor.

But as she came within sight of Dar's defeat, there the Touar-gang beheld what could only make her fear for the worst.

The fear that, despite all her hopes, everything was lost.

. . .

AND SO IT had come to pass. Vorannos had defeated Ancor's pathetic defender and now readied himself to claim the greatest prize in all creation.

For this blessed moment, most of the servants had been sent away. Drayz and Kuln stood as honor guard for him as he approached the great statue. A handful of Pygmesians guarded the perimeter, not that there was anything left to guard against. Zorena was unaccustomedly absent, but that was a matter with which he could deal after he had finished here.

As he neared, he held up the bronze-colored stone. The golden striations shone bright. With cold calculations enhanced by the mechanisms in his mind, it had taken him but a few moments to note the malleability of the stone and, through further computation, reshape it into a seventh and final mandala. True, it was only the crude outline of one, although the striations in the rock did add a suitable effect. What only mattered was that he had the seven . . . the right seven.

In truth, the last few attacks against Dar had been feints, quite successful ones that had given the lord of Ishram the information he needed for his analysis. Now everything had fallen into place. Through additional estimations on his part and triangulation from the monitoring ship above, Vorannos had learned a truth about this ruin that Dar could not have seen from the ground. A connection between the various elements of the stone carried by the Beastmaster, the mandalas, and the construction of Nadeesh.

If uncovered and complete, the ruined city itself was one vast mandala . . . and now Vorannos stood at the heart.

He paused within arm's reach of the massive, marble statue that marked Nadeesh's heart. It was carved in the semblance of a seated, gently smiling elder: a sage. Vorannos had no doubt that it had been meant as the ultimate sign of where those seeking the Fountain had to go.

The skill with which the ancients had carved the sage was lost on him. The serene, handsome face—untouched by time—could have been carved to look like a jester, for all Vorannos cared. The various details down the robed body were of little consequence. Only the symbols inscribed at the waist were of importance . . . for it was one of those that held the key.

He had taken the measure of each of the symbols there, chiseled by the forgotten artisan to be just the perfect size in which to fit the bronze stone if it were of an identical shape. With ease, Vorannos had twisted and bent the malleable stone into the symbol his mechanisms had analyzed as the only choice. It was shaped like what he knew to be the universal Ancorian symbol for water . . . and, thus, the Fountain.

Fitting the stone in place, the lord of Ishram then concentrated on the tattoos. He imagined the chakras opening and the inner strength that they would give him. When Vorannos was certain that those powers were his to wield, the giant stepped back and bellowed, "Behold, powers of creation! I have the keys! I have the right! I claim the Fountain as mine! Let the way be open! Let the Gate of Heaven give up its secret! I am Vorannos and I command it!"

As he spoke, he drew upon the energies within him that his machines made his own. He added them to what he imagined the powers of the chakra would unleash. He pictured the Fountain in his head as he thought it—a grand and glorious, encrusted structure several times his height with gleaming, crystal clear waters—and felt his blood stir.

"Open the way!" he shouted. "By the prophecies and the mandalas, I, lord of all, demand it!"

The air around him crackled—

And still nothing happened.

With a violent roar, Vorannos ripped the stone free, then spun around. His gaze fell upon a random mutate. With a stomach-churning squeal, the hapless creature shriveled within itself until nothing remained but the armor and breathing machine.

"Still nothing! Nothing!" The baleful orbs cast upon Drayz and Kuln, who stood as still as death. Vorannos did not strike them down, though the desire was there.

"Your eyes are blind . . ." said a voice that both chilled him and immediately became the focus of his fury. "They see only without, not within. For that reason alone, you can never reach the Fountain."

The lord of Ishram thrust his empty hand in the direction of the voice. A fearsome, gray-green cloud enveloped the area. Stone sizzled and plant life already dead turned to ash.

And of the one who had spoken, there was no trace.

But even as the grin spread over Vorannos's twisted face, he heard the voice repeat, "Never reach the Fountain . . ."

Vorannos turned again, but this time much more slowly and without unleashing any of his deadly arsenal.

"So . . ." he murmured.

The bleeding figure strode toward him, both hands gripping the mighty sword. Where the skin had been torn free, muscles could be seen shifting and veins could be seen pumping. The hardened mutates stirred in uneasiness at this macabre vision approaching their master. They had witnessed atrocities unbelievable in their service to Vorannos, but to see the dead coming to confront him . . . that was a far more frightening aspect, if only for its uniqueness.

Against all sanity . . . the Beastmaster lived.

20

KING LEARDIUS WAS DEAD . . .

The news reached Tal even as he himself struggled to keep alive. There were too many of the enemy and they were everywhere. Even the land below was not safe, for, having learned from the animals, the invaders had sent their own borers to undermine the defenders and if a few of their own fell with them, they seemed not to care.

King Leardius was dead, which meant that it was now up to Tal to keep Edurac standing. He still prayed that his brother would succeed, but in his heart, doubt began to creep in. It was not for lack of faith in Dar's ability—just that the enemy had so overpowered his forces, he could only imagine what his brother had faced.

We will meet again, he had assured Dar.

If that were to happen, it appeared it would only be in the afterlife . . .

. . .

AS HE NEARED the lord of Ishram, Dar became an even more astounding and unnerving figure to Vorannos's minions, for his skin began to heal, the blood ceasing to flow and then new flesh wrapping over the ruined areas.

The Beastmaster felt his body filled by that which the chakras released. He understood that all that was him, all he had experienced, all he had learned—even his painful sacrifice—had been necessary. The mandalas were no longer necessary, for they had only been needed to unlock the chakras.

All of this was something that the lord of Ishram could never comprehend. Indeed, as Dar's skin healed, Vorannos glanced at his own body and saw the tattoos vanish. His gaze darted back to the Beastmaster's torso, where he furiously sought some sign that the mandalas had returned to the Ancorian.

His rage meant nothing to Dar, who had awoken after a miraculous journey within himself that had begun the moment he had fallen from Vorannos's monstrous attack. The Beastmaster had slipped into a coma so deep that his soul had begun the journey to the beyond, through a tunnel of light. Yet his path had altered, for Ancor and his friends still needed him. Dar had gone through flashes of his own life as he had returned, each of those moments an integral part in his finally achieving total understanding of who he was. As the Beastmaster had at last stirred, it had been with the awareness that his entire life had been steered to this event, this turning point in the existence of all that had been, was, and would be a part of Ancor.

"I ripped those from your hide before; I will do it again!" rasped the lord of Ishram.

In reply, a silent Dar turned the point of his blade toward his foe, beckoning him.

Vorannos twisted his empty hand and a black, glittering sword that emitted an evil hum thrust out of his arm and into his grip. Roaring, he charged the Beastmaster. The clash of their weapons left streaks like lightning. The black blade let out a sinister shriek each time. Dar felt as if tiny lightning bolts sought to assail him, but still he did not flag. Over and over they struck at one another and though Vorannos had the advantage of height and more, he could not break Dar's defenses. Indeed, the Beastmaster beat him back and back.

Kuln and Drayz moved to take Dar from behind, for they knew that their lord had no care for honor, only victory. They readied their sinister tube weapons—

A war cry startled both. From behind a nearby broken wall, out leaped the slim figure of Tara, blocking their way. She used the spear to drive Drayz back, then bashed Kuln in the face with the blunt end. As the one reptile fell, the Touargang planted the tip in the ground and used the weapon to vault at her remaining opponent.

Her feet struck Drayz hard, sending him back against one of the walls. The wall itself cracked as the collision stunned the savage hunter.

But as Tara whirled, she saw a Pygmesian take aim. The female warrior hefted her spear, aware that the duel would be a close one—

Roaring, Ruh fell upon the creature. The tiger ripped apart the would-be assassin before it could fire.

She may have been angry at Ruh for disobeying, but she could not help but be grateful. The situation was desperate.

Barely had Ruh appeared than Sharak flew past Tara. The eagle blinded another attacker, then ripped out the breathing tube.

Even Jalan, Kodo, and Podo sought to assist. The boy hid behind another wall, throwing whatever heavy stones he could find in order to at least distract the enemy, while Seto cheered him on by calling the boy's name each time a stone struck a target. The ferrets, meanwhile, scampered in and among the mutates, tripping them up and moving so quickly none could aim well enough to hit them.

Dar was both pleased to discover that his friends were well and frustrated that they had not fled after his own supposed demise. Yet their presence was a comfort and, in some fashion, contributed to the astounding forces unleashed within him by the chakras. Those forces enabled him to continue to stand strong against the Lord of Ishram's evil power.

Vorannos gritted his teeth. The mirror eyes revealed nothing, but the lord of Ishram's stance finally gave hint of some weakness to Dar. The Beastmaster took advantage of that weakness, at last slipping under Vorannos's guard and bringing the blade across his stomach.

The edge cut cleanly not only into the stomach, but through tubes and odd wires spread throughout the lord of Ishram's flesh. The Beastmaster's eyes widened as he registered this monstrous aspect of his foe.

Vorannos let out a growl. He staggered back, clutching his long wound. A dark, moss-green fluid dripped from it, a fluid whose foul stench burned the Beastmaster's nostrils.

Dar barreled into him, throwing the larger fighter against the statue. Vorannos rolled back, clearly in pain. He muttered something that the Beastmaster could not catch.

A sinister black aura enveloped Vorannos. It pulsated, as if alive and breathing.

Only too late did the Beastmaster register what that meant. He thrust at his adversary—

The aura—and, within it, a snarling Vorannos—disappeared.

Dar started to let out a curse, then saw something lying on the ground surrounded by droplets of still-sizzling green blood. Baraji's gift. It was the one thing Dar had wanted from the invader's master and he had feared that Vorannos had managed to hold onto it even wounded.

Seizing the stone, the Beastmaster turned to aid his friends . . .

only to find they, too, without foes. In their case, though, Dar could see that the mutates had retreated into the jungle, either filled with confusion after their master's frantic departure or possibly responding to some signal unheard by him.

Tara and Jalan ran to him, the animals on their heels. Kodo and Podo ran up into his arms, licking his chest and throat, while Ruh rubbed against his leg. Sharak, ever dignified, alighted onto a branch and screeched his approval of matters.

Dar asked the ferrets to return to their pouch. He then held up the bronze stone. "Their master is wounded. That buys us the time we need."

As the others waited in respectful silence, he considered the stone's purpose. Dar knew it was not the seventh mandala, although it could be shaped, with its striations, to resemble one. The Beastmaster gazed at the great statue and the surrounding buildings. He sensed their purpose now. The true seventh mandala was the city itself. Vorannos had been mistaken, thinking that the city's design only marked where the way to the Fountain lay. He had thought the stone and the six mandalas all he needed. The stone *was* essential, though.

More and more, things fell into place. Vorannos believed owning the mandalas was enough to open the chakras. But he had not earned them and so they had done nothing. Dar could only hope that it would be different for him. He fingered the stone, altering its shape. Suddenly, pieces snapped off, pieces that then fit into other indentations the Beastmaster had not seen earlier. Once in, they fit as snug as if they were supposed to be there.

He worked faster and faster. Time was pressing. Dar was close to finding the key, but was he close enough?

He looked to the statue, studying it with more care than ever. Dar let out a slight gasp. The statue was, he saw with some surprise, composed of the same material as the stone his mentor had given him. More surprising yet, though, was the likeness.

It was *Baraji*—or rather, it looked like the younger Baraji whom he had seen just before departing the mountains. There could be no coincidence and Dar marveled at how near and yet so far Vorannos had been from his goal.

Thinking of Vorannos, Dar stirred himself from staring at Baraji's face and studied the symbols at the waist. Some were symbols he recognized. As the truth began to dawn on him, the Beastmaster manipulated the stone's shape as he wended his way around. The shape of the stone was essential. It had to match some symbol. Like the hands of a master sculptor working clay, Dar manipulated the unique facets of the bronze stone into one form after another. He felt a calmness within him as he worked, even despite time surely running short. The last was emphasized by sounds from beyond Nadeesh, the roars of more flyers in the vicinity, as if the mutates were receiving reinforcements with the intention of flooding into the city. No, there could be little time before that happened—

One symbol caught his attention. Looked at from one direction, it reminded him of a symbol he knew that meant *life*. Yet, when studied from the opposite side, it was so different . . . and hinted of a symbol that the Beastmaster knew referred to death.

Dar stood before the image, studying the delicate patterns of it in order to best understand. As he gazed directly upon it, he saw in it a third meaning . . . a meaning beyond life and death.

Eternity.

Suddenly, Dar felt a sense of absolute certainty within. Confident that he had been shown the way, Dar held up the stone, wondering if he could alter it enough so that it would fit into the carved pattern.

Only as he placed it near did the Beastmaster see that his hands had already shaped it just perfectly.

A tremendous rumbling filled the air. The ground shook. Dar lost his hold on the stone, which fell into some of the flowering vegetation surrounding the statue. Tara gasped and bent to help him find it. They all knew the thundering rumble and the tremor had not been natural. The invaders were closing in. Vorannos likely had given command to take the stone back at any cost.

"Here!" Tara called. She thrust the reshaped stone into his palm.

"This is it," he told the others. A wondrous sensation filled him and he knew that he was near to reaching the legendary Fountain.

Dar set the stone in the symbol he had chosen. It fit *perfectly.*

There was movement above, a slight grinding sound. He looked up.

The stone eyes gazed down on the Beastmaster. In his head, a voice asked, *Who are you?*

Dar knew the answer without hesitation. He was all that his trials had made him. He was the essence of his experience intertwined with his innate nature.

"I *am*," he quietly responded.

The statue raised its gaze. At the same time, it took on an even more distinct likeness to Baraji. The giant figure spread its hands to the side and, as it did, a perfect crack rose from the ground up along the body and even midway between the face. The crack widened, perfectly splitting the statue in twain. Within the statue, Dar beheld a vast, dark gap that could only be the way to the Fountain.

The next second, there was a rumble, like a roaring river. The Beastmaster stared deep into the gap—

What almost appeared to be a hand formed of rushing water burst from the hole. Before Dar could even blink, it enveloped not only him, but everyone else as well. They were thrust through its center and into the gap.

"Dar!" Tara shouted. The Touargang tried to reach for him, but although they did not grow farther apart, neither did the distance shrink. The Beastmaster and the others were carried downward at astounding speed, descending farther and farther into the depths of Ancor. They were carried about in the rushing water, waves constantly spilling over their heads, though never long enough to drown them.

Dar tried to gain some control of the situation, but could find no manner by which to do so. Behind—or actually above—the others tumbled after one or two at a time. Dar caught sight of Jalan once, the boy clinging tightly to Seto, but otherwise it was hard to see how any of them were doing.

The torrent abruptly changed direction. The Beastmaster prepared to be battered against the rocky walls that made up the impossible passage, but at the last moment the water cushioned him.

Down and down and down they plummeted, tossed about as if nothing, yet never in the least bruised . . . thus far. The rocks and earth changed constantly, sometimes rows of black, other times brown, sometimes glittering like diamonds, other times as dull as mud. Dar saw deposits of iron, of silver, and of gold, though all passed in the blink of an eye. It seemed as if all the richness that was Ancor itself, all that made it alive, were there before him.

And still the gargantuan spout carried them down, always without warning changing angles, but ever ultimately descending. The water cushioned Dar and his friends not only on each side, but below as well and, if not for the lightning-swift drop, might have left them secure in their fate. Despite the constant churning of the water—or perhaps because of it—the spout never sucked them into its walls, where surely they would have perished.

As they descended deeper, Dar saw his first chance to seize Tara. The two grasped arms and pulled. For a few moments, they clung together uncertain as to whether the spout would separate them. When that did not happen, Dar peered up in search of Jalan. He saw the boy's legs spinning above him, but Jalan remained well out of reach.

The boy's sandal went flying into the water, where it was immediately battered to shreds against the rock. Jalan still clung tightly to

Seto, whose glittering eyes seemed to hint that the parrot, at least, found the descent amusing. As for the boy, he looked more awestruck than frightened.

The Touargang looked neither amused nor awed, only anxious, for which Dar could not blame her. He held her against him, trying to let his calm radiate to her. At the same time, he sent reassurance to the animals, who, understandably, were as wary as either the woman or the boy.

And then suddenly they sat on a field of long, waving grass and flowers where gossamer butterflies gently rose around them. The soft wings caressed their bodies as the insects fluttered off to some of the many glorious flowers surrounding them.

The transition was so abrupt that no one moved, no one breathed. The spout had not lowered them to this spot; they had simply appeared. In fact, of the tremendous spout, there was not the slightest hint. Dar noticed also that all of them were already nearly dry.

"It—it's beautiful . . ." Tara whispered, the first able to make use of her voice.

Dar felt a sense of serenity surrounding them. "We are in the womb of Ancor. . . ."

They slowly looked around, the Beastmaster also using the moment to make certain that all his companions were with him. Everyone down to Kodo and Podo sat in the idyllic field. The ferrets were, in fact, the first to recover and explore their new surroundings, even if their search mostly involved smelling the brightly colored flowers dotting the area.

"I've never seen flowers like these," Tara remarked. They were funnel-shaped at the base of the petals, then spread out in a star at the upper tips. Each had a rainbow of colors so vivid that the Touargang actually rubbed a few petals, almost as if she thought the colors would come off like some dye.

But the flowers were one of the most minor of miracles, as Dar discovered as he looked up. There were *stars* above, even though they were deep underground. Moreover, those stars were not only different than those seen from any place in his travels, but there were far too many of them. They filled the sky, in some places crowding one another, and all glittered so brightly that, even though there was no visible sun, it was as bright as day.

However, as Dar stared, he began to see other things set between the stars. Frowning, he looked farther to his right.

Miles distant, a vast, unbroken wall of stone covered the horizon . . . and when the Beastmaster followed it up . . . it rose all the way to the stars.

Only . . . they were not stars, he saw now.

"Those are crystal formations," Dar murmured in amazement. "Even perhaps diamonds. Look close, Tara. You can see rock formations between them. Look to every side. The walls rise all the way, arcing into the ceiling . . ."

Even as he spoke, they heard an animal's cry, but like none that the Beastmaster could identify. Dar gazed in the direction of the cry and saw three huge creatures who resembled elephants only in their stocky legs and bulky bodies. The heads were long like those of a crocodile, but the mouths had blunt, plant-eaters' teeth. The odd animals had ears more akin to a horse. They also had stubby tails.

"Look!" Jalan called with delight as he pointed up.

Above, a flock of glistening golden birds serenely flew ahead. They shone like tiny suns, so brilliant was their sweeping auric plumage. Their tail feathers spread out like graceful fans that waved slowly in the wind.

But as the Beastmaster followed their flight, something else on the horizon caught his gaze.

It looked like a lake. But there was more. Even as he saw it, Dar thought he also heard a faint sound like raindrops . . .

Dar instantly felt drawn toward the lake. With Ruh trotting a little before them, the party started forth. An impatient Sharak flew behind the golden flock. The lake did not look all that far, but Dar could delay no longer. The shock of finding themselves in such a paradise had already unwittingly wasted valuable minutes.

However, only barely had they begun walking than the land beneath their feet began flowing . . . as if made of water, not substance. The party slipped gently into it, so gently that what little initial fear some of them had quickly vanished. They did not even sink under the odd, liquid landscape, instead finding that they always floated with their head and shoulders above.

Jalan giggled as Seto perched atop his head. Tara smiled at Dar.

With a smile not only to her but the others, the Beastmaster turned and swam through the "grass." There was no need to explain to the others. Everyone instinctively knew that this was what they were supposed to do.

Here, in the womb of the world, they were now being cleansed of their earthly troubles. Each stroke refreshed the Beastmaster both in body and soul. He had never felt so renewed . . .

As they swam, they sighted other denizens of the underground world. Some were very akin to creatures on the surface, though often in unexpected ways. Over the waving field of grass glided a small group of what at first the Beastmaster thought were birds, but then saw more resembled rays of the deep waters. Their winged bodies rippled over the grass with ease and made perfect sense for this glorious environment.

But despite these wonders, it was the lake that more and more took their attention. As Dar had hoped, the distance was not all that far; this was indeed a compact world compared to those above.

The ground solidified as soon as they reached the end of the "grasslands." Although the land here was still green with life, it behaved like the jungles and solid earth to which Dar was used to. One by one, the party stepped up onto it, filled with a sense of pleasure and gratitude toward Ancor.

The Beastmaster surveyed the glistening lake, searching for some sign of the mythic Fountain. He could still hear the trickling, but could not place from where it originated. Above the waters, the golden birds soared without any care. Sharak did not follow them over the water, but steered close to the shore, seeking for his human brother any clue to their goal.

A massive, silver form broke the surface. Jalan let out a cry of awe. Like the birds, the whale gleamed. Water shot from its spout as it breached. Behind it came a second, then a third. Dar finally counted seven in all.

Whales? The Beastmaster marveled at the notion of such huge, magnificent creatures here, no matter how vast the lake. Was the body of water salted, as the sea was? And how had they gotten here? Could there be a passage from the seas above to this place?

So many questions, especially as to what purpose the whales might have here, continued to run through Dar's head, but he forced them aside. The shoreline lay only yards away. Eager to reach the lake, Dar pushed ahead of the rest. His feet kicked up gleaming white sand.

Waves gently lapped onto the sand. Dar stepped into the water, the sense of serenity filling him more than ever. He had been cleansed by his previous, intriguing swim, but that had merely been to prepare him for the ultimate peace that was the lake . . . and goal of his quest.

And as the Beastmaster thought of the last, he felt, rather than saw, something awaken in the lake. It stirred as if a living thing . . . and who was he to think it not? Dar raised his hands in pleasure and honor as the waters beyond began to bubble—

A sharp, burning pain struck him in the back of the head. Dar screamed and fell face-first into the lake. As he dropped, he heard the cries, both human and animal, of his friends. Struggling with all his might, the Beastmaster managed to push his head up enough to glance back. There he saw two blurry forms, one female . . . and not Tara.

Zorena . . . and behind her, his mocking grin the last thing the Beastmaster saw before blacking out, Vorannos.

ZORENA HAD FIRED, but her shots had only come after her master had fired upon Dar and the mutates had done so at the rest. The wide and deadly stream of crimson beams had enabled her to aim as she pleased, not as she had been commanded. Mixed in with so many other shots, no one could see that hers had done little but add to the damage done by those preceding her. It was not that the huntress had not wanted to obey, just that she had felt some unusual guilt for doing so. In this place, this striking place, it had almost felt *wrong* to bring forth violence.

It was a feeling that had arisen in her more and more above, but in this most pure of realms, it was magnified beyond her ability to comprehend.

The Beastmaster had been naive to think that Vorannos had been badly hurt. Even before he had been transported to his vessel, the mechanisms implanted throughout his body had begun the repairs. It had taken the ship's devices only a few moments more to fix what was still damaged.

For her part, Zorena—along with Drayz and Kuln—had reorganized those mutates that would follow along with the master's plot. Vorannos knew that although he could not open the way, surely the Beastmaster would be able to. It had then been only a matter of precision timing.

Throughout his reconstruction, the lord of Ishram had kept careful watch through a number of horach secreted among Nadeesh's structures. Zorena had awaited his signal and when it had come, she and the rest had transported to the location given.

There, they had witnessed the spout rising from the hidden entrance. It had begun to fade, but Vorannos had then appeared before it. Stretching forth a hand, he had, to Zorena, seemed to summon it forth again.

"Gather around me!" the giant had roared and his servants had quickly obeyed.

The spout had engulfed them, taking the entire band as if combined they weighed no more than a leaf. They had been carried through the stone gateway. The massive gates shut behind them with a resounding clash like thunder, a sound that had reverberated in Zorena's ears for several seconds after.

She surveyed the carnage as the memory faded. In the end, all would be as she had always expected it to be. The Fountain would be Vorannos's, and Ancor would become as tragic a place as Ishram, assuming that Vorannos left even that much.

The Gate of Heaven would be no more.

The huntress frowned. Not even *this* holy place would remain.

Her grip on her weapon tightened at the thought.

"I THANK YOU very much, Beastmaster," Vorannos mocked as he walked past the body without glancing at it. All that mattered to the lord of Ishram was the Fountain. Even the ripples of water that slowly began carrying Dar's still form out into the lake did not garner his interest in the least.

Nor did Vorannos care one whit about the Beastmaster's companions, whose still bodies were also added to the lake by the Pygmesians. As for the birds, Drayz and Kuln took pleasure in firing shots at the pair, and although they missed the swift avians, they also kept both from reaching Dar and the others.

"I can feel it . . . can't you, Zorena?" the lord of Ishram murmured as he gazed at the lake. "The mandalas, the stone, nothing is needed anymore. My destiny will be fulfilled. You will open both the gates of Heaven and Hell, my Fountain . . . and make their reality mine . . ." His laugh was filled with disdain as he added, "Only the pure may drink of the Fountain? Well, I am *pure* power! Pure domination! That is the only 'purity' that matters! You will be mine, Fountain, for nothing can be denied me now! I have crushed everything and everyone! I am lord of all! I am—*Vorannos,* now *lord of Eternity!*"

He raised his hands toward the pristine waters.

The lake began to bubble.

DAR SANK DEEP into the lake. As he did, he began to stir. With that hint of consciousness came dark thoughts of how he had failed everyone and everything.

But then something bumped his right side, sending him twirling. His eyes opened and he saw light far above. The surface came into sight, but although Dar feebly stretched his right hand toward that direction, he could not reach the surface. His lungs strained as he instinctively tried to keep from swallowing water.

Large, silver shapes surrounded him. The whales he and the others had witnessed earlier. Three of them converged on the Beastmaster.

And when they reached him, they shoved him *down.*

THE GOLDEN BIRDS abruptly fluttered up in a panic. The glittering crystals far above in the ceiling grew dimmer.

The waters before Vorannos churned mightily. The mirror eyes reflected a surge that suddenly shot up more than halfway to the great cavern's ceiling. As the surge reached its peak, tons of water spilled back down to the lake. Yet, as it struck, it did not simply became part of the shining body again, but built up above the surface.

Vorannos laughed, and his laugh was dark and terrible in its triumph. He gestured impatiently as a huge shape coalesced, a broad, elegant shape. It was a layered structure with a wide wall as tall as its summoner and upon which were the faces of smiling dryads with long tresses that wrapped around their beautiful faces. The wall was shaped to resemble arcing fish and whales identical to the silver ones, albeit much smaller.

As the next level formed, on it appeared an array of fantastic birds and other winged creatures, including the golden ones above. All seemed to be frolicking, and their numbers were staggering, as was their detail.

And yet, above them, a third and even more glorious level came into being, this one populated by sea creatures of myth and legend. There were intricate images of kraken, mermaids, seahorses, and more. Like the rest, they were posed in positions of wonder and pleasure and were so lifelike that one could almost expect them to go splashing into the lake again.

At the top, a glorious mandala with a thousand tiny star points glistened with the reflected colors of all around it. A hundred sages could not have completed its detail in as many generations. It moved as the water moved, spilling down and constantly replenishing itself.

And through its center, a spout of water shot high, the spray cascading down upon the other levels, constantly soaking them . . . which was of no trouble at all, for the entire structure itself was made of nothing less than water that constantly flowed yet somehow retained this overall shape to the minutest aspect.

As all this came to fruition, a strip of sand rose from the edge of the lake to the Fountain. Without hesitation, the lord of Ishram stepped onto it. Vorannos gazed up at the towering Fountain that he had summoned and grinned.

"The Fountain of Eternity . . ." he whispered as if to a lover. "You are mine . . ."

21

THE BEASTMASTER SHOULD HAVE DROWNED BY NOW. IT HAD been impossible to hold his breath for more than a few minutes. Unable to resist the might of the whales, he had been dragged ever under the surface farther and farther toward the center of the lake . . . until at last his mouth had forced itself open and swallowed.

And once that had happened, the struggle for air had ended.

He breathed, breathed as a fish might, though he had no gills. It did not matter whether he swallowed or sniffed, the lake was to him like fresh, sweet air. Dar's wounds were utterly healed, too, even the fiercely burning one at the back of his head. He understood immediately that it was because he had finally swallowed. The lake's wondrous waters had gone through his body, cleansing everything.

Even as the Beastmaster came to grips with both these miracles, he thought of Vorannos and the Fountain. Dar immediately reached out to the whales' minds, trying to warn them of the terrible threat to not only their realm, but all Ancor.

But even as he sought to warn them, the whales changed direction of their own accord and quickened their speed. An image that he could only assume came from one of the aquatic titans abruptly filled Dar's head, an image of a laughing Vorannos standing on a newly risen strip of sand just beyond the shore, arms raised before a gargantuan magical construct of water. Then the lord of Ishram lowered his arms and even knelt, as if in prayer.

No . . . not prayer, for the master of evil reached with one hand toward the edge of the Fountain. Water from its great spout poured into the edge of the lake just close enough for him to catch it. Cupping his hands, he lifted high the empyrean liquid.

He will drink! Dar feared. *There must be a way to stop him! Hurry!* he urged his aquatic companions, though they were already likely racing as quickly as they could.

The whales brought him above water. Dar blinked and saw a kneeling Vorannos seemingly entranced by the glorious Fountain. Its splendor was greater than the treasures of a hundred kings. It shone like a mountain of jewels . . .

The whales brought Dar under again, this time the Beastmaster unafraid to breathe deep. They created a swell that lifted the human up.

Dar flew from the water, a living missile aimed at Vorannos. Had the Fountain not so enchanted him, Vorannos would surely have spotted his enemy, but no sooner had he lifted the water to his lips then the two collided with a heavy thud. The water spilled from Vorannos's hands as he was thrown back to where the strip of sand met the shoreline, the Beastmaster atop him.

Vorannos flung Dar aside the moment they landed. The lord of Ishram's face was monstrous to behold. He stared at his palms, where not even a drop remained.

Then the arrogant confidence returned. Vorannos grinned.

"You are very, very annoying, little beast," he mocked, "and the tasting of the Fountain's gifts will be that much sweeter after tasting your blood! This time, I will strip *all* flesh from your body, then twist your insides to the outside . . . and even then, you will live long enough for me to drag your carcass to the edge of the lake where you can witness my glory!"

He smiled. A black aura formed around his hand. He pointed at the Beastmaster expectantly.

Dar leaped.

The Beastmaster did not expect to reach his adversary unscathed, but nothing happened after Vorannos's declaration. The power that Vorannos had used earlier to take the mandalas no longer seemed available to the invaders' master. Dar's skin did not rip free and the puzzled look on the lord of Ishram's face was enough to tell him that it was not due to any sudden mercy.

And as he grappled again with Vorannos, Dar realized just what—or who—was responsible for this reprieve. A pair of sleek black forms dropped from the lord of Ishram's back and scampered into the safety of the nearby landscape before the giant could react.

Sharak let out a cry from far above. It was he who had alerted the ferrets. Kodo and Podo had surely run at their swiftest to have made it at this crucial moment. It was not the first time that they had saved the Beastmaster's life, but surely it had been the closest.

"Even the littlest can strike a powerful blow," he told Vorannos. "Those many wires along your arm and back, the ones that guide your dark power . . . they're perfect for a quick bite from a pair of ferrets!"

Vorannos growled, then retorted, "Then I shall just have the pleasure of tearing you to pieces with my bare hands . . ."

But there was something in his tone that warned Dar of further treachery and it was Vorannos's own mirror eyes that warned the Beastmaster of just what that treachery consisted. Reflected in the eyes was one of the sinister scaled hunters, who now stood a short distance from the battling duo.

And in his hands he wielded a weapon whose design was far

beyond Dar's comprehension but whose purpose was very clear . . . especially as it was nearly even now focused on the Beastmaster's back.

Vorannos gripped him tight. Dar tried to spin them around, but the lord of Ishram held fast to his position.

The reptilian assassin steadied his weapon—

HALF-CONSCIOUS AND UTTERLY in pain, Tara had nonetheless tried to move. She felt water all around her and knew that she must be in the lake. The natural fear that she might drown vied with that concerning Dar and Jalan. Images of the Beastmaster's falling body, struck but a moment before by a sinister beam of crimson light, repeated itself over and over in her mind.

The water closed around her. Tara tried to reach for Jalan, although she did not know in which direction he lay.

But as the waters covered the Touargang, the fear abruptly left her. Her lungs filled only with what seemed air.

And, more, the pain vanished. Tara felt her wounds fading and her strength returning.

With the return of that strength also came renewed determination. With a gasp, Tara raised her head above water. As she did, Jalan's head also bobbed up. Beyond Jalan, she saw Ruh stir as well. The boy looked wide-eyed at the Touargang, his younger mind clearly not certain what had happened. Tara hoped that he had already forgotten the brief but terrible moment when the invaders had fired upon them with their monstrous weapons.

Thinking of their foes, she looked to the shore. The mutates' attention was elsewhere, but from her angle, Tara could not immediately see what it was. She squinted—

It was Dar . . . Dar fighting against Vorannos. Dar, alive despite all reason.

No . . . Dar alive because of this wondrous realm.

But that might not last, especially as the mutates were beginning to move to assist their lord against his adversary.

Tara swam toward the shore, Jalan in tow and Ruh beside. Of the ferrets, Tara did not see any immediate sign, but she hoped for the best. As they reached land, she warned Jalan to stay back. Unfortunately, the boy's face gave every indication that he would not obey and, in truth, at this point she could not blame him.

"Just try to be safe, all right?"

In answer, he picked up a sturdy piece of wood. Tara grimaced, then grabbed her fallen spear and blade. Ruh let out a low growl.

"Yes . . ." she responded, somehow knowing what he said. Perhaps it had to do with this realm. She seemed to understand all the creatures' intentions. "Yes, surprise is on our side . . . for now . . ."

In silence, she led them swiftly toward the enemy. The first mutate came within range of her spear.

Tara let out a war cry as she ran the point through where the neck joint demanded softer material. The Pygmesian clacked wildly, then tumbled face-down.

Ruh leaped upon the next nearest pair, bringing them to the ground. His great claws ripped through their protection. As that happened, Kodo and Podo jumped into the fray from the other direction. Where they had come from and how they had gotten there was not as important to the Touargang as the fact that they were not only also healed, but aiding in the fight.

Tara punctured the breathing tube of another foe. She started toward the direction of Dar . . . and Zorena blocked her path. Behind the crimson-haired woman, a line of mutates formed to prevent the Touargang and her companions from interrupting their master in his hour of triumph.

"You should've left Nadeesh when I gave you the chance . . ." muttered the huntress.

"Why stand in my way? You helped us before! Why—"

"You *are* a fool . . ." Zorena cut in. Instead of firing on her rival, she brandished her blade.

Tara instinctively attacked. Zorena blocked her strike but did not follow through. The Touargang lunged again, with the same results. Tara was proud of her skills as a warrior, but even still, she wondered at both her ability to stave off Zorena and the other's hesitancy to strike back. The huntress was certainly among Vorannos's favorites, which meant that her own skills should have been extraordinary. Yet thus far they had battled to a stalemate, with Tara the aggressor.

It seems I've overestimated her, the Touargang finally decided. She pressed the red-haired fighter back.

Over Zorena's shoulder, Tara spotted Jalan. The boy was quick and wiry and could handle a stick well, but he was no match for the three Pygmesians quickly cutting him off from Tara and Ruh.

But though it looked as if Jalan were doomed, an odd thing happened. Seto flew in front of his human friend, the parrot making himself an easy target for the deadly weapons.

However, the helmeted abominations did not fire. The lead Pygmesian froze. The other two Pygmesians hesitated, then joined the first in collectively gazing at Seto as if never seeing such a sight before. They appeared mesmerized by his bright plumage and child-like antics.

Tara let out a gasp as Zorena's blade drew a red line on her arm. The huntress's face was without emotion.

"Dreaming is for the dead," she commented. "Trust me, I know . . ."

Tara would have asked her what she meant, but then Zorena lunged and it was all the Touargang could do to deflect the blade with the tip of her spear. But Zorena suddenly paused in midswing, leaving herself wide open for what from a warrior of Tara's training would have been a fatal strike.

The huntress glanced away from the Touargang. There was such a peculiar, almost *concerned,* look on the other's face that, despite it probably being one of the oldest ploys . . . Tara could not help but turn her gaze in the same direction.

And, to her horror, she saw Dar about to be fired upon by the other reptile, the one called Drayz. Tara had no idea what sort of weapon the fiend carried, but she doubted that he would need more than a single chance to slay the Beastmaster even at the great range between the two.

A startled cry filled her ears, but it was not *hers,* as she at first thought. Instead, Tara's foe plunged in the direction of the assassin.

And before Tara could comprehend what had happened, the huntress threw herself at the reptile, shouting, "Drayz!"

BETRAYAL WAS UNTHINKABLE. Those like Zorena or Drayz or Kuln had been bred with the desire to serve Vorannos utterly. Zorena had outlasted many others of her kind, rising to become his favored enforcer even over the reptiles. She, of all, should have been the one ready to shoot the Beastmaster, not seek to save his life.

It had been a subtle conversion. Ancor was different from all the other worlds. It was a primal paradise, the absolute opposite of Ishram as she knew it . . . and, in addition, it had birthed a warrior like Dar.

She had been drawn to him from the start, first by the skills that she had observed, then his determined demeanor. He was truly a creature of Ancor, as much a part of it as the trees, the fauna, and the mountains. That awoke in her a new, astonishing affinity for the pureness of his world, a world that she began to explore with her heart and soul—things Zorena had imagined long grown cold—in order to better understand him.

And in her observations and inner reflection, she had come to marvel at the life so abundant here. Destruction was simple, she saw . . . creation, not so.

But all she knew how to do was destroy. Zorena looked into

herself and was suddenly repulsed. Her existence had been nothing but cruelty. So many lives she had willingly slaughtered for the sake of her lord.

Her betrayal had started small, with attacks held back or even avoided, such as when she had confronted the woman that Dar *preferred*. Still feeling as if she served Vorannos, she had not been able to completely turn against him, even if she had secretly hoped that something would save the Beastmaster.

She had not even been able to bring herself now to slay the other female, who had the heart that Zorena could never win. It was, of course, due in great part to the Beastmaster, who had instigated the metamorphosis through which the huntress had gone.

And then . . . seeing Dar about to be slain had proven the final straw for the huntress, stripping away the last of her loyalty to the lord of evil. With Dar dead, the Fountain would be Vorannos's and all this would be ravaged.

No more Ancor. No more peace and creation.

Only Ishram.

Only Ishram . . . *everywhere.*

And so Zorena had ceased toying with the woman and lunged for Drayz. A part of her knew that she was mad, but the huntress cared not. She was about to make some slight amends for her monstrous deeds. A new instinct for *defending* life—and especially, those who instilled in her a passion for such—gloriously filled Zorena. For the first time, the huntress felt alive.

"Zzzoreennna?" he hissed in surprise. "Are yyyou mad?"

"Yes . . . mad with sanity!" She raised her voice for Vorannos to hear as well. "Something you will never understand, either, my grand lord, and so will forever be condemned for it!"

In her head—and in Drayz's, she knew—the lord of Ishram's voice came even as he struggled with the Beastmaster.

Slay her . . .

Drayz gave her a toothy grin. He had always resented her dominant place and now he had the perfect opportunity to not only act on that resentment but raise himself in the estimation of his master.

The reptile fired.

Zorena had no chance to avoid his shot. She felt her body burn with electricity. The tiny mechanisms throughout her system sought to compensate but perished before they could do anything much. The huntress, her skin blackening, staggered, then fell a few steps short of her former comrade.

Tara flung herself forward, catching the burnt body. She stared into the huntress's eyes, finally understanding the change in Zorena.

"Fool . . ." Drayz rasped at his traitorous comrade.

"Let me get you into the lake!" Tara whispered frantically. She stretched her hand toward a slight puddle of water left by the lake's tides, gathering a few precious drops. Tara let the drops dribble into the other woman's mouth. "Drink this! It can help—"

"No . . . too late . . ." But as Zorena's life slipped away, the pain suddenly gave way to a sense of peace. The huntress beheld a shimmering form: a mandala. No longer seeing Tara or anything else, she reached out to the mandala and knew that her sacrifice had been worth it. She was a part of Ancor now, not Ishram . . . not Vorannos.

She also knew that her sacrifice had not been in vain.

DRAYZ EYED THE charred remnants of his former rival with immense satisfaction, then turned back to the struggle between his master and the primitive. He would be Vorannos's favored after this, rewarded more than any other.

The reptile raised his weapon to fire again—

And only at the last did he sense the huge form falling upon him. Highly trained reflexes were not enough as more than four hundred pounds of striped predator brought the mutate crashing to the ground. Aware of the greater threat Drayz represented, Ruh had broken through the line of mutates and headed directly for the hunter.

With a hiss, Drayz tried to fire upon his attacker, but Ruh swiped at the reptile with one mighty paw—

The brief struggle between the pair ended.

But not far away, a vicious Kuln batted away Kodo from his side, then, after checking his weapon for severed connections, aimed for Tara. The grinning mutate fired—

His weapon exploded, engulfing him a in violent plume of crimson and black that left little of the reptile in its wake.

As what was left of Kuln rained down on the vicinity, a racing Kodo spat out a small component that he had taken from the mutate's weapon.

Tara and Ruh turned to help Jalan, but, there the tableau they witnessed left even the tiger hesitant. Seto still mesmerized the remaining Pygmesians. The mutates stood like children. Their tube weapons lay forgotten at their feet.

Then the parrot perched atop the lead mutate's hand. As the creature drew Seto to it, the bird casually leaned forward—and plucked free the breathing tube, which had clearly already been damaged.

The Pygmesian did not react . . . not immediately. A green-tinged smoke briefly vented. A rasping sound echoed from within the helmet but quickly subsided.

With its free hand, the Pygmesian suddenly attempted to remove its helmet. When one hand would not suffice, it gently let Seto fly back to Jalan.

Clutching both sides of the helmet, the creature adjusted a series of latches.

With a hiss, the helmet swung open . . . and a twisted face both human and animal peered out in wonder. To anyone of Ancor, it was as if some blind god had taken a man and some feline and randomly put elements of each together to form the new countenance.

One eye was nearly human, the other absolutely catlike. The mouth bent at a harsh angle and the nose was a pointed, prickly mass. The ears were rounded save at the very tip.

Ruh let out a slight growl at this disturbing sight, but was wise enough not to disturb matters. As Dar's friends watched, the other Pygmesians peered at their comrade. Gloved hands touched the lost breathing tube, the opened helmet, the face.

A second invader undid its helmet. Underneath was a different hybrid of man and beast, the latter only barely recognizable as being of canine traits.

The lord of Ishram had spent lifetimes indulging in his corrections of Creation's lackings. Vorannos had manipulated the very basics of all his subjects, leaving none untouched, unchanged. While the life upon Ancor was the result of a natural blending of animals and people, Ishram's had become a parody, a mockery.

But what was also clear by the Pygmesians' fascinated expressions was that they should not have survived without whatever source of air they used. Always in the past, they had perished almost immediately. Yet, here in this realm, they breathed as either Tara or Jalan.

The parrot flapped his wings. "Seto!"

The helmetless Pygmesians noticed him again. They stretched their wondering hands toward the avian. From their misshapen mouths first emerged the clacking sounds . . . and then a single understandable word.

"*Seto* . . ." they intoned, sounding very much like Jalan or some other small child. "*Seto* . . ."

DAR WITNESSED ZORENA'S sacrifice. He mourned her, knowing that she had done it for him and Ancor. Yet the Beastmaster could not concern himself much with the huntress's demise, for he still feared for his friends.

Vorannos had also witnessed Zorena's betrayal, and although her heinous act filled him with righteous anger, he also saw how the distraction touched his foe in another, deeper way. With a mocking laugh, the lord of Ishram used the distraction to twist under Dar's arms and finally gain a suffocating grip on the Beastmaster's chest.

Dar struck him on the side of the neck. The lord of Ishram roared, raised his foe high, and, with a tremendous thrust, threw Dar far into the lake.

Plunging deep into the waters, Dar momentarily struggled. If he did not return to Vorannos instantly, then his adversary would have time to sip and all would be lost. The Beastmaster rose through the center of the lord of Ishram's discovery—

And knew then that what Vorannos had summoned was a false vision.

This was not the Fountain of Eternity. This was only what those who lusted for power, what those who lived for greed, could summon. Grandiose it was, but its waters did nothing. They did not even satiate, but rather would make Vorannos thirst even more for what he desired.

As Dar comprehended that, he also knew exactly where the true Fountain lay. It was within him, at least the thinking of it.

He suddenly sensed the whales returning to him. They swam once around the Beastmaster, then led him *down*. Dar sensed in the leviathans a great urge so he went without a struggle. They guided him all the way to the bottom, a place where only darkness dwelled. Yet their bodies glowed as they neared the floor, giving Dar the illumination he needed.

Able to breathe, Dar had no fear. He knew what needed to be done. Stretching his fingers to the bottom of the lake, he opened himself up to the needs of all Ancor.

A faint blue light rose from the spot the Beastmaster touched. He pulled back, admiring the beauty of its simplicity. There was a faint surge of water, but a trickle compared with what Vorannos had initially unleashed.

And that had been the lord of Ishram's greatest mistake. He had expected the grandeur, but that was not what the Fountain was. It was the soul of Creation, the seed of all. It needed no grandeur; it *was*.

The trickle grew. Unafraid, Dar swam into it and it raised him toward the surface, spreading as it went. At the same time, Dar felt the rest of the lake stir. He smiled, knowing what that meant.

His head broke the surface as the water spread. The simple trickle had now become the great churning column that had brought everyone to this miraculous realm.

Dar watched in awe as another spout and another rose from the edges of the lake. They shot forth until they reached the very ceiling of this inner world, then spilled through rock and dirt, moving on upward in the direction of the Beastmaster's world.

The whales came to him yet again, guiding Dar to the shore. As Dar stood at the edge, the silver behemoths headed in the direction of the spout that he had first stirred.

A heavy hand struck him in the back. Dar tumbled forward into the water, not entirely surprised by the attack but doing nothing to stop it.

"You *are* an amazing fool, Beastmaster!" Vorannos marveled. The giant stepped into the shallows, then pushed himself eagerly toward the deeper areas, until at last he reached a place where the water from the true Fountain fell upon him like a light spring rain. He cupped his hands, shouting to Dar, "And when all is my domain, I will honor you for that foolhardiness!"

Dar straightened. He took a step toward the lord of Ishram, but then stopped.

Stopped and let Vorannos drink.

22

Vorannos swallowed deep. The mirror eyes shone bright with triumph.

And suddenly, the lord of Ishram doubled over in agony.

"Noooo! How—how dare you?" he roared at the Fountain. His gaze wandered, as a drunken man's might. "I—I will not be denied!"

From the area of Vorannos's stomach, a blue light akin to that which Dar had awakened in the lake radiated. The light rose up the giant's gullet and although Vorannos struggled to keep it in, eventually it burst from his mouth . . . and became once more the simple drops of water that he had swallowed.

Undaunted, he grasped for new drops falling from the continually swelling spout. Yet now they refused to even touch his lips, as if repelled.

Dar shook his head in pity. "You cannot imbibe of its true,

wondrous nature, Vorannos, for your evil is its opposite. You can never have its gifts; I see that now."

But Vorannos paid him no mind, his fixation still on the Fountain itself. "No!" cried the lord of Ishram, his expression growing ferocious. "You cannot deny me! I will drink!"

Vorannos cupped his hands, letting the water fill them. As soon as he had enough, he swallowed. Vorannos clamped his mouth shut, but this time no light burst forth. Instead, nothing happened. He might as well have been swallowing water from a stream on Ancor's surface. Twice more he madly drank and twice more nothing happened afterward.

"I have destroyed *worlds* for this!" he shouted at Dar, all but slavering from anger. "I have followed this hunt throughout reality!"

"And with each world that you tortured, you further kept yourself from ever being able to be worthy of its gifts. You are the only reason that the Fountain is beyond you, lord of Ishram. Nothing else. And you will ever be forbidden it."

Vorannos's body shook. "No!" he roared, the cry reverberating throughout the great cavern and perhaps even everywhere beyond. "I will not accept it! No!" He held out his hands and swallowed drop after drop after drop, punctuating each gulp with more denials.

Dar turned from the master of a thousand worlds, the conqueror of billions of innocents. What interested the Beastmaster more now were the many spouts. Each had now separated into two or three or even more and all shot high, bursting effortlessly through the exterior of the underground world in what looked at first like random directions.

But the Beastmaster smiled . . . for he knew that the directions were hardly random. No, indeed, they had each been chosen with particular precision.

. . .

EVEN AS EDURAC fought in what was desperation, in other parts of Ancor the burrowers continued their relentless assault. Ever one to maintain multiple options in regard to his ultimate goal, Vorannos had commanded his servants to continue their dread work, even if all they did was tear this world apart.

In what had once been the area of Jalan's village, the massive burrower encountered a sudden moisture near its nose. The fiery green beams turned the first puddle to vapor, but then more puddles developed.

The mutates increased the burrower's power levels. They had run across small pockets of water beneath the surface of worlds before. This was no different.

But then the entire machine shook. Outside, the walls of the pit began to crack. Huge masses of dirt and rock began to spill in on the burrower.

A crushing torrent of water erupted from the walls and the bottom of the great pit. The burrower lurched, throwing most of those within about. Tons of rock joined with the pressure of the spout to squeeze the frame of the burrower together.

The thick, metal plates gave way. Explosions erupted all over the huge machine. Mutates attempted to flee, but there was nowhere to go.

The forces of nature engulfed the crumbling burrower, reducing it to little more than metal scrap even as the explosions within destroyed what was left of its villainous crew.

A different and more brief plume of smoke rose from the collapsing pit as Pygmesians and others fled in panic. The upheaval below opened great cracks, down which many of the survivors perished. Those that lived called for help and listened in their ears for commands from their master, for Vorannos had ever guided his invasion even as he had hunted the Fountain . . . but there was no voice. Nothing.

And as the one pit fell in on itself, burying forever that which had created it, its destruction was duplicated throughout Ancor. Wherever Vorannos's monstrous burrowers worked, the spouts reached them. They were guided by the Beastmaster's desire to save his world in the only way possible.

Within moments, not one of the great burrowers remained. Panic ensued and Vorannos's commanders beseeched him for orders that would make sense of this monumental and entirely impossible calamity.

But the lord of Ishram did not answer . . .

VORANNOS SHIVERED WITH uncontrollable anger. He kept scooping water and watching it drip between his fingers. Now and then he would taste it, then mutter, "Nothing . . . nothing . . ."

Then, without warning, he looked up. He spun not to face Dar, but the Pygmesians.

"Why do you stand there?" the giant raged. "Why do you stand there?" He waved wildly in the direction of the Beastmaster, Tara, and the rest. "I want them all destroyed! I want everything destroyed! Tear this foul place apart! Tear this foul world apart! I will have it done! I will!"

The Pygmesians did nothing, continuing to cluster near Seto in fascination.

Vorannos roared at this insubordination. He touched his side and a small sphere emerged from his torso. The lord of Ishram threw it.

Guided by both his arm and his desire, the tiny sphere shot forward at Seto with blinding speed.

One of the Pygmesians saw it. The mutate lunged in front.

The explosion was small but powerful. The Pygmesian was torn to shreds. The fringes of the explosion still caught Seto unaware. The force sent the parrot wheeling to the ground.

The remaining mutates stirred, then looked at Vorannos.

"Destroy everything!" the maddened ruler roared again. He thrust a finger at the Beastmaster, crying, "Slay him! Slay him!"

The Pygmesians howled. No longer trained warriors but a frenzied mob, they charged . . . but at a disbelieving Vorannos.

The lord of Ishram vanished beneath a torrent of sharp teeth and claws, but he was by no means undone. A hand burst free, crushing within it the throat of the lead Pygmesian. Another mutate went flying back, part of his skull crushed in.

Heedless of their losses, the mutates continued to swarm him. Their tremendous fury was not simply due to the parrot's injury, either. Dar knew that each of these surely had to have suffered as well, tortured throughout their growth to make them obedient, vicious soldiers of the mad conqueror. More to the point, the mutates were stirred on by something long buried within their original selves. Whether it was some trace of whatever had passed for their humanity or original animal nature, it now held an unbreakable grip on them.

There had been hints before, Dar realized, opportunities when some of the mutates could have fired but had not. Most of all, though, Jalan had spoken with him of that first time that Seto had fascinated a handful of the invaders, possibly even some of this very band, before the attack in Sravasi's clearing. Dar should have wondered then, but he had been too focused on the quest for what had seemed more a child's fanciful story at the time.

And, indeed, even now, there were far more urgent matters. He had been gone so long from Edurac, would that it were still standing. He needed to find out, to help, as he was the one who had been chosen as Ancor's guardian long before his birth.

Dar understood his destiny. More important, he now *accepted* what he should have known from the very beginning. There was no doubt that he was Ancor's guardian, the essence of its nature. Born of an animal but human in creation, his natural instincts exceeded those of both. The Beastmaster accepted now that he was forever the link between the former, which knew by instinct that it had to live in harmony with the environment, and the latter, which had the greatest ability to defend it.

Yet Dar's destiny was to come not only to the aid of Ancor . . . but wherever help was needed, wherever the balance of nature had been upset. Vorannos and his monstrous legions were, for all their horror, but an example of the prodigious challenge facing the Beastmaster, a challenge he more than willingly accepted now. He could do no less, for Ancor *was* him as he was Ancor.

Ancor, the Gate of Heaven . . . as Ishram was the Gate of Hell.

Dar knew what must be done. Gently, he whispered a single word.

"Stop."

The enraged Pygmesians paused. With a touching humbleness, they stepped back as Dar loomed over a frothing Vorannos.

"Come to slay me, Beastmaster?" Vorannos mocked. He grinned. "You cannot, for I am Eternity! I am the lord of Ishram!" Vorannos abruptly spat. "Come! Try to slay me! All I desired has proven nothing! Nothing!"

The Beastmaster did not reply. Instead, he looked with pity at his adversary, an expression that only served to fuel Vorannos's wild rage.

"*Do it*—or I will yet return to destroy all you love, all that *is*! I will tear that which is most precious to bloody gobbets, raze to the ground the jungles, and let flutter on poles the skins of animals and men! I will—"

Dar shook his head . . . and suddenly the lord of Ishram's voice failed him. He screamed and shouted, but only silence emerged.

"It is not my place to slay you, Vorannos. The Gate of Hell must have its guardian, and that is you. You will be sent back and Ishram will be your prison. All other worlds will be given their life again through the power of the Fountain."

He let Vorannos speak again. A bestial laugh first erupted before the lord of Ishram managed coherent words. "My prison?" He laughed again. The mirror eyes darted back and forth. "The Fountain . . . so much power . . . there must be a way! I—"

"Farewell, Vorannos . . ."

"It can change worlds in an instant . . ." babbled the lord of Ishram bitterly. "I must have it somehow! I will have it somehow, some day! This was a mistake! It will still—"

The glory of the Fountain of Eternity filled Dar. The Beastmaster raised a hand and a spout of water shot from the lake, striking Vorannos. Yet instead of smashing him into the ground, it swiftly raised the giant up, thrusting him to the ceiling.

At the last moment, the spout flung Vorannos through the gap through which Dar and the others had all arrived. The lord of Ishram vanished from the underworld. The spout abruptly ceased, droplets from it gently raining down on Dar.

But Dar was not done with his foe. The water had simply thrust Vorannos from Ancor's womb. The true power of the Fountain now enabled the Beastmaster to do so much more. The lord of Ishram was no longer within the world, no longer on its *surface*.

Through the Fountain, Dar saw the mad giant in his mind. Vorannos now stood on the deck of his *flagship*, the lord of Ishram still ranting. Dar heard him repeat the same thing over and over: *A mistake . . . the Fountain would still be mine . . . all a mistake . . .*

Dar gave a gentle wave of his hand, more an affectation than necessity. The Fountain did not need anything but his wish.

The lord of Ishram's ship faded, returned by the Fountain to the dread world. Once there, it would never function again.

The Beastmaster stood calm and determined. Vorannos was

gone, but his command to destroy *all* Ancor remained. His monstrous horde and their human allies still had to be stopped.

He turned to Tara and the others. "We go to Edurac."

Raising his arms, Dar looked to the vast flock of golden birds. They came at his bidding, landing upon he and all the others, save the two avians. Dar summoned Sharak to his arms while Jalan held onto Seto—a fully recovered Seto, thanks to the Fountain's touch.

The flock lifted the party up as if each weighed no more than a feather. The golden birds quickly soared to the glittering ceiling, not even slowing as they approached.

"We're going to strike it!" Tara cried. Kodo and Podo buried themselves deep in the Beastmaster's pouch.

"No . . ." Dar assured her quietly. "Not at all . . ."

They reached the ceiling . . . and passed through it without harm. Ruh let out a triumphant roar that echoed the others' swelling emotions as they were carried up. Into fields of diamonds and past other ancient caverns they briefly flew. Dar smiled at this miracle, even though he had known it would happen.

But, unlike their journey down, they did not continue to rise through layer after countless layer of rock and earth. Barely had the party adjusted to the flight up than the jungles of Ancor surrounded them. Yet even that scene was a brief one, and suddenly the walls of Edurac rose up around the Beastmaster's companions.

Dar, however, was no longer with them.

The golden birds continued to carry him higher, higher. From his great vantage point, he witnessed below him the terrible struggle and knew that, even though the invaders and their human allies were without Vorannos, desperation and strength made them a threat so very terrible.

Nodding to himself, Dar looked out onto the far reaches of Ancor and called, "Come to me . . . come to me, all my brothers and sisters . . ."

It was as if a shroud of silence fell over Edurac. The warriors still battled, but without sound.

Then a new sound rose up from all directions. First a buzzing, then the screeches of birds, then the growls and hisses of animals . . .

Ancor gave up to its champion *all* of its animal children, be they the smallest of the small or the largest of giants. There were creatures recognizable and others fantastic, such as apes as tall as trees and scaled hounds large enough to ride. Birds with vast wings soared through the air at miles per beat and great mounds gave hint of huge diggers boring their way toward Edurac. Drawn by the Fountain and the world, they gathered so quickly it almost seemed that they simply materialized.

Through the Fountain, the Beastmaster spoke to all simultaneously, told them what he needed. Ranks formed as they joined those other animals that Dar had earlier sent. An army such as this never had been seen on Ancor—on *any* world—surged toward the horde.

Dar was not merely satisfied with using their numbers, though. He directed his forces as any general. The sky was his first obstacle, and against the flyers—both living and otherwise—he sent the swarms of insects. Guided by his eye, they did not waste their numbers simply surrounding and seeking crevices and open joints on the mechanical ones; now they knew immediately where the vulnerable points were. The metal flyers fell by the scores, by the hundreds.

And when it was only the living flyers, he sent in the birds. Already harassed by the stings of a million insects, they did not see the raptors and other avians until it was too late. From great ripping beaks to tiny pecking ones, from talons longer than Dar's hand to those smaller than his fingernail, the birds ripped into the savage creatures. Outnumbered already, the invaders' beasts were quickly routed.

With the sky under control, Dar had the golden birds lower him.

Several times, bolts of lightning shot up at him, only to veer off oddly. The power of the Fountain protected him from such feeble attacks.

He alighted onto a waiting elephant, a male giant even among its own kind. As Dar adjusted his position, the bull elephant quickly used his tusks to toss away one, then two spiderlike mutates seeking the Beastmaster.

Jalan was safe within Edurac, but Dar's other companions were a part of the battle. Tara already stood among the defenders, the Touargang princess a terrible foe for any of the invaders. As ever, Ruh fought in the thick of things, leading a massive pack of predators who tore ribbons through Xorot's Vorundites. Sharak flew among the raptors as they, with the sky claimed, began dropping down on the heads of any fighter within sight. Seto added his own beak to the assault. Even Kodo and Podo assisted greatly, the ferrets guiding the moles and other diggers in their underground assaults.

An opening in the defenders' ranks led to a counterattack by a force of mutates. They pushed through, threatening to cut Edurac's lines in half.

But the gap had been Dar's doing, his ability to touch minds now not restricted merely to the animals, but also his brother. Tal had agreed without pause, certain that his brother would have a good reason.

And that reason came trampling down on the mutates but a moment later. A stampede of epic proportions that included Dar's elephants, countless buffalo, antelope, horses, and other animals poured into the invaders, hooves crushing in helmets and skulls. The human defenders suddenly pressed from the sides, packing the invaders together. Several animals in the stampede perished, as did many of Edurac's defenders, but for every one that did, two took its place.

The Beastmaster nodded in grim satisfaction. Keeping the

stampede moving, he summoned the birds again. They easily lifted him up.

As he rose above the fray, he saw that for which he had been searching. Several reptilian mutates were organizing the invaders and surviving human allies for a counterassault. Of all Vorannos's minions, they were the most dedicated, the most cunning.

Take me there, he asked of the birds and they did. The Beastmaster readied his sword, then had the shimmering avians drop him among the mutate commanders.

And with a roar worthy of Ruh, Dar plunged through Ancor's enemies . . .

TARA HAD NO time to think about the miraculous journey to Edurac, for she, like Dar, understood that the fate of the world was not yet decided. If Edurac fell, it would not matter if Vorannos had been defeated.

Her spear was not sufficient for this heavy task, and so the Touargang princess plucked up a bow and two quivers from a dead archer, grabbed a horse whose rider was also slain . . . and began firing at will while riding at full gallop.

She knew now the best points of vulnerability and quickly downed three, four, five mutates in a row. When Dar unleashed the stampede, Tara joined it, reveling at the natural might of thousands of animals. Wherever she could, the Touargang slew those she saw trying to stem the tide by slaying the foremost creatures.

Then, among the lead horses, Tara spotted one that made her heart skip a beat. Even though there were hundreds of steeds, she had no doubt that this was the large mustang from Sravasi's clearing. From the very first, she had felt a kinship to this steed as strong as if it were her own blood.

And so, when she saw it in danger at enemy hands, Tara let out a scream of rage and fired shot after shot. Two Pygmesians fell with bolts through their breathing tubes, a Vorundite with another arrow in his rib cage. Nothing . . . *nothing* could happen to the white horse.

But in her eagerness to protect the mustang, her own horse was struck by a Vorundite ax. The valiant horse tumbled and even as Tara leaped to avoid being injured, she cursed herself for not being as kind to one equine as she had the other.

However, now she was in terrible danger. The shifting struggle forced her to the outskirts of what remained of the nearby jungle. Shadowy forms flitted between the trees, some of them allies, others enemies.

A warrior in a breastplate marked by an insignia she did not recognize nearly beheaded her. His heavy sword cut into her bow. Bereft of the weapon, Tara could only dodge . . . until she felt a tree at her back.

The enemy fighter grinned. Behind him, four of his fellow warriors rushed to join in the kill. Tara was honored by their numbers, though shamed that she could not even defend herself from the one.

Long, hairy arms reached down and seized one of those in the back. As he went screaming into the treetops, another was grabbed. At the same time, a huge white form cut in front of her, kicking at her foremost adversary.

It was the white mustang. It lashed out at the warrior, crushing in his breastplate and no doubt several of his ribs.

But the horse was not alone. A rider joined in her defense, a diminutive figure she had met once before. General Om leaped to the ground, an act that at first Tara thought foolhardy, considering the disadvantage in height. However, as the first of the remaining warriors swung at him, Om moved nimbly aside, struck his much larger foe in the knee with his foot, then used the side of his hand on the back of the neck once the warrior's leg buckled.

A second lunged for the short figure, but Om seized one arm

and threw the man over his shoulder. Before the warrior could re-cover, the dwarf downed him with a chop of the hand.

"What manner of fighting is that?" Tara asked, wide-eyed.

"One that can be taught," Om offered. He suddenly looked over his shoulder. "At a more appropriate time."

Mutates swarmed the area. Their jerky movements indicated their anxiety, which made them all the more dangerous, for they would be less predictable. One spotted Tara and Om and alerted the others.

"It would be wise to depart," suggested the dwarf.

Tara tried to grab hold of the mustang, but although it had been willing to save her, letting her ride was apparently another matter. It pulled away.

"Come with me!" called Om, already mounted on his horse.

As Tara reached for his hand, a mutate ahead of the rest aimed for her. Before it could fire, though, from the trees dropped a heavy, hirsute form, a male chimpanzee. The creature landed atop the in-vader, crashing the latter to the ground.

But as the mutate fell, its weapon also discharged. The bolt struck near the hooves of Om's steed. It turned and fled in panic.

Tara was dragged along. She tried to maintain her hold on Om's hand, but the strain was too much. Her fingers slipped.

A trained warrior, she quickly rolled to her feet and looked for a weapon. Finding a sword, Tara barely saved herself from being run down by an enemy rider. She slashed her foe across the chest and as he fell, the Touargang tried to seize the reins of his horse. Unfortu-nately, they evaded her.

Swearing, Tara looked around. To her surprise, she saw Dar being carried by the golden birds. He descended into the thickest part of the battle, where Tara also spotted several of the reptile men.

Determined to reach him, Tara fought toward that direction.

To her dismay, though, the continually shifting lines pushed her instead *back*, toward the part of the jungle from which she had just escaped.

She was not alone in her predicament, either. Not far from her, the mustang, too, was struggling to survive. A creature that reminded Tara of a bear and warthog mixed together, then coated with an iron hide, sought to seize the horse in what would surely be a grip of death.

The Touargang slashed through a Pygmesian's breathing tube, then closed on the two inhuman combatants. As she neared the mustang's monstrous adversary, the woman warrior let out a shout certain to attract its attention.

It did, much to her sudden concern. There was no pity in the glowing red orbs, only a desire to dismember.

But as the abomination turned, the mustang kicked out, striking the side of the head. As the metallic beast bent, Tara lunged, aiming for a softer spot at the neck. A thick black liquid poured from the wound as the creature stiffened. Another kick by the mustang finished the duel.

Tara stepped up to the willful steed. "We've saved one another's lives! Better to fight together than die separately! What do you say?"

She felt a little foolish speaking to the horse as if he understood her—for she was certainly no Dar—but to Tara's surprise, the mustang snorted and then turned so that she could better mount.

With some relief, she sat atop. There were no reins, but she held to his mane.

A short distance away, Om, now depending on his sword, saw her. Dispatching a foe, the dwarf joined her. He nodded knowingly as he looked over her new companion.

"Clearly, destiny has much in store for you. So I thought when first we met, so I believe even more now . . ."

"Destiny'll have to wait to see if we live through this first . . ."

Om nodded as if her words had been spoken by a sage. "Yes, so it must . . . so it must . . ."

"The first thing we need to do is to reach Dar! He's there, in the worst of it!"

The dwarf gripped his blade tight. "We shall do what we can, yes?"

But as they turned their mounts in that direction, an awful vision filled their gazes and made Tara shake her head in fearful disbelief.

The area to which Dar had descended was now an inferno.

23

ALTHOUGH THE BATTLE WAS STILL A FEROCIOUS ONE, TAL fought with renewed hope. His brother had returned, bringing with him not only a startling army, but powers that the king of Aruk was certain would save the day for them.

Tal was still more than willing to sacrifice himself were it to ensure Ancor's survival. He shared that trait with Dar. Thus it was, with the enemy more and more on the run, that he sought out one of the few that kept it from entirely routing . . . and who also was responsible for the death of a friend.

Xorot bullied his Vorundites and the warriors of some of his allies forward, they still more fearful of him than all the animals and warriors facing their dwindling horde. The blood of many a good man including Leardius stained his garments.

A righteous fury filled Tal. Urging his mount on, he struck down one, two, three warriors in a row. At the same time, he shouted Xorot's name over and over, seeking the warlord's attention.

He finally had it, although not in the manner he desired. Xorot glared at the young king, then shouted a command to his minions.

More than a score of Vorundites converged on Tal, Xorot coming up behind them to no doubt finish his foe once his warriors had "softened" Tal up for him. Realizing that his impetuousness had sent him into disaster, Dar's brother nonetheless drove his steed into the thick of his enemies, cutting down two in the first moments. His mount, trained for war, kicked and bit, sending several more Vorundites sprawling or fleeing.

But there were still too many. A savage strike to his horse's midsection sent the animal stumbling. Tal jumped from the valiant steed just as it crashed. The king brought down another foe as he landed, then spun in a circle with his sword extended to its full reach.

Vorundites surrounded him, their brutish, bearded faces eager for more bloodshed. Xorot rode up behind the circle.

"Maybe should I take you alive, Tal of Aruk, as hostage, eh? Valuable to all, especially Beastmaster . . ."

Tal was very aware that his brother would likely hold back if he indeed thought it worth the younger sibling's life. That might endanger everything for which they had fought.

"I'll slay myself before letting you do that, Xorot!"

The warlord's shaggy brow furrowed in thought. "Yes, you would! A Vorundite in soul, Tal of Aruk!" He laughed harshly. "So, I give you a warrior's death! How kind of me!"

The Vorundites moved in on Tal. He whirled from one direction to the next, trying to gauge which eager fighter would be the first and wondering if somehow he could yet reach Xorot himself.

Then some sight behind him so astounded the warlord's men that they froze and stared past their prey. Despite his situation, Tal followed their gaze.

A huge plume of flames rose high above the battle.

What its meaning was, the king of Aruk did not know, but it served one great purpose for him. The circle splintered as some of the Vorundites turned and fled. Others stood their ground, but looked uncertain as to what to do.

But Tal *knew* . . .

Yelling at the top of his voice, he rammed into those between him and Xorot. One put up a feeble resistance and perished because of it. The other scrambled away as if Tal were a giant beast about to devour him.

Xorot shouted something in his native tongue. Some of the Vorundites rallied from their earlier shock. Tal could only assume that whatever the plume of flame meant, it was something detrimental to their cause.

But it was not enough to deter Xorot himself. Furiously striking down a retreating warrior, he urged the remaining one at Tal. Dar's brother easily dispatched the first, then was forced back by two working in concert.

Then Xorot, clearly impatient, broke through with his horse and tried to run Tal down. As he rolled out of the way, the young king slashed at the warlord's leg but missed.

The area suddenly filled with more warriors, but they were not Vorundites nor their allies. Eduracian fighters poured into the enemy with such force that the collision sounded like thunder. The Vorundites were swept back.

Standing, Tal looked for Xorot . . . and nearly lost his head for it, for the warlord came in behind him. Only the last-minute attack by an Eduracian deflected the warlord's weapon, though in the next instant it cost Tal's defender his life.

However, he had given Tal the moment that the king needed. Tal thrust at his mounted foe and although Xorot dodged the blade, the attack and the wild movements of his animal forced him from the saddle.

Now both on foot, the two rulers fought in earnest. Xorot attempted to cut a swathe across Tal's midsection, the ax scraping the latter's breastplate. Tal fell to one knee, barely deflecting the blow that immediately followed.

Xorot grinned and brought the ax around—

Tal lunged.

As he had planned, the blade came under the warlord's swinging arm. It sank in between the breastplate and the waist.

Xorot let out a gurgling sound. Blood spilled from the wound. The warlord teetered but did not fall. All but frothing at the mouth, he slashed wildly at Tal.

The king of Aruk drove the tip of his sword into the Vorundite's throat.

The warlord stumbled back. His mouth stretched in a ghoulish grin. His eyes lost focus . . . and he fell dead at Tal's feet.

You are avenged, Leardius, Tal thought. Yet Xorot's death was minor so long as the battle raged. Tal wondered where his brother was, for he had seen no sign in far too long a time.

His gaze whipped back to the terrible plume, still burning high.

"No . . ." he gasped. *"No . . ."*

THE INVADERS WERE aware that they had lost, and some, Dar had seen, were ready to die . . . but only if they took their foes with them.

The reptile men against whom he fought were not, Dar realized too late, attempting to reorganize their forces, but rather using them to delay while they set in place part of their terrible plan. Dar smelled Vorannos's sinister plotting in their efforts and cursed himself for having believed that, with the lord of Ishram defeated and cast out, his machinations would be coming to an end.

But Vorannos had planned even for his absence, as the insidious sphere the reptiles adjusted bespoke. The Beastmaster could sense the finality in the mutates' faces, their awareness that they were to die. Still, they were determined to wreak as much carnage as they could before that happened and as Dar struck down one of their number, he knew that they would finish with setting the mysterious sphere's power into motion before he could reach them.

However, Dar was not alone, not even now. Throughout his own battle, he continued to work with the power of the Fountain—power that not only had given him inner peace and enhanced his physical abilities but granted him insight into what needed to be done—to guide his "troops," his animal friends. Where the human defenders weakened from their long struggle, rhinos, bears, wolves, and other creatures added their ferocity and, by doing so, reinforced those lines. Every creature of Ancor was using its natural abilities to its utmost, thanks to Dar.

And that included those below ground.

As the sky belonged to the defenders, so, too, did the earth beneath their feet. Vorannos's burrowers were already long gone and, in like manner, the spouts had rid Dar of any concern for smaller versions of the fiendish devices. Now the moles, voles, worms, ants, and all other animals that dug beneath the surface did so with organized diligence. They undermined the legs of gargantuan golems, opened up vast pits that sank under the weight of armored mutates and their maneuvering weapons.

And now, in the case of the reptiles and their deadly task, created a sinkhole large enough to engulf the villains and the sinister mechanism.

Most of the mutates plunged to their doom, buried under tons of collapsing soil. One managed to cling to the sphere, his six-fingered hands also seeking to press several buttons on it.

Dar jumped into the collapsing hole, colliding with the reptile and the sphere. The mutate slashed at Dar with one hand even as they and the deadly device, caught in the avalanche created by the collapse, sank beneath the surface.

Torrents of dirt flew in his face, both blinding Dar and cutting off his breath. He struck the reptile's other hand as hard as he could and the mutate lost its grip. The scaled fiend slipped below Dar and the sphere and was buried under the still-collapsing earth.

As he tumbled deeper into Ancor, Dar did not fear death. He had done everything that he could for his world. If this was to be his end, then so be it.

Then the sphere began to vibrate. Dar immediately threw himself from it. A torrent of earth and rock descended upon him—

And, to his surprise, he rolled into a large tunnel at the bottom of the collapse. The reason for its sudden and useful existence immediately swarmed over him. Moles and other large burrowers seized hold of the Beastmaster by teeth and claws and dragged him with remarkable strength from the collapse. Among them Dar discovered one ferret: Podo. She had followed his trail all along and had guided the diggers under her command toward him.

Thanking Ancor for such loyal and loving friends, Dar assisted as best he could in his own escape by crawling from the direction of the hole down which he and the sphere had first fallen. Several of the diggers collapsed the end of the tunnel from which he had entered, creating a protective wall between them and where the sphere lay.

Podo squeaked a warning.

The Beastmaster and his rescuers threw themselves forward. A tremendous explosion rocked the makeshift cave and Dar wondered if he would be buried alive. But the walls held and the intentional collapse behind him and his companions kept them from the brunt of the explosion.

So deep beneath the surface, the deadly explosion that the mutates had intended was more safely focused. As the burrowers led him up, Dar emerged to see a huge plume of fire where he had been. Had the sphere exploded on the surface, it would have scorched the area for as far as the eye could see. Now, though, the damage had been minimized.

He was assailed suddenly by animals from all over the battle, who brought him the most joyous news. The invaders' heart for battle was no more. The survivors were fleeing, although Dar knew that they had few places to run. There was only a handful of their larger flying vessels left and those quickly filled. The remaining stragglers were quickly being brought down. Pockets of resistance remained . . . mostly Pygmesians and the reptile men—the most fanatic of Vorannos's evil servants—providing momentary peril before they were overrun.

Kodo surprised him with his sword, the ferret and several furred friends dragging it to Dar. Thanking them, he sheathed the weapon and hurried to put a finish to the struggle.

In the survivors' wake lay the twisted corpses of countless invaders and their human allies. Dar grieved even for them, though there had been no choice in his actions. The Beastmaster trod the landscape, seeking the one he needed.

It was his brother who found him instead. Looking as haggard as Dar felt, Tal nonetheless brightened when he saw the Beastmaster.

"Dar!" he cried, enveloping his brother in a crushing hug. "You've done it! You've saved all of us! Praise be!"

As grateful as he was that Tal had also survived, Dar had no time for reunions. "Where is Leardius?"

"Dead, by Xorot's foul hand . . . but the warlord is himself dispatched by me . . ."

"Then you must also be the one to lead the rest on, to sweep clean what remains of the invaders and Xorot's ilk, Tal!"

"But that role is surely yours—"

The Beastmaster shook his head. "My part here is done. There is something else I must do. It is up to you, Tal."

"Consider it done, brother!" Tal signaled an Eduracian rider.

"Take this horse!" he said to Dar. Hearing no response, the younger sibling glanced back. "But what is it that you—"

Dar was no longer there.

THE FOUNTAIN OF Eternity was only a trickle again, one already vanishing beneath the pristine surface of the underground lake. Even as Dar watched, the last trace vanished from mortal sight, though he still felt its power deep below.

This time, he had needed neither the spouts nor the birds to carry him to the miraculous realm at the center of Ancor. He was still intertwined with the Fountain and that enabled him to do what he needed.

"Has it touched everywhere?" he asked the lake. "All Ancor?"

There was no verbal response, but from the lake rose the silver whales and from the sky descended the brilliant gold birds. They gathered before the Beastmaster . . . and became men and women.

Sages.

And at their forefront stood Brother Ontas.

Dar grinned at sight of the oracle. Ontas smiled back.

"You are—you are a part of this?" the Beastmaster marveled.

"Only through your efforts have I been so blessed," Ontas cheerfully replied. "All of us here have reached the next level of existence and consciousness, Dar, and each, in gratitude, has chosen to be a part of the Fountain's protection and a part of the Fountain itself . . ."

As the oracle explained, Dar sensed that he and the sages were not alone. Though he turned to fight, something made the Beastmaster keep his sword sheathed.

Several shimmering creatures approached from the grasslands. They at first appeared an array of animals, some feline, others ursine . . . and others that Dar could not quite identify. Yet as he studied them, he also saw them briefly change to figures nearly human, then back to animals again.

They were like none of the denizens of the underground world that he had seen previously, but there was no denying that they were very much a part of all surrounding Dar. Yet there was also that which reminded him of something far, far from natural to any place in all the world.

At last the Beastmaster recognized them for what they were . . . or had once been . . . the Pygmesians who, touched by Ancor, had turned on—or perhaps *away from* was a truer way of phrasing it—their vicious master.

The Pygmesians who were clearly far more than the abominations Vorannos had made of them.

"Be not concerned about them," another voice gently told him. "After you left, they one by one did drink from the Fountain. But, unlike their master, they were touched by its waters, although in a different manner from you. Their transformation was as instantaneous as it was complete. They have given themselves wholly now to the Fountain, to all of Ancor . . . they are more, as they would have been, had the dark one never twisted them to resemble his own madness."

They came to Dar. He felt no evil whatsoever in them. Seen now, as somewhere between animal and human, they were almost akin to him.

Then belated recognition of the speaker's voice made Dar turn in yet new surprise.

A young, handsome Baraji bowed his head in great respect to the Beastmaster. "My heartfelt congratulations, my student, for realizing the sacred truth within you. For realizing who is Dar the Beastmaster . . . and how that is intertwined with the life of our world . . ."

There was no sarcasm in the statement, only honest admiration.

Dar marveled at the complexity of even the simplest of the sage's words. The search for one's self was the most basic search of all men, all *creatures*, but few ever attained it.

"You knew this would all come to pass?" Dar asked him.

"All that happened was as fate meant it to be, but fate is the brother of chance, is it not? And are we not ourselves the ones who truly command both?" Baraji, robed as the Beastmaster had seen him last, indicated the other noble figures. "From the start, we recognized you as the chosen one and thus began the long guidance that would help you with the quest to come, the quest that would awaken that part of you that is the Fountain. But does that mean that the quest of the lord of Ishram was doomed to fail? Perhaps, perhaps not. True, he sought that which could never be garnered by terror or violence . . . but at the same time, for you to succeed, the solution to all things had to come from you yourself, or else you would have earned it no more than he."

"I am grateful for all you did to help."

"Help? In the end, my student, we did nothing but hope. Our true parts, our true destinies, demanded that we be neutral, else you not find the way to enlightenment yourself. We could but only trust in your true self."

As Dar nodded in understanding, from the lake there suddenly gushed a new and powerful waterspout. The sages stepped to each side, letting him watch as it not only shot higher and higher but also wider than the Beastmaster had ever seen it.

"We are honored by your presence, Dar," Baraji continued. "honored to have touched the path walked by he who is the hand of Ancor, he who is its champion . . ."

The sages bowed to Dar.

He opened his mouth to protest this undesired honor, but at that moment, the top of the great spout erupted, spraying water down on the shore. Dar instinctively shielded his eyes as the rain fell upon the sages and him.

"We are honored . . ." he heard Baraji say one last time before the downpour drowned out all other sound.

Drenched, the Beastmaster stood there, eyes covered, waiting for the downpour to cease. Only when it did, did Dar look again.

Yet it was not on the lake and the Fountain's holy guardians that he now gazed, nor any other part of the mystic realm.

Instead, Dar stood, alone and quite dry again, at the gates of Edurac.

24

I T TOOK BUT A HANDFUL OF DAYS TO CRUSH WHAT REMAINED of the enemy. A few of the mutates escaped, but they were not bred to survive on their own in Ancor. Others were captured, their fates—along with those of the surviving Vorundites and other traitors to humanity—to be decided by a council of rulers.

As all this took place, Dar reunited one by one with the others. Sharak spotted him first, the eagle spying him at the gates from high in the sky. The eagle circled Dar once, then flew off to alert the others. Before long, Ruh, Kodo, and Podo returned to him, but equally welcome—if not more in some ways—was the wonderful sight of Tara, her hair loose and her expression matching the feeling in his heart, riding up a short time later. The hug she gave him lasted long. Once inside the city, Jalan—on his shoulder a merry Seto chirping the Beastmaster's name—clutched Dar as if the latter were his own father.

When it was clear that the fighting was over, the mourning began in earnest. King Leardius's body, brought from the field on the first day along with those other lords who had perished, was given great honor for all that Edurac's monarch had done to defend his kingdom and Ancor. His pyre stretched thirty feet high and more than twice that across. A hundred trumpeters sounded the funeral notes and Edurac was filled to overflowing with those coming to pay their respects.

Although they were not given individual funeral pyres of their own, the rest of the heroic dead were not forgotten. Tal, Heratos, and the other surviving leaders and commanders led a ceremony honoring all those who had given of themselves to the cause. It was yet again a tragic scene, and there were so many mass pyres that lit up the surrounding region for miles around.

The enemy dead also got their pyres, though without any trappings or ceremony. Rather, they were dumped as quickly as they could be gathered, and that which did not burn was soon thereafter buried deep, where it would never be uncovered.

Tal took charge of all things, including watching over the heir to Edurac. He also sent word to Aruk of his own survival and what should be done in his absence there.

The Beastmaster, the two kings, and Jalan stood within the gates. The sun—for the first time with no shroud to mask its morning glory—was just beginning to rise. Jalan looked tearful and Tal was not much better, but the Beastmaster had to leave. He felt the yearning growing within him. Ancor's wilds called, and despite many wishes otherwise, he knew that he could not resist that call.

"There is much rebuilding needed everywhere, not just Edurac," Dar's brother commented. "I pray we can all stay at peace with one another during that, at least."

"There'll be no fight from the Vorundites, for one," Heratos grimly remarked. "Nor any of those jackals who thought to profit from siding with Xorot . . ."

"Someone'll always try to take advantage of weakness . . . but still, Ancor as a whole should be at peace for some time to come, I'd think!" Tal offered. "This struggle has brought so many of us together! What say you, Dar? Can you not at least wait and ride back with me to Aruk? 'Tis barely a week since Leardius's funeral, and in that time we've hardly seen one another due to all the matters of state! Say yes! There will be such a feast there to honor you—"

Dar shook his head. "I must go. Aruk is your kingdom. Mine"— he paused as a vast and distinctly varied flock of birds passed by overhead, flying toward the jungle lands, part of the mass exodus still going on beyond Edurac, Dar's "army" returning to the wild— "is theirs. The jungle is where I must go."

Tal and Jalan nodded somewhat disappointedly. Tal quietly replied, "I remember, Dar. I remember and understand."

"But if it is meant to be," the Beastmaster added with a smile for their sakes, "we may meet again . . ."

The two brothers embraced. Heratos thrust out his remaining hand for Dar to shake.

Jalan suddenly hugged Dar. "No! I want to go with you!"

"Not this time. Besides, who will watch Seto and Tal?" Dar bent so that he could look the boy in the eyes. "Can you do that for me?"

Although his eyes remained moist, Jalan nodded. "I will."

From Jalan's shoulder, the parrot chirped, "Seto!"

The truth was that Dar had earlier asked his brother to take care of Jalan and give the boy the decent life he should have had if not for the dread invasion.

He is so very much like me, Dar thought. The Beastmaster was curious how Jalan would finally grow up. Time would tell . . .

"There's so much we owe you," Tal said.

"There is nothing anyone owes me." Dar picked up his pouch, in which Kodo and Podo already curled up. They poked their heads out to let Jalan pet them one last time. Ruh, sensing that they were at last departing, rose and gave the others an impatient rumble.

"What if we need you?" asked Heratos.

"You likely will not . . . but if you do . . . tell the jungle and I will know."

Heratos looked a bit awed, while Tal chuckled. He clasped his brother's hand. "Are you sure you don't want a horse?"

"No."

"Then . . . this is truly farewell, brother . . ."

Dar nodded to them, then raised his arm. Sharak, who had been perched atop a nearby building, dropped down and alighted on the arm.

The one-armed king grumbled, "There should be a damned parade or some honor escort . . . something . . ."

Dar gave him a rueful smile that indicated just how much he did *not* want any such honors. The Beastmaster turned. Tal signaled the gates to open. Heratos stayed behind while Tal and Jalan followed the Beastmaster out. The morning mists still prevailed, giving the surrounding landscape a mystical quality.

The trio were joined outside by another party, one that even Dar found unusual. Tara was there—her absence in the city earlier this day one that the Beastmaster had particularly noted—but she had with her some unlikely companions.

Om, already mounted, bowed his head to Dar. The Touargang led the white mustang he had seen her riding at the end of the battle. Seated atop the horse was an even more unusual figure . . . a familiar-looking male chimpanzee.

"This is *Pouf,* as I call him," she said of the chimpanzee. "He and his clan saved our lives more than once, if you remember. He came to my aid in the battle."

Pouf gave a wide, cheerful grin and bobbed his head up and down several times as if to agree with Tara's declaration.

"I remember." Dar acknowledged the primate's role. He knew the origin of the name and the honor the Touargang princess had bestowed on Pouf. "Furred brother."

She patted the mustang on the neck. "And this is *Diva*, after the warrior guardian of my tribe."

"I am honored by both of you," he said to the animals. Diva gave him a courteous snort while Pouf grinned.

Tara suddenly handed the reins to Om, then went to Dar. They stepped beyond the hearing of the rest. The Touragang's expression was troubled. Dar, aware of his own feelings, understood what troubled her.

"Dar . . . I . . ."

He cupped her chin. She trembled at his touch. Eyes locked, they both instinctively embraced.

At that moment, a smaller figure collided with them. Jalan, face soaked with tears, wrapped his arms around both as best as he could.

"I am sorry!" Tal spouted the next moment, Dar's brother red with embarrassment at his failure. "He just suddenly ran—"

"It is all right," Dar replied, unable to feel any anger toward Jalan.

Tara pulled away. Although she sought to hide it, her eyes were filled with sorrow for the interruption. Still, she also held nothing against the boy, for whom she clearly had much affection. She tousled the youth's hair. "I will always think of you, Jalan."

"You both don't have to go—"

"Sometimes people must," Tal interceded. "Take my word for it." He gently steered Jalan back again. "Come."

Tara and Dar watched as Tal led the boy out of hearing, then the Touragang quietly said, "I thought at first that we would ride together, Dar—"

He frowned, already knowing that such was not to be their fate. Still, something had clearly also changed for her. "What is it?"

Tara's sadness deepened, but with it also came a curious determination. "I—I must to go another direction, Dar. I have this feeling—it has grown in me these past few days—that there are others of my people still alive and that they need me! I belong to them! I have to find them . . . for their sake and mine . . ."

He knew such feelings. Her ties to her people were calling her. She could no more ignore such a chance than he could ignore his own path. "You must follow what feels true, Tara—"

"But I will find you again," the Touargang whispered as she stepped back. "I will find you again." She returned to her new friends, and with one lithe leap, she mounted Diva.

Steeling himself against his own regrets, Dar turned his attention to the dwarf. "And you go, also?"

"He only told me last night that he was leaving," Tal muttered. "Said that he was done teaching and protecting me, that I no longer needed his guidance."

"So it is," said Om. "The path this one rides now parallels the warrior maiden. I have offered to tutor Tara in the ways of the spirit as we seek her people. She has accepted."

"For what little I'll likely understand of it."

"To be humble is a virtue. To underestimate oneself is a common failing." To the Beastmaster, Om added, "There are many destinies that mark Ancor, and it is this one's belief that she follows such." The dwarf looked to the Touargang. "She has the potential to reach understanding perhaps as great as yours, master of beasts . . ."

Tara shook her head. "Never . . ."

Utterly serious, the dwarf indicated Diva and Pouf. "But they clearly see it also and, thus, there can be no arguing."

His tone put a finality on that point that Tara grudgingly accepted. "I only know that I am grateful for their company and yours, Om. I don't know how long I'll search, but I have to go on until I am certain one way or another . . ." She patted Diva near the shoulder and the mustang started to turn. Her determined gaze swept over the Beastmaster one last time. "Farewell . . . for *now*, Dar . . ."

He wanted to say something, but there was nothing either could add at this point. Dar gave her a smile and nodded.

The Touargang smiled back . . . then rode off, Om close behind.

Dar watched her vanish, then glanced back at his brother and a still-tearful Jalan.

"Everything's been said," Tal commented. "But one thing I must repeat . . ." He swallowed. "Thank you . . ."

The Beastmaster nodded. Then, with Ruh at his side, Kodo and Podo in the pouch, and Sharak taking to the air once more, he set off for the jungle.

TAL AND JALAN watched until Dar could no longer be seen, then the king put a comforting arm around the boy's shoulder. "Do you know anything about Aruk?"

Wiping away the tears, Jalan shook his head. The boy made no move to leave, even though he could see nothing.

"When we return inside," Tal said as cheerfully as he could, "let me tell you all about it . . . and my adventures with Dar when I was about your age . . . about when I first met the one called the Beast-master—"

"Beastmaster!" chirped Seto. "Beastmaster!"

Jalan smiled.

DAR HEARD THE parrot's call even though Edurac was long behind him. He knew that Tal and Jalan were still standing beyond the gates, eyeing the jungle. He mourned the separation from them, just as Tara's departure had left a pang in a different part of his heart. Yet all was as it had to be.

Dar focused instead on the jungle around him. The trees were healing. Fresh growth sprouted everywhere. Birds, insects, and animals called out. For having occurred over only the space of a few days, the changes were phenomenal . . . *magical.*

Which, of course, they were.

The Fountain's waters had seeped up everywhere, slipping through earth and rock to feed and renew the life of Ancor. Already, the lushness of the jungle was well on its way to what it had been before Vorannos, and Dar knew that the longer he journeyed, the more such miracles he would come upon.

Witnessing Ancor's rebirth brought to the forefront the inner peace and acceptance he had learned. He now knew exactly who and what he was. He would never truly be alone, not only because of Ruh, Sharak, Kodo, and Podo's presence or the love that Tara, Tal, and Jalan carried for him, no matter what the distance separating them, but because Ancor itself—Ancor, the Gate of Heaven, and he as the guardian of Creation—was and always would be a part of him, just as he was so very much a part of it.

He was both its child and its guardian, the epitome of its primal nature and vivid life. He was the one who would stand against all that threatened it, using the gifts he had been granted.

Ruh suddenly let out a majestic roar, both to acknowledge that he knew who and what his human brother was and that the tiger would always be there to stand beside him. Kodo and Podo added their vow with determined squeaks and from above all of them, Sharak screeched his agreement. They would be there to aid against whatever he faced, for they were as much a part of him as he was a part of Ancor.

As much as he was . . . and would always be . . . the *Beastmaster.*

About the Authors

RICHARD A. KNAAK is the *New York Times* bestselling author of forty novels, including many from the worlds of Warcraft and Diablo and his own Dragonrealm series. In addition to his contemporary fantasy and tie-in novels, he also writes manga for Tokyopop. His works have been published in dozens of languages. Visit his website at www.richardaknaak.com

SYLVIO TABET has directed hundreds of commercials, documentaries, and the feature film *Beastmaster II*. He has realized many films and television episodes as a producer and executive producer, with such projects as *The Cotton Club, Dead Ringers*, and the Beastmaster franchise. He is the author of *A Journey to Shanti* and *Tara: Queen of the Touargang*. He lives in Los Angeles. Visit his website at www.smtabet.com